George A. Aitken

The Tatler

Vol. III

George A. Aitken

The Tatler
Vol. III

ISBN/EAN: 9783741103537

Manufactured in Europe, USA, Canada, Australia, Japa

Cover: Foto ©Andreas Hilbeck / pixelio.de

Manufactured and distributed by brebook publishing software
(www.brebook.com)

George A. Aitken

The Tatler

Jonathan Swift.

Engraved by Wm. & Wm'd... 20 from the Original by Bindmaes after Jervas

The Tatler

Edited with Introduction & Notes

by

George A. Aitken

Author of

"The Life of Richard Steele," &c.

VOL. III.

London

Duckworth & Co.

3 Henrietta Street, Covent Garden

1899

To the Right Honourable

William Lord Cowpei

Baron of Wingham[1]

MY LORD,

A fter having long celebrated the superior graces and excellences among men, in an imaginary character, I do myself the honour to show my veneration for transcendent merit, under my own name, in this address to your lordship. The just application of those high accom-

[1] William Cowper was appointed King's counsel about 1694; he succeeded Sir Nathan Wright, as Lord Keeper of the Great Seal, October 11, 1705; was created Baron Cowper of Wingham, November 9, 1706; and was appointed Lord Chancellor, May 4, 1707, which post he held till September 14, 1710. On the accession of King George, he was again appointed Lord Chancellor, and, on resigning the Great Seal, was created Earl Cowper and Viscount Fordwich, March 18, 1717–18. He died in 1723. Lord Cowper refused to accept New Year's gifts from the counsellors at law, which had been long given to his predecessors, and, when he was Chancellor, though in friendship with the Duke of Marlborough, and of the same political principles, he refused to put the broad seal of his office to a commission for making his Grace generalissimo for life. "When Steele's patent, as Governor of the Theatre Royal, passed the Great Seal, Lord Chancellor Cowper, in compliment to Sir Richard, would receive no fee" (Cibber's "Apology"). He was praised by Hughes, under the name of "Manilius," in No. 467 of the *Spectator*.

plishments of which you are master, has been an advantage to all your fellow subjects ; and it is from the common obligation you have laid upon all the world, that I, though a private man, can pretend to be affected with, or take the liberty to acknowledge your great talents and public virtues.

It gives a pleasing prospect to your friends, that is to say, to the friends of your country, that you have passed through the highest offices, at an age when others usually do but form to themselves the hopes of them.[1] They may expect to see you in the House of Lords as many years as you were ascending to it. It is our common good, that your admirable eloquence can now no longer be employed but in the expression of your own sentiments and judgment. The skilful pleader is now for ever changed into the just judge ; which latter character your lordship exerts with so prevailing an impartiality, that you win the approbation even of those who dissent from you, and you always obtain favour, because you are never moved by it.

This gives you a certain dignity peculiar to your present situation, and makes the equity, even of a Lord High Chancellor, appear but a degree towards the magnanimity of a peer of Great Britain.

Forgive me, my lord, when I cannot conceal from you, that I shall never hereafter behold you, but I shall behold you, as lately, defending the brave, and the unfortunate.[2]

When we attend to your lordship, engaged in a discourse, we cannot but reflect upon the many requisites

[1] The date of Lord Cowper's birth is not known, but in 1710 he was probably about 46. He entered the Middle Temple in 1682.
[2] In a pamphlet entitled "A Letter to Isaac Bickerstaff," 1710, Lord Cowper defended the character of the Duchess of Marlborough against an attack by Bolingbroke in a "Letter to the *Examiner*."

which the vainglorious speakers of antiquity have demanded in a man who is to excel in oratory ; I say, my lord, when we reflect upon the precepts by viewing the example, though there is no excellence proposed by those rhetoricians wanting, the whole art seems to be resolved into that one motive of speaking, sincerity in the intention. The graceful manner, the apt gesture, and the assumed concern, are impotent helps to persuasion, in comparison of the honest countenance of him who utters what he really means. From hence it is, that all the beauties which others attain with labour, are in your lordship but the natural effects of the heart that dictates.

It is this noble simplicity which makes you surpass mankind in the faculties wherein mankind are distinguished from other creatures, reason and speech.

If these gifts were communicated to all men in proportion to the truth and ardour of their hearts, I should speak of you with the same force as you express yourself on any other subject. But I resist my present impulse, as agreeable as it is to me ; though indeed, had I any pretensions to a fame of this kind, I should, above all other themes, attempt a panegyric upon my Lord Cowper : for the only sure way to a reputation for eloquence, in an age wherein that perfect orator lives, is to choose an argument, upon which he himself must of necessity be silent. I am,

> My Lord, your Lordship's
>
> Most devoted, most obedient, and
>
> Most humble Servant,
>
> RICHARD STEELE.

By ISAAC BICKERSTAFF, Esq.

No. 115.

[STEELE.

From *Saturday, Dec.* 31, 1709, to *Tuesday, Jan.* 3, 1709–10.

—— Novum intervenit vitium et calamitas,
Ut neque spectari, neque cognosci potuerit :
Ita populus studio stupidus in funambulo
Animum occupârat.—Ter., Hecyra, Prologue.

Sheer Lane, January 2.

I went on Friday last to the opera, and was surprised to find a thin house at so noble an entertainment, till I heard that the tumbler[1] was not to make his appearance that night. For my own part, I was fully satisfied with the sight of an actor, who, by the grace and propriety of his action and gesture, does honour to a human figure, as much as the other vilifies and degrades it. Every one will easily imagine I mean Signor Nicolini,[2] who sets off

[1] See No. 108.

[2] Cavalier Nicolini Grimaldi was a Neapolitan actor and singer, who appeared first in England in McSwiney's "Pyrrhus and Demetrius." He is often mentioned in the *Spectator* (see Nos. 5, 13, 405), and seems to have been a friend of both Addison and Steele. Addison praises him alike as an actor and as a singer. The following letter from Hughes to Nicolini, dated February 4, 1709–10, is given in Hughes' "Correspondence" (Dublin, 1773, i. 33–4): "Depuis que j'ai eu l'honneur d'être chez vous à la répétition de

5

the character he bears in an opera by his action, as much
as he does the words of it by his voice.   Every limb, and
every finger, contributes to the part he acts, insomuch that
a deaf man might go along with him in the sense of it.
There is scarce a beautiful posture in an old statue which
he does not plant himself in, as the different circumstances

l'opéra, j'ai diné avec Mr. Steele, et la conversation roulante sur vous,
je lui dis la manière obligeante dont je vous avois ou parler de Mr.
Bickerstaff, en disant que vous aviez beaucoup d'inclination à étudier
l'Anglois pour avoir seulement le plaisir de lire le *Tatler*.   Il trouvre
que votre compliment à l'auteur du *Tatler* est fort galant."   Nicolini
sang in Italian to the English of Mrs. Tofts (see No. 20, and *Spectator*,
No. 22), but Cibber observes that "whatever defect the fashionably
skilful might find in her manner, she had, in the general sense of her
spectators, charms that few of the most learned singers ever arrive at."
A letter from Lady Wentworth, dated December 10, 1708, gives us
a curious glimpse of Nicolini and Mrs. Tofts : "My dearest and
best of children. . . Yesterday I had lyke to have been ketched in a
trap, your Brother Wentworth had almoste persuaded me to have gon
last night to hear the fyne muisick the famous Etallion sing att the
rehersall of the Operer, which he asured me it was soe dark none
could see me.   Indeed musick was the greatest temtation I could
have, but I was afraid he deceaved me, soe Betty only went with his
wife and him ; and I rejoysed I did not, for thear was a vast deal of
company and good light—but the Dutchis of Molbery had gott the
Etallion to sing and he sent an excuse, but the Dutchis of Shrosberry
made him com, brought him in her coach, but Mrs. Taufs huft and
would not sing becaus he had first put it ofe ; though she was thear
yet she would not, but went away.   I wish the house would al joyne
to humble her and not receav her again.   This man out dus Sefachoe,
they say that has hard both" ("Wentworth Papers," 1883, p. 66).
Mr. Cartwright quotes from a letter in Lord Egmont's collection,
dated March 17, 1709 : "This day the opera of 'Camilla' is acted
expressly for Lord Marlborough.   Our famous Nicolini got 800
guineas for his day ; and 'tis thought Mrs. Tofts, whose turn it is on
Tuesday next, will get a vast deal.   She was on Sunday last at the
Duke of Somerset's, where there was about thirty gentlemen, and
every kiss was one guinea ; some took three, others four, others five,
at that rate, but none less than one" (Seventh Report of Hist. MSS.
Commission, p. 246).

6

of the story give occasion for it. He performs the most ordinary action in a manner suitable to the greatness of his character, and shows the prince even in the giving of a letter, or the despatching of a message. Our best actors are somewhat at a loss to support themselves with proper gesture, as they move from any considerable distance to the front of the stage ; but I have seen the person of whom I am now speaking, enter alone at the remotest part of it, and advance from it with such greatness of air and mien, as seemed to fill the stage, and at the same time commanding the attention of the audience with the majesty of his appearance. But notwithstanding the dignity and elegance of this entertainment, I find for some nights past, that Punchinello has robbed the gentleman of the greater part of his female spectators. The truth of it is, I find it so very hard a task to keep that sex under any manner of government, that I have often resolved to give them over entirely, and leave them to their own inventions. I was in hopes that I had brought them to some order, and was employing my thoughts on the reformation of their petticoats, when on a sudden I received informa-tion from all parts, that they run gadding after a puppet-show. I know very well, that what I here say will be thought by some malicious persons to flow from envy to Mr. Powell ; for which reason, I shall set the late dispute between us in a true light.[1] Mr. Powell and I had some difference about four months ago, which we managed by way of letter, as learned men ought to do ; and I was very well contented to bear such sarcasms as he was pleased to throw upon me, and answered them with the same freedom. In the midst of this our misunderstanding and correspondence, I happened to give the world an account of the order of esquires[2]; upon which, Mr. Powell was so

[1] See Nos. 11, 44, 45.   [2] See No. 19.

7

disingenuous, as to make one of his puppets (I wish I
knew which of them it was) declare by way of prologue,
that one Isaac Bickerstaff, a pretended esquire, had wrote a
scurrilous piece to the dishonour of that rank of men ; and
then, with more art than honesty, concluded, that all the
esquires in the pit were abused by his antagonist as much
he was. This public accusation made all the esquires of that
county, and several of other parts, my professed enemies. I
do not in the least question but that he will proceed in his
hostilities ; and I am informed, that part of his design in
coming up to town was to carry the war into my own
quarters. I do therefore solemnly declare (notwithstanding that I am a great lover of art and ingenuity) that if I
hear he opens any of his people's mouths against me, I
shall not fail to write a critique upon his whole performance ; for I must confess, that I have naturally so strong
a desire of praise, that I cannot bear reproach, though
from a piece of timber. As for Punch, who takes all
opportunities of bespattering me, I know very well his
original, and have been assured by the joiner who put him
together, that he was in long dispute with himself, whether
he should turn him into several pegs and utensils, or make
him the man he is. The same person confessed to me,
that he had once actually laid aside his head for a nut-
cracker. As for his scolding wife (however she may value
herself at present), it is very well known that she is but a
piece of crabtree. This artificer further whispered in my
ear, that all his courtiers and nobles were taken out of a
quickset hedge not far from Islington ; and that Dr.
Faustus himself, who is now so great a conjurer, is supposed to have learned his whole art from an old woman in
that neighbourhood, whom he long served in the figure of
a broomstaff.

But perhaps it may look trivial to insist so much upon

men's persons; I shall therefore turn my thoughts rather to examine their behaviour, and consider, whether the several parts are written up to that character which Mr. Powell piques himself upon, of an able and judicious dramatist. I have for this purpose provided myself with the works of above twenty French critics, and shall examine (by the rules which they have laid down upon the art of the stage) whether the unity of time, place and action, be rightly observed in any one of this celebrated author's productions; as also, whether in the parts of his several actors, and that of Punch in particular, there is not sometimes an impropriety of sentiments, and an impurity of diction.

White's Chocolate-house, January 2.

I came in here to-day at an hour when only the dead appear in places of resort and gallantry, and saw hung up the escutcheon of Sir Hannibal,[1] a gentleman who used to frequent this place, and was taken up and interred by the Company of Upholders, as having been seen here at an unlicensed hour. The coat of the deceased is, three

[1] Sir James Baker, known as the "Knight of the Peak"; see No. 118. Steele's comments on gambling in the *Tatler* brought upon him the anger of many of the sharpers. There is a well-known story that Lord Forbes, Major-General Davenport, and Brigadier Bisset were in the St. James's Coffee-house when some well-dressed men entered, and began to abuse Steele as the author of the *Tatler*. One of them swore that he would cut Steele's throat or teach him better manners. "In this country," said Lord Forbes, "you will find it easier to cut a purse than to cut a throat"; and the cut-throats were soon turned out of the house with every mark of disgrace. A similar incident is described in a recently published letter from Lady Marow to her daughter, Lady Kaye ("Manuscripts of the Earl of Dartmouth," iii. 148; Hist. MSS. Comm., Fifteenth Report, Part I.). Writing on January 5, 1709–10, Lady Marow says: "All the town are full of the *Tatler*, which I hope you have to prepare you for discourse, for no

bowls and a jack in a green field ; the crest, a dice-box, with the king of clubs and Pam for supporters. Some days ago the body was carried out of town with great pomp and ceremony, in order to be buried with his ancestors at the Peak. It is a maxim in morality, that we are to speak nothing but truth of the living, nothing but good of the dead. As I have carefully observed the first during his lifetime, I shall acquit myself as to the latter now he is deceased.

He was knighted very young, not in the ordinary form, but by the common consent of mankind.

He was in his person between round and square ; in the motion and gesture of his body he was unaffected and free, as not having too great a respect for superiors. He was in his discourse bold and intrepid ; and as every one has an excellence as well as a failing which distinguishes him from other men, eloquence was his predominant quality, which he had to so great a perfection, that it was easier to him to speak than to hold his tongue. This sometimes exposed him to the derision of men who had much less parts than himself : and indeed his great volubility and inimitable manner of speaking, as well as the great courage he showed on those occasions, did sometimes betray him into that figure of speech which is commonly distinguished by the name of "gasconade." To mention no other, he professed in this very place some few days before he died, that he would be one of the six that would under-

visit is made that I hear of but Mr. Bickerstaff is mentioned, and I am told he has done so much good that the sharpers cannot increase their stocks as they did formerly ; for one Young came into the chocolate-house, and said he would stop Mr. Bickerstaff if he knew him. Mr. Steele, who is thought to write the *Tatler*, heard Young say so, and, when he went out of the house, said he should walk in St. James's Park an hour, if any would speak with him ; but the Hector took no notice."

take to assault me ; for which reason I have had his figure upon my wall till the hour of his death : and am resolved for the future to bury every one forthwith who I hear has an intention to kill me.

Since I am upon the subject of my adversaries, I shall here publish a short letter which I have received from a well-wisher, and is as follows :

"SAGE SIR,

" **Y**ou cannot but know, there are many scribblers and others who revile you and your writings. It is wondered that you do not exert yourself, and crush them at once. I am,

"Sir (with great respect),

"Your most humble Admirer

"and Disciple."

In answer to this, I shall act like my predecessor Æsop, and give him a fable instead of a reply.

It happened one day, as a stout and honest mastiff (that guarded the village where he lived against thieves and robbers) was very gravely walking, with one of his puppies by his side, all the little dogs in the street gathered about him, and barked at him. The little puppy was so offended at this affront done to his sire, that he asked him why he would not fall upon them, and tear them to pieces ?

To which the sire answered, with a great composure of mind, " If there were no curs, I should be no mastiff."[1]

[1] In the original folio number, after indication of certain errata in No. 114, comes the following note : " The reader is desired not to pronounce anything in any one of these writings *nonsense*, till the following paper comes out."

No. 116.   [ADDISON.

From *Tuesday, Jan.* 3, to *Thursday, Jan.* 5, 1709–10.

—— Pars minima est ipsa puella sui.
OVID, Rem. Amor. 344.

Sheer Lane, January 4.

The court being prepared for proceeding on the cause of the petticoat, I gave orders to bring in a criminal who was taken up as she went out of the puppet-show about three nights ago, and was now standing in the street with a great concourse of people about her. Word was brought me, that she had endeavoured twice or thrice to come in, but could not do it by reason of her petticoat, which was too large for the entrance of my house, though I had ordered both the folding-doors to be thrown open for its reception. Upon this, I desired the jury of matrons, who stood at my right hand, to inform themselves of her condition, and know whether there were any private reasons why she might not make her appearance separate from her petticoat. This was managed with great discretion, and had such an effect, that upon the return of the verdict from the bench of matrons, I issued out an order forthwith, that the criminal should be stripped of her encumbrances, till she became little enough to enter my house. I had before given directions for an engine of several legs, that could contract or open itself like the top of an umbrello,[1] in order to place the petticoat upon it, by which means I might take a leisurely survey of it, as it should appear in its proper dimensions. This was all done accordingly ; and

---

[1] Swift uses this form of the word : "It served him for a nightcap when he went to bed, and for an umbrello in rainy whether."

forthwith, upon the closing of the engine, the petticoat was brought into court. I then directed the machine to be set upon the table, and dilated in such a manner as to show the garment in its utmost circumference; but my great hall was too narrow for the experiment; for before it was half unfolded, it described so immoderate a circle, that the lower part of it brushed upon my face as I sate in my chair of judicature. I then inquired for the person that belonged to the petticoat; and to my great surprise, was directed to a very beautiful young damsel, with so pretty a face and shape, that I bid her come out of the crowd, and seated her upon a little crock at my left hand. " My pretty maid," said I, " do you own yourself to have been the inhabitant of the garment before us ? " The girl I found had good sense, and told me with a smile, that notwithstanding it was her own petticoat, she should be very glad to see an example made of it ; and that she wore it for no other reason, but that she had a mind to look as big and burly as other persons of her quality ; that she had kept out of it as long as she could, and till she began to appear little in the eyes of all her acquaintance ; that if she laid it aside, people would think she was not made like other women. I always give great allowances to the fair sex upon account of the fashion, and therefore was not displeased with the defence of my pretty criminal. I then ordered the vest which stood before us to be drawn up by a pulley to the top of my great hall, and afterwards to be spread open by the engine it was placed upon, in such a manner, that it formed a very splendid and ample canopy over our heads, and covered the whole court of judicature with a kind of silken rotunda, in its form not unlike the cupola of St. Paul's. I entered upon the whole cause with great satisfaction as I sat under the shadow of it.

13

The counsel for the petticoat was now called in, and ordered to produce what they had to say against the popular cry which was raised against it.   They answered the objections with great strength and solidity of argument, and expatiated in very florid harangues, which they did not fail to set off and furbelow (if I may be allowed the metaphor) with many periodical sentences and turns of oratory.   The chief arguments for their client were taken, first, from the great benefit that might arise to our woollen manufactury from this invention, which was calculated as follows : the common petticoat has not above four yards in the circumference ; whereas this over our heads had more in the semi-diameter ; so that by allowing it twenty-four yards in the circumference, the five millions of woollen petticoats, which (according to Sir William Petty) supposing what ought to be supposed in a well-governed state, that all petticoats are made of that stuff, would amount to thirty millions of those of the ancient mode. A prodigious improvement of the woollen trade ! and what could not fail to sink the power of France in a few years.

To introduce the second argument, they begged leave to read a petition of 'the ropemakers, wherein it was represented, that the demand for cords, and the price of them, were much risen since this fashion came up.   At this, all the company who were present lifted up their eyes into the vault ; and I must confess, we did discover many traces of cordage which were interwoven in the stiffening of the drapery.

A third argument was founded upon a petition of the Greenland trade, which likewise represented the great consumption of whalebone which would be occasioned by the present fashion, and the benefit which would thereby accrue to that branch of the British trade.

To conclude, they gently touched upon the weight and unwieldiness of the garment, which they insinuated might be of great use to preserve the honour of families.

These arguments would have wrought very much upon me (as I then told the company in a long and elaborate discourse) had I not considered the great and additional expense which such fashions would bring upon fathers and husbands ; and therefore by no means to be thought of till some years after a peace. I further urged, that it would be a prejudice to the ladies themselves, who could never expect to have any money in the pocket, if they laid out so much on the petticoat. To this I added, the great temptation it might give to virgins, of acting in security like married women, and by that means give a check to matrimony, an institution always encouraged by wise societies.

At the same time, in answer to the several petitions produced on that side, I showed one subscribed by the women of several persons of quality, humbly setting forth, that since the introduction of this mode, their respective ladies had, instead of bestowing on them their cast gowns, cut them into shreds, and mixed them with the cordage and buckram, to complete the stiffening of their under-petticoats. For which, and sundry other reasons, I pronounced the petticoat a forfeiture : but to show that I did not make that judgment for the sake of filthy lucre, I ordered it to be folded up, and sent it as a present to a widow gentlewoman, who has five daughters, desiring she would make each of them a petticoat out of it, and send me back the remainder, which I design to cut into stomachers, caps, facings of my waistcoat sleeves, and other garnitures suitable to my age and quality.

I would not be understood, that, while I discard this monstrous invention, I am an enemy to the proper ornaments of the fair sex. On the contrary, as the hand of nature has poured on them such a profusion of charms and graces, and sent them into the world more amiable and finished than the rest of her works ; so I would have them bestow upon themselves all the additional beauties that art can supply them with, provided it does not interfere with, disguise, or pervert, those of nature.

I consider woman as a beautiful romantic animal, that may be adorned with furs and feathers, pearls and diamonds, ores and silks. The lynx shall cast its skin at her feet to make her a tippet ; the peacock, parrot, and swan, shall pay contributions to her muff ; the sea shall be searched for shells, and the rocks for gems ; and every part of nature furnish out its share towards the embellishment of a creature that is the most consummate work of it. All this I shall indulge them in ; but as for the petticoat I have been speaking of, I neither can, nor will allow it.

No. 117. [ADDISON.

From *Thursday, Jan.* 5, to *Saturday, Jan.* 7, 1709–10.

Durate, et vosmet rebus servate secundis.
VIRG., Æn. i. 207.

Sheer Lane, January 6.

When I look into the frame and constitution of my own mind, there is no part of it which I observe with greater satisfaction, than that tenderness and concern which it bears for the good and happiness of mankind. My own circumstances are indeed so narrow and scanty, that I should taste but very little pleasure, could I receive it only from those enjoyments which are in my own possession ; but by this great tincture of humanity, which I find in all my thoughts and reflections, I am happier than any single person can be, with all the wealth, strength, beauty, and success, that can be conferred upon a mortal, if he only relishes such a proportion of these blessings as is vested in himself, and is his own private property. By this means, every man that does himself any real service, does me a kindness. I come in for my share in all the good that happens to a man of merit and virtue, and partake of many gifts of fortune and power that I was never born to. There is nothing in particular in which I so much rejoice, as the deliverance of good and generous spirits out of dangers, difficulties, and distresses. And because the world does not supply instances of this kind to furnish out sufficient entertainments for such a humanity and benevolence of temper, I have ever delighted in reading the history of ages past, which draws together into a narrow compass the great occurrences and events that are but thinly sown in those tracts of time which lie within our own knowledge and observation. When I see the life of a great man, who has deserved well of his country, after having struggled through all the opposi- tions of prejudice and envy, breaking out with lustre, and shining forth in all the splendour of success, I close my book, and am a happy man for a whole evening.

But since in history events are of a mixed nature, and often happen alike to the worthless and the deserving, insomuch that we frequently see a virtuous man dying in the midst of disappointments and calamities, and the vicious ending their days in prosperity and peace, I love to amuse myself with the accounts I meet with in fabulous histories and fictions : for in this kind of writings we have always the pleasure of seeing vice punished, and virtue rewarded. Indeed, were we able to view a man in the whole circle of his existence, we should have the satisfaction of seeing it close with happiness or misery, according to his proper merit : but though our view of him is interrupted by death before the finishing of his adventures (if I may so speak), we may be sure that the conclusion and catastrophe is altogether suitable to his behaviour. On the contrary, the whole being of a man, considered as a hero, or a knight-errant, is comprehended within the limits of a poem or romance, and therefore always ends to our satisfaction ; so that inventions of this kind are like food and exercise to a good-natured disposition, which they please and gratify at the same time that they nourish and strengthen. The greater the affliction is in which we see our favourites in these relations engaged, the greater is the pleasure we take in seeing them relieved.

Among the many feigned histories which I have met with in my reading, there is none in which the hero's perplexity is greater, and the winding out of it more difficult, than that in a French author whose name I have forgot. It so happens, that the hero's mistress was the sister of his most intimate friend, who for certain reasons was given out to be dead, while he was preparing to leave his country in quest of adventures. The hero having heard of his friend's death, immediately repaired to his mistress, to condole with her, and comfort her. Upon his arrival in her garden, he discovered at a distance a man clasped in her arms, and embraced with the most endearing tenderness. What should he do ? It did not consist with the gentleness of a knight-errant either to kill his mistress, or the man whom she was pleased to favour. At the same time, it would have spoiled a romance, should he have laid violent hands on himself. In short, he immediately entered upon his adventures ; and after a long series of exploits, found out by degrees, that the person he saw in his mistress's arms was her own brother, taking leave of her before he left his country, and the embrace she gave him nothing else but the affectionate farewell of a sister : so that he had at once the two greatest satisfactions that could enter into the heart of man, in finding his friend alive, whom he thought dead ; and his mistress faithful, whom he had believed inconstant.

There are indeed some disasters so very fatal, that it is impossible for any accidents to rectify them. Of this kind was that of poor Lucretia ; and yet we see Ovid has found an expedient even in this case. He describes a beautiful and royal virgin walking on the seashore, where she was discovered by Neptune, and violated after a long and unsuccessful importunity. To mitigate her sorrow, he offers her whatever she would wish for. Never certainly was the wit of woman more puzzled in finding out a stratagem to retrieve her honour. Had she desired to be changed into a stock or stone, a beast, fish or fowl, she would have been a loser by it : or had she desired to have been made a sea-nymph, or a goddess, her immortality would but have perpetuated her disgrace. "Give me therefore," said she, "such a shape as may make me incapable of suffering again the like calamity, or of being reproached for what I have already suffered." To be short, she was turned into a man, and by that only means avoided the danger and imputation she so much dreaded.

I was once myself in agonies of grief that are unutterable, and in so great a distraction of mind, that I thought myself even out of the possibility of receiving comfort. The occasion was as follows : When I was a youth in a part of the army which was then quartered at Dover, I fell in love with an agreeable young woman, of a good family in those parts, and had the satisfaction of seeing my addresses kindly received, which occasioned the perplexity I am going to relate.

The Tatler   No. 117. January 7, 1709–10

We were in a calm evening diverting ourselves upon the top of the cliff with the prospect of the sea, and trifling away the time in such little fondnesses as are most ridiculous to people in business, and most agreeable to those in love.

In the midst of these our innocent endearments, she snatched a paper of verses out of my hand, and ran away with them. I was following her, when on a sudden the ground, though at a considerable distance from the verge of the precipice, sank under her, and threw her down from so prodigious a height upon such a range of rocks, as would have dashed her into ten thousand pieces, had her body been made of adamant. It is much easier for my reader to imagine my state of mind upon such an occasion, than for me to express it. I said to myself, " It is not in the power of heaven to relieve me ! " when I awoke, equally transported and astonished, to see myself drawn out of an affliction which the very moment before appeared to me altogether inextricable.

The impressions of grief and horror were so lively on this occasion, that while they lasted, they made me more miserable than I was at the real death of this beloved person (which happened a few months after, at a time when the match between us was concluded), inasmuch as the imaginary death was untimely, and I myself in a sort an accessory ; whereas her real decease had at least these alleviations, of being natural and inevitable.

The memory of the dream I have related still dwells so strongly upon me, that I can never read the description of Dover Cliff in Shakespeare's tragedy of " King Lear,"[1] without a fresh sense of my escape. The prospect from that place is drawn with such proper incidents, that whoever can read it without growing giddy, must have a good head, or a very bad one.

[1] " King Lear," act iv. sc. 6.

" Come on, sir, here's the place ; stand still! How fearful
And dizzy 'tis to cast one's eyes so low ?
The crows and choughs that wing the midway air,
Show scarce as gross as beetles,   Half-way down
Hangs one that gathers samphire.   Dreadful trade !
Methinks he seems no bigger than his head.
The fishermen that walk upon the beach,
Appear like mice, and yond' tall anchoring bark
Diminished to her boat ;[1] her boat /[1] a buoy
Almost too small for sight.   The murmuring surge
(That on the unnumbered idle pebble beats)
Cannot be heard so high.   I'll look no more,
Lest my brain turn."[2]

No. 118.   [STEELE.[3]

From *Saturday*, Jan. 7, to *Tuesday*, Jan. 10, 1709–10.

Lusisti satis, edisti satis atque bibisti ;
Tempus abire tibi. . . .—HOR., 2 Ep. ii. 214.

From my own Apartment, January 8.

I thought to have given over my prosecution of the dead
for this season, having by me many other projects for
the reformation of mankind ; but I have received so many
complaints from such different hands, that I shall disoblige
multitudes of my correspondents, if I do not take notice
of them.   Some of the deceased, who I thought had been
laid quietly in their graves, are such hobgoblins in public
assemblies, that I must be forced to deal with them as
Evander did with his triple-lived adversary, who, according

[1] Altered from Shakespeare's " cock."
[2] " The parcel of letters, value 10s. 3d., with the subsequent letter,
is received, for which Mr. Bickerstaff gives his thanks and humble
service " (folio).
[3] Nichols suggests that Addison was at least partly responsible for
this paper.

to Virgil, was forced to kill him thrice over before he could despatch him.

" Ter leto sternendus erat."[1]

I am likewise informed, that several wives of my dead men have, since the decease of their husbands, been seen in many public places without mourning, or regard to common decency.

I am further advised, that several of the defunct, contrary to the Woollen Act,[2] presume to dress themselves in lace, embroidery, silks, muslins, and other ornaments forbidden to persons in their condition.   These and other the like informations moving me thereunto, I must desire, for distinction-sake, and to conclude this subject for ever, that when any of these posthumous persons appear, or are spoken of, their wives may be called "widows"; their houses, "sepulchres" ; their chariots, "hearses" ; and their garments, "flannel": on which condition, they shall be allowed all the conveniences that dead men can in reason desire.

As I was writing this morning on this subject, I received the following letter :

"MR. BICKERSTAFF,   *From the Banks of Styx.*

" **I** must confess I treated you very scurrilously when you first sent me hither ; but you have despatched such multitudes after me to keep me in countenance, that I am very well reconciled both to you and my condition.   We

[1] " Æneid," viii. 566.
[2] The Act "for burying in wool" (30 Charles II. cap. 3) was intended to protect homespun goods. Sometimes a fine was paid for allowing a person of position to be " buried in linen, contrary to the Act of Parliament."   The widow in Steele's " Funeral " (act v. sc. 2} says : " Take care I ain't buried in flannel ; 'twould never become me, I'm sure." See, too, Pope's " Moral Essays," i. 246 :
　　" ' Odious ! in woollen ! 'twould a saint provoke,'
　　Were the last words that poor Narcissa spoke."

live very lovingly together ; for as death makes us all equal, it makes us very much delight in one another's company. Our time passes away much after the same manner as it did when we were among you : eating, drinking, and sleeping, are our chief diversions. Our quidnuncs between whiles go to a coffee-house, where they have several warm liquors made of the waters of Lethe, with very good poppy tea. We that are the sprightly geniuses of the place, refresh ourselves frequently with a bottle of mum,[1] and tell stories till we fall asleep. You would do well to send among us Mr. Dodwell's[2] book against the immortality of the soul, which would be of great consolation to our whole fraternity, who would be very glad to find that they are dead for good and all, and would in particular make me rest for ever,

" Yours,

" John Partridge.

" P.S.—Sir James [3] is just arrived here in good health."

The foregoing letter was the more pleasing to me, because I perceive some little symptoms in it of a resuscitation ; and having lately seen the predictions of this author, which are written in a true Protestant spirit of prophecy, and a particular zeal against the French king, I have some thoughts of sending for him from the Banks

---

[1] Ale brewed with wheat. John Philips (" Cyder," ii. 231) speaks of " bowls of fattening mum."

[2] Henry Dodwell, the nonjuror, died in 1711, in his seventieth year. He tried to prove that immortality was conferred on the soul only at baptism, by the gift of God, through the hands of the ordained clergy. The title of the book alluded to is " An Epistolary Discourse concerning the Soul's Immortality."

[3] Sir James Baker. See No. 115.

of Styx, and reinstating him in his own house, at the sign of the Globe in Salisbury Street. For the encouragement of him and others, I shall offer to their consideration a letter which gives me an account of the revival of one of their brethren :

"SIR,　　　　　　　　　　　　　　*December* 31.

"I have perused your *Tatler* of this day,[1] and have wept over it with great pleasure : I wish you would be more frequent in your family pieces. For as I consider you under the notion of a great designer, I think these are not your least valuable performances. I am glad to find you have given over your face painting for some time, because, I think, you have employed yourself more in grotesque figures, than in beauties ; for which reason, I would rather see you work upon history pieces, than on single portraits. Your several draughts of dead men appear to me as pictures of still life, and have done great good in the place where I live. The squire of a neighbouring village, who had been a long time in the number of nonentities, is entirely recovered by them. For these several years past, there was not a hare in the county that could be at rest for him ; and I think, the greatest exploit he ever boasted of, was, that when he was high sheriff of the county, he hunted a fox so far, that he could not follow him any farther by the laws of the land. All the hours he spent at home, were in swilling[2] himself with October, and rehearsing the wonders he did in the field. Upon reading your papers, he has sold his dogs, shook off his dead companions, looked into his estate, got the multiplication table by heart, paid his tithes, and intends to take upon him the office of churchwarden next year. I wish the same success with your other patients, and am, &c."

[1] No. 114.　　　[2] The original editions read "swelling."

Ditto, January 9.

When I came home this evening, a very tight middle-aged woman presented to me the following petition :

" *To the Worshipful Isaac Bickerstaff, Esq., Censor of Great Britain.*

" The humble petition of Penelope Prim, widow ;

" Sheweth,

" That your petitioner was bred a clear-starcher and sempstress, and for many years worked to the Exchange ; and to several aldermen's wives, lawyers' clerks, and merchants' apprentices.

" That through the scarcity caused by regraters of bread-corn (of which starch is made) and the gentry's immoderate frequenting the operas, the ladies, to save charges, have their heads washed at home, and the beaus put out their linen to common laundresses, so that your petitioner hath little or no work at her trade : for want of which she is reduced to such necessity, that she and her seven fatherless children must inevitably perish, unless relieved by your worship.

" That your petitioner is informed, that in contempt of your judgment pronounced on Tuesday the third instant against the new-fashioned petticoat, or old-fashioned farthingale,[1] the ladies design to go on in that dress. And since it is presumed your worship will not suppress them by force, your petitioner humbly desires you would order, that ruffs may be added to the dress ; and that she may be heard by her counsel, who has assured your petitioner, he has such cogent reasons to offer to your court, that ruffs and farthingales are inseparable; and that he questions

[1] See No. 116.

not but two-thirds of the greatest beauties about town
will have cambric collars on their necks before the end of
Easter Term next.   He further says, that the design of our
great-grandmothers in this petticoat, was to appear much
bigger than the life ; for which reason, they had false
shoulder-blades, like wings, and the ruff above mentioned,
to make their upper and lower parts of their bodies appear
proportionable ; whereas the figure of a woman in the
present dress, bears (as he calls it) the figure of a cone,
which (as he advises) is the same with that of an extin-
guisher, with a little knob at the upper end, and widening
downward, till it ends in a basis of a most enormous
circumference.

" Your petitioner therefore most humbly prays, that
you would restore the ruff to the farthingale, which in their
nature ought to be as inseparable as the two Hungarian
twins.[1]

" And your Petitioner shall ever pray."

I have examined into the allegations of this petition,

[1] Helen and Judith, two united twin-sisters, were born at Tzoni, in
Hungary, October 26, 1701 ; lived to the age of twenty-one, and
died in a convent at Petersburg, February 23, 1723.   The mother, it
is said, survived their birth, bore another child afterwards, and was
alive when her singular twins were shown here, at a house in the
Strand, near Charing Cross, in 1708.   The writers of a periodical
publication at that time seem to have examined them carefully, with
a view to enable themselves to answer the many questions of their
correspondents concerning them.   See " The British Apollo," vol. i.
Nos. 35, 36, 37, &c. (1708), and the Royal Society's "Phil.
Transact." vol. l. part 1, for the year 1757, art. 39.   Nothing
more can be well said of the Hungarian twins here, but that they
were well shaped, had beautiful faces, and loved each other tenderly ;
they could read, write, and sing very prettily ; they spoke the Hungarian, High and Low Dutch, and French languages, and learnt
English when they were in this country (Nichols).

and find, by several ancient pictures of my own predecessors, particularly that of Dame Deborah Bickerstaff,
my great-grandmother, that the ruff and farthingale are
made use of as absolutely necessary to preserve the
symmetry of the figure ; and Mrs. Pyramid Bickerstaff,
her second sister, is recorded in our family-book, with
some observations to her disadvantage, as the first female
of our house that discovered, to any besides her nurse and
her husband, an inch below her chin or above her instep.
This convinces me of the reasonableness of Mrs. Prim's
demand ; and therefore I shall not allow the reviving of
any one part of that ancient mode, except the whole is
complied with. Mrs. Prim is therefore hereby empowered
to carry home ruffs to such as she shall see in the above-
mentioned petticoats, and require payment on demand.

Mr. Bickerstaff has under consideration the offer from
the Corporation of Colchester of four hundred pounds
per annum, to be paid quarterly, provided that all his
dead persons shall be obliged to wear the baize of that
place.

No. 119. [ADDISON.

From *Tuesday, Jan.* 10, to *Thursday, Jan.* 12, 1709–10.

In tenui labor.—VIRG., Georg. iv. 6.

Sheer Lane, January 11.

I have lately applied myself with much satisfaction to the
curious discoveries that have been made by the help of
microscopes, as they are related by authors of our own and
other nations. There is a great deal of pleasure in prying
into this world of wonders, which Nature has laid out of

sight, and seems industrious to conceal from us. Philosophy had ranged over all the visible creation, and began to want objects for her inquiries, when the present age, by the invention of glasses, opened a new and inexhaustible magazine of rarities, more wonderful and amazing than any of those which astonished our forefathers. I was yesterday amusing myself with speculations of this kind, and reflecting upon myriads of animals that swim in those little seas of juices that are contained in the several vessels of a human body. While my mind was thus filled with that secret wonder and delight, I could not but look upon myself as in an act of devotion, and am very well pleased with the thought of the great heathen anatomist,[1] who calls his description of the parts of a human body, " A Hymn to the Supreme Being." The reading of the day produced in my imagination an agreeable morning's dream, if I may call it such ; for I am still in doubt, whether it passed in my sleeping or waking thoughts. However it was, I fancied that my good genius stood at my bed's head, and entertained me with the following discourse ; for upon my rising, it dwelt so strongly upon me, that I wrote down the substance of it, if not the very words.

" If," said he, " you can be so transported with those productions of nature which are discovered to you by those artificial eyes that are the works of human invention, how great will your surprise be, when you shall have it in your power to model your own eye as you please, and adapt it to the bulk of objects, which, with all these helps, are by infinite degrees too minute for your perception. We who are unbodied spirits can sharpen our sight to what degree we think fit, and make the least work of the creation distinct and visible. This gives us such ideas as cannot possibly enter into your present conceptions.

[1] Galen, " De Usu Partium."

There is not the least particle of matter which may not furnish one of us sufficient employment for a whole eternity. We can still divide it, and still open it, and still discover new wonders of Providence, as we look into the different texture of its parts, and meet with beds of vegetables, mineral and metallic mixtures, and several kinds of animals that lie hid, and as it were lost in such an endless fund of matter. I find you are surprised at this discourse ; but as your reason tells you there are infinite parts in the smallest portion of matter, it will likewise convince you, that there is as great a variety of secrets, and as much room for discoveries, in a particle no bigger than the point of a pin, as in the globe of the whole earth. Your microscopes bring to sight shoals of living creatures in a spoonful of vinegar ; but we who can distinguish them in their different magnitudes, see among them several huge leviathans, that terrify the little fry of animals about them, and take their pastime as in an ocean, or the great deep." I could not but smile at this part of his relation, and told him, I doubted not but he could give me the history of several invisible giants, accompanied with their respective dwarfs, in case that any of these little beings are of a human shape. "You may assure yourself," said he, " that we see in these little animals different natures, instincts and modes of life, which correspond to what you observe in creatures of bigger dimensions. We descry millions of species subsisted on a green leaf, which your glasses represent only in crowds and swarms. What appears to your eye but as hair or down rising on the surface of it, we find to be woods and forests, inhabited by beasts of prey, that are as dreadful in those their little haunts, as lions and tigers in the deserts of Libya." I was much delighted with his discourse, and could not forbear telling him, that I should be wonderfully pleased to

see a natural history of imperceptibles, containing a true
account of such vegetables and animals as grow and live
out of sight. " Such disquisitions," answered he, " are
very suitable to reasonable creatures ; and you may be
sure, there are many curious spirits amongst us who
employ themselves in such amusements. For as our
hands, and all our senses, may be formed to what degree
of strength and delicacy we please, in the same manner as
our sight, we can make what experiments we are inclined
to, how small soever the matter be in which we make
them. I have been present at the dissection of a mite,
and have seen the skeleton of a flea. I have been shown
a forest of numberless trees, which has been picked out of
an acorn. Your microscope can show you in it a complete oak in miniature ; and could you suit all your organs
as we do, you might pluck an acorn from this little oak,
which contains another tree ; and so proceed from tree to
tree, as long as you would think fit to continue your disquisitions. It is almost impossible," added he, "to talk
of things so remote from common life, and the ordinary
notions which mankind receive from blunt and gross
organs of sense, without appearing extravagant and
ridiculous. You have often seen a dog opened, to observe
the circulation of the blood, or make any other useful
inquiry ; and yet would be tempted to laugh if I should
tell you, that a circle of much greater philosophers than
any of the Royal Society, were present at the cutting up of
one of those little animals which we find in the blue of a
plum : that it was tied down alive before them ; and that
they observed the palpitations of the heart, the course of
the blood, the working of the muscles, and the convulsions
in the several limbs, with great accuracy and improvement."
" I must confess," said I, " for my own part, I go along with
you in all your discoveries with great pleasure ; but it is

certain, they are too fine for the gross of mankind, who are more struck with the description of everything that is great and bulky. Accordingly we find the best judge of human nature setting forth his wisdom, not in the formation of these minute animals (though indeed no less wonderful than the other) but in that of the leviathan and behemoth, the horse and the crocodile."[1] " Your observation," said he, " is very just ; and I must acknowledge for my own part, that although it is with much delight that I see the traces of Providence in these instances, I still take greater pleasure in considering the works of the creation in their immensity, than in their minuteness. For this reason, I rejoice when I strengthen my sight so as to make it pierce into the most remote spaces, and take a view of those heavenly bodies which lie out of the reach of human eyes, though assisted by telescopes. What you look upon as one confused white in the Milky Way, appears to me a long tract of heavens, distinguished by stars that are ranged in proper figures and constellations. While you are admiring the sky in a starry night, I am entertained with a variety of worlds and suns placed one above another, and rising up to such an immense distance, that no created eye can see an end of them."

The latter part of his discourse flung me into such an astonishment, that he had been silent for some time before I took notice of it ; when on a sudden I started up and drew my curtains, to look if any one was near me, but saw nobody, and cannot tell to this moment whether it was my good genius or a dream that left me.

[1] See Job, chaps. 39–41.

No. 120.   [ADDISON.

From *Thursday, Jan.* 12, to *Saturday, Jan.* 14, 1709–10.

—— Velut silvis, ubi passim
Palantes error certo de tramite pellit ;
Ille sinistrorsum, hic dextrorsum abit.
                                        HOR., 2 Sat. iii. 48.

Sheer Lane, January 13.

Instead of considering any particular passion or character
in any one set of men, my thoughts were last night
employed on the contemplation of human life in general ;
and truly it appears to me, that the whole species are
hurried on by the same desires, and engaged in the same
pursuits, according to the different stages and divisions
of life. Youth is devoted to lust, middle age to ambition, old age to avarice. These are the three general
motives and principles of action both in good and bad
men ; though it must be acknowledged, that they change
their names, and resign their natures, according to the
temper of the person whom they direct and animate. For
with the good, lust becomes virtuous love ; ambition, true
honour ; and avarice, the care of posterity. This scheme
of thought amused me very agreeably till I retired to rest,
and afterwards formed itself into a pleasing and regular
vision, which I shall describe in all its circumstances, as
the objects presented themselves, whether in a serious or
ridiculous manner.

I dreamed that I was in a wood, of so prodigious an
extent, and cut into such a variety of walks and alleys,
that all mankind were lost and bewildered in it. After
having wandered up and down some time, I came into the
centre of it, which opened into a wide plain, that was

filled with multitudes of both sexes. I here discovered three great roads, very wide and long, that led into three different parts of the forest. On a sudden, the whole multitude broke into three parts, according to their different ages, and marched in their respective bodies into the three great roads that lay before them. As I had a mind to know how each of these roads terminated, and whither it would lead those who passed through them, I joined myself with the assembly that were in the flower and vigour of their age, and called themselves, "The Band of Lovers." I found to my great surprise, that several old men besides myself had intruded into this agreeable company ; as I had before observed, there were some young men who had united themselves to the Band of Misers, and were walking up the path of avarice ; though both made a very ridiculous figure, and were as much laughed at by those they joined, as by those they forsook. The walk which we marched up, for thickness of shades, embroidery of flowers, and melody of birds, with the distant purling of streams, and falls of water, was so wonderfully delightful, that it charmed our senses, and intoxicated our minds with pleasure. We had not been long here, before every man singled out some woman to whom he offered his addresses and professed himself a lover ; when on a sudden we perceived this delicious walk to grow more narrow as we advanced in it, till it ended in many intricate thickets, mazes and labyrinths, that were so mixed with roses and brambles, brakes of thorns, and beds of flowers, rocky paths and pleasing grottoes, that it was hard to say, whether it gave greater delight or perplexity to those who travelled in it.

It was here that the lovers began to be eager in their pursuits. Some of their mistresses, who only seemed to retire for the sake of form and decency, led them into plantations that were disposed into regular walks ; where, after they had wheeled about in some turns and windings, they suffered themselves to be overtaken, and gave their hands to those who pursued them. Others withdrew from their followers into little wildernesses, where there were so many paths interwoven with each other in so much confusion and irregularity, that several of the lovers quitted the pursuit, or broke their hearts in the chase. It was sometimes very odd to see a man pursuing a fine woman that was following another, whose eye was fixed upon a fourth, that had her own game in view in some other quarter of the wilderness. I could not but observe two things in this place which I thought very particular, that several persons who stood only at the end of the avenues, and cast a careless eye upon the nymphs during their whole flight, often caught them, when those who pressed them the most warmly through all their turns and doubles, were wholly unsuccessful : and that some of my own age, who were at first looked upon with aversion and contempt, by being well acquainted with the wilderness, and by dodging their women in the particular corners and alleys of it, caught them in their arms, and took them from those they really loved and admired. There was a particular grove, which was called, " The Labyrinth of Coquettes " ; where many were enticed to the chase, but few returned with purchase. It was pleasant enough to see a celebrated beauty, by smiling upon one, casting a glance upon another, beckoning to a third, and adapting her charms and graces to the several follies of those that admired her, drawing into the labyrinth a whole pack of lovers, that lost themselves in the maze, and never could find their way out of it. However, it was some satisfaction to me, to see many of the fair ones who had thus deluded their followers, and left them among the intricacies of the labyrinth, obliged when they came out of it, to surrender to the first partner that offered himself. I now had crossed over all the difficult and perplexed passages that seemed to bound our walk, when on the other side of them, I saw the same great road running on a little way, till it was terminated by two beautiful temples. I stood here for some time, and saw most of the multitude who had been dispersed amongst the thickets, coming out two by two, and marching up in pairs towards the temples that stood before us. The structure on the right hand was (as I afterwards found) consecrated to virtuous love, and could not be entered but by such as received a ring, or some other token, from a person who was placed as a guard at the gate of it. He wore a garland of roses and myrtles on his head, and on his shoulders a robe like an imperial mantle, white and unspotted all over, excepting only, that where it was clasped at his breast, there were two golden turtle-doves that buttoned it by their bills, which were wrought in rubies. He was called by the name of Hymen, and was seated near the entrance of the temple, in a delicious bower, made up of several trees, that were embraced by wood-bines, jessamines, and amaranths, which were as so many emblems of marriage, and ornaments to the trunks that supported them. As I was single and unaccompanied, I was not permitted to enter the temple, and for that reason am a stranger to all the mysteries that were performed in it. I had however the curiosity to observe how the several couples that entered were disposed of; which was after the following manner. There were two great gates on the back side of the edifice, at which the whole crowd was let out. At one of these gates were two women, extremely beautiful, though in a different kind, the one having a very careful and composed air, the other a sort of smile and ineffable sweetness in her countenance. The name of the first was Discretion, and of the other Complacency. All who came out of this gate, and put themselves under the direction of these two sisters, were immediately conducted by them into gardens, groves, and meadows, which abounded in delights, and were furnished with everything that could make them the proper seats of happiness. The second gate of this temple let out all the couples that were unhappily married, who came out linked together by chains, which each of them strove to break, but could not. Several of these were such as had never been acquainted with each other before they met in the great walk, or had been too well acquainted in the thicket. The entrance to this gate was possessed by three sisters, who joined themselves with these wretches, and occasioned most of their miseries. The youngest of the sisters was known by the name of Levity, who with the innocence of a virgin, had the dress and behaviour of a harlot. The name of the second was Contention, who bore on her right arm a muff made of the skin of a porcupine; and on her left carried a little lap-dog, that barked and snapped at every one that passed by her.

The eldest of the sisters, who seemed to have a haughty and imperious air, was always accompanied with a tawny Cupid, who generally marched before her with a little mace on his shoulder, the end of which was fashioned into the horns of a stag. Her garments were yellow, and her complexion pale. Her eyes were piercing, but had odd casts in them, and that particular distemper, which makes persons who are troubled with it, see objects double. Upon inquiry, I was informed that her name was Jealousy.

Having finished my observations upon this temple, and its votaries, I repaired to that which stood on the left hand, and was called, "The Temple of Lust." The front of it was raised on Corinthian pillars, with all the meretricious

ornaments that accompany that order ; whereas that of
the other was composed of the chaste and matronlike
Ionic.   The sides of it were adorned with several grotesque
figures of goats, sparrows, heathen gods, satyrs, and
monsters made up of half-man half-beast. The gates
were unguarded, and open to all that had a mind to enter.
Upon my going in, I found the windows were blinded,
and let in only a kind of twilight, that served to discover
a prodigious number of dark corners and apartments, into
which the whole temple was divided.   I was here stunned
with a mixed noise of clamour and jollity : on one side of
me, I heard singing and dancing ; on the other, brawls
and clashing of swords.   In short, I was so little pleased
with the place, that I was going out of it ; but found
I could not return by the gate where I entered, which was
barred against all that were come in, with bolts of iron,
and locks of adamant.   There was no going back from
this temple through the paths of pleasure which led to it:
all who passed through the ceremonies of the place, went
out at an iron wicket, which was kept by a dreadful giant
called Remorse, that held a scourge of scorpions in his
hand, and drove them into the only outlet from that
temple.   This was a passage so rugged, so uneven, and
choked with so many thorns and briars, that it was a
melancholy spectacle to behold the pains and difficulties
which both sexes suffered who walked through it.   The
men, though in the prime of their youth, appeared weak
and enfeebled with old age : the women wrung their hands,
and tore their hair ; and several lost their limbs before
they could extricate themselves out of the perplexities of
the path in which they were engaged. The remaining
part of this vision, and the adventures I met with in the
two great roads of ambition and avarice, must be the
subject of another paper.

ADVERTISEMENT.

I have this morning received the following letter from the famous Mr. Thomas Doggett:[1]

"SIR,

"On Monday next will be acted for my benefit, the comedy of 'Love for Love': if you will do me the honour to appear there, I will publish on the bills, that it is to be performed at the request of Isaac Bicker-staff, Esq.; and question not but it will bring me as great an audience, as ever was at the house since the Morocco ambassador was there.[2] I am, (with the greatest respect)

"Your most obedient and
"Most humble Servant,
"THOMAS DOGGETT."

Being naturally an encourager of wit, as well as bound to it in the quality of censor, I returned the following answer:

"MR. DOGGETT,

"I am very well pleased with the choice you have made of so excellent a play, and have always looked upon you as the best of comedians; I shall therefore come in between the first and second act, and remain in the right-hand box over the pit till the end of the fourth, provided you take care that everything be rightly prepared for my reception."[3]

[1] See No. 1.
[2] The Morocco ambassador made his public entry into London in April 1706. Don Venturo Zary, another Morocco minister, visited the Haymarket Theatre on May 4, 1710, with his "attendants in their several habits, &c., having never as yet appeared in public." There was no play at Drury Lane Theatre that night (*Postboy*, April 29 to May 2, 1710).   [3] See No. 122.

No. 121.   [ADDISON.

From *Saturday*, *Jan.* 14, to *Tuesday*, *Jan.* 17, 1709–10.

—— Similis tibi, Cynthia, vel tibi, cujus
Turbavit nitidos extinctus passer ocellos.

Juv., Sat. vi. 7.

From my own Apartment, January 16.

I was recollecting the remainder of my vision, when my
maid came to me, and told me, there was a gentlewoman below who seemed to be in great trouble, and
pressed very much to see me.   When it lay in my power
to remove the distress of an unhappy person, I thought I
should very ill employ my time in attending matters of
speculation, and therefore desired the lady would walk in.
When she entered, I saw her eyes full of tears.   However,
her grief was not so great as to make her omit rules ; for
she was very long and exact in her civilities, which gave
me time to view and consider her.   Her clothes were
very rich, but tarnished ; and her words very fine, but ill
applied.   These distinctions made me without hesitation
(though I had never seen her before) ask her, if her lady
had any commands for me ?   She then began to weep
afresh, and with many broken sighs told me, that their
family was in very great affliction.   I beseeched her to
compose herself, for that I might possibly be capable of
assisting them.   She then cast her eye upon my little dog,
and was again transported with too much passion to proceed ; but with much ado, she at last gave me to understand, that Cupid, her lady's lap-dog, was dangerously ill,
and in so bad a condition, that her lady neither saw company, nor went abroad, for which reason she did not come

39

herself to consult me ; that as I had mentioned with great
affection my own dog (here she curtsied, and looking first
at the cur, and then on me, said, indeed I had reason, for
he was very pretty) her lady sent to me rather than to any
other doctor, and hoped I would not laugh at her sorrow,
but send her my advice. I must confess, I had some
indignation to find myself treated like something below a
farrier ; yet well knowing, that the best, as well as most
tender way of dealing with a woman, is to fall in with her
humours, and by that means to let her see the absurdity
of them, I proceeded accordingly : " Pray, madam,"
said I, " can you give me any methodical account of this
illness, and how Cupid was first taken ? "   " Sir," said
she, " we have a little ignorant country girl who is kept to
tend him : she was recommended to our family by one,
that my lady never saw but once, at a visit ; and you
know, persons of quality are always inclined to strangers ;
for I could have helped her to a cousin of my own,
but——"   " Good madam," said I, " you neglect the
account of the sick body, while you are complaining of
this girl."   " No, no, sir," said she, " begging your
pardon : but it is the general fault of physicians, they are
so in haste, that they never hear out the case.   I say, this
silly girl, after washing Cupid, let him stand half an hour
in the window without his collar, where he caught cold,
and in an hour after began to bark very hoarse.   He had
however a pretty good night, and we hoped the danger
was over ; but for these two nights last past, neither he
nor my lady have slept a wink."   " Has he," said I,
" taken anything ? "   " No," said she, " but my lady says,
he shall take anything that you prescribe, provided you
do not make use of Jesuits' powder,[1] or the cold bath.
Poor Cupid," continued she, " has always been phthisical,

[1] Peruvian Bark, then comparatively little used.

and as he lies under something like a chin-cough, we are
afraid it will end in a consumption." I then asked her, if
she had brought any of his water to show me. Upon
this, she stared me in the face, and said, "I am afraid,
Mr. Bickerstaff, you are not serious; but if you have
any receipt that is proper on this occasion, pray let us
have it; for my mistress is not to be comforted." Upon
this, I paused a little without returning any answer, and
after some short silence, I proceeded in the following
manner: "I have considered the nature of the distemper,
and the constitution of the patient, and by the best
observation that I can make on both, I think it is safest
to put him into a course of kitchen physic. In the meantime, to remove his hoarseness, it will be the most natural
way to make Cupid his own druggist; for which reason, I
shall prescribe to him, three mornings successively, as
much powder as will lie on a groat, of that noble
remedy which the apothecaries call 'Album Græcum.'"
Upon hearing this advice, the young woman smiled, as if
she knew how ridiculous an errand she had been employed
in; and indeed I found by the sequel of her discourse,
that she was an arch baggage, and of a character that is
frequent enough in persons of her employment, who are
so used to conform themselves in everything to the
humours and passions of their mistresses, that they sacrifice
superiority of sense to superiority of condition, and are
insensibly betrayed into the passions and prejudices of
those whom they serve, without giving themselves leave to
consider, that they are extravagant and ridiculous. However I thought it very natural, when her eyes were thus
open, to see her give a new turn to her discourse, and from
sympathising with her mistress in her follies, to fall a-rail-
ing at her. "You cannot imagine," said she, "Mr.
Bickerstaff, what a life she makes us lead for the sake of

this little ugly cur : if he dies, we are the most unhappy family in town.   She chanced to lose a parrot last year, which, to tell you truly, brought me into her service ; for she turned off her woman upon it, who had lived with her ten years, because she neglected to give him water, though every one of the family says, she was as innocent of the bird's death as the babe that is unborn.   Nay, she told me this very morning, that if Cupid should die, she would send the poor innocent wench I was telling you of, to Bridewell, and have the milkwoman tried for her life at the Old Bailey, for putting water into his milk.   In short, she talks like any distracted creature."

"Since it is so, young woman," said I, "I will by no means let you offend her, by staying on this message longer than is absolutely necessary," and so forced her out.

While I am studying to cure those evils and distresses that are necessary or natural to human life, I find my task growing upon me, since by these accidental cares, and acquired calamities, if I may so call them, my patients contract distempers to which their constitution is of itself a stranger.   But this is an evil I have for many years remarked in the fair sex ; and as they are by nature very much formed for affection and dalliance, I have observed, that when by too obstinate a cruelty, or any other means, they have disappointed themselves of the proper objects of love, as husbands, or children, such virgins have exactly at such a year grown fond of lap-dogs, parrots, or other animals.   I know at this time a celebrated toast, whom I allow to be one of the most agreeable of her sex, that in the presence of her admirers, will give a torrent of kisses to her cat, any one of which a Christian would be glad of. I do not at the same time deny, but there are as great enormities of this kind committed by our sex as theirs.

42

A Roman emperor had so very great an esteem for a horse of his, that he had thoughts of making him a consul; and several moderns of that rank of men whom we call country squires, won't scruple to kiss their hounds before all the world, and declare in the presence of their wives, that they had rather salute a favourite of the pack, than the finest woman in England. These voluntary friendships between animals of different species, seem to arise from instinct ; for which reason, I have always looked upon the mutual goodwill between the squire and the hound, to be of the same nature with that between the lion and the jackal.

The only extravagance of this kind which appears to me excusable, is one that grew out of an excess of gratitude, which I have somewhere met with in the life of a Turkish emperor. His horse had brought him safe out of a field of battle, and from the pursuit of a victorious enemy. As a reward for such his good and faithful service, his master built him a stable of marble, shod him with gold, fed him in an ivory manger, and made him a rack of silver. He annexed to the stable several fields and meadows, lakes, and running streams. At the same time he provided for him a seraglio of mares, the most beautiful that could be found in the whole Ottoman Empire. To these were added a suitable train of domestics, consisting of grooms, farriers, rubbers, &c., accommodated with proper liveries and pensions. In short, nothing was omitted that could contribute to the ease and happiness of his life who had preserved the emperor's.

By reason of the extreme cold, and the changeableness of the weather, I have been prevailed upon to allow the free use of the farthingale, till the 20th of February next ensuing.

13

No. 122.   [ADDISON.

From *Tuesday, Jan.* 17, to *Thursday, Jan.* 19, 1709–10.

Cur in theatrum, Cato severe, venisti ?
MART., Epig. i. Prol. 21.

From my own Apartment, January 18.

I find it is thought necessary, that I (who have taken upon me to censure the irregularities of the age) should give an account of my own actions when they appear doubtful, or subject to misconstruction. My appearing at the play on Monday last,[1] is looked upon as a step in my conduct, which I ought to explain, that others may not be misled by my example. It is true in matter of fact, I was present at the ingenious entertainment of that day, and placed myself in a box which was prepared for me with great civility and distinction. It is said of Virgil, when he entered a Roman theatre, where there were many thousands of spectators present, that the whole assembly rose up to do him honour ; a respect which was never before paid to any but the emperor. I must confess, that universal clap, and other testimonies of applause, with which I was received at my first appearance in the theatre of Great Britain, gave me as sensible a delight, as the above-mentioned reception could give to that immortal poet. I should be ungrateful at the same time, if I did not take this opportunity of acknowledging the great civilities that were shown me by Mr. Thomas Doggett, who made his compliments to me between the acts, after a

---

[1] See No. 120. "A person dressed for Isaac Bickerstaff did appear at the playhouse on this occasion " (Addison's " Works," Birmingham, ii. 246).

most ingenuous and discreet manner ; and at the same
time communicated to me, that the Company of Upholders
desired to receive me at their door at the end of the
Haymarket, and to light me home to my lodgings. That
part of the ceremony I forbad, and took particular care
during the whole play to observe the conduct of the
drama, and give no offence by my own behaviour. Here
I think it will not be foreign to my character, to lay down
the proper duties of an audience, and what is incumbent
upon each individual spectator in public diversions of this
nature. Every one should on these occasions show his
attention, understanding and virtue. I would undertake
to find out all the persons of sense and breeding by the
effect of a single sentence, and to distinguish a gentleman
as much by his laugh, as his bow. When we see the
footman and his lord diverted by the same jest, it very
much turns to the diminution of the one, or the honour of
the other. But though a man's quality may appear in his
understanding and taste, the regard to virtue ought to be
the same in all ranks and conditions of men, however they
make a profession of it under the name of honour, religion, or morality. When therefore we see anything divert
an audience, either in tragedy or comedy, that strikes at
the duties of civil life, or exposes what the best men in all
ages have looked upon as sacred and inviolable, it is the
certain sign of a profligate race of men, who are fallen
from the virtue of their forefathers, and will be contemptible in the eyes of their posterity. For this reason
I took great delight in seeing the generous and disinterested
passion of the lovers in this comedy (which stood so many
trials, and was proved by such a variety of diverting
incidents) received with an universal approbation. This
brings to my mind a passage in Cicero,[1] which I could

[1] "De Amicitia," vii.

never read without being in love with the virtue of a
Roman audience. He there describes the shouts and
applause which the people gave to the persons who acted
the parts of Pylades and Orestes, in the noblest occasion
that a poet could invent to show friendship in perfection.
One of them had forfeited his life by an action which he
had committed ; and as they stood in judgment before the
tyrant, each of them strove who should be the criminal,
that he might save the life of his friend. Amidst the
vehemence of each asserting himself to be the offender,
the Roman audience gave a thunder of applause, and by
that means, as the author hints, approved in others what
they would have done themselves on the like occasion.
Methinks, a people of so much virtue were deservedly
placed at the head of mankind : But alas ! pleasures of
this nature are not frequently to be met with on the
English stage.

The Athenians, at a time when they were the most
polite, as well as the most powerful, government in the
world, made the care of the stage one of the chief parts of
the administration : and I must confess, I am astonished
at the spirit of virtue which appeared in that people upon
some expressions in a scene of a famous tragedy ; an
account of which we have in one of Seneca's epistles.[1] A
covetous person is represented speaking the common sentiments of all who are possessed with that vice in the following
soliloquy, which I have translated literally :

Let me be called a base man, so I am called a rich one.
If a man is rich, who asks if he is good ? The question
is, How much we have ; not from whence, or by what
means, we have it. Every one has so much merit as he
has wealth. For my own part, let me be rich, O ye gods !

[1] L. A. Senecæ Opera, Lips., 1741, ii. 520.

or let me die.   The man dies happily, who dies increasing his treasure.   There is more pleasure in the possession of wealth, than in that of parents, children, wife, or friends."

The audience were very much provoked by the first words of this speech ; but when the actor came to the close of it, they could bear no longer.   In short, the whole assembly rose up at once in the greatest fury, with a design to pluck him off the stage, and brand the work itself with infamy.   In the midst of the tumult, the author came out from behind the scenes, begging the audience to be composed for a little while, and they should see the tragical end which this wretch should come to immediately.   The promise of punishment appeased the people, who sat with great attention and pleasure to see an example made of so odious a criminal.   It is with shame and concern that I speak it ; but I very much question, whether it is possible to make a speech so impious, as to raise such a laudable horror and indignation in a modern audience.   It is very natural for an author to make ostentation of his reading, as it is for an old man to tell stories ; for which reason I must beg the reader will excuse me, if I for once indulge myself in both these inclinations.   We see the attention, judgment, and virtue of a whole audience, in the foregoing instances.   If we would imitate the behaviour of a single spectator, let us reflect upon that of Socrates, in a particular which gives me as great an idea of that extraordinary man, as any circumstance of his life ; or what is more, of his death. This venerable person often frequented the theatre, which brought a great many thither, out of a desire to see him ; on which occasions it is recorded of him, that he sometimes stood to make himself the more conspicuous, and to satisfy the curiosity of the beholders.   He was one day present at the first representation of a tragedy of Euripides, who was his intimate friend, and whom he is said to have assisted in several of his plays. In the midst of the tragedy, which had met with very great success, there chanced to be a line that seemed to encourage vice and immorality.

This was no sooner spoken, but Socrates rose from his seat, and without any regard to his affection for his friend, or to the success of the play, showed himself displeased at what was said, and walked out of the assembly. I question not but the reader will be curious to know what the line was that gave this divine heathen so much offence. If my memory fails me not, it was in the part of Hippolitus, who when he is pressed by an oath, which he had taken to keep silence, returned for answer, that he had taken the oath with his tongue, but not with his heart. Had a person of a vicious character made such a speech, it might have been allowed as a proper representation of the baseness of his thoughts : but such an expression out of the mouth of the virtuous Hippolitus, was giving a sanction to falsehood, and establishing perjury by a maxim.

Having got over all interruptions, I have set apart to-morrow for the closing of my vision.[1]

---

[1] See Nos. 120, 123.

No. 123. [ADDISON.

From *Thursday*, *Jan.* 19, to *Saturday*, *Jan.* 21, 1709–10.

Audire, atque togam jubeo componere, quisquis
Ambitione malâ, aut argenti pallet amore.
HOR., 2 Sat. iii. 77.

From my own Apartment, January 20.

A Continuation of the Vision.[1]

With much labour and difficulty I passed through the first part of my vision, and recovered the centre of the wood, from whence I had the prospect of the three great roads. I here joined myself to the middle-aged party of mankind, who marched behind the standard of Ambition. The great road lay in a direct line, and was terminated by the Temple of Virtue. It was planted on each side with laurels, which were intermixed with marble trophies, carved pillars, and statues of lawgivers, heroes, statesmen, philosophers, and poets. The persons who travelled up this great path, were such whose thoughts were bent upon doing eminent services to mankind, or promoting the good of their country. On each side of this great road were several paths, that were also laid out in straight lines, and ran parallel with it. These were most of them covered walks, and received into them men of retired virtue, who proposed to themselves the same end of their journey, though they chose to make it in shade and obscurity. The edifices at the extremity of the walk were so contrived, that we could not see the Temple of Honour by reason of the Temple of Virtue, which stood before it. At the gates of this temple we were

[1] See No. 120.

met by the goddess of it, who conducted us into that of Honour, which was joined to the other edifice by a beautiful triumphal arch, and had no other entrance into it. When the deity of the inner structure had received us, she presented us in a body to a figure that was placed over the high altar, and was the emblem of eternity. She sat on a globe in the midst of a golden zodiac, holding the figure of a sun in one hand, and a moon in the other. Her head was veiled, and her feet covered. Our hearts glowed within us as we stood amidst the sphere of light which this image cast on every side of it.

Having seen all that happened to this band of adventurers, I repaired to another pile of buildings that stood within view of the Temple of Honour, and was raised in imitation of it, upon the very same model ; but at my approach to it, I found that the stones were laid together without mortar, and that the whole fabric stood upon so weak a foundation, that it shook with every wind that blew. This was called the Temple of Vanity. The goddess of it sat in the midst of a great many tapers, that burned day and night, and made her appear much better than she would have done in open daylight. Her whole art was to show herself more beautiful and majestic than she really was. For which reason, she had painted her face, and wore a cluster of false jewels upon her breast : but what I more particularly observed, was, the breadth of her petticoat, which was made altogether in the fashion of a modern farthingale. This place was filled with hypocrites, pedants, freethinkers, and prating politicians ; with a rabble of those who have only titles to make them great men. Female votaries crowded the temple, choked up the avenues of it, and were more in number than the sand upon the seashore. I made it my business in my return towards that part of the wood from whence I first set out, to observe the walks which led to this temple ; for I met in it several who had begun their journey with the band of virtuous persons, and travelled some time in their company : but upon examination I found, that there were several paths which led out of the great road into the sides of the wood, and ran into so many crooked turns and windings, that those who travelled through them often turned their backs upon the Temple of Virtue, then crossed the straight road, and sometimes marched in it for a little space, till the crooked path which they were engaged in again led them into the wood. The several alleys of these wanderers had their particular ornaments : one of them I could not but take notice of, in the walk of the mischievous pretenders to politics, which had at every turn the figure of a person, whom by the inscription I found to be Machiavel, pointing out the way with an extended finger like a Mercury.

I was now returned in the same manner as before, with a design to observe carefully everything that passed in the region of Avarice, and the occurrences in that assembly, which was made up of persons of my own age. This body of travellers had not gone far in the third great road, before it led them insensibly into a deep valley, in which they journeyed several days with great toil and uneasiness, and without the necessary refreshments of food and sleep. The only relief they met with, was in a river that ran through the bottom of the valley on a bed of golden sand : they often drank of this stream, which had such a particular quality in it, that though it refreshed them for a time, it rather inflamed than quenched their thirst. On each side of the river was a range of hills full of precious ore ; for where the rains had washed off the earth, one might see in several parts of them long veins of gold, and rocks that looked like pure silver. We were told that the deity of the place had forbade any of his votaries to dig into the bowels of these hills, or convert the treasures they contained to any use, under pain of starving. At the end of the valley stood the Temple of Avarice, made after the manner of a fortification, and surrounded with a thousand triple-headed dogs, that were placed there to keep off beggars. At our approach they all fell a-barking, and would have very much terrified us, had not an old woman who had called herself by the forged name of Competency offered herself for our guide. She carried under her garment a golden bow, which she no sooner held up in her hand, but the dogs lay down, and the gates flew open for our reception. We were led through a hundred iron doors, before we entered the temple. At the upper end of it sat the god of Avarice, with a long filthy beard, and a meagre starved countenance, enclosed with heaps of ingots and pyramids of money, but half naked and shivering with cold. On his right hand was a fiend called Rapine, and on his left a particular favourite to whom he had given the title of Parsimony. The first was his collector, and the other his cashier.

There were several long tables placed on each side of the temple, with respective officers attending behind them. Some of these I inquired into. At the first table was kept the office of Corruption. Seeing a solicitor extremely busy, and whispering everybody that passed by, I kept my eye upon him very attentively, and saw him often going up to a person that had a pen in his hand, with a multiplication table and an almanac before him, which as I afterwards heard, was all the learning he was master of. The solicitor would often apply himself to his ear, and at the same time convey money into his hand, for which the other would give him out a piece of paper or parchment, signed and sealed in form. The name of this dexterous and successful solicitor was Bribery. At the next table was the office of Extortion. Behind it sat a person in a bob-wig, counting over a great sum of money. He gave out little purses to several, who after a short tour brought him, in return, sacks full of the same kind of coin. I saw at the same time a person called Fraud, who sat behind a counter with false scales, light weights, and scanty measures ; by the skilful application of which instruments, she had got together an immense heap of wealth. It would be endless to name the several officers, or describe the votaries that attended in this temple. There were many old men panting and breathless, repos-ing their heads on bags of money ; nay many of them actually dying, whose very pangs and convulsions, which rendered their purses useless to them, only made them grasp them the faster. There were some tearing with one hand all things, even to the garments and flesh of many miserable persons who stood before them, and with the other hand, throwing away what they had seized, to harlots, flatterers, and panders, that stood behind them.

On a sudden the whole assembly fell a-trembling, and upon inquiry, I found, that the great room we were in was haunted with a spectre, that many times a day ap-peared to them, and terrified them to distraction.

In the midst of their terror and amazement the appari-tion entered, which I immediately knew to be Poverty. Whether it were by my acquaintance with this phantom, which had rendered the sight of her more familiar to me, or however it was, she did not make so indigent or fright-ful a figure in my eye, as the god of this loathsome temple. The miserable votaries of this place, were, I found, of another mind. Every one fancied himself threatened by the apparition as she stalked about the room, and began to lock their coffers, and tie their bags, with the utmost fear and trembling.

I must confess, I look upon the passion which I saw in this unhappy people to be of the same nature with those unaccountable antipathies which some persons are born with, or rather as a kind of frenzy, not unlike that which throws a man into terrors and agonies at the sight of so useful and innocent a thing as water. The whole assembly was surprised, when, instead of paying my devotions to the deity whom they all adored, they saw me address myself to the phantom.

"O Poverty!" said I, "my first petition to thee is, that thou wouldst never appear to me hereafter; but if thou wilt not grant me this, that thou wouldst not bear a form more terrible than that in which thou appearest to me at present. Let not thy threats and menaces betray me to anything that is ungrateful or unjust. Let me not shut my ears to the cries of the needy. Let me not forget the person that has deserved well of me. Let me not, for any fear of thee, desert my friend, my principles, or my honour. If Wealth is to visit me, and to come with her usual attendants, Vanity and Avarice, do thou, O Poverty! hasten to my rescue; but bring along with thee the two sisters, in whose company thou art always cheerful, Liberty and Innocence."

The conclusion of this vision must be deferred to another opportunity.

No. 124.   [STEELE.

From *Saturday, Jan.* 21, to *Tuesday, Jan.* 24, 1709–10.

—— Ex humili summa ad fastigia rerum
Extollit, quoties voluit Fortuna jocari.
Juv., Sat. iii. 39.

From my own Apartment, January 23.

I went on Saturday last to make a visit in the city ; and as I passed through Cheapside, I saw crowds of people turning down towards the Bank, and struggling who should first get their money into the new-erected lottery.[1]   It gave me a great notion of the credit of our

---

[1] The first State lottery of 1710 ; see No. 87.   Various passages in the "Wentworth Papers" (pages 126, 127, 129, 130, 148, 165) throw light upon this subject.   Thus, "I hear the Million Lottery is drawing and thear is a prise of 400*l.* a year drawn, and Col. St. Pear has gott 5 (*sic*) a year ; it will be hard fate if you mis a pryse that put so much in.   I long tel its all drawn ; they say it will be six weeks drawing" (Aug. 1, 1710).   "It will be a long time first if ever, except I win ye thoussand p^d a year, for mony now adays is the raening passion" (July (?) 1710).   "Some very ordenary creeture has gott 400*l.* a year" (Aug. 4, 1710).   "Thear is a lady gave her footman in the last before this, mony for a lot, and he got five hundred a year, and she would have half, and they had a law suit, but the lawyers gave it all to him" (Aug. 7, 1710).   "Betty has lost all her hopse of the Lottery, als drawn now" (Oct. 6, 1710). "You know your grandfather's Butler (?), they say he put ten thousand pd in the lottry and lost it all, and is really worth forty thousand pd" (Dec. 15, 1710).   Swift refers to the drawing in September : "To-day Mr. Addison, Colonel Freind and I went to see the million lottery drawn at Guildhall.   The jackanapes of blue-coat boys gave themselves such airs in pulling out the tickets, and shewed white hands open to the company to let us see there was no cheat" ("Journal to Stella," Sept. 15, 1710).   See also Nos. 170, 203, and the *Spectator*, No. 191.

present government and administration, to find people press as eagerly to pay money, as they would to receive it ; and at the same time a due respect for that body of men who have found out so pleasing an expedient for carrying on the common cause, that they have turned a tax into a diversion.   The cheerfulness of spirit, and the hopes of success, which this project has occasioned in this great city, lightens the burden of the war, and puts me in mind of some games which they say were invented by wise men who were lovers of their country, to make their fellow citizens undergo the tediousness and fatigues of a long siege.   I think there is a kind of homage due to fortune (if I may call it so), and that I should be wanting to myself if I did not lay in my pretences to her favour, and pay my compliments to her by recommending a ticket to her disposal.   For this reason, upon my return to my lodgings, I sold off a couple of globes and a telescope,[1] which, with the cash I had by me, raised the sum that was requisite for that purpose.   I find by my calculations, that it is but a hundred and fifty thousand to one against my being worth a thousand pounds per annum for thirty-two years ;[2] and if any plum[3] in the City will lay me a hundred and fifty thousand pounds to twenty shillings (which is an even bet), that I am not this fortunate man, I will take the wager, and shall look upon

---

[1] See No. 128.

[2] "There were 150,000 tickets at £10 each, making £1,500,000, the principal of which was to be sunk, and 9 per cent. to be allowed on it for thirty-two years.   Three thousand seven hundred and fifty tickets were prizes from £1000 to £5 per annum ; the rest were blanks—a proportion of thirty-nine to one prize, but, as a consolation, each blank was entitled to fourteen shillings per annum during the thirty-two years" (Ashton's "Social Life in the Reign of Queen Anne," i. 114).

[3] The possessor of a fortune of £100,000.

him as a man of singular courage and fair-dealing, having given orders to Mr. Morphew to subscribe such a policy in my behalf, if any person accepts of the offer. I must confess, I have had such private intimations from the twinkling of a certain star in some of my astronomical observations, that I should be unwilling to take fifty pounds a year for my chance, unless it were to oblige a particular friend. My chief business at present is, to prepare my mind for this change of fortune : for as Seneca, who was a great moralist, and a much richer man than I shall be with this addition to my present income, says, " *Munera ista Fortunæ putatis ? Insidiæ sunt.*"[1] "What we look upon as gifts and presents of Fortune, are traps and snares which she lays for the unwary." I am arming myself against her favours with all my philosophy ; and that I may not lose myself in such a redundance of unnecessary and superfluous wealth, I have determined to settle an annual pension out of it upon a family of Palatines, and by that means give these unhappy strangers a taste of British property. At the same time, as I have an excellent servant-maid, whose diligence in attending me has increased in proportion to my infirmities, I shall settle upon her the revenue arising out of the ten pounds, and amounting to fourteen shillings per annum, with which she may retire into Wales, where she was born a gentlewoman, and pass the remaining part of her days in a condition suitable to her birth and quality. It was impossible for me to make an inspection into my own fortune on this occasion, without seeing at the same time the fate of others who are embarked in the same adventure. And indeed it was a great pleasure to me to observe, that the war, which generally impoverishes those

[1] L. A. Senecæ Opera, Epist. viii. sect. 3 (Lips., Tauchn., 1832, iii. 14).

who furnish out the expense of it, will by this means
give estates to some, without making others the poorer for
it. I have lately seen several in liveries, who will give as
good of their own very suddenly ; and took a particular
satisfaction in the sight of a young country wench, whom
I this morning passed by as she was whirling her mop,[1]
with her petticoats tucked up very agreeably, who, if
there is any truth in my art, is within ten[2] months of
being the handsomest great fortune in town. I must confess, I was so struck with the foresight of what she is to
be, that I treated her accordingly, and said to her, " Pray,
young lady, permit me to pass by." I would for this
reason advise all masters and mistresses to carry it with
great moderation and condescension towards their servants
till next Michaelmas, lest the superiority at that time
should be inverted. I must likewise admonish all my
brethren and fellow adventurers, to fill their minds with
proper arguments for their support and consolation in
case of ill-success. It so happens in this particular, that
though the gainers will have reason to rejoice, the losers
will have no reason to complain. I remember, the day after
the thousand pound prize was drawn in the penny lottery,[3]
I went to visit a splenetic acquaintance of mine, who
was under much dejection, and seemed to me to have

---

[1] Cf. Swift's " City Shower," in No. 238 : " She, singing, still
whirls on her mop."   [2] Cf. No. 128.

[3] This penny lottery seems to have been a private undertaking,
not warranted by Act of Parliament, or intended to raise any part of
the public revenue. In the year 1698, a " Penny Lottery " was
drawn at the theatre in Dorset Garden, as appears from the title of
the following pamphlet, apparently alluded to here : " The Wheel of
Fortune : or, Nothing for a Penny. Being remarks on the drawing of
the Penny Lottery at the Theatre Royal in Dorset Garden. With
the characters of some of the honourable trustees, and all due acknowledgment to his Honour the Undertaker. Written by a person who
was cursed mad that he had not the Thousand Pounds Lot " (Nichols).

suffered some great disappointment. Upon inquiry, I
found he had put twopence for himself and his son into
· the lottery and that neither of them had drawn the
thousand pound. Hereupon this unlucky person took
occasion to enumerate the misfortunes of his life, and
concluded with telling me, that he never was successful in
any of his undertakings. I was forced to comfort him
with the common reflection upon such occasions, that men
of the greatest merit are not always men of the greatest
success, and that persons of his character must not expect
to be as happy as fools. I shall proceed in the like
manner with my rivals and competitors for the thousand
pounds a year which we are now in pursuit of ; and that
I may give general content to the whole body of candi-
dates, I shall allow all that draw prizes to be fortunate,
and all that miss them to be wise.

I must not here omit to acknowledge, that I have
received several letters upon this subject, but find one
common error running through them all, which is,
that the writers of them believe their fate in these cases
depends upon the astrologer, and not upon the stars, as in
the following letter from one, who, I fear, flatters himself
with hopes of success, which are altogether groundless,
since he does not seem to me so great a fool as he takes
himself to be :

"SIR,

"Coming to town, and finding my friend Mr. Partridge
dead and buried, and you the only conjurer in
repute, I am under a necessity of applying myself to you
for a favour, which nevertheless I confess it would better
become a friend to ask, than one who is, as I am
altogether, a stranger to you ; but poverty, you know, is
impudent ; and as that gives me the occasion, so that

alone could give me the confidence to be thus
tunate.

"I am, sir, very poor, and very desirous to be
wise : I have got ten pounds, which I design to
in the lottery now on foot. What I desire of you
by your art, you will choose such a ticket for me
arise a benefit sufficient to maintain me. I mu
leave to inform you, that I am good for nothing, an
therefore insist upon a larger lot than would satisf
who are capable by their own abilities of adding son
to what you should assign them ; whereas I must ex̧
absolute, independent maintenance, because, as I
can do nothing. 'Tis possible, after this free con
of mine, you may think I don't deserve to be rich ;
hope you'll likewise observe, I can ill afford to be
My own opinion is, I am well qualified for an estat
have a good title to luck in a lottery ; but I resig
self wholly to your mercy, not without hopes that yo
consider, the less I deserve, the greater the generos
you. If you reject me, I have agreed with an acquai
of mine to bury me for my ten pounds. I once
recommend myself to your favour, and bid you adiет

I cannot forbear publishing another letter which I
received, because it redounds to my own credit, as w
to that of a very honest footman :

"MR. BICKERSTAFF,   *January* 23, 17:

"I am bound in justice to acquaint you, that I pi
advertisement[1] into your last paper about a v
which was lost, and was brought to me on the very

[1] The following was the advertisement: "A plain gold v
made by Tompion, with a gold hook and chain, a cornelian seal
gold, and a cupid sifting hearts, was dropt from a lady's side

your paper came out by a footman, who told me, that he would [not] have brought it, if he had not read your discourse of that day against avarice ;[1] but that since he had read it, he scorned to take a reward for doing what in justice he ought to do. I am,

" Sir,

" Your most humble Servant,

" JOHN HAMMOND."

No. 125. [STEELE.

From *Tuesday, Jan. 24,* to *Thursday, Jan. 26,* 1709–10.

Quem mala stultitia, et quæcunque inscitia veri
Cæcum agit, insanum Chrysippi porticus, et grex
Autumat. Hæc populos, hæc magnos formula reges,
Excepto sapiente, tenet.—HOR., 2 Sat. iii. 43.

From my own Apartment, January 25.

There is a sect of ancient philosophers, who, I think, have left more volumes behind them, and those better written, than any other of the fraternities in philosophy. It was a maxim of this sect, that all those who do not live up to the principles of reason and virtue, are madmen. Every one, who governs himself by these rules, is allowed the title of wise, and reputed to be in his senses ; and every one in proportion, as he deviates from them, is pronounced frantic and distracted. Cicero having chosen

near Great Marlborough Street on Thursday night last. Whoever took it up, if they will bring it to Mr. Plaistow's, at the Hand and Star between the two Temple Gates, in Fleet Street, shall receive five guineas reward.—Signed JOHN HAMMOND."

[1] See No. 123.

this maxim for his theme, takes occasion to argue from it
very agreeably with Clodius, his implacable adversary, who
had procured his banishment. " A city," says he, " is an
assembly distinguished into bodies of men, who are in
possession of their respective rights and privileges, cast
under proper subordinations, and in all its parts obedient
to the rules of law and equity." He then represents the
government from whence he was banished, at a time when
the consul, senate, and laws, had lost their authority, as a
commonwealth of lunatics. For this reason, he regards
his expulsion from Rome, as a man would being turned
out of Bedlam, if the inhabitants of it should drive him
out of their walls as a person unfit for their community.[1]
We are therefore to look upon every man's brain to be
touched, however he may appear in the general conduct of
his life, if he has an unjustifiable singularity in any part of
his conversation or behaviour : or if he swerves from right
reason, however common his kind of madness may be, we
shall not excuse him for its being epidemical, it being our
present design to clap up all such as have the marks of
madness upon them, who are now permitted to go about
the streets, for no other reason, but because they do no
mischief in their fits. Abundance of imaginary great men
are put in straw to bring them to a right sense of themselves : and is it not altogether as reasonable, that an
insignificant man, who has an immoderate opinion of his
merits, and a quite different notion of his own abilities
from what the rest of the world entertain, should have the
same care taken of him, as a beggar who fancies himself a
duke or a prince ? Or, why should a man, who starves in
the midst of plenty, be trusted with himself, more than he
who fancies he is an emperor in the midst of poverty ? I
have several women of quality in my thoughts, who set so

[1] Cicero, Tusc. Disp. iii. 4, &c. ; Orat. pro Dom. 33, &c.

exorbitant a value upon themselves, that I have often most heartily pitied them, and wished them, for their recovery, under the same discipline with the pewterer's wife. I find by several hints in ancient authors, that when the Romans were in the height of power and luxury, they assigned out of their vast dominions, an island called Anticyra, as an habitation for madmen. This was the Bedlam of the Roman Empire, whither all persons who had left their wits used to resort from all parts of the world in quest of them. Several of the Roman emperors were advised to repair to this island ; but most of them, instead of listening to such sober counsels, gave way to their distraction, till the people knocked them in the head as despairing of their cure. In short, it was as usual for men of distempered brains to take a voyage to Anticyra[1] in those days, as it is in ours for persons who have a disorder in their lungs to go to Montpellier.

The prodigious crops of hellebore[2] with which this whole island abounded, did not only furnish them with incomparable tea, snuff, and Hungary water,[3] but impregnated the air of the country with such sober and salutiferous streams, as very much comforted the heads, and refreshed the senses, of all that breathed in it. A discarded statesman, that at his first landing appeared stark staring mad,

---

[1] Mr. Dobson quotes from Burton's "Anatomie of Melancholy" (1628), p. 18 : "I will evince it, that most men are mad, that they had as much need to go a pilgrimage to the Anticyræ (as in Strabo's time they did) as in our dayes they run to Compostella, our Lady of Sichim, or Lauretta, to seeke for helpe ; that it is likely to be as prosperous a voyage as that of Guiana, and there is much more need of Hellebor than of Tobacco."

[2] Hellebore was much used by the ancients as a cure for madness and melancholy.

[3] The best Hungary water (a popular scent) was made of spirits of wine, rosemary in bloom, lavender flowers, and oil of rosemary.

would become calm in a week's time ; and upon his return home, live easy and satisfied in his retirement. A moping lover would grow a pleasant fellow by that time he had ridden thrice about the island ; and a hair-brained rake, after a short stay in the country, go home again a composed, grave, worthy gentleman.

I have premised these particulars before I enter on the main design of this paper, because I would not be thought altogether notional[1] in what I have to say, and pass only for a projector in morality. I could quote Horace, and Seneca, and some other ancient writers of good repute, upon the same occasion, and make out by their testimony, that our streets are filled with distracted persons ; that our shops and taverns, private and public houses, swarm with them ; and that it is very hard to make up a tolerable assembly without a majority of them.   But what I have already said, is, I hope, sufficient to justify the ensuing project, which I shall therefore give some account of without any further preface.

1. It is humbly proposed, that a proper receptacle or habitation be forthwith erected for all such persons as, upon due trial and examination, shall appear to be out of their wits.

2. That to serve the present exigency, the College in Moorfields[2] be very much extended at both ends ; and that it be converted into a square, by adding three other sides to it.

3. That nobody be admitted into these three additional sides, but such whose frenzy can lay no claim to an apartment in that row of building which is already erected.

---

[1] Dealing in ideas instead of realities.   [2] Bedlam ; see No. 30.

4. That the architect, physician, apothecary, surgeon, keepers, nurses, and porters, be all and each of them cracked, provided that their frenzy does not lie in the profession or employment to which they shall severally and respectively be assigned.

N.B. It is thought fit to give the foregoing notice, that none may present himself here for any post of honour or profit who is not duly qualified.

5. That over all the gates of the additional buildings, there be figures placed in the same manner as over the entrance of the edifice already erected ;[1] provided, they represent such distractions only as are proper for those additional buildings ; as, of an envious man gnawing his own flesh, a gamester pulling himself by the ears, and knocking his head against a marble pillar, a covetous man warming himself over a heap of gold, a coward flying from his own shadow, and the like.

Having laid down this general scheme of my design, I do hereby invite all persons who are willing to encourage so public-spirited a project, to bring in their contributions as soon as possible, and to apprehend forthwith any politician whom they shall catch raving in a coffee-house, or any freethinker whom they shall find publishing his deliriums, or any other person who shall give the like manifest signs of a crazed imagination : and I do at the same time give this public notice to all the madmen about this great city, that they may return to their senses with all imaginable expedition, lest if they should come into my hands, I should put them into a regimen which they would not like ; for if I find any one of them persist in his frantic behaviour, I will make him in a month's time as famous as ever Oliver's porter[2] was.

[1] The statues by C. G. Cibber.   [2] See No. 51.

reduced her to a restlessness in her seat, an impertinent playing of her fan, and many other motions and gestures, before I took the least notice of her. At last I looked at her with a kind of surprise, as if she had before been unobserved by reason of an ill light where she sat. It is not to be expressed what a sudden joy I saw rise in her countenance, even at the approbation of such a very old fellow : but she did not long enjoy her triumph without a rival ; for there immediately entered Castabella, a lady of a quite contrary character, that is to say, as eminent a prude as Lydia is a coquette. Belvidera gave me a glance, which methought intimated, that they were both curiosities in their kind, and worth remarking. As soon as we were again seated, I stole looks at each lady, as if I was comparing their perfections. Belvidera observed it, and began to lead me into a discourse of them both to their faces, which is to be done easily enough ; for one woman is generally so intent upon the faults of another, that she has not reflection enough to observe when her own are represented. "I have taken notice, Mr. Bickerstaff," said Belvidera, " that you have in some parts of your writings drawn characters of our sex, in which you have not, to my apprehension, been clear enough and distinct, particularly in those of a prude and a coquette." Upon the mention of this, Lydia was roused with the expectation of seeing Castabella's picture, and Castabella with the hopes of that of Lydia. "Madam," said I to Belvidera, " when we consider nature, we shall often find very contrary effects flow from the same cause. The prude and coquette (as different as they appear in their behaviour) are in reality the same kind of women : the motive of action in both is the affectation of pleasing men. They are sisters of the same blood and constitution, only one chooses a grave, the other a light, dress. The prude appears more virtuous, the coquette more vicious, than she really is. The distant behaviour of the prude tends to the same purpose as the advances of the coquette ; and you have as little reason to fall into despair from the severity of the one, as to conceive hope from the familiarity of the latter. What leads you into a clear sense of their character is, that you may observe each of them has the distinction of sex in all her thoughts, words and actions. You can never mention any assembly you were lately in, but one asks you with a rigid, the other with a sprightly air, ' Pray, what men were there ? ' As for prudes, it must be confessed, that there are several of them, who, like hypocrites, by long practice of a false part, become sincere ; or at least delude themselves into a belief that they are so."

For the benefit of this society of ladies, I shall propose one rule to them as a test of their virtue. I find in a very celebrated modern author, that the great foundress of the Pietists, Madame de Bourignon,[1] who was no less famous for the sanctity of her life than for the singularity of some of her opinions, was used to boast, that she had not only the spirit of continency in herself, but that she had also the power of communicating it to all who beheld her. This the scoffers of those days called the Gift of Infrigidation, and took occasion from it to rally her face, rather than

---

[1] Bayle, in his life of this devotee, 1697, says that Antoinette Bourignon was born at Lisle in 1616, so deformed, that it was debated for some days in the family, whether it was not proper to stifle her as a monster. Her deformity diminishing, they laid aside the thought. Although she was of a morose and peevish temper, and embroiled in troubles most part of her life, she seemed to be but forty years of age when she was above sixty ; never made use of spectacles, and died at Franeker, in the province of Frise, in 1680. From her childhood to her old age she had an extraordinary turn of mind. She published a multitude of books, filled with singular doctrines, such as might be expected from a person who roundly asserted, on the express declaration, she said, of God Himself, " That the examination of things by

admire her virtue. I would therefore advise the prude, who has a mind to know the integrity of her own heart, to lay her hand seriously upon it, and to examine herself, whether she could sincerely rejoice in such a gift of conveying chaste thoughts to all her male beholders. If she has any aversion to the power of inspiring so great a virtue, whatever notion she may have of her perfection, she deceives her own heart, and is still in the state of prudery. Some perhaps will look upon the boast of Madame de Bourignon as the utmost ostentation of a prude.

If you would see the humour of a coquette pushed to the last excess, you may find an instance of it in the following story, which I will set down at length, because it pleased me when I read it, though I cannot recollect in what author.

A young coquette widow in France having been followed by a Gascon of quality, who had boasted among his companions of some favours which he had never received, to be revenged of him, sent for him one evening, and told him, it was in his power to do her a very particular service. The Gascon, with much profession of his readiness to obey her commands, begged to hear in what manner she designed to employ him. "You know," said the widow, "my friend Belinda, and must often have heard of the jealousy

reason, was the most accursed of all heresies, formal atheism, a rejection of God, and the substitution of corrupt reason in his place." She pretended to inspiration, and boasted of extraordinary communications with God ; but appears to have been exceedingly defective in the essential duties of humility and charity. She was a woman of such ill conditions and odd behaviour, that nobody could live with her ; and she seriously maintained, that anger was a real virtue. She contrived to accumulate money, but continued always uncharitable upon principle, alleging the errors of her understanding in defence of the inhumanity of her conduct.

of that impotent wretch her husband. Now it is absolutely
necessary, for the carrying on a certain affair, that his wife
and I should be together a whole night. What I have to
ask of you, is, to dress yourself in her night-clothes, and
lie by him a whole night in her place, that he may not
miss her while she is with me." The Gascon (though of a
very lively and undertaking complexion) began to startle
at the proposal. "Nay," says the widow, "if you have
not the courage to go through what I ask of you, I must
employ somebody else that will." "Madam," says the
Gascon, "I'll kill him for you if you please; but for lying
with him!—How is it possible to do it without being
discovered?" "If you do not discover yourself," says the
widow, "you will lie safe enough, for he is past all curiosity.
He comes in at night while she is asleep, and goes out in
the morning before she awakes, and is in pain for nothing,
so he knows she is there." "Madam," replied the
Gascon, "how can you reward me for passing a night with
this old fellow?" The widow answered with a laugh,
"Perhaps by admitting you to pass a night with one you
think more agreeable." He took the hint, put on his
night-clothes, and had not been a-bed above an hour before
he heard a knocking at the door, and the treading of one
who approached the other side of the bed, and who he did
not question was the good man of the house. I do not
know, whether the story would be better by telling you in
this place, or at the end of it, that the person who went to
bed to him was our young coquette widow. The Gascon
was in a terrible fright every time she moved in the bed,
or turned towards him, and did not fail to shrink from her
till he had conveyed himself to the very ridge of the bed.
I will not dwell upon the perplexity he was in the whole
night, which was augmented, when he observed that it was
now broad day, and that the husband did not yet offer to

get up and go about his business. All that the Gascon
had for it, was to keep his face turned from him, and to
feign himself asleep, when, to his utter confusion, the
widow at last puts out her arm, and pulls the bell at her
bed's head. In came her friend, and two or three companions, to whom the Gascon had boasted of her favours.
The widow jumped into a wrapping-gown, and joined with
the rest in laughing at this man of intrigue.[1]

[1] " *Advertisement.*—Proposals for printing the Lucubrations of Isaac
Bickerstaff, Esq., by subscriptions, are to be seen, and subscriptions
taken by Charles Lillie, a perfumer, at the corner of Beaufort
Buildings, in the Strand, and John Morphew, near Stationers Hall."
See No. 80, note. The same proposals are advertised at the end of
the subsequent papers in the original folio, with the following variation
and addition : Proposals for printing, &c. by subscriptions, " in two
volumes in octavo, on a large character and fine royal paper," &c.
In No. 134, &c., there was this addition : " All persons that desire to
subscribe to this work are desired to send their subscriptions before the
25th instant, it being intended to print no more than what shall be
subscribed for, and to begin on the 27th in order to have it published
before Easter." In No. 139 (Feb. 25–28) was the announcement,
" this day put to press." The idea of publishing by Easter was
given up after No. 153. The books were not ready for the subscribers
until July 10 (see No. 195, Advertisement). The third and fourth
volumes of the *Tatler* were advertised as " ready to be delivered " in
No. 227 of the *Spectator* (Nov. 20, 1711). The copies on royal
paper were issued at a guinea a volume, and copies on medium paper
at half a guinea. " I am one of your two-guinea subscribers," says
the writer of No. 5 of the *Examiner* (Aug. 31, 1710).

No. 127.   [STEELE.

From *Saturday, Jan.* 28, to *Tuesday, Jan.* 31, 1709–10.

Nimirum insanus paucis videatur, eo quod
Maxima pars hominum morbo jactatur eodem.
                                HOR., 2 Sat. iii. 120.

From my own Apartment, January 30.

There is no affection of the mind so much blended in human nature, and wrought into our very constitution, as pride. It appears under a multitude of disguises, and breaks out in ten thousand different symptoms. Every one feels it in himself, and yet wonders to see it in his neighbour. I must confess, I met with an instance of it the other day where I should very little have expected it. Who would believe the proud person I am going to speak of, is a cobbler upon Ludgate Hill ? This artist being naturally a lover of respect, and considering that his circumstances are such that no man living will give it him, has contrived the figure of a beau in wood, who stands before him in a bending posture, with his hat under his left arm, and his right hand extended in such a manner as to hold a thread, a piece of wax, or an awl, according to the particular service in which his master thinks fit to employ him. When I saw him, he held a candle in this obsequious posture. I was very well pleased with the cobbler's invention, that had so ingeniously contrived an inferior, and stood a little while contemplating this inverted idolatry, wherein the image did homage to the man. When we meet with such a fantastic vanity in one of this order, it is no wonder if we may trace it through all degrees above it, and particularly through all the steps of greatness. We easily see the absurdity of pride when it enters into the heart of a cobbler ; though in reality it is altogether as ridiculous and unreasonable wherever it takes possession of a human creature. There is no temptation to it from the reflection upon our being in general, or upon any comparative perfection, whereby one man may excel another. The greater a man's knowledge is, the greater motive he may seem to have for pride ; but in the same proportion as the one rises, the other sinks, it being the chief office of wisdom to discover to us our weaknesses and imperfections.

As folly is the foundation of pride, the natural superstructure of it is madness. If there was an occasion for the experiment, I would not question to make a proud man a lunatic in three weeks' time, provided I had it in my power to ripen his frenzy with proper applications. It is an admirable reflection in Terence, where it is said of a parasite, " *Hic homines ex stultis facit insanos !* "[1] " This fellow," says he, " has an art of converting fools into madmen." When I was in France (the region of complaisance and vanity), I have often observed, that a great man who has entered a levy of flatterers humble and temperate, has grown so insensibly heated by the court which was paid him on all sides, that he has been quite distracted before he could get into his coach.

If we consult the collegiates of Moorfields, we shall find most of them are beholden to their pride for their introduction into that magnificent palace.[2] I had some years ago the curiosity to inquire into the particular circumstances of these whimsical freeholders, and learned from their own mouths the condition and character of each of them. Indeed I found, that all I spoke to were persons of quality. There were at that time five duchesses, three

[1] " Eunuchus," II. ii. 23. See No. 208.   [2] Bedlam.

earls, two heathen gods, an emperor, and a prophet. There were also a great number of such as were locked up from their estates, and others who concealed their titles. A leather-seller of Taunton whispered me in my ear, that he was the Duke of Monmouth ; but begged me not to betray him. At a little distance from him sat a tailor's wife, who asked me as I went by, if I had seen the sword-bearer ? Upon which I presumed to ask her, who she was ; and was answered, "My Lady Mayoress."

I was very sensibly touched with compassion towards these miserable people ; and indeed, extremely mortified to see human nature capable of being thus disfigured. However, I reaped this benefit from it, that I was resolved to guard myself against a passion which makes such havoc in the brain, and produces so much disorder in the imagination. For this reason, I have endeavoured to keep down the secret swellings of resentment, and stifle the very first suggestions of self-esteem ; to establish my mind in tranquillity, and over-value nothing in my own, or in another's possession.

For the benefit of such whose heads are a little turned, though not to so great a degree as to qualify them for the place of which I have been now speaking, I shall assign one of the sides of the college which I am erecting, for the cure of this dangerous distemper.

The most remarkable of the persons whose disturbance arises from pride, and whom I shall use all possible diligence to cure, are such as are bidden in the appearance of quite contrary habits and dispositions. Among such, I shall in the first place take care of one who is under the most subtle species of pride that I have observed in my whole experience.

This patient is a person for whom I have a great respect, as being an old courtier, and a friend of mine in my youth.

The man has but a bare subsistence, just enough to pay his reckoning with us at the Trumpet :[1] but by having spent the beginning of his life in the hearing of great men and persons of power, he is always promising to do good offices, to introduce every man he converses with into the world ; will desire one of ten times his substance to let him see him sometimes, and hints to him, that he does not forget him. He answers to matters of no consequence with great circumspection ; but however, maintains a general civility in his words and actions, and an insolent benevolence to all whom he has to do with : this he practises with a grave tone and air ; and though I am his senior by twelve years, and richer by forty pounds per annum, he had yesterday the impudence to commend me to my face, and tell me, he should be always ready to encourage me. In a word, he is a very insignificant fellow, but exceeding gracious. The best return I can make him for his favours, is, to carry him myself to Bedlam, and see him well taken care of.[2]

The next person I shall provide for, is of a quite contrary character ; that has in him all the stiffness and insolence of quality, without a grain of sense or good nature to make it either respected or beloved. His pride has infected every muscle of his face ; and yet, after all his

---

[1] In Shire Lane. See No. 132.

[2] "Perhaps the most consummately drawn of all his characters is introduced in the Essay, No. 127. . . . We have a portrait of that kind which, though produced by a few apparently careless touches, never ceases to charm, and is a study for all succeeding time and painters" (Forster's Essay on Steele). "This character," wrote Leigh Hunt, "is one of the finest that ever proceeded from his pen. It shows his contempt of that absurdest of all the passions of mortality—pride. The reader will take notice of the exquisite expression 'insolent benevolence,' and the 'very insignificant fellow, but exceeding gracious'" ("A Book for a Corner," ii. 78–9).

endeavours to show mankind that he contemns them, he is only neglected by all that see him, as not of consequence enough to be hated.

For the cure of this particular sort of madness, it will be necessary to break through all forms with him, and familiarise[1] his carriage by the use of a good cudgel. It may likewise be of great benefit to make him jump over a stick half a dozen times every morning.

A third whom I have in my eye is a young fellow, whose lunacy is such, that he boasts of nothing but what he ought to be ashamed of. He is vain of being rotten, and talks publicly of having committed crimes, which he ought to be hanged for by the laws of his country.

There are several others whose brains are hurt with pride, and whom I may hereafter attempt to recover ; but shall conclude my present list with an old woman, who is just dropping into her grave, that talks of nothing but her birth. Though she has not a tooth in her head, she expects to be valued for the blood in her veins, which she fancies is much better than that which glows in the cheeks of Belinda,[2] and sets half the town on fire.

---

[1] Bring down from its state of superiority.

[2] Nichols suggests an allusion to Mary Ann, daughter of Baron Spanheim, the Bavarian ambassador. She married the Marquis de Montandre in April 1710, and was a Kit-Cat toast. The reference— if there is any personal reference at all—may equally well be to any one of the beauties of the time.

No. 128.   [STEELE.

From *Tuesday*, *Jan.* 31, to *Thursday*, *Feb.* 2, 1709-10.

—— Veniunt a dote sagittæ.—Juv., Sat. vi. 139.

From my own Apartment, February 1.

This morning I received a letter from a fortune-hunter, which being better in its kind than men of that character usually write, I have thought fit to communicate to the public :

"*To Isaac Bickerstaff, Esq.*

"SIR,

"I take the boldness to recommend to your care the enclosed letter, not knowing how to communicate it but by your means to the agreeable country maid you mention with so much honour in your discourse concerning the lottery.[1]

"I should be ashamed to give you this trouble without offering at some small requital : I shall therefore direct a new pair of globes and a telescope of the best maker, to be left for you at Mr. Morphew's, as a testimony of the great respect with which I am

"Your most humble Servant, &c."

"*To Mopsa in Sheer Lane.*

"FAIREST UNKNOWN,

"It being discovered by the stars, that about ten[2] months hence, you will run the hazard of being persecuted by many worthless pretenders to your person, unless

[1] See No. 124.

[2] Altered, in error, to "three," in the 1711 edition. In No. 124 "ten months" remains. The drawing was at Michaelmas 1710.

77

timely prevented, I now offer my service for your security against the persecution that threatens you. This is therefore to let you know, that I have conceived a most extraordinary passion for you ; and that for several days I have been perpetually haunted with the vision of a person I have never yet seen. To satisfy you that I am in my senses, and that I do not mistake you for any one of higher rank, I assure you, that in your daily employment, you appear to my imagination more agreeable in a short scanty petticoat, than the finest woman of quality in her spreading farthingale ; and that the dexterous twirl of your mop has more native charms than the studied airs of a lady's fan. In a word, I am captivated with your menial qualifications : the domestic virtues adorn you like attendant Cupids ; cleanliness and healthful industry wait on all your motions ; and dust and cobwebs fly your approach.

"Now, to give you an honest account of myself, and that you may see my designs are honourable, I am an esquire of an ancient family, born to about fifteen hundred pounds a year, half of which I have spent in discovering myself to be a fool, and with the rest am resolved to retire with some plain honest partner, and study to be wiser. I had my education in a laced coat, and a French dancing school ; and by my travel into foreign parts, have just as much breeding to spare, as you may think you want, which I intend to exchange as fast as I can for old English honesty and good sense. I will not impose on you by a false recommendation of my person, which (to show you my sincerity) is none of the handsomest, being of a figure somewhat short ; but what I want in length, I make out in breadth. But in amends for that and all other defects, if you can like me when you see me, I shall continue to you, whether I find you fair, black or brown,

"THE MOST CONSTANT OF LOVERS.

"*January* 27, 17⅟₀⁹₁₀."

This letter seems to be written by a wag, and for that reason I am not much concerned for what reception Mopsa shall think fit to give it ; but the following certainly proceeds from a poor heart, that languishes under the most deplorable misfortune that possibly can befall a woman. A man that is treacherously dealt with in love may have recourse to many consolations. He may gracefully break through all opposition to his mistress, or explain with his rival ; urge his own constancy, or aggravate the falsehood by which it is repaid. But a woman that is ill-treated has no refuge in her griefs but in silence and secrecy. The world is so unjust, that a female heart which has been once touched is thought for ever blemished. The very grief in this case is looked upon as a reproach, and a complaint almost a breach of chastity. For these reasons, we see treachery and falsehood are become as it were male vices, and are seldom found, never acknowledged, in the other sex. This may serve to introduce Statira's letter, which, without any turn or art, has something so pathetical and moving in it, that I verily believe it to be true, and therefore heartily pity the injured creature that wrote it :

" *To Isaac Bickerstaff, Esq.*

" Sir,

" Y ou seem in many of your writings to be a man of a very compassionate temper, and well acquainted with the passion of love. This encourages me to apply myself to you in my present distress, which I believe you will look upon to be very great, and treat with tenderness, notwithstanding it wholly arises from love, and that it is a woman that makes this confession. I am now in the twenty-third year of my age, and have for a great while entertained the addresses of a man who I thought loved me more than life. I am sure I did him ; and must own to you, not without some confusion, that I have thought

on nothing else for these two long years, but the happy
life we should lead together, and the means I should use
to make myself still dearer to him. My fortune was
indeed much beyond his ; and as I was always in the
company of my relations, he was forced to discover his
inclinations, and declare himself to me by stories of other
persons, kind looks, and many ways which he knew too
well that I understood. Oh ! Mr. Bickerstaff, it is
impossible to tell you, how industrious I have been to
make him appear lovely in my thoughts. I made it a
point of conscience to think well of him, and of no man
else : but he has since had an estate fallen to him, and
makes love to another of a greater fortune than mine. I
could not believe the report of this at first ; but about a
fortnight ago I was convinced of the truth of it by his own
behaviour. He came to give our family a formal visit,
when, as there were several in company, and many things
talked of, the discourse fell upon some unhappy woman
who was in my own circumstances. It was said by one in
the room, that they could not believe the story could be
true, because they did not believe any man could be so
false. Upon which, I stole a look upon him with an
anguish not to be expressed. He saw my eyes full of
tears ; yet had the cruelty to say, that he could see no
falsehood in alterations of this nature, where there had
been no contracts or vows interchanged. Pray, do not
make a jest of misery, but tell me seriously your opinion
of his behaviour ; and if you can have any pity for my
condition, publish this in your next paper, that being the
only way I have of complaining of his unkindness, and
showing him the injustice he has done me. I am

" Your humble Servant,

" The unfortunate

" STATIRA."

The name my correspondent gives herself, puts me in mind of my old reading in romances, and brings into my thoughts a speech of the renowned Don Bellianis, who, upon a complaint made him of a discourteous knight, that had left his injured paramour in the same manner, dries up her tears with a promise of relief. " Disconsolate damsel," quoth he, "a foul disgrace it were to all right worthy professors of chivalry, if such a blot to knighthood should pass unchastised. Give me to know the abode of this recreant lover, and I will give him as a feast to the fowls of the air, or drag him bound before you at my horse's tail."

I am not ashamed to own myself a champion of distressed damsels, and would venture as far to relieve them as Don Bellianis ; for which reason, I do invite this lady to let me know the name of the traitor who has deceived her ; and do promise, not only her, but all the fair ones of Great Britain who lie under the same calamity, to employ my right hand for their redress, and serve them to my last drop of ink.

No. 129. [ADDISON.[1]

From *Thursday, Feb.* 2, to *Saturday, Feb.* 4, 1709-10.

Ingenio manus est et cervix cæsa.—Juv., Sat. x. 120.

From my own Apartment, February 3.

When my paper for to-morrow was prepared for the press, there came in this morning a mail from Holland, which brought me several advices from foreign

[1] There is the following note in No. 130 (orig. folio) : " Errata in the last. Insert the following motto, which was overlooked by the printer," &c. " Col. 2, line 16, for Oration read Ovation." Probably this paper, No. 129, was by Addison, not only because of these cor-

parts, and took my thoughts off domestic affairs.   Among others, I have a letter from a burgher of Amsterdam, who makes me his compliments, and tells me, he has sent me several draughts of humorous and satirical pictures by the best hands of the Dutch nation.   They are a trading people, and in their very minds mechanics.   They express their wit in manufacture, as we do in manuscript.   He informs me, that a very witty hand has lately represented the present posture of public affairs in a landscape, or rather sea-piece, wherein the potentates of the Alliance are figured as their interests correspond with, or affect each other, under the appearance of commanders of ships. These vessels carry the colours of the respective nations concerned in the present war.   The whole design seems to tend to one point, which is, that several squadrons of British and Dutch ships are battering a French man-of-war, in order to make her deliver up a long-boat with Spanish colours.   My correspondent informs me, that a man must understand the compass perfectly well, to be able to comprehend the beauty and invention of this piece, which is so skilfully drawn, that the particular views of every prince in Europe are seen according as the ships lie to the main figure in the picture, and as that figure may help or retard their sailing.   It seems this curiosity is now on board a ship bound for England, and with other rarities made a present to me.   As soon as it arrives, I design to expose it to public view at my secretary Mr. Lillie's, who shall have an explication of all the terms of art ; and I doubt not but it will give as good content as the moving picture in Fleet Street.[1]

rections, but because of the allusions to medals, &c., in the letter from Pasquin.   The paper is, however, not included in Addison's Works.

[1] " To be seen daily, at the Duke of Marlborough's Head in Fleet Street, a new moving picture, drawn by the best hand, with great

But above all the honours I have received from the learned world abroad, I am most delighted with the following epistle from Rome :

" *Pasquin of Rome, to Isaac Bickerstaff of Great Britain, greeting.*

" Sir,

" Your reputation has passed the Alps, and would have come to my ears by this time, if I had any. In short, sir, you are looked upon here as a Northern droll, and the greatest virtuoso among the Tramontanes. Some indeed say, that Mr. Bickerstaff and Pasquin are only names invented, to father compositions which the natural parent does not care for owning. But however that is, all agree, that there are several persons, who, if they durst attack you, would endeavour to leave you no more limbs than I have. I need not tell you that my adversaries have joined in a confederacy with Time to demolish me, and that, if I were not a very great wit, I should make the worst figure in Europe, being abridged of my legs, arms, nose, and ears. If you think fit to accept of the correspondence of so facetious a cripple, I shall from time to time send you an account of what happens at Rome. You have only heard of it from Latin and Greek authors ; may, perhaps, have read no accounts from hence, but of a triumph, ovation, or apotheosis, and will, doubtless, be surprised to

variety of curious motions and figures, which form a most agreeable prospect. It has the general approbation of all who see it, and far exceeds the original formerly shown at the same place.—N.B. This picture was never exposed to public view, before the beginning of the present year 1710 " (No. 127, Advertisement). "The famous and curious original moving picture, which came from Germany, that was designed for the Elector of Bavaria, is still to be seen at the Duke of Marlborough's Head, in Fleet Street ;" &c.—*Postman*, March 1-3, 1709 [-10].

see the description of a procession, jubilee, or canonisation.
I shall however send you what the place affords, in return
to what I shall receive from you.   If you will acquaint me
with your next promotion of general officers, I will send
you an account of our next advancement of saints.   If you
will let me know who is reckoned the bravest warrior in
Great Britain, I'll tell you who is the best fiddler in Rome.
If you will favour me with an inventory of the riches that
were brought into your nation by Admiral Wager,[1] I will
not fail giving you an account of a pot of medals that has
been lately dug up here, and are now under the examination of our ministers of state.

"There is one thing in which I desire you would be
very particular.   What I mean is an exact list of all the
religions in Great Britain, as likewise the habits, which are
said here to be the great points of conscience in England,
whether they are made of serge or broadcloth, of silk or
linen.   I should be glad to see a model of the most con-
scientious dress amongst you, and desire you would send

---

[1] Charles Wager was first made a captain at the battle of La Hogue
by Admiral Russell, who recommended him on the most important
services.   He was sent commodore to the West Indies in 1707, where
he attacked the Spanish galleons, May 28, 1708, with three ships,
though they were fourteen in number drawn up in line of battle, and
defeated them.   His services Queen Anne distinguished by sending
him a flag as Vice-admiral of the Blue, intended for him before this
engagement, and by honouring him at his return with knighthood.
His share of prize-money amounted to 100,000*l.*   But the riches he
acquired, on this and other occasions, were regarded by him only as
instruments of doing good ; accordingly he gave fortunes to his relations, that he might see them happy in his lifetime ; and to persons
in distress, his liberality was such, that whole families were supported,
and their estates and fortunes saved, by his generosity.   He was promoted to be Rear-admiral of the Red, November 9, 1709 ; and in that
year was returned for Portsmouth to Parliament, where he continued
to sit till his death.   In April 1726, he was sent up the Baltic as
Vice-admiral of the Red, with a large fleet on an important expedition ;

hat of each religion; as likewise, if it be not too
trouble, a cravat. It would also be very acceptable
:o receive an account of those two religious orders
. are lately sprung up amongst you, the Whigs and
'ories, with the points of doctrine, severities in discip-
penances, mortifications, and good works, by which
iiffer one from another. It would be no less kind
a would explain to us a word which they do not
·stand even at our English monastery toasts, and
; know whether the ladies so called are nuns or lay-
;.

a return, I will send you the secret history of several
als, which I have by me in manuscript, with gal-
:s, amours, politics, and intrigues, by which they
their way to the Holy Purple.

·ut when I propose a correspondence, I must not tell
·hat I intend to advise you of hereafter, and neglect
·e you what I have at present. The Pope has been
·or this fortnight of a violent toothache, which has
much raised the French faction, and put the conclave
great ferment. Every one of the pretenders to the

rformed all that could be expected from the wisdom and skill
English admiral. He dined with the King of Denmark; had
:ence of the King of Sweden; and exchanged many civilities
'rince Menzikoff, then Prime Minister of Russia. He was
:ed Comptroller of the Navy in February 1714; a Lord of the
ilty in March 1717; and, on the death of Lord Torrington in
r 1732–3, he was placed at the head of that Board, and
:ed president of the corporation for relief of poor sea-officers'
i, and also president of the corporation of the Trinity House.
i appointed one of the Lords Regent in 1741; Vice-admiral of
d and Treasurer of the Navy in 1742; and died May 24, 1743,
r. A prudent, temperate, wise, and honest man, he was easy
ss to all, unaffected in his manners, steady and resolute in his
t, affable and cheerful in his behaviour, and in time of action
inent danger was never hurried or discomposed (Nichols).

The Tatler   No. 129. February 4, 1709-10

succession is grown twenty years older than he was a
fortnight ago. Each candidate tries who shall cough and
stoop most ; for these are at present the great gifts that
recommend to the apostolical seat, which he stands the
fairest for, who is likely to resign it the soonest. I have
known the time when it used to rain louis-d'ors on such
occasions ; but whatever is the matter, there are very few
of them to be seen at present at Rome, insomuch that
it is thought a man might purchase infallibility at a
very reasonable rate. It is nevertheless hoped that his
Holiness may recover, and bury these his imaginary suc-
cessors.

" There has lately been found a human tooth in a
catacomb, which has engaged a couple of convents in a
lawsuit ; each of them pretending that it belonged to the
jawbone of a saint who was of their Order. The colleges
have sat upon it thrice, and I find there is a disposition
among them to take it out of the possession of both the
contending parties, by reason of a speech which was made
by one of the cardinals, who, by reason of its being
found out of the company of any other bones, asserted,
that it might be one of the teeth which was coughed
out by Ælia, an old woman whose loss is recorded in
Martial.[1]

" I have nothing remarkable to communicate to you of
State affairs, excepting only, that the Pope has lately
received a horse from the German ambassador, as an
acknowledgment for the kingdom of Naples, which is a
fief of the Church. His Holiness refused this horse from
the Germans ever since the Duke of Anjou has been
possessed of Spain ; but as they lately took care to accompany it with a body of ten thousand more, they have at

[1] "Epig." i. 20.
86

last overcome his Holiness's modesty, and prevailed upon him to accept the present.   I am,

> "Sir,

>> "Your most obedient,

>>> "Humble Servant,

>>>> "Pasquin.

"P.S. Morforio is very much yours."[1]

No. 130.   [? Addison.[2]

From *Saturday, Feb. 4,* to *Tuesday, Feb. 7,* 1709-10.

—— At me
Cum magnis vixisse invita fatebitur usque
Invidia.—Hor., 2 Sat. i. 75.

Sheer Lane, February 6.

I find some of the most polite Latin authors, who wrote at a time when Rome was in its glory, speak with a certain noble vanity of the brightness and splendour of the age in which they lived.   Pliny often compliments his Emperor Trajan upon this head ; and when he would

---

[1] See No. 130, Advertisement.

[2] Nichols suggests that this paper may be by Addison, because in No. 131 Addison has the following note : " For the benefit of my readers, I think myself obliged here to let them know that I always make use of an old-fashioned e, which very little differs from an o. This has been the reason that my printer sometimes mistakes the one for the other ; as in my last paper, I find, *those* for *these, beheld* for *behold,* Corvix for Cervix, and the like." The internal evidence supports this view ; but the paper is not included in Addison's Works.

animate him to anything great, or dissuade him from anything that was improper, he insinuates, that it is befitting
or unbecoming the *claritas et nitor sæculi*, that period
of time which was made illustrious by his reign.   When
we cast our eyes back on the history of mankind, and trace
them through their several successions to their first original,
we sometimes see them breaking out in great and memorable actions, and towering up to the utmost heights of
virtue and knowledge ; when, perhaps, if we carry our
observation to a little distance, we see them sunk into
sloth and ignorance, and altogether lost in darkness and
obscurity.   Sometimes the whole species is asleep for two
or three generations, and then again awakens into action,
flourishes in heroes, philosophers, and poets, who do honour
to human nature, and leave such tracts of glory behind
them, as distinguish the years in which they acted their
part from the ordinary course of time.

Methinks a man cannot, without a secret satisfaction,
consider the glory of the present age, which will shine as
bright as any other in the history of mankind.   It is still
big with great events, and has already produced changes
and revolutions which will be as much admired by
posterity, as any that have happened in the days of our
fathers, or in the old times before them.   We have seen
kingdoms divided and united, monarchs erected and
deposed, nations transferred from one sovereign to another ;
conquerors raised to such a greatness as has given a terror
to Europe, and thrown down by such a fall, as has moved
their pity.

But it is still a more pleasing view to an Englishman, to
see his own country give the chief influence to so illustrious
an age, and stand in the strongest point of light amidst the
diffused glory that surrounds it.

If we begin with learned men, we may observe, to the

honour of our country, that those who make the greatest
figure in most arts and sciences, are universally allowed to
be of the British nation ; and what is more remarkable,
that men of the greatest learning are among the men of
the greatest quality.

A nation may indeed abound with persons of such
uncommon parts and worth, as may make them rather a
misfortune than a blessing to the public. Those who
singly might have been of infinite advantage to the age
they live in, may, by rising up together in the same crisis
of time, and by interfering in their pursuits of honour,
rather interrupt than promote the service of their country.
Of this we have a famous instance in the Republic of Rome,
when Cæsar, Pompey, Cato, Cicero, and Brutus, endeavoured to recommend themselves at the same time to
the admiration of their contemporaries. Mankind was not
able to provide for so many extraordinary persons at once,
or find out posts suitable to their ambition and abilities.
For this reason, they were all as miserable in their deaths
as they were famous in their lives, and occasioned, not
only the ruin of each other, but also that of the commonwealth.

It is therefore a particular happiness to a people, when
the men of superior genius and character are so justly
disposed in the high places of honour, that each of them
moves in a sphere which is proper to him, and requires
those particular qualities in which he excels.

If I see a general commanding the forces of his country,
whose victories are not to be paralleled in story, and who is
as famous for his negotiations as his victories ;[1] and at the
same time see the management of a nation's treasury in the
hands of one who has always distinguished himself by a
generous contempt of his own private wealth, and an

[1] The Duke of Marlborough.

The *Tatler*

exact frugality of that which belongs to the public ;[1] I
cannot but think a people under such an Administration
may promise themselves conquest abroad, and plenty at
home.   If I were to wish for a proper person to preside
over the public councils, it should certainly be one as much
admired for his universal knowledge of men and things,
as for his eloquence, courage and integrity, in the exerting
of such extraordinary talents.[2]

Who is not pleased to see a person in the highest
station in the law, who was the most eminent in his
profession, and the most accomplished orator at the Bar ?[3]
Or at the head of the fleet a commander, under whose
conduct the common enemy received such a blow as he has
never been able to recover ?[4]

Were we to form to ourselves the idea of one whom we
should think proper to govern a distant kingdom, consisting chiefly of those who differ from us in religion, and
are influenced by foreign politics, would it not be such a
one as had signalised himself by a uniform and unshaken
zeal for the Protestant interest, and by his dexterity in
defeating the skill and artifice of its enemies ?[5]   In short, if
we find a great man popular for his honesty and humanity,
as well as famed for his learning and great skill in all the
languages of Europe, or a person eminent for those
qualifications which make men shine in public assemblies,
or for that steadiness, constancy, and good sense, which
carry a man to the desired point through all the opposition
of tumult and prejudice, we have the happiness to behold
them all in posts suitable to their characters.

Such a constellation of great persons, if I may so speak,

[1] Sidney, Lord Godolphin.   [2] Lord Somers. See No. 4.
[3] Lord Chancellor Cowper.   See the Dedication to this volume.
[4] Edward Russell, Earl of Oxford. See No. 4.
[5] Thomas, Earl of Wharton, the Lord-Lieutenant of Ireland.

while they shine out in their own distinct capacities, reflect a lustre upon each other, but in a more particular manner on their Sovereign, who has placed them in those proper situations, by which their virtues become so beneficial to all her subjects. It is the anniversary of the birthday of this glorious Queen which naturally led me into this field of contemplation, and instead of joining in the public exultations that are made on such occasions, to entertain my thoughts with the more serious pleasure of ruminating upon the glories of her reign.

While I behold her surrounded with triumphs, and adorned with all the prosperity and success which Heaven ever shed on a mortal, and still considering herself as such; though the person appears to me exceeding great that has these just honours paid to her, yet I must confess, she appears much greater in that she receives them with such a glorious humility, and shows she has no further regard for them, than as they arise from these great events which have made her subjects happy. For my own part, I must confess, when I see private virtues in so high a degree of perfection, I am not astonished at any extraordinary success that attends them, but look upon public triumphs as the natural consequences of religious retirements.

ADVERTISEMENT.

Finding some persons have mistaken Pasquin who was mentioned in my last, for one who has been pilloried at Rome; I must here advertise them, that it is only a maimed statue so called, on which the private scandal of that city is generally pasted. Morforio is a person of the same quality, who is usually made to answer whatever is published by the other : the wits of that place, like too many of our own country, taking pleasure in setting innocent people together by the ears. The mentioning of

this person, who is a great wit, and a great cripple, put me
in mind of Mr. Estcourt,[1] who is under the same circumstances.   He was formerly my apothecary, and being at
present disabled by the gout and stone, I must recommend
him to the public on Thursday next, that admirable play
of Ben Jonson's, called, "The Silent Woman," being
appointed to be acted for his benefit.   It would be
indecent for me to appear twice in a season at these
ludicrous diversions ; but as I always give my man and my
maid one day in the year, I shall allow them this, and am
promised by Mr. Estcourt, my ingenious apothecary, that
they shall have a place kept for them in the first row of
the middle gallery.

No. 131.   [Addison.
From *Tuesday, Feb.* 7, to *Thursday, Feb.* 9, 1709–10.

—— Scelus est jugulare Falernum,
Et dare Campano toxica sæva mero.
MART., Epig. i. 18.

Sheer Lane, February 8.

There is in this city a certain fraternity of chemical
operators, who work under ground in holes, caverns,
and dark retirements, to conceal their mysteries from the
eyes and observation of mankind.   These subterraneous
philosophers are daily employed in the transmutation of
liquors, and, by the power of magical drugs and incanta-
tions, raising under the streets of London the choicest
products of the hills and valleys of France.   They can

[1] See Nos. 20, 51.   Estcourt was apprenticed to an apothecary,
and is said to have tried that business before going on the stage.

squeeze bordeaux out of the sloe, and draw champagne from an apple. Virgil in that remarkable prophecy,

Incultisque rubens pendebit sentibus uva,[1]

(*The ripening grape shall hang on every thorn*),

seems to have hinted at this art which can turn a plantation of Northern hedges into a vineyard. These adepts are known among one another by the name of "wine-brewers," and I am afraid do great injury, not only to her Majesty's customs, but to the bodies of many of her good subjects.

Having received sundry complaints against these invisible workmen, I ordered the proper officer of my court to ferret them out of their respective caves, and bring them before me, which was yesterday executed accordingly.

The person who appeared against them was a merchant, who had by him a great magazine of wines that he had laid in before the war : but these gentlemen (as he said) had so vitiated the nation's palate, that no man could believe his to be French, because it did not taste like what they sold for such. As a man never pleads better than where his own personal interest is concerned, he exhibited to the court with great eloquence, that this new corporation of druggists had inflamed the bills of mortality, and puzzled the College of Physicians with diseases, for which they neither knew a name nor cure. He accused some of giving all their customers colics and megrims ; and mentioned one who had boasted, he had a tun of claret by him, that in a fortnight's time should give the gout to a dozen of the healthiest men in the city, provided that their constitutions were prepared for it by wealth and idleness. He then enlarged, with a great show of reason,

---

[1] Eclog. iv. 29.

upon the prejudice which these mixtures and compositions had done to the brains of the English nation ; as is too visible (said he) from many late pamphlets, speeches and sermons, as well as from the ordinary conversations of the youth of this age. He then quoted an ingenious person, who would undertake to know by a man's writings, the wine he most delighted in ; and on that occasion named a certain satirist, whom he had discovered to be the author of a lampoon, by a manifest taste of the sloe, which showed itself in it by much roughness, and little spirit.

In the last place, he ascribed to the unnatural tumults and fermentations which these mixtures raise in our blood, the divisions, heat and animosities, that reign among us ; and in particular, asserted most of the modern enthusiasms and agitations to be nothing else but the effects of adulterated port.

The counsel for the brewers had a face so extremely inflamed and illuminated with carbuncles, that I did not wonder to see him an advocate for these sophistications. His rhetoric was likewise such as I should have expected from the common draught, which I found he often drank to a great excess. Indeed, I was so surprised at his figure and parts, that I ordered him to give me a taste of his usual liquor ; which I had no sooner drunk, but I found a pimple rising in my forehead ; and felt such a sensible decay in my understanding, that I would not proceed in the trial till the fume of it was entirely dissipated.

This notable advocate had little to say in the defence of his clients, but that they were under a necessity of making claret if they would keep open their doors, it being the nature of mankind to love everything that is prohibited. He further pretended to reason, that it might be as profitable to the nation to make French wine as French hats ; and concluded with the great advantage that this had already brought to part of the kingdom. Upon which he informed the court, that the lands in Hertfordshire were raised two years' purchase since the beginning of the war.

When I had sent out my summons to these people, I gave at the same time orders to each of them to bring the several ingredients he made use of in distinct phials, which they had done accordingly, and ranged them into two rows on each side of the court. The workmen were drawn up in ranks behind them. The merchant informed me, that in one row of phials were the several colours they dealt in, and in the other the tastes. He then showed me on the right hand one who went by the name of Tom Tintoret, who (as he told me) was the greatest master in his colouring of any vintner in London.[1] To give me a proof of his art, he took a glass of fair water ; and by the infusion of three drops out of one of his phials, converted it into a most beautiful pale burgundy. Two more of the same kind heightened it into a perfect languedoc : from thence it passed into a florid hermitage : and after having gone through two or three other changes, by the addition of a single drop, ended in a very deep pontack.[2] This ingenious virtuoso seeing me very much surprised at his art, told me, that he had not an opportunity of showing it in perfection, having only made use of water for the groundwork of his colouring : but that if I were to see an operation upon liquors of stronger bodies, the art would appear to a much greater advantage. He added, that he doubted not that it would please my curiosity to see the cider of one apple take only a vermilion, when

[1] See No. 138.
[2] A fashionable eating-house in Abchurch Lane, kept by one Pontack, who was son of the President of Bordeaux, then owner, as Evelyn tells us, of the excellent vineyards of Pontaq and Haut Brion.

another, with a less quantity of the same infusion, would rise into a dark purple, according to the different texture of parts in the liquor. He informed me also, that he could hit the different shades and degrees of red, as they appear in the pink and the rose, the clove and the carnation, as he had Rhenish or Moselle, perry, or white port, to work in.

I was so satisfied with the ingenuity of this virtuoso, that, after having advised him to quit so dishonest a profession, I promised him, in consideration of his great genius, to recommend him as a partner to a friend of mine, who has heaped up great riches, and is a scarlet dyer.

The artists on my other hand were ordered in the second place to make some experiments of their skill before me : upon which the famous Harry Sippet stepped out, and asked me what I would be pleased to drink. At the same time he filled out three or four white liquors in a glass, and told me, that it should be what I pleased to call for ; adding very learnedly, that the liquor before him was as the naked substance or first matter of his compound, to which he and his friend, who stood over against him, could give what accidents or form they pleased. Finding him so great a philosopher, I desired he would convey into it the qualities and essence of right bordeaux. "Coming, coming, sir," said he, with the air of a drawer ; and after having cast his eye on the several tastes and flavours that stood before him, he took up a little cruet that was filled with a kind of inky juice, and pouring some of it out into the glass of white wine, presented it to me, and told me, this was the wine over which most of the business of the last term had been despatched. I must confess, I looked upon that sooty drug which he held up in his cruet as the quintessence of English bordeaux, and therefore desired him to give me a glass of it by itself, which he did with great unwillingness. My cat at that time sat by me upon the elbow of my chair ; and as I did not care for making the experiment upon myself, I reached it to her to sip of it, which had like to have cost her her life ; for notwithstanding it flung her at first into freakish tricks, quite contrary to her usual gravity, in less than a quarter of an hour she fell into convulsions ; and had it not been a creature more tenacious of life than any other, would certainly have died under the operation.

I was so incensed by the tortures of my innocent domestic, and the unworthy dealings of these men, that I told them, if each of them had as many lives as the injured creature before them, they deserved to forfeit them for the pernicious arts which they used for their profit. I therefore bid them look upon themselves as no better than as a kind of assassins and murderers within the law. However, since they had dealt so clearly with me, and laid before me their whole practice, I dismissed them for that time ; with a particular request, that they would not poison any of my friends and acquaintance, and take to some honest livelihood without loss of time.

For my own part, I have resolved hereafter to be very careful in my liquors, and have agreed with a friend of mine in the army, upon their next march, to secure me two hogsheads of the best stomach-wine in the cellars of Versailles, for the good of my Lucubrations, and the comfort of my old age.

No. 132.

From *Thursday, Feb.* 9, to *Saturday, Feb.* 11, 1709-10.

Habeo senectuti magnam gratiam, quæ mihi sermonis aviditatem
auxit, potionis et cibi sustulit.—CICERO, De Sen. 46.

Sheer Lane, February 10.

After having applied my mind with more than ordinary
attention to my studies, it is my usual custom to
relax and unbend it in the conversation of such as are
rather easy than shining companions. This I find particularly necessary for me before I retire to rest, in order
to draw my slumbers upon me by degrees, and fall asleep
insensibly. This is the particular use I make of a set of
heavy honest men, with whom I have passed many hours,
with much indolence, though not with great pleasure.
Their conversation is a kind of preparative for sleep : it
takes the mind down from its abstractions, leads it into
the familiar traces[1] of thought, and lulls it into that state
of tranquillity, which is the condition of a thinking man
when he is but half awake. After this, my reader will not
be surprised to hear the account which I am about to give
of a club of my own contemporaries, among whom I pass
two or three hours every evening. This I look upon as
taking my first nap before I go to bed. The truth of it
is, I should think myself unjust to posterity, as well as to
the society at the Trumpet,[2] of which I am a member, did
not I in some part of my writings give an account of the

---

[1] Paths.
[2] The Trumpet stood about half-way up Shire Lane, between
Temple Bar and Carey Street, at the widest and best part of the lane,
and remained almost entirely in its original state until demolished to

persons among whom I have passed almost a sixth part of my time for these last forty years. Our club consisted originally of fifteen ; but partly by the severity of the law in arbitrary times, and partly by the natural effects of old age, we are at present reduced to a third part of that number : in which however we have this consolation, that the best company is said to consist of five persons.   I must confess, besides the aforementioned benefit which I meet with in the conversation of this select society, I am not the less pleased with the company, in that I find myself the greatest wit among them, and am heard as their oracle in all points of learning and difficulty.

Sir Jeoffrey Notch, who is the oldest of the club, has been in possession of the right-hand chair time out of mind, and is the only man among us that has the liberty of stirring the fire. This our foreman is a gentleman of an ancient family, that came to a great estate some years before he had discretion, and run it out in hounds, horses, and cock-fighting ; for which reason he looks upon himself as an honest worthy gentleman who has had misfortunes in the world, and calls every thriving man a pitiful upstart.

Major Matchlock is the next senior, who served in the last civil wars, and has all the battles by heart. He does not think any action in Europe worth talking of since the fight of Marston Moor ;[1] and every night tells us of his having been knocked off his horse at the rising of the London apprentices ;[2] for which he is in great esteem amongst us.

make way for the new Law Courts. It had the old sign of the Trumpet to the last, as it is figured in Limbard's " Mirror," in a picture where it is placed side by side with a view of the house in Fulwood's Rents where papers for the *Spectator* were taken in.

[1] July 2, 1644.

[2] In July 1647 the London apprentices presented a petition, and forced their way into the House of Commons.

The Tatler No. 132. February 11, 1709-10

Honest old Dick Reptile is the third of our society : he is a good-natured indolent man, who speaks little himself, but laughs at our jokes, and brings his young nephew along with him, a youth of eighteen years old, to show him good company, and give him a taste of the world. This young fellow sits generally silent; but whenever he opens his mouth, or laughs at anything that passes, he is constantly told by his uncle, after a jocular manner, "Ay, ay, Jack, you young men think us fools ; but we old men know you are." [1]

The greatest wit of our company, next to myself, is a bencher of the neighbouring inn, who in his youth frequented the ordinaries about Charing Cross, and pretends to have been intimate with Jack Ogle.[2] He has about ten distichs of "Hudibras" without book, and never leaves the club till he has applied them all. If any modern

---

[1] This retort, in almost identical words, occurs in Swift's "Genteel Conversation" (1739), and in Defoe's "Life of Duncan Campbell" (1720).

[2] Jack Ogle, said to have been descended from a decent family in Devonshire, was a man of some genius and great extravagance, but rather artful than witty. Ogle had an only sister, more beautiful, it is said, than was necessary to arrive, as she did, at the honour of being a mistress to the Duke of York. This sister Ogle laid under very frequent contributions to supply his wants and support his extravagance. It is said that, by the interest of her royal keeper, Ogle was placed, as a private gentleman, in the first troop of foot guards, at that time under the command of the Duke of Monmouth. To this era of Ogle's life the story of the red petticoat refers. He had pawned his trooper's cloak, and to save appearances at a review, had borrowed his landlady's red petticoat, which he carried rolled up *en croupe* behind him. The Duke of Monmouth "smoked" it, and willing to enjoy the confusion of a detection, gave order to "cloak all," with which Ogle, after some hesitation, was obliged to comply ; although he could not cloak, he said he would petticoat with the best of them. Such as are curious to know more of the history, the duels, and odd pranks of this mad fellow, may consult the account of them in the "Memoirs of Gamesters," 1714, 12mo, p. 183 (Nichols).

wit be mentioned, or any town frolic spoken of, he shakes his head at the dulness of the present age, and tells us a story of Jack Ogle.

For my own part, I am esteemed among them, because they see I am something respected by others, though at the same time I understand by their behaviour, that I am considered by them as a man of a great deal of learning, but no knowledge of the world ; insomuch that the Major sometimes, in the height of his military pride, calls me the philosopher : and Sir Jeoffrey no longer ago than last night, upon a dispute what day of the month it was then in Holland, pulled his pipe out of his mouth, and cried, " What does the scholar say to it ? "

Our club meets precisely at six o'clock in the evening ; but I did not come last night till half an hour after seven, by which means I escaped the battle of Naseby, which the Major usually begins at about three-quarters after six ; I found also, that my good friend, the bencher, had already spent three of his distichs, and only waiting an opportunity to hear a sermon spoken of, that he might introduce the couplet where "a stick" rhymes to "ecclesiastic."[1] At my entrance into the room, they were naming a red petticoat and a cloak, by which I found that the bencher had been diverting them with a story of Jack Ogle.

I had no sooner taken my seat, but Sir Jeoffrey, to show his goodwill towards me, gave me a pipe of his own tobacco, and stirred up the fire. I look upon it as a point .of morality, to be obliged by those who endeavour to oblige me ; and therefore in requital for his kindness, and to set the conversation a-going, I took the best occasion I could, to put him upon telling us the story of old Gantlett,

---

[1] " When pulpit drum ecclesiastic
Was beat with fist instead of a stick."
—" Hudibras," Part I. c. i. line 10.

which he always does with very particular concern. He
traced up his descent on both sides for several generations,
describing his diet and manner of life, with his several
battles, and particularly that in which he fell. This
Gantlett was a game-cock, upon whose head the knight in
his youth had won five hundred pounds, and lost two
thousand. This naturally set the major upon the account
of Edge Hill fight, and ended in a duel of Jack Ogle's.

Old Reptile was extremely attentive to all that was said,
though it was the same he had heard every night for these
twenty years, and upon all occasions, winked upon his
nephew to mind what passed.

This may suffice to give the world a taste of our innocent conversation, which we spun out till about ten of the
clock, when my maid[1] came with a lantern to light me
home. I could not but reflect with myself as I was going
out upon the talkative humour of old men, and the little
figure which that part of life makes in one who cannot
employ this natural propensity in discourses which would
make him venerable. I must own, it makes me very
melancholy in company, when I hear a young man begin a
story ; and have often observed, that one of a quarter of an
hour long in a man of five and twenty, gathers circumstances every time he tells it, till it grows into a long
Canterbury tale of two hours by that time he is threescore.

The only way of avoiding such a trifling and frivolous
old age, is, to lay up in our way to it such stores of knowledge and observation as may make us useful and agreeable in our declining years. The mind of man in a long
life will become a magazine of wisdom or folly, and will

---

[1] Cf. No. 130, Advertisements. The dangers of the streets at the
beginning of the eighteenth century are described in Gay's " Trivia,"
iii. 335 *seq.*

consequently discharge itself in something impertinent or improving. For which reason, as there is nothing more ridiculous than an old trifling story-teller, so there is nothing more venerable than one who has turned his experience to the entertainment and advantage of mankind.

In short, we who are in the last stage of life, and are apt to indulge ourselves in talk, ought to consider, if what we speak be worth being heard, and endeavour to make our discourse like that of Nestor, which Homer compares to the flowing of honey for its sweetness.[1]

I am afraid I shall be thought guilty of this excess I am speaking of, when I cannot conclude without observing, that Milton certainly thought of this passage in Homer, when in his description of an eloquent spirit, he says, "His tongue dropped manna."[2]

No. 133.   [ADDISON.

From *Saturday, Feb.* 11, to *Tuesday, Feb.* 14, 1709–10.

Dum tacent, clamant.—TULL.

Sheer Lane, February 13.

Silence is sometimes more significant and sublime than the most noble and most expressive eloquence, and is on many occasions the indication of a great mind. Several authors have treated of silence as a part of duty and discretion, but none of them have considered it in this

[1] " Iliad," i. 249.
[2] Milton says of Belial ("Paradise Lost," ii. 112) :
" But all was false and hollow, though his tongue
Dropped manna, and could make the worse appear
The better cause."

light.   Homer compares the noise and clamour of the
Trojans advancing towards the enemy, to the cackling of
cranes when they invade an army of pigmies.[1]   On the
contrary, he makes his countrymen and favourites, the
Greeks, move forward in a regular determined march, and
in the depth of silence.   I find in the accounts which are
given us of some of the more Eastern nations, where the
inhabitants are disposed by their constitutions and climates
to higher strains of thought, and more elevated raptures
than what we feel in the northern regions of the world,
that silence is a religious exercise among them.   For when
their public devotions are in the greatest fervour, and
their hearts lifted up as high as words can raise them,
there are certain suspensions of sound and motion for a
time, in which the mind is left to itself, and supposed to
swell with such secret conceptions as are too big for utterance.   I have myself been wonderfully delighted with a
masterpiece of music, when in the very tumult and ferment
of their harmony, all the voices and instruments have
stopped short on a sudden, and after a little pause
recovered themselves again as it were, and renewed the
concert in all its parts.   Methought this short interval of
silence has had more music in it than any the same space
of time before or after it.   There are two instances of
silence in the two greatest poets that ever wrote, which
have something in them as sublime as any of the speeches
in their whole works.   The first is that of Ajax, in the
eleventh book of the Odyssey.[2]   Ulysses, who had been the
rival of this great man in his life, as well as the occasion
of his death, upon meeting his shade in the region of
departed heroes, makes his submission to him with a
humility next to adoration, which the other passes over
with dumb sullen majesty, and such a silence, as (to use

[1] "Iliad," iii. 3.   [2] "Odyssey," xi. 563.

the words of Longinus) had more greatness in it than any-thing he could have spoken.

The next instance I shall mention is in Virgil, where the poet, doubtless, imitates this silence of Ajax in that of Dido ;[1] though I do not know that any of his commentators have taken notice of it. Æneas finding among the shades of despairing lovers, the ghost of her who had lately died for him, with the wound still fresh upon her, addresses himself to her with expanded arms, floods of tears, and the most passionate professions of his own innocence as to what had happened ; all which Dido receives with the dignity and disdain of a resenting lover, and an injured Queen ; and is so far from vouchsafing him an answer, that she does not give him a single look. The poet represents her as turning away her face from him while he spoke to her ; and after having kept her eyes for some time upon the ground, as one that heard and con-temned his protestations, flying from him into the grove of myrtle, and into the arms of another, whose fidelity had deserved her love.[1]

I have often thought our writers of tragedy have been very defective in this particular, and that they might have given great beauty to their works, by certain stops and pauses in the representation of such passions, as it is not in the power of language to express. There is something like this in the last act of "Venice Preserved," where Pierre is brought to an infamous execution, and begs of his friend,[3] as a reparation for past injuries, and the only favour he could do him, to rescue him from the ignominy of the wheel by stabbing him. As he is going to make this dreadful request, he is not able to communicate it, but withdraws his face from his friend's ear, and bursts into

---

[1] "Æneid," vi. 46.   [2] Sichæus.
[3] Jaffier. See Otway's "Venice Preserved," act v. sc. 3.

tears. The melancholy silence that follows hereupon, and continues till he has recovered himself enough to reveal his mind to his friend, raises in the spectators a grief that is inexpressible, and an idea of such a complicated distress in the actor as words cannot utter. It would look as ridiculous to many readers to give rules and directions for proper silences, as for penning a whisper : but it is certain, that in the extremity of most passions, particularly surprise, admiration, astonishment, nay, rage itself, there is nothing more graceful than to see the play stand still for a few moments, and the audience fixed in an agreeable suspense during the silence of a skilful actor.

But silence never shows itself to so great an advantage, as when it is made the reply to calumny and defamation, provided that we give no just occasion for them. One might produce an example of it in the behaviour of one in whom it appeared in all its majesty, and one whose silence, as well as his person, was altogether divine. When one considers this subject only in its sublimity, this great instance could not but occur to me ; and since I only make use of it to show the highest example of it, I hope I do not offend in it. To forbear replying to an unjust reproach, and overlook it with a generous, or (if possible) with an entire neglect òf it, is one of the most heroic acts of a great mind. And I must confess, when I reflect upon the behaviour of some of the greatest men in antiquity, I do not so much admire them that they deserved the praise of the whole age they lived in, as because they contemned the envy and detraction of it.

All that is incumbent on a man of worth, who suffers under so ill a treatment, is to lie by for some time in silence and obscurity, till the prejudice of the times be over, and his reputation cleared. I have often read with a great deal of pleasure a legacy of the famous Lord Bacon, one of the greatest geniuses that our own or any country has produced : after having bequeathed his soul, body, and estate, in the usual form, he adds, " My name and memory I leave to foreign nations, and to my countrymen, after some time be passed over."

At the same time that I recommend this philosophy to others, I must confess I am so poor a proficient in it myself, that if in the course of my Lucubrations it happens, as it has done more than once, that my paper is duller than in conscience it ought to be, I think the time an age till I have an opportunity of putting out another, and growing famous again for two days.

I must not close my discourse upon silence, without informing my reader, that I have by me an elaborate treatise on the Aposiopesis called an " Et cætera," it being a figure much used by some learned authors, and particularly by the great Littleton, who, as my Lord Chief Justice Coke observes, had a most admirable talent at an et cetera.[1]

ADVERTISEMENT.

To oblige the Pretty Fellows, and my fair readers, I have thought fit to insert the whole passage above mentioned relating to Dido, as it is translated by Mr. Dryden :

> *Not far from thence, the mournful fields appear ;*
> *So called, from lovers that inhabit there.*
> *The souls, whom that unhappy flame invades,*
> *In secret solitude, and myrtle shades,*
> *Make endless moans, and pining with desire,*
> *Lament too late their unextinguished fire.*

[1] In the preface to his " Institutes of the Laws of England ; or, a Commentary upon Littleton," Coke says, " Certain it is, that there is never a period, nor (for the most part) a word, nor an &c., but affordeth excellent matter of learning."

Here Procris, Eryphile here, he found
Baring her breast, yet bleeding with the wound
Made by her son.   He saw Pasiphae there,
With Phædra's ghost, a foul incestuous pair;
There Laodamia with Evadne moves:
Unhappy both, but loyal in their loves.
Cæneus, a woman once, and once a man;
But ending in the sex she first began.
Not far from these, Phœnician Dido stood;
Fresh from her wound, her bosom bathed in blood.
Whom, when the Trojan hero hardly knew,
Obscure in shades, and with a doubtful view
(Doubtful as he who runs through dusky night,
Or thinks he sees the moon's uncertain light)
With tears he first approached the sullen shade;
And, as his love inspired him, thus he said:
" Unhappy queen!   Then is the common breath
Of rumour true, in your reported death;
And I, alas, the cause!   By Heaven, I vow,
And all the powers that rule the realms below,
Unwilling I forsook your friendly state,
Commanded by the gods, and forced by Fate.
Those gods, that Fate, whose unresisted might,
Have sent me to these regions, void of light,
Through the vast empire of eternal night.
Nor dared I to presume, that, pressed with grief,
My flight should urge you to this dire relief.
Stay, stay your steps, and listen to my vows;
'Tis the last interview that Fate allows!"
In vain he thus attempts her mind to move,
With tears and prayers, and late repenting love.
Disdainfully she looked, then turning round;
But fixed her eyes unmoved upon the ground;
And, what he says, and swears, regards no more
Than the deaf rocks, when the loud billows roar;
But whirled away, to shun his hateful sight,
Hid in the forest, and the shades of night.
Then sought Sichæus through the shady grove,
Who answered all her cares, and equalled all her love.

No. 134.   [STEELE.

From *Tuesday*, *Feb.* 14, to *Thursday*, *Feb.* 16, 1709-10.

—— Quis talia fando
Myrmidonum, Dolopumve, aut duri miles Ulixi,
Temperet a lachrimis !—VIRG., Æn. ii. 6.

Sheer Lane, February 15.

I was awakened very early this morning by the distant crowing of a cock, which I thought had the finest pipe I ever heard. He seemed to me to strain his voice more than ordinary, as if he designed to make himself heard to the remotest corner of this lane. Having entertained myself a little before I went to bed with a discourse on the transmigration of men into other animals, I could not but fancy that this was the soul of some drowsy bellman who used to sleep upon his post, for which he was condemned to do penance in feathers, and distinguish the several watches of the night under the outside of a cock. While I was thinking of the condition of this poor bellman in masquerade, I heard a great knocking at my door, and was soon after told by my maid, that my worthy friend the tall black gentleman, who frequents the coffee-houses hereabouts, desired to speak with me. This ancient Pythagorean, who has as much honesty as any man living, but good nature to an excess, brought me the following petition, which I am apt to believe he penned himself, the petitioner not being able to express his mind in paper under his present form, however famous he might have been for writing verses when he was in his original shape.

The Tatler   No. 134. February 16, 1709–10

" *To Isaac Bickerstaff, Esq., Censor of Great Britain.*

" The humble petition of Job Chanticleer, in behalf of himself, and many other poor sufferers in the same condition ;

"Sheweth,

" That whereas your petitioner is truly descended of the ancient family of the Chanticleers at Cock Hall near Romford in Essex, it has been his misfortune to come into the mercenary hands of a certain ill-disposed person, commonly called a 'higgler,' who, under the close confinement of a pannier, has conveyed him and many others up to London ; but hearing by chance of your worship's great humanity towards robin-redbreasts and tom-tits,[1] he is emboldened to beseech you to take his deplorable condition into your tender consideration, who otherwise must suffer (with many thousands more as innocent as himself) that inhumane barbarity of a Shrove Tuesday persecution.[2] We humbly hope that our courage and vigilance may plead for us on this occasion.

" Your poor petitioner most earnestly implores your immediate protection from the insolence of the rabble, the batteries of catsticks,[3] and a painful lingering death.

" And your petitioner, &c.

"From my coup in Clare Market, *February* 13, 1709."

Upon delivery of this petition, the worthy gentleman who presented it, told me the customs of many wise nations of the East, through which he had travelled ; that

---

[1] See No. 112.   [2] See the date of this number.
[3] Sticks used in the games of tip-cat and trap-ball.

nothing was more frequent than to see a dervish lay out a whole year's income in the redemption of larks or linnets that had unhappily fallen into the hands of bird-catchers :[1] that it was also usual to run between a dog and a bull to keep them from hurting one another, or to lose the use of a limb in parting a couple of furious mastiffs. He then insisted upon the ingratitude and disingenuity[2] of treating in this manner a necessary and domestic animal, that has made the whole house keep good hours, and called up the cook maid for five years together. " What would a Turk say," continued he, " should he hear, that it is a common entertainment in a nation which pretends to be one of the most civilised of Europe, to tie an innocent animal to a stake, and put him to an ignominious death, who has perhaps been the guardian and proveditor of a poor family, as long as he was able to get eggs for his mistress ? "

I thought what this gentleman said was very reasonable ; and have often wondered, that we do not lay aside a custom which makes us appear barbarous to nations much more rude and unpolished than ourselves. Some French writers have represented this diversion of the common people much to our disadvantage, and imputed it to natural fierceness and cruelty of temper ; as they do some other entertainments peculiar to our nation : I mean those elegant diversions of bull-baiting and prize-fighting, with the like ingenious recreations of the bear-garden.[3] I wish I knew how to answer this reproach which is cast upon us, and excuse the death of so many innocent cocks, bulls, dogs, and bears, as have been set together by the ears, or died untimely deaths only to make us sport.

[1] Cf. the *Spectator*, No. 343, where Addison refers to Sir Paul Rycaut's work on the Ottoman Empire.
[2] Disingenuousness.   [3] See Nos. 28, 31.

The Tatler No. 134. February 16, 1709-10

It will be said, that these are the entertainments of common people. It is true ; but they are the entertainments of no other common people.[1] Besides, I am afraid there is a tincture of the same savage spirit in the diversions of those of higher rank, and more refined relish. Rapin observes, that the English theatre very much delights in bloodshed, which he likewise represents as an indication of our tempers. I must own, there is something very horrid in the public executions of an English tragedy. Stabbing and poisoning, which are performed behind the

[1] "Cock-fighting is diverting enough, the anger and eagerness of these little creatures, and the triumphant crowing of a cock when he strutts haughtily on the body of his enemy, has something in't singular and pleasant. What renders these shows less agreeable is the great number of wagerers, who appear as angry as the cocks themselves, and make such a noise that one would believe every minute they were going to fight ; but combats among the men are another kind of diversion, where the spectators are more peaceable " (" Letters describing the Character and Customs of the English and French Nations ; by Mr. Muralt, a Gentleman of Switzerland. 2nd ed. ; translated from the French." London, 1726, p. 41). In Hogarth's picture of a cock-fight a Frenchman is depicted turning away in disgust (see Lecky's " History of England in the Eighteenth Century," 1878, i. 552). "There will be a cock-match fought at Leeds in Yorkshire, the 19th of March next ; and another at Wakefield the 23rd of April next. At each meeting 40 Cocks on each side will be shewn. These are fought betwixt the people of the West and North Riding of Yorkshire ; And every Battel 5*l.* each side, and 50*l.* the odd Battel, and four Shake Bags for 10*l.* each Cock" (*London Gazette*, March 8-12, 1687). A cock-match between Surrey and Sussex was to commence on May 4, 1703, "and will continue the whole week " (*London Gazette*, April 12-15, 1703) " The Royal Pastime of Cock-fighting, or, the Art of Breeding, Feeding, Fighting and Curing Cocks of the Game. Published purely for the good and benefit of all such as take Delight in that Royal and Warlike Sport. To which is prefixed, a Short Treatise, wherein Cocking is proved not only ancient and honourable, but also useful and profitable. By R. H., a Lover of the Sport, and a friend to such as delight in Military Discipline " (*Post Boy*, Jan. 15-18, 1708-9).

scenes in other nations, must be done openly among us, to gratify the audience.[1]

When poor Sandford[2] was upon the stage, I have seen him groaning upon a wheel, stuck with daggers, impaled alive, calling his executioners, with a dying voice, cruel dogs and villains! And all this to please his judicious spectators, who were wonderfully delighted with seeing a man in torment so well acted. The truth of it is, the politeness of our English stage, in regard to decorum, is very extraordinary. We act murders to show our intrepidity, and adulteries to show our gallantry: both of them are frequent in our most taking plays, with this difference only, that the first are done in sight of the audience, and the other wrought up to such a height upon the stage, that they are almost put in execution before the actors can get behind the scenes.

I would not have it thought, that there is just ground for those consequences which our enemies draw against us from these practices; but methinks one would be sorry for any manner of occasion for such misrepresentations of

---

[1] Addison, also referring to Rapin, writes to the same effect in the *Spectator*, No. 44. Rapin said, in his "Reflections on Aristotle's Treatise of Poetry," translated in 1694: "The English, our neighbours, love blood in their sports, by the quality of their temperament. . . . The English have more of genius for tragedy than other people, as well by the spirit of their nation, which delights in cruelty, as also by the character of their language, which is proper for great expressions." There is an "Address to the Cock-killers" in Lillie's "Letters sent to the *Tatler* and *Spectator*," i. 25–29.

[2] Samuel Sandford seems to have left the stage about 1700. He had a low and crooked person, and Cibber describes him as "an excellent actor in disagreeable parts." Charles II. called him the best villain in the world. There is a story of a new play being damned because Sandford played the part of an honest statesman, and the pit was therefore disappointed at not seeing the usual Iago-like or Machiavelian character.

us. The virtues of tenderness, compassion and humanity, are those by which men are distinguished from brutes, as much as by reason itself; and it would be the greatest reproach to a nation to distinguish itself from all others by any defect in these particular virtues. For which reasons, I hope that my dear countrymen will no longer expose themselves by an effusion of blood, whether it be of theatrical heroes, cocks, or any other innocent animals, which we are not obliged to slaughter for our safety, convenience, or nourishment. Where any of these ends are not served in the destruction of a living creature, I cannot but pronounce it a great piece of cruelty, if not a kind of murder.

No. 135.   [STEELE.

From *Thursday, Feb.* 16, to *Saturday, Feb.* 18, 1709-10.

Quod si in hoc erro, quod animos hominum immortales esse credam, libenter erro : nec mihi hunc errorem, quo delector, dum vivo, extorqueri volo : sin mortuus (ut quidam minuti philosophi censent) nihil sentiam ; non vereor, ne hunc errorem meum mortui philosophi irrideant.—CICERO, De Sen., cap. ult.

Sheer Lane, February 17.

Several letters which I have lately received give me information, that some well-disposed persons have taken offence at my using the word "freethinker" as a term of reproach. To set therefore this matter in a clear light, I must declare, that no one can have a greater veneration than myself for the freethinkers of antiquity, who acted the same part in those times, as the great men of the Reformation did in several nations of Europe, by exerting themselves against the idolatry and superstition of the times in which they lived. It was by this noble impulse

that Socrates and his disciples, as well as all the philosophers
of note in Greece, and Cicero, Seneca, with all the learned
men of Rome, endeavoured to enlighten their contemporaries amidst the darkness and ignorance in which the
world was then sunk and buried.   The great points which
these freethinkers endeavoured to establish and inculcate
into the minds of men, were, the formation of the universe,
the superintendency of Providence, the perfection of the
divine nature, the immortality of the soul, and the future
state of rewards and punishments.   They all complied
with the religion of their country, as much as possible, in
such particulars as did not contradict and pervert these
great and fundamental doctrines of mankind.   On the
contrary, the persons who now set up for freethinkers, are
such as endeavour by a little trash of words and sophistry,
to weaken and destroy those very principles, for the
vindication of which, freedom of thought at first became
laudable and heroic.[1]   These apostates, from reason and
good sense, can look at the glorious frame of Nature,
without paying an adoration to Him that raised it ; can
consider the great revolutions in the universe, without
lifting up their minds to that Superior Power which hath
the direction of it ; can presume to censure the Deity in
His ways towards men ; can level mankind with the
beasts that perish ; can extinguish in their own minds all
the pleasing hopes of a future state, and lull themselves
into a stupid security against the terrors of it.   If one
were to take the word "priestcraft" out of the mouths of

[1] In speaking of Collins' "Discourse of Free-Thinking" (1713) in
the *Guardian* (No. 9), Steele says : "I cannot see any possible inter-
pretation to give this work, but a design to subvert and ridicule the
authority of scripture. The peace and tranquillity of the nation, and
regards even above those, are so much concerned in this matter, that
it is difficult to express sufficient sorrow for the offender, or indignation against him."

these shallow monsters, they would be immediately struck dumb. It is by the help of this single term that they endeavour to disappoint the good works of the most learned and venerable order of men, and harden the hearts of the ignorant against the very light of Nature, and the common received notions of mankind. We ought not to treat such miscreants as these upon the foot of fair disputants, but to pour out contempt upon them, and speak of them with scorn and infamy, as the pests of society, the revilers of human nature, and the blasphemers of a Being, whom a good man would rather die than hear dishonoured. Cicero, after having mentioned the great heroes of knowledge that recommended this divine doctrine of the immortality of the soul, calls those small pretenders to wisdom who declared against it, certain minute philosophers,[1] using a diminutive even of the word " little," to express the despicable opinion he had of them. The contempt he throws upon them in another passage[2] is yet more remarkable, where, to show the mean thoughts he entertains of them, he declares, he would rather be in the wrong with Plato, than in the right with such company. There is indeed nothing in the world so ridiculous as one of these grave philosophical freethinkers, that hath neither passions nor appetites to gratify, no heats of blood nor vigour of constitution that can turn his systems of infidelity to his advantage, or raise pleasures out of them which are inconsistent with the belief of a hereafter. One that has neither wit, gallantry, mirth, nor youth, to indulge by these notions, but only a poor, joyless, uncomfortable vanity of distinguishing himself from the rest of mankind, is rather to be regarded as a mis-

[1] See the motto at the head of this paper.
[2] " Tusc. Disp." i. 17. Cicero calls those who differ from Plato and Socrates " plebii omnes philosophi " (*ib.* i. 23).

chievous lunatic, than a mistaken philosopher. A chaste infidel, a speculative libertine, is an animal that I should not believe to be in Nature, did I not sometimes meet with this species of men, that plead for the indulgence of their passions in the midst of a severe studious life, and talk against the immortality of the soul over a dish of coffee.

I would fain ask a minute philosopher, what good he proposes to mankind by the publishing of his doctrines? Will they make a man a better citizen, or father of a family; a more endearing husband, friend, or son? Will they enlarge his public or private virtues, or correct any of his frailties or vices? What is there either joyful or glorious in such opinions? Do they either refresh or enlarge our thoughts? Do they contribute to the happiness, or raise the dignity of human nature? The only good that I have ever heard pretended to, is, that they banish terrors, and set the mind at ease. But whose terrors do they banish? It is certain, if there were any strength in their arguments, they would give great disturbance to minds that are influenced by virtue, honour, and morality, and take from us the only comforts and supports of affliction, sickness, and old age. The minds therefore which they set at ease, are only those of impenitent criminals and malefactors, and which, to the good of mankind, should be in perpetual terror and alarm.

I must confess, nothing is more usual than for a free-thinker, in proportion as the insolence of scepticism is abated in him by years and knowledge, or humbled and beaten down by sorrow or sickness, to reconcile himself to the general conceptions of reasonable creatures; so that we frequently see the apostates turning from their revolt toward the end of their lives, and employing the refuse of their parts in promoting those truths which they had before endeavoured to invalidate.

The Tatler   No. 135. February 18, 1709–10

The history of a gentleman in France is very well known, who was so zealous a promoter of infidelity, that he had got together a select company of disciples, and travelled into all parts of the kingdom to make converts. In the midst of his fantastical success he fell sick, and was reclaimed to such a sense of his condition, that after he had passed some time in great agonies and horrors of mind, he begged those who had the care of burying him, to dress his body in the habit of a Capuchin, that the devil might not run away with it ; and to do further justice upon himself, desired them to tie a halter about his neck, as a mark of that ignominious punishment, which in his own thoughts he had so justly deserved.

I would not have persecution so far disgraced, as to wish these vermin might be animadverted on by any legal penalties ; though I think it would be highly reasonable, that those few of them who die in the professions of their infidelity, should have such tokens of infamy fixed upon them, as might distinguish those bodies which are given up by the owners to oblivion and putrefaction, from those which rest in hope, and shall rise in glory.   But at the same time that I am against doing them the honour of the notice of our laws, which ought not to suppose there are such criminals in being, I have often wondered how they can be tolerated in any mixed conversations while they are venting these absurd opinions ; and should think, that if on any such occasion half a dozen of the most robust Christians in the company would lead one of these gentle- men to a pump, or convey him into a blanket, they would do very good service both to Church and State.   I do not know how the laws stand in this particular ; but I hope, whatever knocks, bangs or thumps might be given with such an honest intention, would not be construed as a breach of the peace.   I daresay they would not be returned by the person who receives them ; for whatever these fools may say in the vanity of their hearts, they are too wise to risk their lives upon the uncertainty of their opinions.

When I was a young man about this town, I frequented the ordinary of the Black Horse, in Holborn, where the person that usually presided at the table was a rough old-fashioned gentleman, who, according to the custom of those times, had been the major and preacher of a regiment. It happened one day that a noisy young officer, bred in France, was venting some new-fangled notions, and speaking, in the gaiety of his humour, against the dispensations of Providence. The major at first only desired him to talk more respectfully of one for whom all the company had an honour ; but finding him run on in his extravagance, began to reprimand him after a more serious manner. " Young man," said he, " do not abuse your Benefactor whilst you are eating His bread. Consider whose air you breathe, whose presence you are in, and who it is that gave you the power of that very speech which you make use of to His dishonour." The young fellow, who thought to turn matters into a jest, asked him if he was going to preach ; but at the same time desired him to take care what he said when he spoke to a man of honour. " A man of honour ? " says the major, " thou art an infidel and a blasphemer, and I shall use thee as such." In short, the quarrel ran so high, that the major was desired to walk out. Upon their coming into the garden, the old fellow advised his antagonist to consider the place into which one pass might drive him ; but finding him grow upon him to a degree of scurrility, as believing the advice proceeded from fear ; " Sirrah," says he, " if a thunderbolt does not strike thee dead before I come at thee, I shall not fail to chastise thee for thy profaneness to thy Maker, and thy sauciness to His servant." Upon this he drew his sword, and cried out with a loud voice, " The sword of the Lord and of Gideon " ; which so terrified his antagonist, that he was immediately disarmed, and thrown upon his knees.   In this posture he begged his life ; but the major refused to grant it, before he had asked pardon for his offence in a short extemporary prayer which the old gentleman dictated to him upon the spot, and which his proselyte repeated after him in the presence of the whole ordinary, that were now gathered about him in the garden.

No. 136.

From *Saturday, Feb.* 18, to *Tuesday, Feb.* 21, 1709–10.

Deprendi miserum est ; Fabio vel judice vincam.
HOR., 1 Sat. ii. 134.

White's Chocolate-house, February 18.

The History of Tom Varnish.

Because I have a professed aversion to long beginnings of stories, I will go into this at once, by telling you, that there dwells near the Royal Exchange as happy a couple as ever entered into wedlock.   These live in that mutual confidence of each other, which renders the satisfactions of marriage even greater than those of friendship, and makes wife and husband the dearest appellations of human life.   Mr. Ballance is a merchant of good consideration, and understands the world not from speculation, but practice.   His wife is the daughter of an honest house, ever bred in a family-way ; and has, from a natural good

[1] Nichols suggests that this paper may be by Addison, and it is certainly not unlikely that he was the author of the " History of Tom Varnish."

understanding, and great innocence, a freedom which men of sense know to be the certain sign of virtue, and fools take to be an encouragement to vice.

Tom Varnish, a young gentleman of the Middle Temple, by the bounty of a good father who was so obliging as to die, and leave him in his twenty-fourth year, besides a good estate, a large sum, which lay in the hands of Mr. Ballance, had by this means an intimacy at his house ; and being one of those hard students who read plays for improvement in the law, took his rules of life from thence. Upon mature deliberation, he conceived it very proper, that he, as a man of wit and pleasure of the town, should have an intrigue with his merchant's wife. He no sooner thought of this adventure, but he began it by an amorous epistle to the lady, and a faithful promise to wait upon her, at a certain hour the next evening, when he knew her husband was to be absent.

The letter was no sooner received, but it was communicated to the husband, and produced no other effect in him, than that he joined with his wife to raise all the mirth they could out of this fantastical piece of gallantry. They were so little concerned at this dangerous man of mode, that they plotted ways to perplex him without hurting him. Varnish comes exactly at his hour ; and the lady's well-acted confusion at his entrance, gave him opportunity to repeat some couplets very fit for the occasion with very much grace and spirit. His theatrical manner of making love was interrupted by an alarm of the husband's coming ; and the wife, in a personated terror, beseeched him, if he had any value for the honour of a woman that loved him, he would jump out of the window. He did so, and fell upon feather-beds placed on purpose to receive him.

It is not to be conceived how great the joy of an amorous man is when he has suffered for his mistress, and is never the worse for it. Varnish the next day writ a most elegant billet, wherein he said all that imagination could form upon the occasion. He violently protested, going out of the window was no way terrible, but as it was going from her ; with several other kind expressions, which procured him a second assignation. Upon his second visit, he was conveyed by a faithful maid into her bedchamber, and left there to expect the arrival of her mistress. But the wench, according to her instructions, ran in again to him, and locked the door after her to keep out her master. She had just time enough to convey the lover into a chest before she admitted the husband and his wife into the room.

You may be sure that trunk was absolutely necessary to be opened ; but upon her husband's ordering it, she assured him, she had taken all the care imaginable in packing up the things with her own hand, and he might send the trunk aboard as soon as he thought fit. The easy husband believed his wife, and the good couple went to bed ; Varnish having the happiness to pass the night in his mistress's bedchamber without molestation. The morning arose, but our lover was not well situated to observe her blushes ; so that all we know of his sentiments on this occasion, is, that he heard Ballance ask for the key, and say, he would himself go with this chest, and have it opened before the captain of the ship, for the greater safety of so valuable a lading.

The goods were hoisted away, and Mr. Ballance marching by his chest with great care and diligence, omitted nothing that might give his passenger perplexity. But to consummate all, he delivered the chest, with strict charge, in case they were in danger of being taken, to throw it overboard, for there were letters in it, the matter of which might be of great service to the enemy.

N.B. It is not thought advisable to proceed further in this account, Mr. Varnish being just returned from his travels, and willing to conceal the occasion of his first applying himself to the languages.

St. James's Coffee-house, February 20.

This day came in a mail from Holland, with a confirmation of our late advices, that a treaty of peace would very suddenly be set on foot, and that yachts were appointed by the States to convey the Ministers of France from Moerdyk to Gertruydenburg, which is appointed for the place wherein this important negotiation is to be transacted. It is said, this affair has been in agitation ever since the close of the last campaign ; Monsieur Petticum having been appointed to receive from time to time the overtures of the enemy. During the whole winter, the Ministers of France have used their utmost skill in forming such answers as might amuse the Allies, in hopes of a favourable event ; either in the north, or some other part of Europe, which might affect some part of the alliance too nearly to leave it in a capacity of adhering firmly to the interest of the whole. In all this transaction, the French king's own name has been as little made use of as possible : but the season of the year advancing too fast to admit of much longer delays in the present condition of France, Monsieur Torcy, in the name of the king, sent a letter to Monsieur Petticum, wherein he says, that " the king is willing all the preliminary articles shall rest as they are during the treaty for the 37th."

Upon the receipt of this advice, passports were sent to the French Court, and their Ministers are expected at Moerdyk on the 5th of the next month.

Sheer Lane, February 20.

I have been earnestly solicited for a further term, for wearing the farthingale by several of the fair sex, but more especially by the following petitioners :

" The humble petition of Deborah Hark, Sarah Thread-paper and Rachael Thimble, spinsters, and single women, commonly called Waiting-maids, in behalf of themselves and their sisterhood ;

"S H E W E T H,

" That your Worship hath been pleased to order and command, that no person or persons shall presume to wear quilted petticoats, on forfeiture of the said petticoats, or penalty of wearing ruffs, after the 17th instant now expired.

" That your petitioners have time out of mind been entitled to wear their ladies' clothes, or to sell the same.

" That the sale of the said clothes is spoiled by your Worship's said prohibition.

" Your petitioners therefore most humbly pray, that your Worship would please to allow, that all gentlewomen's gentlewomen may be allowed to wear the said dress, or to repair the loss of such a perquisite in such manner as your Worship shall think fit.

" And your petitioners," &c.

I do allow the allegations of this petition to be just, and forbid all persons but the petitioners, or those who shall purchase from them, to wear the said garment after the date hereof.

No. 137.

[Steele.

From *Tuesday, Feb.* 21, to *Thursday, Feb.* 23, 1709–10.

Ter centum tonat ore deos, Erebumque, Chaosque,
Tergeminamque Hecaten.—Virg., Æn. iv. 510.

Sheer Lane, February 22.

Dick Reptile and I sat this evening later than the rest of the club ; and as some men are better company when only with one friend, others when there is a large number, I found Dick to be of the former kind. He was bewailing to me in very just terms, the offences which he frequently met with in the abuse of speech : some use ten times more words than they need, some put in words quite foreign to their purpose, and others adorn their discourses with oaths and blasphemies by way of tropes and figures. What my good friend started, dwelt upon me after I came home this evening, and led me into an inquiry with myself, whence should arise such strange excrescences in discourse ? Whereas it must be obvious to all reasonable beings, that the sooner a man speaks his mind, the more complaisant he is to the man with whom he talks : but upon mature deliberation, I am come to this resolution, that for one man who speaks to be understood, there are ten who talk only to be admired.

The ancient Greeks had little independent syllables called "expletives," which they brought into their discourses both in verse and prose, for no other purpose but for the better grace and sound of their sentences and periods. I know no example but this which can authorise the use of more words than are necessary. But whether it be from this freedom taken by that wise nation, or however it

arises, Dick Reptile hit upon a very just and common
cause of offence in the generality of the people of all orders.
We have one here in our lane who speaks nothing without
quoting an authority ; for it is always with him, so and
so, " as the man said." He asked me this morning, how I
did, " as the man said " ; and hoped I would come now and
then to see him, " as the man said." I am acquainted with
another, who never delivers himself upon any subject, but
he cries, he only speaks his " poor judgment " ; this is his
humble opinion ; or as for his part, if he might presume to
offer anything on that subject. But of all the persons
who add elegances and superfluities to their discourses,
those who deserve the foremost rank, are the swearers ;
and the lump of these may, I think, be very aptly divided
into the common distinction of high and low. Dulness
and barrenness of thought is the original of it in both
these sects, and they differ only in constitution : the low
is generally a phlegmatic, and the high a choleric coxcomb.
The man of phlegm is sensible of the emptiness of his
discourse, and will tell you, that " I'fackins," such a thing is
true : or if you warm him a little, he may run into passion,
and cry, "Odsbodikins," you do not say right. But the high
affects a sublimity in dulness, and invokes hell and damnation at the breaking of a glass, or the slowness of a
drawer.

I was the other day trudging along Fleet Street on
foot, and an old army friend came up with me. We were
both going towards Westminster, and finding the streets
were so crowded that we could not keep together, we
resolved to club for a coach. This gentleman I knew to
be the first of the order of the choleric. I must confess
(were there no crime in it), nothing could be more diverting than the impertinence of the high juror : for whether
there is remedy or not against what offends him, still he is

to show he is offended ; and he must sure not omit to be
magnificently passionate, by falling on all things in his
way.   We were stopped by a train of coaches at Temple
Bar.   " What the devil ! " says my companion, " cannot
you drive on, coachman ?   D——n you all, for a set of
sons of whores, you will stop here to be paid by the
hour !   There is not such a set of confounded dogs as the
coachmen unhanged !   But these rascally Cits—— 'Ounds,
why should not there be a tax to make these dogs widen
their gates ?   Oh !   but the hell-hounds move at last."
" Ay," said I, " I knew you would make them whip on if
once they heard you."   " No," says he ; " but would it
not fret a man to the devil, to pay for being carried slower
than he can walk ?   Lookee, there is for ever a stop at
this hole by St. Clement's Church.   Blood, you dog !—
Harkee, sirrah,—why, and be d——d to you, do not you
drive over that fellow ?   Thunder, furies, and damnation !
I'll cut your ears off, you fellow before there.   Come
hither, you dog you, and let me wring your neck round
your shoulders."   We had a repetition of the same
eloquence at the Cockpit,[1] and the turning into Palace
Yard.

This gave me a perfect image of the insignificancy of
the creatures who practise this enormity ; and made me
conclude, that it is ever want of sense makes a man guilty
in this kind.   It was excellently well said, that this folly
had no temptation to excuse it, no man being born of a
swearing constitution.   In a word, a few rumbling words
and consonants clapped together, without any sense, will
make an accomplished swearer : and it is needless to dwell
long upon this blustering impertinence, which is already

[1] A portion of Henry VIII.'s palace at Whitehall.   When Whitehall was burned down in 1697, the Cockpit escaped, and was used as
a Court for the Committee of the Privy Council.

banished out of the society of well-bred men, and can be useful only to bullies and ill tragic writers, who would have sound and noise pass for courage and sense.

St. James's Coffee-house, February 22.

There arrived a messenger last night from Harwich, who left that place just as the Duke of Marlborough was going on board. The character of this important general going out by the command of his Queen, and at the request of his country, puts me in mind of that noble figure which Shakespeare gives Harry the Fifth upon his expedition against France. The poet wishes for abilities to represent so great a hero :

> " *Oh for a muse of fire !*" says he,
> " *Then should the warlike Harry, like himself,*
> *Assume the port of Mars ; and at his heels,*
> *Leashed in, like hounds, should Famine, Sword and Fire*
> *Crouch for employment.*"[1]

A conqueror drawn like the god of battle, with such a dreadful leash of hell-hounds at his command, makes a picture of as much majesty and terror as is to be met with in any poet.

Shakespeare understood the force of this particular allegory so well, that he had it in his thoughts in another passage, which is altogether as daring and sublime as the former. What I mean, is in the tragedy of "Julius Cæsar," where Antony, after having foretold the bloodshed and destruction that should be brought upon the earth by the death of that great man ; to fill up the horror of his description, adds the following verses :

> " *And Cæsar's spirit ranging for revenge,*
> *With Ate by his side, come hot from Hell,*
> *Shall in these confines, with a monarch's voice,*
> *Cry ' Havoc'; and let slip the dogs of war.*"[2]

[1] "Henry the Fifth," Prologue.   [2] "Julius Cæsar," act iii. sc. i.

I do not question but these quotations will call to mind in my readers of learning and taste, that imaginary person described by Virgil with the same spirit. He mentions it upon the occasion of a peace which was restored to the Roman Empire, and which we may now hope for from the departure of that great man who has given occasion to these reflections. "The Temple of Janus," says he, "shall be shut, and in the midst of it Military Fury shall sit upon a pile of broken arms, loaded with a hundred chains, bellowing with madness, and grinding his teeth in blood.

> "*Claudentur belli portæ ; Furor impius intus,*
> *Sæva sedens super arma, et centum vinctus ahenis*
> *Post tergum nodis, fremit horridus ore cruento.*" [1]

> "*Janus himself before his fane shall wait,*
> *And keep the dreadful issues of his gate,*
> *With bolts and iron bars. Within remains*
> *Imprisoned Fury bound in brazen chains ;*
> *High on a trophy raised of useless arms,*
> *He sits, and threats the world with vain alarms.*"

DRYDEN.

ADVERTISEMENT.

The tickets which were delivered out for the benefit of Signor Nicolini Grimaldi [2] on the 24th instant, will be taken on Thursday the 2nd of March, his benefit being deferred till that day.

N.B. In all operas for the future, where it thunders and lightens in proper time and in tune, the matter of the said lightning is to be of the finest resin ; and, for the sake of harmony, the same which is used to the best Cremona fiddles.

Note also, that the true perfumed lightning is only prepared and sold by Mr. Charles Lillie, at the corner of Beauford Buildings.

[1] "Æneid," i. 294.   [2] See Nos. 115, 142.

The Tatler   No. 138. February 25, 1709–10

The lady who has chosen Mr. Bickerstaff for her valentine, and is at a loss what to present him with, is desired to make him, with her own hands, a warm nightcap.[1]

No. 138.   [STEELE.

From *Thursday, Feb.* 23, to *Saturday, Feb.* 25, 1709-10.

Secretosque pios, his dantem jura Catonem.
VIRG., Æn. viii. 670.

Sheer Lane, February 24.

It is an argument of a clear and worthy spirit in a man, to be able to disengage himself from the opinions of others, so far as not to let the deference due to the sense of mankind ensnare him to act against the dictates of his own reason. But the generality of the world are so far from walking by any such maxim, that it is almost a standing rule to do as others do, or be ridiculous. I have heard my old friend Mr. Hart[2] speak it as an observation among the players, that it is impossible to act with grace, except the actor has forgot that he is before an audience. Till he has arrived at that, his motion, his air, his every step and gesture, has something in them which discovers he is under a restraint for fear of being ill received ; or if he considers himself as in the presence of those who approve his behaviour, you see an affectation of that pleasure run through his whole carriage. It is as common in life, as upon the stage, to behold a man in the most indifferent action betray a sense he has of doing what he

[1] A description of the custom of drawing valentines, and of the hope and fear shown on the faces of the drawers, who in their earnestness gave to a scrap of paper the same effect as the person represented, is to be found in Lillie's "Letters sent to the *Tatler* and *Spectator*" (1725), i. 30. See No. 141.   [2] See No. 99.

is about gracefully. Some have such an immoderate relish for applause, that they expect it for things, which in themselves are so frivolous, that it is impossible, without this affectation, to make them appear worthy either of blame or praise. There is Will Glare, so passionately intent upon being admired, that when you see him in public places, every muscle of his face discovers his thoughts are fixed upon the consideration of what figure he makes. He will often fall into a musing posture to attract observation, and is then obtruding himself upon the company when he pretends to be withdrawn from it. Such little arts are the certain and infallible tokens of a superficial mind, as the avoiding observation is the sign of a great and sublime one. It is therefore extremely difficult for a man to judge even of his own actions, without forming to himself an idea of what he should act, were it in his power to execute all his desires without the observation of the rest of the world. There is an allegorical fable in Plato,[1] which seems to admonish us, that we are very little acquainted with ourselves, while we know our actions are to pass the censures of others ; but had we the power to accomplish all our wishes unobserved, we should then easily inform ourselves how far we are possessed of real and intrinsic virtue. The fable I was going to mention, is that of Gyges, who is said to have had an enchanted ring, which had in it a miraculous quality, making him who wore it visible or invisible, as he turned it to or from his body. The use Gyges made of his occasional invisibility, was, by the advantage of it, to violate a queen, and murder a king. Tully takes notice of this allegory, and says very handsomely, that a man of honour who had such a ring, would act just in the same manner as he would do without it.[2] It is indeed no small pitch of virtue under the tempta-

[1] " Republic," ii. 359.　　　　[2] "De Officiis," iii. 9.

tion of impunity, and the hopes of accomplishing all a
man desires, not to transgress the rules of justice and
virtue ; but this is rather not being an ill man, than being
positively a good one ; and it seems wonderful, that so
great a soul as that of Tully, should not form to himself a
thousand worthy actions which a virtuous man would be
prompted to by the possession of such a secret. There
are certainly some part of mankind who are guardian
beings to the other. Sallust could say of Cato, "that he
had rather be than appear good " ;[1] but indeed, this
eulogium rose no higher than (as I just now hinted) to
an inoffensiveness, rather than an active virtue. Had it
occurred to the noble orator to represent, in his language,
the glorious pleasures of a man secretly employed in
beneficence and generosity, it would certainly have made a
more charming page than any he has now left behind him.
How might a man, furnished with Gyges' secret, employ
it in bringing together distant friends, laying snares for
creating goodwill in the room of groundless hatred ; in
removing the pangs of an unjust jealousy, the shyness of
an imperfect reconciliation, and the tremor of an awful
love ! Such a one could give confidence to bashful merit,
and confusion to overbearing impudence.

Certain it is, that secret kindnesses done to mankind,
are as beautiful as secret injuries are detestable. To be
invisibly good, is as godlike, as to be invisibly ill,
diabolical. As degenerate as we are apt to say the age we
live in is, there are still amongst us men of illustrious
minds, who enjoy all the pleasures of good actions, except
that of being commended for them. There happens
among others very worthy instances of a public spirit, one
of which I am obliged to discover, because I know not
otherwise how to obey the commands of the Benefactor.

[1] " Bell. Cat," ad fin.

A citizen of London has given directions to Mr. Rayner, the writing-master of Paul's School,[1] to educate at his charge ten boys (who shall be nominated by me) in writing and accounts, till they shall be fit for any trade. I desire therefore such as know any proper objects for receiving this bounty, to give notice thereof to Mr. Morphew, or Mr. Lillie, and they shall, if properly qualified, have instructions accordingly.

Actions of this kind have in them something so transcendent, that it is an injury to applaud them, and a diminution of that merit which consists in shunning our approbation. We shall therefore leave them to enjoy that glorious obscurity, and silently admire their virtue, who can contemn the most delicious of human pleasures, that of receiving due praise. Such celestial dispositions very justly suspend the discovery of their benefactions, till they come where their actions cannot be misinterpreted, and receive their first congratulations in the company of angels.

ADVERTISEMENT.

Whereas Mr. Bickerstaff, by a letter bearing date this 24th of February, has received information, that there are in and about the Royal Exchange a sort of persons commonly known by the name of " whetters,"[2] who drink

---

[1] " The Paul's scholar's copy-book, containing the round and round-text hands, with alphabets at large of the Greek and Hebrew, and joining-pieces of each. Embellished with proper ornaments of command of hand. By John Rayner, at the Hand and Pen, in St. Paul's Churchyard, London. Published for the use of schools. Sold by the author, and Jonathan Robinson, at the Golden Lion, in St. Paul's Churchyard. Price 1*s*." (No. 135, Advertisement). Rayner's book was dedicated to the Master and Wardens of the Mercers' Company, and was reissued in 1716 (W. Massey's 'Origin and Progress of Letters," 1763, part ii. p. 120).

[2] See No. 141.

themselves into an intermediate state of being neither drunk nor sober before the hours of 'change, or business, and in that condition buy and sell stocks, discount notes, and do many other acts of well-disposed citizens ; this is to give notice, that from this day forward, no whetter shall be able to give or endorse any note, or execute any other point of commerce, after the third half pint, before the hour of one : and whoever shall transact any matter or matters with a whetter (not being himself of that order) shall be conducted to Moorfields [1] upon the first application of his next of kin.

N.B. No tavern near the 'Change shall deliver wine to such as drink at the bar standing, except the same shall be three parts of the best cider ; and the master of the house shall produce a certificate of the same from Mr. Tintoret,[2] or other credible wine-painter.

Whereas the model of the intended Bedlam [3] is now finished, and that the edifice itself will be very suddenly begun ; it is desired, that all such as have relations, whom they would recommend to our care, would bring in their proofs with all speed, none being to be admitted of course but lovers, who are put into an immediate regimen. Young politicians also are received without fees or examination.

No. 139. [STEELE.

From *Saturday*, *Feb.* 25, to *Tuesday*, *Feb.* 28, 1709-10.

—— Nihil est, quod credere de se
Non possit, cum laudatur Dis æqua potestas.
Juv., Sat. iv. 70.

Sheer Lane, February 27.

When I reflect upon the many nights I have sat up for some months last past in the greatest anxiety for the good of my neighbours and contemporaries, it is no small discouragement to me, to see how slow a progress I make in the reformation of the world. But indeed I must do my female readers the justice to own, that their tender hearts are much more susceptible of good impressions, than the minds of the other sex. Business and ambition take up men's thoughts too much to leave room for philosophy : but if you speak to women in a style and manner proper to approach them, they never fail to improve by your counsel. I shall therefore for the future turn my thoughts more particularly to their service, and study the best methods to adorn their persons, and inform their minds in the justest methods to make them what Nature designed them, the most beauteous objects of our eyes, and the most agreeable companions of our lives. But when I say this, I must not omit at the same time to look into their errors and mistakes, that being the readiest way to the intended end of adorning and instructing them. It must be acknowledged, that the very inadvertencies of this sex are owing to the other ; for if men were not flatterers, women could not fall into that general cause of all their follies, and our misfortunes, their love of flattery. Were the commendation of these agreeable creatures built

upon its proper foundation, the higher we raised their
opinion of themselves, the greater would be the advantage
to our sex ; but all the topic of praise is drawn from very
senseless and extravagant ideas we pretend we have of
their beauty and perfection.   Thus when a young man
falls in love with a young woman, from that moment she
is no more Mrs. Alice such-a-one, born of such a father,
and educated by such a mother ; but from the first minute
that he casts his eye upon her with desire, he conceives a
doubt in his mind, what heavenly power gave so unexpected
a blow to a heart that was ever before untouched.   But
who can resist Fate and Destiny, which are lodged in Mrs.
Alice's eyes ?   After which he desires orders accordingly,
whether he is to live or breathe ; the smile or frown of his
goddess is the only thing that can now either save or
destroy him.   By this means, the well-humoured girl, that
would have romped with him before she received this
declaration, assumes a state suitable to the majesty he has
given her, and treats him as the vassal he calls himself.
The girl's head is immediately turned by having the power
of life and death, and takes care to suit every motion and
air to her new sovereignty.   After he has placed himself
at this distance, he must never hope to recover his former
familiarity, till she has had the addresses of another, and
found them less sincere.

   If the application to women were justly turned, the
address of flattery, though it implied at the same time
an admonition, would be much more likely to succeed.
Should a captivated lover, in a billet, let his mistress
know, that her piety to her parents, her gentleness of
behaviour, her prudent economy with respect to her own
little affairs in a virgin condition, had improved the
passion which her beauty had inspired him with, into so
settled an esteem for her, that of all women breathing he

wished her his wife; though his commending her for qualities she knew she had as a virgin, would make her believe he expected from her an answerable conduct in the character of a matron, I will answer for it, his suit would be carried on with less perplexity.

Instead of this, the generality of our young women, taking all their notions of life from gay writings, or letters of love, consider themselves as goddesses, nymphs, and shepherdesses.

By this romantic sense of things, all the natural relations and duties of life are forgotten, and our female part of mankind are bred and treated, as if they were designed to inhabit the happy fields of Arcadia, rather than be wives and mothers in old England. It is indeed long since I had the happiness to converse familiarly with this sex, and therefore have been fearful of falling into the error which recluse men are very subject to, that of giving false representations of the world from which they have retired, by imaginary schemes drawn from their own reflections. An old man cannot easily gain admittance into the dressing-room of ladies; I therefore thought it time well spent, to turn over Agrippa, and use all my occult art, to give my old cornelian ring the same force with that of Gyges, which I have lately spoken of.[1] By the help of this, I went unobserved to a friend's house of mine, and followed the chamber-maid invisibly about twelve of the clock into the bed-chamber of the beauteous Flavia, his fine daughter, just before she got up.

I drew the curtains, and being wrapped up in the safety of my old age, could with much pleasure, without passion, behold her sleeping with Waller's poems, and a letter fixed in that part of him, where every woman thinks herself described. The light flashing upon her face, awakened

[1] See No. 138.

her : she opened her eyes, and her lips too, repeating that piece of false wit in that admired poet :

> *Such Helen was, and who can blame the boy,*
> *That in so bright a flame consumed his Troy ?*[1]

This she pronounced with a most bewitching sweetness ; but after it fetched a sigh, that methought had more desire than languishment, then took out her letter, and read aloud, for the pleasure, I suppose, of hearing soft words in praise of herself, the following epistle :

"MADAM,

"I sat near you at the Opera last night ; but knew no entertainment from the vain show and noise about me, while I waited wholly intent upon the motion of your bright eyes, in hopes of a glance, that might restore me to the pleasures of sight and hearing in the midst of beauty and harmony. It is said, the hell of the accursed in the next life arises from an incapacity to partake the joys of the blessed, though they were to be admitted to them. Such I am sure was my condition all this evening ; and if you, my deity, cannot have so much mercy as to make me by your influence capable of tasting the satisfactions of life, my being is ended, which consisted only in your favour."

The letter was hardly read over, when she rushed out of bed in her wrapping-gown, and consulted her glass for the truth of his passion. She raised her head, and turned it to a profile, repeating the last lines, " my being is ended, which consisted only in your favour." The goddess immediately called her maid, and fell to dressing that

[1] " Under a Lady's Picture" (Waller's Poems : " Epigrams, Epitaphs," &c.).

mischievous face of hers, without any manner of consideration for the mortal who had offered up his petition.
Nay, it was so far otherwise, that the whole time of her
woman's combing her hair was spent in discourse of the
impertinence of his passion, and ended, in declaring a
resolution, if she ever had him, to make him wait. She
also frankly told the favourite gipsy that was prating to
her, that her passionate lover had put it out of her power
to be civil to him, if she were inclined to it; "for," said
she, "if I am thus celestial to my lover, he will certainly
so far think himself disappointed, as I grow into the
familiarity and form of a mortal woman."

I came away as I went in, without staying for other
remarks than what confirmed me in the opinion, that it is
from the notions the men inspire them with, that the
women are so fantastical in the value of themselves. This
imaginary pre-eminence which is given to the fair sex, is
not only formed from the addresses of people of condition;
but it is the fashion and humour of all orders to go
regularly out of their wits, as soon as they begin to make
love. I know at this time three goddesses in the New
Exchange;[1] and there are two shepherdesses who sell
gloves in Westminster Hall.[2]

[1] See No. 26.
[2] See No. 145. Part of Westminster Hall was devoted to shop-
keepers' stalls, where toys, books, &c., could be brought. Tom
Brown ("Amusements," &c. 1700) says: "On your left hand you
hear a nimble-tongued painted sempstress with her charming treble
invite you to buy some of her knick-knacks, and on your right a deep-
mouthed crier, commanding impossibilities, viz., silence to be kept
among women and lawyers."

No. 140.   [Steele.

From *Tuesday, Feb.* 28, to *Thursday, March* 2, 1709-10.

—— Aliena negotia centum
Per caput, et circa saliunt latus—
Hor., 2 Sat. vi. 33.

Sheer Lane, March 1.

Having the honour to be by my great-grandmother a Welshman, I have been among some choice spirits of that part of Great Britain, where we solaced ourselves in celebration of the day of St. David I am, I confess, elevated above that state of mind which is proper for lucubration : but I am the less concerned at this, because I have for this day or two last past observed, that we novelists have been condemned wholly to the pastry-cooks, the eyes of the nation being turned upon greater matters.[1] This therefore being a time when none but my immediate correspondents will read me, I shall speak to them chiefly at this present writing. It is the fate of us who pretend to joke, to be frequently understood to be only upon the droll when we are speaking the most seriously, as appears by the following letter to Charles Lillie :

" Mr. Lillie,   " London, *February* 28, 17$\frac{09}{10}$.

" It being professed by 'Squire Bickerstaff, that his intention is to expose the vices and follies of the age, and to promote virtue and goodwill amongst man-

[1] The trial of Dr. Sacheverell, which extended from February 27 to March 23, 1710. A Tory pamphlet, " A Letter to the Rev. Dr. Henry Sacheverell, by Isaac Bickerstaff, Esq.," 1709, appeared in

kind; it must be a comfort, to a person labouring under
great straits and difficulties, to read anything that has the
appearance of succour.   I should be glad to know therefore, whether the intelligence given in his *Tatler* of Saturday
last,[1] of the intended charity of a certain citizen of London,
to maintain the education of ten boys in writing and
accounts till they be fit for trade, be given only to
encourage and recommend persons to the practice of such
noble and charitable designs, or whether there be a person
who really intends to do so.   If the latter, I humbly beg
Squire Bickerstaff's pardon for making a doubt, and
impute it to my ignorance ; and most humbly crave, that
he would be pleased to give notice in his *Tatler*, when he
thinks fit, whether his nomination of ten boys be disposed
of, or whether there be room for two boys to be recommended to him ; and that he will permit the writer of this
to present him with two boys, who, it is humbly presumed, will be judged to be very remarkable objects of
such charity.

" Sir,

" Your most humble Servant."

I am to tell this gentleman in sober sadness, and without
jest, that there really is so good and charitable a man as
the benefactor inquired for in his letter, and that there are
but two boys yet named.   The father of one of them was
killed at Blenheim, the father of the other at Almanza.   I
do not here give the names of the children, because I
should take it to be an insolence in me to publish them, in
a charity which I have only the direction of as a servant,

January 1710.   Another pamphlet was called " The Character of
Don Sacheverello, Knight of the Firebrand, in a Letter to Isaac
Bickerstaff, Esq., Censor of Great Britain."

[1] See No. 138.

to that worthy and generous spirit who bestows upon them this bounty, without laying the bondage of an obligation. What I have to do is to tell them, they are· beholden only to their Maker, to kill in them as they grow up the false shame of poverty, and let them know, that their present fortune, which is come upon them by the loss of their poor fathers on so glorious occasions, is much more honourable, than the inheritance of the most ample ill-gotten wealth.

The next letter which lies before me is from a man of sense, who strengthens his own authority with that of Tully, in persuading me to what he very justly believes one cannot be averse :

"MR. BICKERSTAFF,   "London, *Feb.* 27, 1709.

" I am so confident of your inclination to promote anything that is for the advancement of liberal arts, that I lay before you the following translation of a paragraph in Cicero's oration in defence of Archias the poet, as an incentive to the agreeable and instructive reading of the writings of the Augustan age. Most vices and follies proceed from a man's incapacity of entertaining himself, and we are generally fools in company, because we dare not be wise alone. I hope, on some future occasions, you will find this no barren hint. Tully, after having said very handsome things of his client, commends the arts of which he was master as follows :

" ' If so much profit be not reaped in the study of letters, and if pleasure only be found ; yet, in my opinion, this relaxation of the mind should be esteemed most humane and ingenuous. Other things are not for all ages, places and seasons. These studies form youth, delight old age, adorn prosperity, and soften, and even remove adversity, entertain at home, are no hindrance abroad ;

don't leave us at night, and keep us company on the road and in the country.' I am,

"Your humble Servant,

"STREPHON."

The following epistle seems to want the quickest despatch, because a lady is every moment offended till it is answered ; which is best done by letting the offender see in her own letter how tender she is of calling him so :

"SIR,

"This comes from a relation of yours, though unknown to you, who, besides the tie of consanguinity, has some value for you on the account of your lucubrations, those being designed to refine our conversation, as well as cultivate our minds. I humbly beg the favour of you, in one of your *Tatlers* (after what manner you please), to correct a particular friend of mine, for an indecorum he is guilty of in discourse, of calling his acquaintance, when he speaks of them, ' Madam ' : as for example, my cousin Jenny Distaff, ' Madam Distaff' ; which I am sure you are sensible is very unpolite, and 'tis what makes me often uneasy for him, though I cannot tell him of it myself, which makes me guilty of this presumption, that I depend upon your goodness to excuse ; and I do assure you, the gentleman will mind your reprehension, for he is, as I am,

"Sir,

"Your most humble

"Servant and Cousin,

"DOROTHY DRUMSTIC...

"I write this in a thin under-petticoat,[1] and never did or will wear a farthingale."

[1] See No. 136.

The Tatler

No. 140. March 2, 1709–10

I had no sooner read the just complaint of Mrs. Drumstick, but I received an urgent one from another of the fair sex, upon faults of more pernicious consequence : -

"Mᴿ. Bɪᴄᴋᴇʀsᴛᴀғғ,

"Observing that you are entered into a correspondence with Pasquin,[1] who is, I suppose, a Roman Catholic, I beg of you to forbear giving him any account of our religion, or manners, till you have rooted out certain misbehaviours even in our churches ; among others, that of bowing, saluting, taking snuff, and other gestures. Lady Autumn made me a very low curtsy the other day from the next pew, and, with the most courtly air imaginable, called herself ' Miserable sinner.' Her niece soon after, in saying, ' Forgive us our trespasses,' curtsied with a gloating look at my brother. He returned it, opening his snuff-box and repeating yet a more solemn expression. I beg of you, good Mr. Censor, not to tell Pasquin anything of this kind, and to believe this does not come from one of a morose temper, mean birth, rigid education, narrow fortune, or bigotry in opinion, or from one in whom Time had worn out all taste of pleasure. I assure you, it is far otherwise, for I am possessed of all the contrary advantages ; and hope, wealth, good humour, and good breeding, may be best employed in the service of religion and virtue ; and desire you would, as soon as possible, remark upon the above-mentioned indecorums, that we may not longer transgress against the latter, to preserve our reputation in the former.

" Your humble Servant,

" Lʏᴅɪᴀ."

[1] See No. 129.

The last letter I shall insert is what follows. This is written by a very inquisitive lady ; and I think, such interrogative gentlewomen are to be answered no other way than by interrogation. Her billet is this :

"DEAR MR. BICKERSTAFF,

"Are you quite as good as you seem to be ?

" CHLOE."

To which I can only answer :

"DEAR CHLOE,

"Are you quite as ignorant as you seem to be ?

" I. B."

No. 141. [STEELE.

From *Thursday, March 2,* to *Saturday, March 4,* 1709–10.

Sheer Lane, March 3.

While the attention of the town is drawn aside from the reading us writers of news, we all save ourselves against it is at more leisure. As for my own part, I shall still let the labouring oar be managed by my correspondents, and fill my paper with their sentiments, rather than my own, till I find my readers more disengaged than they are at present.[1] When I came home this evening, I found several letters and petitions, which I shall insert with no other order, than as I accidentally opened them, as follows :

[1] The whole attention of the town in March 1710 was devoted to the Sacheverell trial. See Nos. 140, 142, 157.

"*March* 1, 17$\frac{09}{10}$.

"SIR,

"Having a daughter about nine years of age, I would-endeavour she might have education ; I mean such as may be useful, as working well, and a good deportment. In order to it, I am persuaded to place her at some boarding-school, situate in a good air. My wife opposes it, and gives for her greatest reason, that she is too much a woman, and understands the formalities of visiting and a tea-table so very nicely, that none, though much older, can exceed her ; and with all these perfections, the girl can scarce thread a needle : but however, after several arguments, we have agreed to be decided by your judg-ment ; and knowing your abilities, shall manage our daughter exactly as you shall please to direct. I am serious in my request, and hope you will be so in your answer, which will lay a deep obligation upon,

"Sir,

"Your humble Servant,

"T. T.

"Sir, pray answer it in your *Tatler*, that it may be serviceable to the public."

I am as serious on this subject as my correspondent can be, and am of opinion, that the great happiness or mis-fortune of mankind depends upon the manner of educating and treating that sex. I have lately said, I design to turn my thoughts more particularly to them and their service : I beg therefore a little time to give my opinion on so important a subject, and desire the young lady may fill tea one week longer, till I have considered whether she shall be removed or not.[1]

---

[1] See No. 145.

" Chancery Lane, *February* 27, 1709.

" Mr. Bickerstaff,

" Your notice in the advertisement in your *Tatler* of Saturday last[1] about 'whetters' in and about the Royal Exchange, is mightily taken notice of by gentlemen who use the coffee-houses near the Chancery office in Chancery Lane ; and there being a particular certain set of both young and old gentlemen that belong to and near adjoining to the Chancery office, both in Chancery Lane and Bell Yard, that are not only 'whetters' all the morning long, but very musically given about twelve at night the same days, and mightily taken with the union of the dulcimer, violin, and song ; at which recreation they rejoice together with perfect harmony, however their clients disagree : you are humbly desired by several gentlemen to give some regulation concerning them ; in which you will contribute to the repose of us, who are

" Your very humble Servants,

" L. T., N. F., T. W."

These " whetters " are a people I have considered with much pains, and find them to differ from a sect I have heretofore spoken of, called " snuff-takers," [2] only in the expedition they take in destroying their brains : the " whetter " is obliged to refresh himself every moment with a liquor, as the " snuff-taker " with a powder.   As for their harmony in the evening, I have nothing to object, provided they remove to Wapping or the Bridge-Foot,[3] where

---

[1] See No. 138.   [2] See No. 35.
[3] The foot of London Bridge.   There was a tavern, famous in the seventeenth century, called " The Bear at the Bridge-foot," below London Bridge.

it is not to be supposed that their vociferations will annoy the studious, the busy, or the contemplative. I once had lodgings in Gray's Inn, where we had two hard students, who learned to play upon the hautboy ; and I had a couple of chamber fellows over my head not less diligent in the practice of backsword and single-rapier. I remember these gentlemen were assigned by the benchers the two houses at the end of the Terrace Walk, as the only places fit for their meditations. Such students as will let none improve but themselves, ought indeed to have their proper distances from societies.

The gentlemen of loud mirth above mentioned I take to be, in the quality of their crime, the same as eaves-droppers ; for they who will be in your company whether you will or no, are to as great a degree offenders, as they who hearken to what passes without being of your company at all. The ancient punishment for the latter, when I first came to this town, was the blanket, which I humbly conceive may be as justly applied to him that bawls, as to him that listens. It is therefore provided for the future, that (except in the Long Vacation) no retainers to the law, with dulcimer, violin, or any other instrument, in any tavern within a furlong of an inn of court, shall sing any tune, or pretended tune whatsoever, upon pain of the blanket, to be administered according to the discretion of all such peaceable people as shall be within the annoyance. And it is further directed, that all clerks who shall offend in this kind shall forfeit their indentures, and be turned over as assistants to the clerks of parishes within the bills of mortality, who are hereby empowered to demand them accordingly.

I am not to omit the receipt of the following letter, with a nightcap, from my valentine ;[1] which nightcap I find

[1] See No. 137.

was finished in the year 1588, and is too finely wrought to be of any modern stitching. Its antiquity will better appear by my valentine's own words :

" SIR,

" Since you are pleased to accept of so mean a present as a nightcap from your valentine, I have sent you one, which I do assure you has been very much esteemed of in our family ; for my great-grandmother's daughter who worked it, was maid of honour to Queen Elizabeth, and had the misfortune to lose her life by pricking her finger in the making of it, of which she bled to death, as her tomb now at Westminster will show : for which reason, myself, nor none of my family, have loved work ever since ; otherwise you should have had one as you desired, made by the hands of,

" Sir,

" Your affectionate

" VALENTINE."

" *To the Right Worshipful Isaac Bickerstaff, Esq., Censor of Great Britain, and Governor of the Hospital erected, or to be erected, in Moorfields.*

" The petition of the inhabitants of the parish of Goatham in the county of Middlesex ;

" HUMBLY SHEWETH,

" That whereas 'tis the undoubted right of your said petitioners to repair on every Lord's Day to a chapel of ease in the said parish, there to be instructed in their duties in the known or vulgar tongue ; yet so it is (may it please your Worship) that the preacher of the said chapel has of late given himself wholly up to matters of controversy, in no wise tending to the edification of your said petitioners ; and in handling (as he calls it) the same, has used divers hard and crabbed words ; such as, among many others, are ' orthodox' and ' heterodox,' which are in no sort understood by your said petitioners ; and it is with grief of heart that your petitioners beg leave to represent to you, that in mentioning the aforesaid words or names (the latter of which, as we have reason to believe, is his deadly enemy), he will fall into ravings and foamings, ill-becoming the meekness of his office, and tending to give offence and scandal to all good people.

"Your petitioners further say, that they are ready to prove the aforesaid allegations ; and therefore humbly hope, that from a true sense of their condition, you will please to receive the said preacher into the hospital, until he shall recover a right use of his senses.

"And your petitioners," &c.

No. 142.   [STEELE.

From *Saturday, March* 4, to *Tuesday, March* 7, 1709-10.

Sheer Lane, March 6.

All persons who employ themselves in public, are still interrupted in the course of their affairs : and it seems, the admired Cavalier Nicolini himself is commanded by the ladies, who at present employ their time with great assiduity in the care of the nation, to put off his day till he shall receive their commands, and notice that they are at leisure for diversions.[1] In the meantime it is not to

[1] See No. 137. In No. 140 there was the following advertisement : "At the request of all the ladies of quality, who are at present engaged in politics, the benefit night for Cavalier Nicolini is put off to Tuesday the 7th instant."

be expressed, how many cold chickens the fair ones have eaten since this day sennight for the good of their country. This great occasion has given birth to many discoveries of high moment for the conduct of life. There is a toast of my acquaintance told me, she had now found out, that it was day before nine in the morning ;[1] and I am very confident, if the affair holds many days longer, the ancient hours of eating will be revived among us, many having by it been made acquainted with the luxury of hunger and thirst.

There appears, methinks, something very venerable in all assemblies : and I must confess, I envied all who had youth and health enough to make their appearance there, that they had the happiness of being a whole day in the best company in the world. During the adjournment of that awful court, a neighbour of mine was telling me, that it gave him a notion of the ancient grandeur of the English hospitality, to see Westminster Hall a dining-room.[2] There is a cheerfulness at such repasts, which is very delightful to tempers which are so happy as to be clear of spleen and vapour ; for to the jovial to see others pleased, is the greatest of all pleasures.

But since age and infirmities forbid my appearance at such public places, the next happiness is to make the best use of privacy, and acquit myself of the demands of my correspondents. The following letter is what has given me no small inquietude, it being an accusation of partiality, and disregard to merit, in the person of a virtuoso, who is the most eloquent of all men upon small occasions, and is the more to be admired for his prodigious fertility of

[1] Cf. "Wentworth Papers," p. 113. " Sacheverell will make all the Ladys good huswis, they goe att seven every mornin'," says Lady Wentworth.

[2] The spectators brought their lunch with them.

invention, which never appears but upon subjects which others would have thought barren. But in consideration of his uncommon talents, I am contented to let him be the hero of my next two days, by inserting his friends' recommendation of him at large:

"DEAR COUSIN,   "Nando's,' *Feb.* 28, 1709.

"I am just come out of the country, and upon perusing your late Lucubrations, I find Charles Lillie to be the darling of your affections, that you have given him a place, and taken no small pains to establish him in the world ; and at the same time have passed by his namesake[2] at this end of the town, as if he was a citizen defunct, and one of no use in a commonwealth. I must own, his circumstances are so good, and so well known, that he does not stand in need of having his fame published to the world ; but being of an ambitious spirit, and an aspiring soul, he would be rather proud of the honour, than desirous of the profit, which might result from your recommendation. He is a person of a particular genius, the first that brought toys in fashion, and baubles to perfection. He is admirably well versed in screws, springs, and hinges, and deeply read in knives, combs or scissors, buttons or buckles. He is a perfect master of words, which, uttered with a smooth voluble tongue, flow into a most persuasive eloquence ; insomuch that I have known a gentleman of distinction find several ingenious faults with a toy of his, and show his utmost dislike to it, as being either useless, or ill-contrived ; but when the orator behind the counter had harangued upon it for an hour and a half, displayed its hidden beauties, and revealed its secret

---

[1] A coffee-house in Fleet Street, at the east corner of Inner Temple Lane.
[2] Charles Mather, the toyman (see Nos. 27, 113).

perfections, he has wondered how he had been able to spend so great a part of his life without so important an utensil. I won't pretend to furnish out an inventory of all the valuable commodities that are to be found at his shop.

" I shall content myself with giving an account of what I think most curious. Imprimis, his pocket-books are very neat, and well contrived, not for keeping bank bills or goldsmiths' notes,[1] I confess ; but they are admirable for registering the lodgings of Madonnas, and for preserving letters from ladies of quality : his whips and spurs are so nice, that they'll make one that buys them ride a fox-hunting, though before he hated noise and early rising, and was afraid of breaking his neck. His seals are curiously fancied, and exquisitely well cut, and of great use to encourage young gentlemen to write a good hand. Ned Puzzlepost had been ill-used by his writing-master, and writ a sort of a Chinese, or downright scrawlian : however, upon his buying a seal of my friend, he is so much improved by continual writing, that it is believed in a short time one may be able to read his letters, and find out his meaning, without guessing. His pistols and fusees are so very good, that they are fit to be laid up among the finest china. Then his tweezer-cases are incomparable : you shall have one not much bigger than your finger, with seventeen several instruments in it, all necessary every hour of the day, during the whole course of a man's life. But if this virtuoso excels in one thing more than another, it is in canes ; he has spent his most select hours in the knowledge of them, and is arrived at that perfection, that he is able to hold forth upon canes longer than upon any

---

[1] Goldsmiths' receipts for coin lodged with them as bankers were sometimes transferred from hand to hand, but this was always limited to a few merchants.

one subject in the world. Indeed his canes are so finely
clouded, and so well made up, either with gold or amber
heads, that I am of the opinion it is impossible for a
gentleman to walk, talk, sit or stand as he should do,
without one of them. He knows the value of a cane, by
knowing the value of the buyer's estate. Sir Timothy
Shallow has two thousand pounds per annum, and Tom
Empty one. They both at several times bought a cane
of Charles : Sir Timothy's cost ten guineas, and Tom
Empty's five. Upon comparing them, they were perfectly
alike. Sir Timothy surprised there should be no difference in the canes, and so much in the price, comes to
Charles. 'Damn it, Charles,' says he, ' you have sold me a
cane here for ten pieces, and the very same to Tom Empty
for five.' 'Lord, Sir Timothy,' says Charles, ' I am concerned that you, whom I took to understand canes better
than any baronet in town, should be so overseen ;[1] why,
Sir Timothy, yours is a true jambee, and Squire Empty's
only a plain dragon.'[2]

" This virtuoso has a parcel of jambees now growing in
the East Indies, where he keeps a man on purpose to look
after them, which will be the finest that ever landed in
Great Britain, and will be fit to cut about two years hence.
Any gentleman may subscribe for as many as he pleases.
Subscriptions will be taken in at his shop at ten guineas
each joint. They that subscribe for six, shall have a
dragon gratis. This is all I have to say at present concerning Charles' curiosities ; and hope it may be sufficient to

[1] Deceived.
[2] A dragon is a small malacca cane, so called from its blood-red
colour. It comes from Penang, Singapore, and other islands in the
Straits of Malacca. A jambee, on the contrary, is a knotty bamboo
of a pale brown hue. As an article of commerce it is now extinct.
The "clouded cane" of Sir Plume was a large malacca artificially
coloured (Dobson).

prevail with you to take him into your consideration, which if you comply with, you will oblige,

> " Your humble Servant.

" N.B. Whereas there came out last term several gold snuff-boxes and others : this is to give notice, that Charles[1] will put out a new edition on Saturday next, which will be the only one in fashion till after Easter.   The gentleman that gave fifty pounds for the box set with diamonds, may show it till Sunday night, provided he goes to church ; but not after that time, there being one to be published on Monday which will cost fourscore guineas."

No. 143.   [STEELE.
From *Tuesday, March* 7, to *Thursday, March* 9, 1709–10.

Sheer Lane, March 8.

I was this afternoon surprised with a visit from my sister Jenny, after an absence of some time. She had, methought, in her manner and air, something that was a little below that of the women of first breeding and quality, but at the same time above the simplicity and familiarity of her usual deportment.   As soon as she was seated, she began to talk to me of the odd place I lived in, and begged of me to remove out of the lane where I have been so long acquainted ; " for," said she, " it does so spoil one's horses, that I must beg your pardon if you see me much seldomer, when I am to make so great a journey with a single pair, and make visits and get home the same night." I understood her pretty well, but would not ; therefore desired her to pay off her coach, for I had a great deal to

---

[1] Charles Mather.

talk to her. She very pertly told me, she came in her own
chariot. "Why," said I, " is your husband in town ? And
has he set up an equipage ?" "No," answered she, "but I have
received £500 by his order ; and his letters, which came
at the same time, bade me want for nothing that was
necessary." I was heartily concerned at her folly, whose
affairs render her but just able to bear such an expense.
However I considered, that according to the British custom
of treating women, there is no other method to be used
in removing any of their faults and errors, but conducting
their minds from one humour to another, with as much
ceremony as we lead their persons from one place to
another. I therefore dissembled my concern, and in compliance with her, as a lady that was to use her feet no
more, I begged of her, after a short visit, to let me persuade her not to stay out till it was late, for fear of catching
cold as she went into her coach in the dampness of the
evening. The Malapert knew well enough I laughed at
her, but was not ill-pleased with the certainty of her
power over her husband, who, she knew, would support
her in any humour he was able, rather than pass through
the torment of an expostulation, to gainsay anything she
had a mind to. As soon as my fine lady was gone, I writ
the following letter to my brother :

"DEAR BROTHER,

"I am at present under very much concern at the
splendid appearance I saw my sister make in an
equipage which she has set up in your absence. I beg
of you not to indulge her in this vanity ; and desire you
to consider, the world is so whimsical, that though it will
value you for being happy, it will hate you for appearing so. The possession of wisdom and virtue (the only
solid distinctions of life) is allowed much more easily than

that of wealth and quality. Besides which, I must entreat you to weigh with yourself, what it is that people aim at in setting themselves out to show in gay equipages, and moderate fortunes. You are not by this means a better man than your neighbour is ; but your horses are better than his are. And will you suffer care and inquietude, to have it said as you pass by, 'Those are very pretty punch nags !'[1] Nay, when you have arrived at this, there are a hundred worthless fellows who are still four horses happier than you are. Remember, dear brother, there is a certain modesty in the enjoyment of moderate wealth, which to transgress, exposes men to the utmost derision ; and as there is nothing but meanness of spirit can move a man to value himself upon what can be purchased with money, so he that shows an ambition that way, and cannot arrive at it, is more emphatically guilty of that meanness. I give you only my first thoughts on this occasion, but shall, as I am a censor, entertain you in my next with my sentiments in general upon the subject of equipage ; and show, that though there are no sumptuary laws amongst us, reason and good sense are equally binding, and will ever prevail in appointing approbation or dislike in all matters of an indifferent nature, when they are pursued with earnestness. I am,

"Sir," &c.

ADVERTISEMENTS.

To all Gentlemen, Ladies, and others, that delight in soft lines.

These are to give notice, that the proper time of the year for writing pastorals now drawing near, there is a

[1] A punch nag is a horse well set and well knit, having a short back and thin shoulders, with a broad neck, and well lined with flesh ("Farrier's Dictionary").

stage-coach settled from the One Bell in the Strand to Dorchester, which sets out twice a week, and passes through Basingstoke, Sutton, Stockbridge, Salisbury, Blandford, and so to Dorchester, over the finest downs in England. At all which places, there are accommodations of spreading beeches, beds of flowers, turf seats, and purling streams, for happy swains ; and thunderstruck oaks, and left-handed ravens, to foretell misfortunes to those that please to be wretched ; with all other necessaries for pensive passion.

And for the convenience of such whose affairs will not permit them to leave this town, at the same place they may be furnished, during the season, with opening buds, flowering thyme, warbling birds, sporting lambkins, and fountain water, right and good, and bottled on the spot, by one sent down on purpose.

N.B. The nymphs and swains are further given to understand, that in those happy climes, they are so far from being troubled with wolves, that for want of even foxes, a considerable pack of hounds have been lately forced to eat sheep.

Whereas on the 6th instant at midnight, several persons of light honour and loose mirth, having taken upon them in the shape of men, but with the voice of the players belonging to Mr. Powell's[1] company, to call up surgeons at midnight, and send physicians to persons in sound sleep, and perfect health : this is to certify, that Mr. Powell had locked up the legs of all his company for fear of mischief that night ; and that Mr. Powell will not pay for any damages done by the said persons. It is also further advised, that there were no midwives wanted when those persons called them up in the several parts of Westminster ; but that those gentlewomen who were in the company of

[1] The puppet-show man.

158

the said impostors, may take care to call such useful persons on the 6th of December next.

The Censor having observed, that there are fine wrought ladies' shoes and slippers put out to view at a great shoe-maker's shop towards St. James's end of Pall Mall, which create irregular thoughts and desires in the youth of this nation; the said shopkeeper is required to take in those eyesores, or show cause the next court-day why he continues to expose the same ; and he is required to be prepared particularly to answer to the slippers with green lace and blue heels.

It is impossible for me to return the obliging things Mr. Joshua Barnes[1] has said to me upon the account of our mutual friend Homer. He and I have read him now forty years with some understanding, and great admiration. A work to be produced by one who has enjoyed so great

[1] "The learned and ingenious Mr. Joshua Barnes has lately writ an eulogium (after the manner of learned men to each other) upon me ; and after having made me his compliments in the behalf of his beloved Homer, and thanked me for the justice I have done him, in the 'Table of Fame,' has desired me to recommend the following advertisement: 'Whereas Mr. Joshua Barnes, B.D., her Majesty's Greek professor in the University of Cambridge, hath some time since published proposals for printing a new and accurate edition of all Homer's "Works," enlarged, corrected, and amended, by the help of ancient MSS. the best editions, scholiographers, &c. : These are to certify, that the "Iliad" and "Odyssey" are now both actually printed off, only a small part of the hymns, other poems, and fragments remaining, with the indexes, Life of Homer, and Prolegomena, which are carried on with all possible expedition. All gentlemen therefore, scholars and masters of great schools, that are willing to reap the benefit of subscription, being ten shillings down, and on the delivery of the two volumes in sheets twenty shillings more, are desired to make their first payment to the said Mr. Barnes, now lodging at the printing house at Cambridge, before the end of March ; after which

an intimacy with an author, is certainly to be valued more than any comment made by persons of yesterday : therefore, according to my friend Joshua's request, I recommend· his [1] work ; and having used a little magic in the case, I give this recommendation by way of amulet or charm, against the malignity of envious backbiters, who speak evil of performances whereof themselves were never capable.   If I may use my friend Joshua's own words, I shall at present say no more, but that we, Homer's oldest acquaintance now living, know best his ways ; and can inform the world, that they are often mistaken when they think he is in lethargic fits, which we know he was never subject to ; and shall make appear to be rank scandal and envy that of the Latin poet :

"—— *Aliquando bonus dormitat Homerus.*" [2]

No. 144.

From *Thursday, March* 9, to *Saturday, March* 11, 1709–10.

Sheer Lane, March 10.

In a nation of liberty, there is hardly a person in the whole mass of the people more absolutely necessary than a censor.   It is allowed, that I have no authority for

time no more single subscriptions to be admitted'" (*Tatler*, orig. folio, No. 139).   Joshua Barnes (1654–1712), Greek scholar and antiquary, was educated at Christ's Hospital and Emanuel College, Cambridge. He was appointed professor of Greek at Cambridge in 1695.   The expenses incurred in the production of his "Homer" involved him in considerable difficulties.   Bentley paid a doubtful compliment to Barnes when he said that Barnes knew as much Greek as a Greek cobbler.   See the *Spectator*, No. 245.

[1] Mr. Joshua Barnes' new and accurate edition of all Homer's Works, &c. (Steele).

[2] Horace, "Ars Poet." 359 ("Quandoque bonus," &c.).

assuming this important appellation, and that I am censor
of these nations, just as one is chosen king at the game of
questions and commands :[1] but if, in the execution of this
fantastical dignity, I observe upon things which do not fall
within the cognisance of real authority, I hope it will be
granted, that an idle man could not be more usefully employed. Among all the irregularities of which I have
taken notice, I know none so proper to be presented to
the world by a censor, as that of the general expense and
affectation in equipage. I have lately hinted, that this
extravagance must necessarily get footing where we have
no sumptuary laws, and where every man may be dressed,
attended, and carried, in what manner he pleases. But
my tenderness to my fellow subjects will not permit me to
let this enormity go unobserved.

As the matter now stands, every man takes it in his
head, that he has a liberty to spend his money as he pleases.
Thus, in spite of all order, justice, and decorum, we the
greater number of the Queen's loyal subjects, for no reason
in the world but because we want money, do not share
alike in the division of her Majesty's high-road. The
horses and slaves of the rich take up the whole street,
while we peripatetics are very glad to watch an opportunity to whisk across a passage, very thankful that we are
not run over for interrupting the machine, that carries in
it a person neither more handsome, wise, nor valiant than
the meanest of us. For this reason, were I to propose a
tax, it should certainly be upon coaches and chairs : for
no man living can assign a reason why one man should
have half a street to carry him at his ease, and perhaps
only in pursuit of pleasures, when as good a man as him-

---

[1] Cf. Steele's "Lover," No. 13 : "I might have been a king at
questions and commands." This game is mentioned several times in
the *Spectator*.

self wants room for his own person to pass upon the most
necessary and urgent occasion. Till such an acknowledgment is made to the public, I shall take upon me to
vest certain rights in the scavengers of the cities of London
and Westminster, to take the horses and servants of all
such as do not become or deserve such distinctions into
their peculiar custody. The offenders themselves I shall
allow safe conduct to their places of abode in the carts of
the said scavengers, but their horses shall be mounted by
their footmen, and sent into the service abroad : and I
take this opportunity in the first place to recruit the regiment of my good old friend the brave and honest Sylvius,[1]
that they be as well taught as they are fed. It is to me
most miraculous, so unreasonable an usurpation as this I
am speaking of should so long have been tolerated. We
hang a poor fellow for taking any trifle from us on the
road, and bear with the rich for robbing us of the road
itself. Such a tax as this would be of great satisfaction to
us who walk on foot ; and since the distinction of riding
in a coach is not to be appointed according to a man's
merit or service to their country, nor that liberty given as

[1] General Cornelius Wood, son of the Rev. Seth Wood, was born
in 1636. He served for four years as a private soldier, before he was
advanced to be a sub-brigadier ; after which his rise was rapid, owing
entirely to his signal valour, his strict justice, and extensive humanity.
The Prince of Orange, on his accession to the throne, gave him a
troop of horse, in the regiment commanded by George Lord Huet ;
he was made a colonel of horse in 1693 ; and a brigadier-general in
1702. His conduct and conversation in Ireland rendered him very
acceptable to Marshal Schomberg ; his valour was conspicuous
at the Battle of Blenheim, after which the Duke of Marlborough
declared him a major-general ; it was no less signally manifested at
Ramillies in 1706 ; the year following he was made a lieutenant-
general of horse, in which post he arrived to be the eldest. In 1708,
he was Governor of Ghent, and honoured by the burghers, in testimony of their singular satisfaction, with a large piece of plate, which

a reward for some eminent virtue, we should be highly contented to see them pay something for the insult they ·do us in the state they take upon them while they are drawn by us.

Till they have made us some reparation of this kind, we the peripatetics of Great Britain cannot think ourselves well treated, while every one that is able is allowed to set up an equipage.

As for my part, I cannot but admire how persons, conscious to themselves of no manner of superiority above others, can out of mere pride or laziness expose themselves at this rate to public view, and put us all upon pronouncing those three terrible syllables, Who is that? When it comes to that question, our method is to consider the mien and air of the passenger, and comfort ourselves for being dirty to the ankles, by laughing at his figure and appearance who overlooks us. I must confess, where it not for the solid injustice of the thing, there is nothing could afford a discerning eye greater occasion for mirth, than this licentious huddle of qualities and characters in the equipages about this town. The overseers of the highway and constables have so little skill or power to rectify this matter, that you may often see the equipage

he left as a legacy to the Duke of Ormond, to evince his gratitude for services received, and his esteem for that nobleman's illustrious character. In 1709, he gathered fresh laurels in the bloody field of Tanieres, and next year was again appointed Governor of Ghent; but in his march to that garrison, an unruly horse on which he rode, reared on end, and fell backwards upon him; his collar-bone was broken, and his stomach so bruised by this accident, that he never was well after. He languished about two years, and died at the Gravel-pits near Kensington, on the 17th of May 1712, in the 75th year of his age. He never married (Nichols). Prior, in his poem on the Battle of Blenheim, says:

"Let generous Sylvius stand for honest Wood."

of a fellow whom all the town knows to deserve hanging, make a stop that shall interrupt the Lord High Chancellor and all the judges on their way to Westminster.

For the better understanding of things and persons in this general confusion, I have given directions to all the coachmakers and coach-painters in town, to bring me in lists of their several customers ; and doubt not, but with comparing the orders of each man, in the placing his arms on the doors of his chariot, as well as the words, devices and ciphers to be fixed upon them, to make a collection which shall let us into the nature, if not the history, of mankind, more usefully than the curiosities of any medallist in Europe.

But this evil of vanity in our figure, with many, many others, proceeds from a certain gaiety of heart, which has crept into men's very thoughts and complexions. The passions and adventures of heroes, when they enter the lists for the tournament in romances, are not more easily distinguishable by their palfreys and their armour, than the secret springs and affections of the several pretenders to show amongst us are known by their equipages in ordinary life. The young bridegroom with his gilded cupids, and winged angels, has some excuse in the joy of his heart to launch out into something that may be significant of his present happiness : but to see men, for no reason upon earth but that they are rich, ascend triumphant chariots, and ride through the people, has at the bottom nothing else in it but an insolent transport, arising only from the distinction of fortune.

It is therefore high time that I call in such coaches as ᵗe in their embellishments improper for the character of eir owners. But if I find I am not obeyed herein, and ᵗ I cannot pull down these equipages already erected, I ll take upon me to prevent the growth of this evil for the future, by inquiring into the pretensions of the persons who shall hereafter attempt to make public entries with ornaments and decorations of his own appointment. If a man, who believed he had the handsomest leg in this kingdom, should take a fancy to adorn so deserving a limb with a blue garter, he would justly be punished for offending against the most noble order : and, I think, the general prostitution of equipage and retinue is as destructive to all distinction, as the impertinence of one man, if permitted, would certainly be to that illustrious fraternity.

ADVERTISEMENT.

The Censor having lately received intelligence, that the ancient simplicity in the dress and manners of that part of this island, called Scotland, begins to decay ; and that there are at this time in the good town of Edinburgh, beaus, fops, and coxcombs : his late correspondent[1] from that place is desired to send up their names and characters with all expedition, that they may be proceeded against accordingly, and proper officers named to take in their canes, snuff-boxes, and all other useless necessaries commonly worn by such offenders.

No. 145.   [Steele.

From *Saturday, March* 11, to *Tuesday, March* 14, 1709–10.

Nescio quis teneros oculus mihi fascinat agnos.
Virg., Eclog. iii. 103.

White's Chocolate-house, March 13.

This evening was allotted for taking into consideration a late request of two indulgent parents, touching the care of a young daughter, whom they design to send to a

---

[1] "Osyris" ; see No. 143.

boarding-school, or keep at home, according to my determination;[1] but I am diverted from that subject by letters which I have received from several ladies, complaining of a certain sect of professed enemies to the repose of the fair sex, called Oglers. These are, it seems, gentlemen who look with deep attention on one object at the playhouses, and are ever staring all round them in churches. It is urged by my correspondents, that they do all that is possible to keep their eyes off these ensnarers; but that, by what power they know not, both their diversions and devotions are interrupted by them in such a manner, as that they cannot attend either without stealing looks at the persons whose eyes are fixed upon them. By this means, my petitioners say, they find themselves grow insensibly less offended, and in time enamoured, of these their enemies. What is required of me on this occasion, is, that as I love and study to preserve the better part of mankind, the females, I would give them some account of this dangerous way of assault, against which there is so little defence, that it lays ambush for the sight itself, and makes them seeingly, knowingly, willingly, and forcibly go on to their own captivity.

This representation of the present state of affairs between the two sexes gave me very much alarm; and I had no more to do, but to recollect what I had seen at any one assembly for some years last past, to be convinced of the truth and justice of this remonstrance. If there be not a stop put to this evil art, all the modes of address, and the elegant embellishments of life, which arise out of the noble passion of love, will of necessity decay. Who would be at the trouble of rhetoric, or study the *bon mien*, when his introduction is so much easier obtained by a sudden reverence in a downcast look at the meeting the

[1] See No. 141.

eye of a fair lady, and beginning again to ogle her as soon as
she glances another way ?   I remember very well, when I
.was last at an opera, I could perceive the eyes of the
whole audience cast into particular cross angles one upon
another, without any manner of regard to the stage,
though King Latinus was himself present when I made that
observation.   It was then very pleasant to look into the
hearts of the whole company ; for the balls of sight are
so formed, that one man's eyes are spectacles to another to
read his heart with.   The most ordinary beholder can
take notice of any violent agitation in the mind, any
pleasing transport, or any inward grief, in the person he
looks at ; but one of these oglers can see a studied indifference, a concealed love, or a smothered resentment, in
the very glances that are made to hide those dispositions of
thought.   The naturalists tell us, that the rattlesnake will
fix himself under a tree where he sees a squirrel playing ;
and when he has once got the exchange of a glance from
the pretty wanton, will give it such a sudden stroke on its
imagination, that though it may play from bough to
bough, and strive to avert its eyes from it for some time,
yet it comes nearer and nearer by little intervals of looking
another way, till it drops into the jaws of the animal,
which it knew gazed at it for no other reason but to ruin
it.   I did not believe this piece of philosophy till that
night I was just now speaking of ; but I then saw the
same thing pass between an ogler and a coquette. Mirtillo,
the most learned of the former, had for some time discon-
tinued to visit Flavia, no less eminent among the latter.
They industriously avoided all places where they might
probably meet, but chance brought them together to the
playhouse, and seated them in a direct line over against
each other, she in a front box, he in the pit next the stage.
As soon as Flavia had received the looks of the whole

crowd below her with that air of insensibility which is
necessary at the first entrance, she began to look round
her and saw the vagabond Mirtillo, who had so long·
absented himself from her circle ; and when she first
discovered him, she looked upon him with that glance,
which, in the language of oglers, is called the scornful, but
immediately turned her observation another way, and
returned upon him with the indifferent. This gave
Mirtillo no small resentment ; but he used her accordingly.
He took care to be ready for her next glance. She found
his eyes full in the indolent, with his lips crumpled up in
the posture of one whistling. Her anger at this usage
immediately appeared in every muscle of her face ; and
after many emotions, which glistened in her eyes, she cast
them round the whole house, and gave them softnesses in
the face of every man she had ever seen before. After
she thought she had reduced all she saw to her obedience,
the play began, and ended their dialogue. As soon as that
was over, she stood up with a visage full of dissembled
alacrity and pleasure, with which she overlooked the
audience, and at last came to him : he was then placed in
a side-way, with his hat slouching over his eyes, and
gazing at a wench in the side-box,[1] as talking of that
gipsy to the gentleman who sat by him. But as she was
fixed upon him, he turned suddenly with a full face upon
her, and with all the respect imaginable, made her the
most obsequious bow in the presence of the whole theatre.
This gave her a pleasure not to be concealed, and she
made him the recovering or second curtsy, with a smile
that spoke a perfect reconciliation. Between the ensuing
acts, they talked to each other with gestures and glances so
significant, that they ridiculed the whole house in this
silent speech, and made an appointment that Mirtillo
should lead her to her coach.

[1] See No. 50.

The peculiar language of one eye, as it differs from another, as much as the tone of one voice from another, and the fascination or enchantment which is lodged in the optic nerves of the persons concerned in these dialogues, is, I must confess, too nice a subject for one who is not an adept in these speculations ; but I shall, for the good and safety of the fair sex, call my learned friend Sir William Read[1] to my assistance, and, by the help of his observations on this organ, acquaint them when the eye is to be believed, and when distrusted. On the contrary, I shall conceal the true meaning of the looks of ladies, and indulge in them all the art they can acquire in the management of their glances : all which is but too little against creatures who triumph in falsehood, and begin to forswear with their eyes, when their tongues can be no longer believed.

ADVERTISEMENT.

A very clean, well-behaved young gentleman, who is in a very good way in Cornhill, has writ to me the following lines, and seems in some passages of his letter (which I omit) to lay it very much to heart, that I have not spoken of a supernatural beauty whom he sighs for, and complains to in most elaborate language. Alas ! what can a monitor do ? All mankind live in romance :

"Royal Exchange, *March* 11.

"MR. BICKERSTAFF,

"Some time since you were pleased to mention the beauties in the New Exchange and Westminster Hall,[2] and in my judgment were not very impartial ; for if you were pleased to allow there was one goddess in the New Exchange, and two shepherdesses in Westminster Hall, you very well might say, there was and is at present one angel in the Royal Exchange : and I humbly beg the

[1] See No. 9. [2] See No. 139.

favour of you to let justice be done her, by inserting this in your next *Tatler;* which will make her my good angel, and me your most humble servant,

"A. B."[1]

No. 146.   [ADDISON.

From *Tuesday, March* 14, to *Thursday, March* 16, 1709–10.

Permittes ipsis expendere numinibus, quid
Conveniat nobis, rebusque sit utile nostris.
Nam pro jucundis aptissima quæque dabunt Di.
Carior est illis homo, quam sibi.   Nos animorum
Impulsu et cæca magnaque cupidine ducti
Conjugium petimus, partumque uxoris ; at illis
Notum, qui pueri qualisque futura sit uxor.

Juv., Sat. x. 347.

From my own Apartment, March 15.

Among the various sets of correspondents who apply to me for advice, and send up their cases from all parts of Great Britain, there are none who are more importunate with me, and whom I am more inclined to answer, than the complainers.   One of them dates his letter to me from the banks of a purling stream, where he used to ruminate in solitude upon the divine Clarissa, and where he is now looking about for a convenient leap, which he tells me he is resolved to take, unless I support him under the loss of that charming perjured woman.   Poor Lavinia presses as much for consolation on the other side, and is reduced to such an extremity of despair by the inconstancy of Philander, that she tells me she writes her letter with her pen in one hand and her garter in the other.   A gentleman of an ancient family in Norfolk is almost out of his

---

[1] Perhaps Alexander Bayne ; see No. 84.

wits upon account of a greyhound, that after having been his inseparable companion for ten years, is at last run mad. Another (who I believe is serious) complains to me, in a very moving manner, of the loss of a wife ; and another, in terms still more moving, of a purse of money that was taken from him on Bagshot Heath, and which, he tells me, would not have troubled him if he had given it to the poor. In short, there is scarce a calamity in human life that has not produced me a letter.

It is indeed wonderful to consider, how men are able to raise affliction to themselves out of everything. Lands and houses, sheep and oxen, can convey happiness and misery into the hearts of reasonable creatures. Nay, I have known a muff, a scarf, or a tippet, become a solid blessing or misfortune. A lap-dog has broke the hearts of thousands. Flavia, who had buried five children, and two husbands, was never able to get over the loss of her parrot. How often has a divine creature been thrown into a fit by a neglect at a ball or an assembly ? Mopsa has kept her chamber ever since the last masquerade, and is in greater danger of her life upon being left out of it, than Clarinda from the violent cold which she caught at it. Nor are these dear creatures the only sufferers by such imaginary calamities : many an author has been dejected at the censure of one whom he ever looked upon as an idiot ; and many a hero cast into a fit of melancholy, because the rabble have not hooted at him as he passed through the streets. Theron places all his happiness in a running horse, Suffenus in a gilded chariot, Fulvius in a blue string, and Florio in a tulip root. It would be endless to enumerate the many fantastical afflictions that disturb mankind ; but as a misery is not to be measured from the nature of the evil, but from the temper of the sufferer, I shall present my readers, who are unhappy either in reality or imagination, with an allegory, for which I am indebted to the great father and prince of poets.

As I was sitting after dinner in my elbow-chair, I took up Homer, and dipped into that famous speech of Achilles to Priam, in which he tells him, that Jupiter has by him two great vessels, the one filled with blessings, and the other with misfortunes ; out of which he mingles a composition for every man that comes into the world. This passage so exceedingly pleased me, that as I fell insensibly into my afternoon's slumber, it wrought my imagination into the following dream :

When Jupiter took into his hands the government of the world, the several parts of nature, with their presiding deities, did homage to him. One presented him with a mountain of winds, another with a magazine of hail, and a third with a pile of thunderbolts. The stars offered up their influences ; the ocean gave in his trident, the earth her fruits, and the sun his seasons. Among the several deities who came to make their court on this occasion, the destinies advanced with two great tuns carried before them, one of which they fixed at the right hand of Jupiter as he sat upon his throne, and the other on his left. The first was filled with all the blessings, and the other with all the calamities of human life. Jupiter, in the beginning of his reign, finding the world much more innocent than it is in this iron age, poured very plentifully out of the tun that stood at his right hand ; but as mankind degenerated, and became unworthy of his blessings, he set abroach the other vessel, that filled the world with pain and poverty, battles and distempers, jealousy and falsehood, intoxicating pleasures and untimely deaths.

He was at length so very much incensed at the great depravation of human nature, and the repeated provocations which he received from all parts of the earth, that having resolved to destroy the whole species, except Deucalion and Pyrrha, he commanded the Destinies to gather up the blessings which he had thrown away upon the sons of men, and lay them up till the world should be inhabited by a more virtuous and deserving race of mortals.

The three sisters immediately repaired to the earth, in search of the several blessings that had been scattered on it ; but found the task which was enjoined them, to be much more difficult than they had imagined. The first places they resorted to, as the most likely to succeed in, were cities, palaces, and courts ; but instead of meeting with what they looked for here, they found nothing but envy, repining, uneasiness, and the like bitter ingredients of the left-hand vessel. Whereas, to their great surprise, they discovered content, cheerfulness, health, innocence, and other the most substantial blessings of life, in cottages, shades, and solitudes.

There was another circumstance no less unexpected than the former, and which gave them very great perplexity in the discharge of the trust which Jupiter had committed to them. They observed, that several blessings had degenerated into calamities, and that several calamities had improved into blessings, according as they fell into the possession of wise or foolish men. They often found power, with so much insolence and impatience cleaving to it, that it became a misfortune to the person on whom it was conferred. Youth had often distempers growing about it, worse than the infirmities of old age : wealth was often united to such a sordid avarice, as made it the most uncomfortable and painful kind of poverty. On the contrary, they often found pain made glorious by fortitude, poverty lost in content, deformity beautified with virtue. In a word, the blessings were often like good fruits planted in a bad soil, that by degrees fall off from their natural relish, into tastes altogether insipid or unwholesome ; and the calamities, like harsh fruits, cultivated in a good soil, and enriched by proper grafts and inoculations, till they swell with generous and delightful juices.

There was still a third circumstance that occasioned as great a surprise to the three sisters as either of the foregoing, when they discovered several blessings and calamities which had never been in either of the tuns that stood by the throne of Jupiter, and were nevertheless as great occasions of happiness or misery as any there. These were that spurious crop of blessings and calamities which were never sown by the hand of the Deity, but grow of themselves out of the fancies and dispositions of human creatures. Such are dress, titles, place, equipage, false shame, and groundless fear, with the like vain imaginations that shoot up in trifling, weak, and irresolute minds.

The Destinies finding themselves in so great a perplexity, concluded, that it would be impossible for them to execute the commands that had been given them according to their first intention ; for which reason they agreed to throw all the blessings and calamities together into one large vessel, and in that manner offer them up at the feet of Jupiter.

This was performed accordingly, the eldest sister presenting herself before the vessel, and introducing it with an apology for what they had done.

" O Jupiter ! " says she, " we have gathered together all the good and evil, the comforts and distresses of human life, which we thus present before thee in one promiscuous heap. We beseech thee that thou thyself wilt sort them out for the future, as in thy wisdom thou shalt think fit. For we acknowledge, that there is none beside thee that can judge what will occasion grief or joy in the heart of a human creature, and what will prove a blessing or a calamity to the person on whom it is bestowed..

No. 147.   [ADDISON AND STEELE.

From *Thurs.*, *March* 16, to *Satur.*, *March* 18, 1709-10.

—— Ut ameris, amabilis esto.—OVID., Ars Am. ii. 107.

From my own Apartment, March 17.

R eading is to the mind what exercise is to the body. As by the one, health is preserved, strengthened and invigorated ; by the other, virtue (which is the health of the mind) is kept alive, cherished and confirmed. But as exercise becomes tedious and painful when we make use of it only as the means of health, so reading is apt to grow uneasy and burdensome, when we apply ourselves to it only for our improvement in virtue. For this reason, the virtue which we gather from a fable, or an allegory, is like the health we get by hunting ; as we are engaged in an agreeable pursuit that draws us on with pleasure, and makes us insensible of the fatigues that accompany it.

After this preface, I shall set down a very beautiful allegorical fable out of the great poet whom I mentioned in my last paper, and whom it is very difficult to lay aside when one is engaged in the reading of him. And this I particularly design for the use of several of my fair correspondents, who in their letters have complained to me, that they have lost the affections of their husbands, and desire my advice how to recover them.

Juno, says Homer,[1] seeing her Jupiter seated on the top of Mount Ida, and knowing that he had conceived an

[1] "Iliad," xiv. 157.

175

aversion to her, began to study how she should regain his affections, and make herself amiable to him. With this thought she immediately retired into her chamber, where she bathed herself in ambrosia, which gave her person all its beauty, and diffused so divine an odour, as refreshed all nature, and sweetened both heaven and earth. She let her immortal tresses flow in the most graceful manner, and took a particular care to dress herself in several ornaments, which the poet describes at length, and which the goddess chose out as the most proper to set off her person to the best advantage. In the next place, she made a visit to Venus, the deity who presides over love, and begged of her, as a particular favour, that she would lend her for a while those charms with which she subdued the hearts both of gods and men. " For," says the goddess, " I would make use of them to reconcile the two deities who took care of me in my infancy, and who, at present, are at so great a variance, that they are estranged from each other's bed." Venus was proud of an opportunity of obliging so great a goddess, and therefore made her a present of the cestus which she used to wear about her own waist, with advice to hide it in her bosom till she had accomplished her intention. This cestus was a fine particoloured girdle, which, as Homer tells us, had all the attractions of the sex wrought into it. The four principal figures in the embroidery were Love, Desire, Fondness of Speech, and Conversation, filled with that sweetness and complacency, which, says the poet, insensibly steal away the hearts of the wisest men.

Juno, after having made these necessary preparations, came as by accident into the presence of Jupiter, who is said to have been as much inflamed with her beauty, as when he first stole to her embraces without the consent of their parents. Juno, to cover her real thoughts, told him

as she had told Venus, that she was going to make a visit
to Oceanus and Tethys. He prevailed upon her to stay
with him, protesting to her, that she appeared more amiable
in his eye than ever any mortal, goddess, or even herself,
had appeared to him till that day. The poet then represents him in so great an ardour, that (without going up to
the house which had been built by the hands of Vulcan
according to Juno's direction) he threw a golden cloud
over their heads as they sat upon the top of Mount Ida,
while the earth beneath them sprung up in lotuses,[1]
saffrons, hyacinths, and a bed of the softest flowers for
their repose.

This close translation of one of the finest passages in
Homer, may suggest abundance of instruction to a woman
who has a mind to preserve or recall the affection of her
husband. The care of the person and the dress, with the
particular blandishments woven in the cestus, are so plainly
recommended by this fable, and so indispensably necessary
in every female who desires·to please, that they need no
further explanation. The discretion likewise in covering
all matrimonial quarrels from the knowledge of others, is
taught in the pretended visit to Tethys, in the speech
where Juno addresses herself to Venus ; as the chaste and
prudent management of a wife's charms is intimated by
the same pretence for her appearing before Jupiter, and by
the concealment of the cestus in her bosom.

I shall leave this tale to the consideration of such good
housewives who are never well dressed but when they are
abroad, and think it necessary to appear more agreeable to

---

[1] Lotus is the name of a native genus akin to the trefoil and clovers.
It is best known as the supposed opium-like food of a people on the
shores of the Mediterranean, visited by Ulysses,—Tennyson's "mild-
eyed melancholy lotos-eaters," living in a land where all things always
seemed the same.

all men living than their husbands : as also to those
prudent ladies, who, to avoid the appearance of being over-
fond, entertain their husband with indifference, aversion,
sullen silence, or exasperating language.[1]

Sheer Lane, March 17.

Upon my coming home last night, I found a very handsome present of wine left for me, as a taste of 216 hogsheads which are to be put to sale at £20 a hogshead, at
Garraway's Coffee-house in Exchange Alley, on the 22nd
instant, at three in the afternoon, and to be tasted in
Major Long's vaults from the 20th instant till the time of
sale.[2] This having been sent to me with a desire that I
would give my judgment upon it, I immediately im-
panelled a jury of men of nice palates and strong heads,
who being all of them very scrupulous, and unwilling to
proceed rashly in a matter of so great importance, refused
to bring in their verdict till three in the morning ; at
which time the foreman pronounced, as well as he was
able, " Extra—a—ordinary French claret."   For my own
part, as I love to consult my pillow in all points of
moment, I slept upon it before I would give my sentence,
and this morning confirmed the verdict.

Having mentioned this tribute of wine, I must give
notice to my correspondents for the future, who shall
apply to me on this occasion, that as I shall decide nothing
unadvisedly in matters of this nature, I cannot pretend to
give judgment of a right good liquor, without examining
at least three dozen bottles of it.   I must at the same
time do myself the justice to let the world know, that I
have resisted great temptations in this kind ; as it is well
known to a butcher in Clare Market, who endeavoured to

[1] The preceding portion of this paper was by Addison (Tickell)
[2] This sale was advertised in No. 145.

corrupt me with a dozen and a half of marrow-bones. I had likewise a bribe sent me by a fishmonger, consisting of a collar of brawn, and a joll of salmon ; but not finding them excellent in their kinds, I had the integrity to eat them both up, without speaking one word of them. However, for the future, I shall have an eye to the diet of this great city, and will recommend the best and most whole-some food to them, if I receive these proper and respectful notices from the sellers, that it may not be said hereafter, my readers were better taught than fed.

No. 148.   [Addison.

From *Saturday, March* 18, to *Tuesday, March* 21, 1709-10.

—— Gustus elementa per omnia quærunt,
Nunquam animo pretiis obstantibus.

Juv., Sat. xi. 14.

From my own Apartment, March 20.

Having intimated in my last paper, that I design to take under my inspection the diet of this great city, I shall begin with a very earnest and serious exhortation to all my well-disposed readers, that they would return to the food of their forefathers, and reconcile themselves to beef and mutton. This was the diet which bred that hardy race of mortals who won the fields of Cressy and Agin-court. I need not go up so high as the history of Guy Earl of Warwick, who is well known to have eaten up a dun cow of his own killing.[1] The renowned King Arthur

[1] Butler, speaking of Talgol ("Hudibras," Part 1. canto ii. 305), says :

> "He many a boar and huge dun-cow
> Did, like another Guy, o'erthrow,
> But Guy, with him in fight compared,
> Had like the boar or dun-cow fared."

179

is generally looked upon as the first who ever sat down to a whole roasted ox (which was certainly the best way to preserve the gravy), and it is further added, that he and his knights sat about it at his Round Table, and usually consumed it to the very bones before they would enter upon any debate of moment. The Black Prince was a professed lover of the brisket ; not to mention the history of the sirloin, or the institution of the Order of Beef-eaters, which are all so many evident and undeniable marks of the great respect which our warlike predecessors have paid to this excellent food. The tables of the ancient gentry of this nation were covered thrice a day with hot roast beef ; and I am credibly informed, by an antiquary who has searched the registers in which the bills of fare of the Court are recorded, that instead of tea and bread and butter, which have prevailed of late years, the maids of honour in Queen Elizabeth's time were allowed three rumps of beef for their breakfast. Mutton has like-wise been in great repute among our valiant countrymen, but was formerly observed to be the food rather of men of nice and delicate appetites, than those of strong and robust constitutions. For which reason, even to this day, we use the word " sheep-biter " as a term of reproach, as we do " beef-eater " in a respectful and honourable sense. As for the flesh of lamb, veal, chicken, and other animals under age, they were the invention of sickly and degenerate palates, according to that wholesome remark of Daniel the historian,[1] who takes notice, that in all taxes upon provisions, during the reigns of several of our kings, there is nothing men-tioned besides the flesh of such fowl and cattle as were arrived at their full growth, and were mature for slaughter. The common people of this kingdom do still keep up the taste of their ancestors ; and it is to this that we in a great

---

[1] Samuel Daniel's "History" was published in 1613.

measure owe the unparalleled victories that have been gained in this reign : for, I would desire my reader to consider, what work our countrymen would have made at Blenheim and Ramillies, if they had been fed with fricassees and ragouts.

For this reason, we at present see the florid complexion, the strong limb, and the hale constitution, are to be found chiefly among the meaner sort of people, or in the wild gentry, who have been educated among the woods or mountains. Whereas many great families are insensibly fallen off from the athletic constitution of their progenitors, and are dwindled away into a pale, sickly, spindle-legged, generation of valetudinarians.

I may perhaps be thought extravagant in my notion ; but I must confess, I am apt to impute the dishonours that sometimes happen in great families to the inflaming kind of diet which is so much in fashion. Many dishes can excite desire without giving strength, and heat the body without nourishing it ; as physicians observe, that the poorest and most dispirited blood is most subject to fevers. I look upon a French ragout to be as pernicious to the stomach as a glass of spirits ; and when I have seen a young lady swallow all the instigations of high soups, seasoned sauces, and forced meats, I have wondered at the despair or tedious sighing of her lovers.

The rules among these false delicates are to be as con-tradictory as they can be to nature.

Without expecting the return of hunger, they eat for an appetite, and prepare dishes not to allay, but to excite it.

They admit of nothing at their tables, in its natural form, or without some disguise.

They are to eat everything before it comes in season, and to leave it off as soon as it is good to be eaten.

They are not to approve anything that is agreeable to ordinary palates ; and nothing is to gratify their senses, but what would offend those of their inferiors.

I remember I was last summer invited to a friend's house, who is a great admirer of the French cookery, and (as the phrase is) eats well. At our sitting down, I found the table covered with a great variety of unknown dishes. I was mightily at a loss to learn what they were, and therefore did not know where to help myself. That which stood before me, I took to be a roasted porcupine, however did not care for asking questions ; and have since been informed, that it was only a larded turkey. I afterwards passed my eye over several hashes, which I do not know the names of to this day ; and hearing that they were delicacies, did not think fit to meddle with them.

Among other dainties, I saw something like a pheasant, and therefore desired to be helped to a wing of it ; but to my great surprise, my friend told me it was a rabbit, which is a sort of meat I never cared for. At last I discovered, with some joy, a pig at the lower end of the table, and begged a gentleman that was near it to cut me a piece of it. Upon which the gentleman of the house said, with great civility, " I am sure you will like the pig, for it was whipped to death." I must confess, I heard him with horror, and could not eat of an animal that had died so tragical a death. I was now in great hunger and confusion, when, methought, I smelt the agreeable savour of roast beef, but could not tell from which dish it arose, though I did not question but it lay disguised in one of them. Upon turning my head, I saw a noble sirloin on the side-table smoking in the most delicious manner. I had recourse to it more than once, and could not see, without some indignation, that substantial English dish banished in so ignominious a manner, to make way for French kickshaws.

· The dessert was brought up at last, which in truth was as extraordinary as anything that had come before it. The whole, when ranged in its proper order, looked like a very beautiful winter-piece. There were several pyramids of candied sweetmeats, that hung like icicles, with fruit scattered up and down, and hid in an artificial kind of frost. At the same time there were great quantities of cream beaten up into a snow, and near them little plates of sugar-plums, disposed like so many heaps of hailstones, with a multitude of congelations in jellies of various colours. I was indeed so pleased with the several objects which lay before me, that I did not care for displacing any of them, and was half angry with the rest of the company, that for the sake of a piece of lemon-peel, or a sugar-plum, would spoil so pleasing a picture. Indeed, I could not but smile to see several of them cooling their mouths with lumps of ice which they had just before been burning with salts and peppers.

As soon as this show was over I took my leave, that I might finish my dinner at my own house : for as I in every thing love what is simple and natural, so particularly in my food ; two plain dishes, with two or three good-natured, cheerful, ingenious friends, would make me more pleased and vain, than all that pomp and luxury can bestow. For it is my maxim, that he keeps the greatest table, who has the most valuable company at it.

No. 149.   [STEELE.

From *Tuesday, March* 21, to *Thursday, March* 23, 1709–10.

From my own Apartment, March 22.

It has often been a solid grief to me, when I have re-
flected on this glorious nation, which is the scene of
public happiness and liberty, that there are still crowds of
private tyrants, against whom there neither is any law now
in being, nor can there be invented any by the wit of man.
These cruel men are ill-natured husbands.   The commerce
in the conjugal state is so delicate, that it is impossible to
prescribe rules for the conduct of it, so as to fit ten
thousand nameless pleasures and disquietudes which arise
to people in that condition.   But it is in this as in some
other nice cases, where touching upon the malady tenderly,
is half way to the cure ; and there are some faults which
need only to be observed to be amended.   I am put into
this way of thinking by a late conversation which I am
going to give an account of.

I made a visit the other day to a family for which I
have a great honour, and found the father, the mother,
and two or three of the younger children, drop off de-
signedly to leave me alone with the eldest daughter, who
was but a visitant there as well as myself, and is the wife
of a gentleman of a very fair character in the world.   As
soon as we were alone, I saw her eyes full of tears, and methought she had much to say to me, for which she wanted
encouragement.   " Madam," said I, " you know I wish you
all as well as any friend you have : speak freely what I see
you are oppressed with, and you may be sure, if I cannot
relieve your distress, you may at least reap so much present

advantage, as safely to give yourself the ease of uttering it." She immediately assumed the most becoming composure of countenance, and spoke as follows : "It is an aggravation of affliction in a married life, that there is a sort of guilt in communicating it : for which reason it is, that a lady of your and my acquaintance, instead of speaking to you herself, desired me the next time I saw you, as you are a professed friend to our sex, to turn your thoughts upon the reciprocal complaisance which is the duty of a married state.

"My friend was neither in fortune, birth nor education, below the gentleman whom she has married. Her person, her age, and her character, are also such as he can make no exception to. But so it is, that from the moment the marriage ceremony was over, the obsequiousness of a lover was turned into the haughtiness of a master. All the kind endeavours which she uses to please him, are at best but so many instances of her duty. This insolence takes away that secret satisfaction, which does not only excite to virtue, but also rewards it. It abates the fire of a free and generous love, and embitters all the pleasures of a social life." The young lady spoke all this with such an air of resentment, as discovered how nearly she was concerned in the distress.

When I observed she had done speaking, "Madam," said I, "the affliction you mention is the greatest that can happen in human life, and I know but one consolation in it, if that be a consolation, that the calamity is a pretty general one. There is nothing so common as for men to enter into marriage, without so much as expecting to be happy in it. They seem to propose to themselves a few holidays in the beginning of it ; after which they are to return at best to the usual course of their life ; and for aught they know, to constant misery and uneasiness. From this false

sense of the state they are going into, proceeds the immediate coldness and indifference, or hatred and aversion,
which attend ordinary marriages, or rather bargains to
cohabit." Our conversation was here interrupted by company which came in upon us.

The humour of affecting a superior carriage, generally
rises from a false notion of the weakness of a female
understanding in general, or an overweening opinion that
we have of our own : for when it proceeds from a natural
ruggedness and brutality of temper, it is altogether incorri-
gible, and not to be amended by admonition. Sir Francis
Bacon, as I remember, lays it down as a maxim, that no
marriage can be happy in which the wife has no opinion
of her husband's wisdom ;[1] but without offence to so great
an authority, I may venture to say, that a sullen-wise man is
as bad as a good-natured fool. Knowledge, softened with
complacency and good breeding, will make a man equally
beloved and respected ; but when joined with a severe,
distant and unsociable temper, it creates rather fear than
love. I who am a bachelor, have no other notion of conjugal tenderness, but what I learn from books, and shall
therefore produce three letters of Pliny,[2] who was not only
one of the greatest, but the most learned men in the whole
Roman Empire. At the same time I am very much
ashamed, that on such occasions I am obliged to have
recourse to heathen authors, and shall appeal to my readers,
if they would not think it a mark of a narrow education in
a man of quality to write such passionate letters to any
woman but a mistress. They were all three written at a
time when she was at a distance from him : the first of

[1] Bacon, Essay viii., "Of marriage and single life" : "It is one
of the best bonds, both of chastity and obedience, in the wife, if she
thinks her husband wise, which she will never do if she finds him
jealous."   [2] "Epist.," vi. 4, 7, 5.

them puts me in mind of a married friend of mine, who said, sickness itself is pleasant to a man that is attended in it by one whom he dearly loves.

Pliny to Calphurnia.

"I never was so much offended at business, as when it hindered me from going with you into the country, or following you thither : for I more particularly wish to be with you at present, that I might be sensible of the progress you make in the recovery of your strength and health ; as also of the entertainment and diversions you can meet with in your retirement. Believe me, it is an anxious state of mind to live in ignorance of what happens to those whom we passionately love. I am not only in pain for your absence, but also for your indisposition. I am afraid of everything, fancy everything, and, as it is the nature of men in fear, I fancy those things most which I am most afraid of. Let me therefore earnestly desire you to favour me under these my apprehensions with one letter every day, or, if possible, with two ; for I shall be a little at ease while I am reading your letters, and grow anxious again as soon as I have read them."

Second Letter.

"You tell me that you are very much afflicted at my absence, and that you have no satisfaction in anything but my writings, which you often lay by you upon my pillow. You oblige me very much in wishing to see me, and making me your comforter in my absence. In return, I must let you know, I am no less pleased with the letters which you writ to me, and read them over a thousand times with new pleasure. If your letters are capable of giving me so much pleasure, what would your conversation do ? Let me beg of you to write to me often ; though at the same time I must confess, your letters give me anguish whilst they give me pleasure."

Third Letter.

"It is impossible to conceive how much I languish for you in your absence ; the tender love I bear you is the chief cause of this my uneasiness, which is still the more insupportable, because absence is wholly a new thing to us. I lie awake most part of the night in thinking of you, and several times of the day go as naturally to your apartment, as if you were there to receive me ; but when I miss you, I come away dejected, out of humour, and like a man that had suffered a repulse. There is but one part of the day in which I am relieved from this anxiety, and that is when I am engaged in public affairs.

"You may guess at the uneasy condition of one who has no rest but in business, no consolation but in trouble."

I shall conclude this paper with a beautiful passage out of Milton,[1] and leave it as a lecture to those of my own sex, who have a mind to make their conversation agreeable as well as instructive, to the fair partners who are fallen into their care. Eve, having observed that Adam was entering into some deep disquisitions with the angel, who was sent to visit him, is described as retiring from their company, with a design of learning what should pass there from her husband.

> *So spake our sire, and by his countenance seemed*
> *Entering on studious thoughts abstruse, which Eve*
> *Perceiving where she sat retired in sight,*
> *With lowliness majestic from her seat*
> *Rose, and went forth among her fruits and flowers.*
> *Yet went she not, as not with such discourse*

[1] "Paradise Lost," viii. 39.

Delighted, or not capable her ear
Of what was high : such pleasure she reserved,
Adam relating, she sole auditress ;
Her husband the relater she preferred
Before the angel, and of him to ask
Chose rather : he, she knew, would intermix
Grateful digressions, and solve high dispute
With conjugal caresses ; from his lip
Not words alone pleased her.   O I when meet now
Such pairs, in love and mutual honour joined ?

No. 150.   [STEELE.

From *Thursday, March* 23, to *Saturday, March* 25, 1710.

Hæc sunt jucundi causa, cibusque mali.
OVID, Rem. Amor. 138.

From my own Apartment, March 24.

I have received the following letter upon the subject of
my last paper. The writer of it tells me, I there
spoke of marriage as one that knows it only by speculation, and for that reason he sends me his sense of it, as
drawn from experience:

"MR. BICKERSTAFF,

" I have read your paper of this day, and think you
have done the nuptial state a great deal of justice in
the authority you give us of Pliny, whose letters to his
wife you have there translated : but give me leave to tell
you, that it is impossible for you, that are a bachelor, to
have so just a notion of this way of life, as to touch the
affections of your readers in a particular wherein every
man's own heart suggests more than the nicest observer
can form to himself without experience.   I therefore, who
am an old married man, have sat down to give you an

189

account of the matter from my own knowledge, and the observations which I have made upon the conduct of others in that most agreeable or wretched condition.

"It is very commonly observed, that the most smart pangs which we meet with are in the beginning of wedlock, which proceed from ignorance of each other's humour, and want of prudence to make allowances for a change from the most careful respect to the most unbounded familiarity. Hence it arises, that trifles are commonly occasions of the greatest anxiety; for contradiction being a thing wholly unusual between a new married couple, the smallest instance of it is taken for the highest injury; and it very seldom happens, that the man is slow enough in assuming the character of a husband, or the woman quick enough in condescending to that of a wife. It immediately follows, that they think they have all the time of their courtship been talking in masks to each other, and therefore begin to act like disappointed people. Philander finds Delia ill-natured and impertinent; and Delia, Philander surly and inconstant.

"I have known a fond couple quarrel in the very honeymoon about cutting up a tart: nay, I could name two, who after having had seven children, fell out and parted beds upon the boiling of a leg of mutton. My very next neighbours have not spoken to one another these three days, because they differed in their opinions, whether the clock should stand by the window, or over the chimney. It may seem strange to you, who are not a married man, when I tell you how the least trifle can strike a woman dumb for a week together. But if you ever enter into this state, you will find, that the soft sex as often express their anger by an obstinate silence, as by an ungovernable clamour.

"Those indeed who begin this course of life without jars at their setting out, arrive within few months at a pitch of benevolence and affection, of which the most perfect friendship is but a faint resemblance. As in the unfortunate marriage, the most minute and indifferent things are objects of the sharpest resentment; so in a happy one, they are occasions of the most exquisite satisfaction. For what does not oblige in one we love? What does not offend in one we dislike? For these reasons I take it for a rule, that in marriage, the chief business is to acquire a prepossession in favour of each other. They should consider one another's words and actions with a secret indulgence: there should be always an inward fondness pleading for each other, such as may add new beauties to everything that is excellent, give charms to what is indifferent, and cover everything that is defective. For want of this kind propensity and bias of mind, the married pair often take things ill of each other, which no one else would take notice of in either of them.

"But the most unhappy circumstance of all is, where each party is always laying up fuel for dissension, and gathering together a magazine of provocations to exasperate each other with when they are out of humour. These people in common discourse make no scruple to let those who are by know they are quarrelling with one another, and think they are discreet enough, if they conceal from the company the matters which they are hinting at. About a week ago, I was entertained for a whole dinner with a mysterious conversation of this nature; out of which I could learn no more, than that the husband and wife were angry at one another. We had no sooner sat down, but says the gentleman of the house, in order to raise discourse, ' I thought Margarita[1] sung extremely well

---

[1] Francesca Margarita de l'Epine, a native of Tuscany. This celebrated singer performed in many of the earlier Italian operas represented in England. She and Mrs. Tofts were rivals for the

last night.' Upon this, says the lady, looking as pale as ashes, ' I suppose she had cherry-coloured ribands¹ on.' ' No,' answered the husband, with a flush in his face, ' but she had laced shoes.'² I look upon it, that a bystander on such occasions has as much reason to be out of countenance as either of the combatants. To turn off my confusion, and seem regardless of what had passed, I desired the servant who attended to give me the vinegar, which unluckily created a new dialogue of hints ; for as far as I could gather by the subsequent discourse, they had dissented the day before about the preference of elder

public favour, and it seems they divided pretty equally the applause of the town. She sung on the stage, at public entertainments, in concerts at York Buildings and Stationers' Hall, and once in the hall of the Middle Temple, in a musical performance at the Christmas revels of that society. One Greber, a German musician, who studied some few years in Italy, brought this Italian with him to England, whence she was known by the name of Greber's Peg. It is said that she had afterwards a criminal connection with Daniel Earl of Nottingham. In a shrewd epigram written by Lord Halifax, she is styled "The Tawny Tuscan," and he is called "Tall Nottingham." Margarita continued a singer till about the year 1718, when, having, as Downes relates, scraped together above ten thousand guineas, she retired, and was afterwards married to Dr. Pepusch. The epithet "tawny" was very characteristic of her, for she was remarkably swarthy, and in general so destitute of personal charms, that her husband seldom called her by any other name than Hecate, to which she answered very readily. She died about 1740. See Sir J. Hawkins's "History of Music," vol. v. p. 153 (Nichols).—The statement that she had an improper connection with the Earl of Nottingham appears to rest solely on statements in party poems of the time.

¹ Ladies wore "commodes" as head-dresses, sometimes backed by dark-coloured ribbons. The prevailing fashion about 1712 was cherry colour ; see *Spectator*, No. 271.

² In a song in D'Urfey's "Wit and Mirth"—"The Young Maid's Portion"—the lady speaks of her laced shoes of Spanish leather. Malcolm says that Spanish leather shoes laced with gold were common about this time (Planché's "Cyclopædia of Costume ").

to wine vinegar. In the midst of their discourse, there appeared a dish of chickens and asparagus, when the husband seemed disposed to lay aside all disputes ; and looking upon her with a great deal of good nature, said, 'Pray, my dear, will you help my friend to a wing of the fowl that lies next you, for I think it looks extremely well.' The lady, instead of answering him, addressing herself to me, 'Pray, sir,' said she, 'do you in Surrey reckon the white- or the black-legged fowls the best ? ' I found the husband changed colour at the question ; and before I could answer, asked me, whether we did not call hops ' broom ' in our country ? I quickly found, they did not ask questions so much out of curiosity as anger : for which reason I thought fit to keep my opinion to myself, and, as an honest man ought (when he sees two friends in warmth with each other), I took the first opportunity I could to leave them by themselves.

"You see, sir, I have laid before you only small incidents, which are seemingly trivial ; but take it from a man who am very well experienced in this state, they are principally evils of this nature which make marriages unhappy. At the same time, that I may do justice to this excellent institution, I must own to you, there are unspeakable pleasures which are as little regarded in the computation of the advantages of marriage, as the others are in the usual survey that is made of its misfortunes.

"Lovemore and his wife live together in the happy possession of each other's hearts, and by that means have no indifferent moments, but their whole life is one continued scene of delight. Their passion for each other communicates a certain satisfaction, like that which they themselves are in, to all that approach them. When she enters the place where he is, you see a pleasure which he cannot conceal, nor he or any one else describe. In so consummate

an affection, the very presence of the person beloved has the effect of the most agreeable conversation. Whether they have matter to talk of or not, they enjoy the pleasures of society, and at the same time the freedom of solitude. Their ordinary life is to be preferred to the happiest moments of other lovers. In a word, they have each of them great merit, live in the esteem of all who know them, and seem but to comply with the opinions of their friends, in the just value they have for each other."

No. 151.   [STEELE.[1]

From *Saturday, March* 25, to *Tuesday, March* 28, 1710.

—— Ni vis boni
In ipsa inesset forma, hæc formam extinguerent.
          TER., Phorm. I. ii. 58.

From my own Apartment, March 27.

When artists would expose their diamonds to an advantage, they usually set them to show in little cases of black velvet. By this means the jewels appear in their true and genuine lustre, while there is no colour that can infect their brightness, or give a false cast to the water. When I was at the opera the other night, the assembly of ladies in mourning[2] made me consider them in the same kind of view. A dress wherein there is so little variety, shows

---

[1] This paper, though not included in Addison's Works, may, as Nichols suggested, be his. Two slight corrections were made in the following number in the folio issue.

[2] See No. 8, with reference to the long-continued mourning, on the decease of the Queen's husband, George Prince of Denmark, who died in October 1708. Lewis Duke of Bourbon, eldest son to the Dauphin of France, died on March 3, about three weeks before the

the face in all its natural charms, and makes one differ
from another only as it is more or less beautiful. Painters
are ever careful of offending against a rule which is so
essential in all just representation. The chief figure must
have the strongest point of light, and not be injured by
any gay colourings that may draw away the attention to
any less considerable part of the picture. The present
fashion obliges everybody to be dressed with propriety,
and makes the ladies' faces the principal objects of sight.
Every beautiful person shines out in all the excellence with
which Nature has adorned her : gaudy ribands and glaring
colours being now out of use, the sex has no opportunity
given them to disfigure themselves, which they seldom fail
to do whenever it lies in their power. When a woman
comes to her glass, she does not employ her time in
making herself look more advantageously what she really
is, but endeavours to be as much another creature as she
possibly can. Whether this happens, because they stay so
long, and attend their work so diligently, that they forget
the faces and persons which they first sat down with, or
whatever it is, they seldom rise from the toilet the same
women they appeared when they began to dress. What
jewel can the charming Cleora place in her ears, that can
please her beholders so much as her eyes? The cluster of
diamonds upon the breast can add no beauty to the fair
chest of ivory which supports it. It may indeed tempt a
man to steal a woman, but never to love her. Let
Thalestris change herself into a motley parti-coloured
animal : the pearl necklace, the flowered stomacher, the

date of this paper. A month before, on February 2, 1709-10, in
consequence of a petition presented by the mercers, &c., complaining
of their sufferings from the length and frequency of public mourn-
ings, leave was given to bring in a Bill for ascertaining and limiting
the time of them.

artificial nosegay, and shaded furbelow,[1] may be of use to attract the eye of the beholder, and turn it from the imperfections of her features and shape. But if ladies will take my word for it (and as they dress to please men, they ought to consult our fancy rather than their own in this particular), I can assure them, there is nothing touches our imagination so much as a beautiful woman in a plain dress. There might be more agreeable ornaments found in our own manufacture, than any that rise out of the looms of Persia.

This, I know, is a very harsh doctrine to womankind, who are carried away with everything that is showy, and with what delights the eye, more than any other species of living creatures whatsoever. Were the minds of the sex laid open, we should find the chief idea in one to be a tippet, in another a muff, in a third a fan, and in a fourth a farthingale. The memory of an old visiting lady is so filled with gloves, silks, and ribands, that I can look upon it as nothing else but a toy-shop. A matron of my acquaintance complaining of her daughter's vanity, was observing, that she had all of a sudden held up her head higher than ordinary, and taken an air that showed a secret satisfaction in herself, mixed with a scorn of others. " I did not know," says my friend, " what to make of the carriage of this fantastical girl, until I was informed by her elder sister, that she had a pair of striped garters on." This odd turn of mind often makes the sex unhappy, and disposes them to be struck with everything that makes a show, however trifling and superficial.

Many a lady has fetched a sigh at the toss of a wig, and been ruined by the tapping of a snuff-box. It is impos-

---

[1] The furbelow was a puckered flounce ornamenting the dress. D'Urfey wrote a play, "The Old Mode and the New, or Country Miss with her Furbelow,"

sible to describe all the execution that was done by the shoulder-knot[1] while that fashion prevailed, or to reckon up all the virgins that have fallen a sacrifice to a pair of fringed gloves.[2] A sincere heart has not made half so many conquests as an open waistcoat,[3] and I should be glad to see an able head make so good a figure in a woman's company as a pair of red heels.[4] A Grecian hero,[5] when he was asked whether he could play upon the lute, thought he had made a very good reply when he answered, "No, but I can make a great city of a little one." Notwithstanding his boasted wisdom, I appeal to the heart of any toast in town, whether she would not think the lutenist preferable to the statesman. I do not speak this out of any aversion that I have to the sex : on the contrary, I have always had a tenderness for them ; but I must confess, it troubles me very much to see the generality of them place their affections on improper objects, and give up all the pleasures of life for gewgaws and trifles.

Mrs. Margery Bickerstaff, my great aunt, had a thousand pounds to her portion, which our family was desirous of keeping among themselves, and therefore used all possible means to turn off her thoughts from marriage. The method they took was, in any time of danger to throw a new gown or petticoat in her way. When she was about twenty-five years of age, she fell in love with a man of an agreeable temper, and equal fortune, and would certainly have married him, had not my grandfather, Sir Jacob, dressed her up in a suit of flowered satin ; upon which, she set so immoderate a value upon herself, that the lover was contemned and discarded. In the

[1] Introduced from France at the Restoration.
[2] Gloves with silver fringe round the wrists. A Fringe-Glove Club is mentioned in No. 30 of the *Spectator*.
[3] See No. 95.   [4] See No. 45.   [5] Themistocles.

fortieth year of her age, she was again smitten, but very luckily transferred her passion to a tippet, which was presented to her by another relation who was in the plot. This, with a white sarcenet hood, kept her safe in the family till fifty.   About sixty, which generally produces a kind of latter spring[1] in amorous constitutions, my Aunt Margery had again a colt's-tooth[2] in her head, and would certainly have eloped from the mansion-house, had not her brother Simon, who was a wise man, and a scholar, advised to dress her in cherry-coloured ribands,[3] which was the only expedient that could have been found out by the wit of man to preserve the thousand pounds in our family, part of which I enjoy at this time.

This discourse puts me in mind of a humorist mentioned by Horace,[4] called Eutrapelus, who, when he designed to do a man a mischief, made him a present of a gay suit ; and brings to my memory another passage of the same author, when he describes the most ornamental dress that a woman can appear in with two words, *simplex munditiis*,[5] which I have quoted for the benefit of my female readers.

[1] Cf. " 1 Henry IV." act i. sc. 2, where Prince Hal says to Falstaff, " Farewell, thou latter spring ! "

[2] A love of youthful pleasure.   Cf. " Henry VIII." act i. sc. 3,
" Well said, Lord Sands,
Your colt's tooth is not cast yet."

[3] See No. 150.   [4] 1 Epist. xviii. 31.   [5] 1 Od. v. 5.

No. 152.　　　　　　　　　　　[ADDISON.

From *Tuesday, March* 28, to *Thursday, March* 30, 1710.

Di, quibus imperium est animarum, Umbræque silentes,
Et Chaos, et Phlegethon, loca nocte silentia late,
Sit mihi fas audita loqui ; sit numine vestro
Pandere resalta terra et caligine mersas.

　　　　　　　　　　　　　VIRG., Æn. vi. 264.

From my own Apartment, March 29.

A man who confines his speculations to the time present, has but a very narrow province to employ his
thoughts in. For this reason, persons of studious and
contemplative natures often entertain themselves with the
history of past ages, or raise schemes and conjectures upon
futurity. For my own part, I love to range through that
half of eternity which is still to come, rather than look
on that which is already run out ; because I know I have
a real share and interest in the one, whereas all that was
transacted in the other can be only matter of curiosity to
me.

Upon this account, I have been always very much
delighted with meditating on the soul's immortality, and
in reading the several notions which the wisest of men,
both ancient and modern, have entertained on that subject.
What the opinions of the greatest philosophers have been,
I have several times hinted at, and shall give an account
of them from time to time as occasion requires. It may
likewise be worth while to consider, what men of the
most exalted genius, and elevated imagination, have
thought of this matter. Among these, Homer stands up
as a prodigy of mankind, that looks down upon the rest
of human creatures as a species beneath him. Since he

is the most ancient heathen author, we may guess from his relation, what were the common opinions in his time concerning the state of the soul after death.

Ulysses, he tells us, made a voyage to the regions of the dead, in order to consult Tiresias how he should return to his own country, and recommend himself to the favour of the gods. The poet scarce introduces a single person, who does not suggest some useful precept to his reader, and designs his description of the dead for the amendment of the living.

Ulysses, after having made a very plenteous sacrifice, sat him down by the pool of holy blood, which attracted a prodigious assembly of ghosts of all ages and conditions, that hovered about the hero, and feasted upon the steams of his oblation. The first he knew, was the shade of Elpenor, who, to show the activity of a spirit above that of body, is represented as arrived there long before Ulysses, notwithstanding the winds and seas had contributed all their force to hasten his voyage thither. This Elpenor, to inspire the reader with a detestation of drunkenness, and at the same time with a religious care of doing proper honours to the dead, describes himself as having broken his neck in a debauch of wine ; and begs Ulysses, that for the repose of his soul, he would build a monument over him, and perform funeral rites to his memory. Ulysses with great sorrow of heart promises to fulfil his request, and is immediately diverted to an object much more moving than the former. The ghost of his own mother Anticlea, whom he still thought living, appears to him among the multitude of shades that surrounded him, and sits down at a small distance from him by the lake of blood, without speaking to him, or knowing who he was. Ulysses was exceedingly troubled at the sight, and could not forbear weeping as he looked upon her ;

but being all along set forth as a pattern of consummate wisdom, he makes his affection give way to prudence; and therefore, upon his seeing Tiresias, does not reveal himself to his mother, till he had consulted that great prophet, who was the occasion of this his descent into the empire of the dead. Tiresias having cautioned him to keep himself and his companions free from the guilt of sacrilege, and to pay his devotions to all the gods, promises him a safe return to his kingdom and family, and a happy old age in the enjoyment of them.

The poet having thus with great art kept the curiosity of his reader in suspense, represents his wise man, after the despatch of his business with Tiresias, as yielding himself up to the calls of natural affection, and making himself known to his mother. Her eyes are no sooner opened, but she cries out in tears, "Oh my son!" and inquires into the occasions that brought him thither, and the fortune that attended him.

Ulysses on the other hand desires to know, what the sickness was that had sent her into those regions, and the condition in which she had left his father, his son, and more particularly his wife. She tells him, they were all three inconsolable for his absence; "and as for myself," says she, "that was the sickness of which I died. My impatience for your return, my anxiety for your welfare, and my fondness for my dear Ulysses, were the only distempers that preyed upon my life, and separated my soul from my body." Ulysses was melted with these expressions of tenderness, and thrice endeavoured to catch the apparition in his arms, that he might hold his mother to his bosom and weep over her.

This gives the poet occasion to describe the notion the heathens at that time had of an unbodied soul, in the excuse which the mother makes for seeming to withdraw herself from her son's embraces. " The soul," says she, " is composed neither of bones, flesh, nor sinews, but leaves behind her all those encumbrances of mortality to be consumed on the funeral pile. As soon as she has thus cast her burden she makes her escape, and flies away from it like a dream."

When this melancholy conversation is at an end, the poet draws up to view as charming a vision as could enter into man's imagination. He describes the next who appeared to Ulysses, to have been the shades of the finest women that had ever lived upon the earth, and who had either been the daughters of kings, the mistresses of gods, or mothers of heroes, such as Antiope, Alcmena, Leda, Ariadne, Iphimedia, Eriphyle, and several others of whom he gives a catalogue, with a short history of their adventures. The beautiful assembly of apparitions were all gathered together about the blood : " each of them," says Ulysses (as a gentle satire upon female vanity), " giving me an account of her birth and family." This scene of extraordinary women seems to have been designed by the poet as a lecture of mortality to the whole sex, and to put them in mind of what they must expect, notwithstanding the greatest perfections, and highest honours, they can arrive at.

The circle of beauties at length disappeared, and was succeeded by the shades of several Grecian heroes who had been engaged with Ulysses in the siege of Troy. The first that approached was Agamemnon, the generalissimo of that great expedition, who at the appearance of his old friend wept very bitterly, and without saying anything to him, endeavoured to grasp him by the hand. Ulysses, who was much moved at the sight, poured out a flood of tears, and asked him the occasion of his death, which Agamemnon related to him in all its tragical circumstances ;

how he was murdered at a banquet by the contrivance of his own wife, in confederacy with her adulterer : from whence he takes occasion to reproach the whole sex, after a manner which would be inexcusable in a man who had not been so great a sufferer by them. "My wife," says he, "has disgraced all the women that shall ever be born into the world, even those who hereafter shall be innocent. Take care how you grow too fond of your wife. Never tell her all you know. If you reveal some things to her, be sure you keep others concealed from her. You indeed have nothing to fear from your Penelope, she will not use you as my wife has treated me ; however, take care how you trust a woman." The poet, in this and other instances, according to the system of many heathen as well as Christian philosophers, shows how anger, revenge, and other habits which the soul had contracted in the body, subsist and grow in it under its stage of separation.

I am extremely pleased with the companions which the poet in the next description assigns to Achilles. "Achilles, says the hero, "came up to me with Patroclus and Antilochus." By which we may see that it was Homer's opinion, and probably that of the age he lived in, that the friendships which are made among the living will likewise continue among the dead. Achilles inquires after the welfare of his son, and of his father, with a fierceness of the same character that Homer has everywhere expressed in the actions of his life. The passage relating to his son is so extremely beautiful, that I must not omit it. Ulysses, after having described him as wise in council and active in war, and mentioned the foes whom he had slain in battle, adds an observation that he himself had made of his behaviour whilst he lay in the wooden horse. "Most of the generals," says he, "that were with us either wept or trembled : as for your son, I neither saw him wipe a tear from his cheeks, nor change his countenance. On the contrary, he would often lay his hand upon his sword, or grasp his spear, as impatient to employ them against the Trojans." He then informs his father of the great honour and rewards which he had purchased before Troy, and of his return from it without a wound. The shade of Achilles, says the poet, was so pleased with the account he received of his son, that he inquired no further, but stalked away with more than ordinary majesty over the green meadow that lay before them.

This last circumstance of a deceased father's rejoicing in the behaviour of his son is very finely contrived by Homer, as an incentive to virtue, and made use of by none that I know besides himself.

The description of Ajax, which follows, and his refusing to speak to Ulysses, who had won the armour of Achilles from him, and by that means occasioned his death, is admired by every one that reads it. When Ulysses relates the sullenness of his deportment, and considers the greatness of the hero, he expresses himself with generous and noble sentiments. "Oh! that I had never gained a prize which cost the life of so brave a man as Ajax! Who, for the beauty of his person, and greatness of his actions, was inferior to none but the divine Achilles." The same noble condescension, which never dwells but in truly great minds, and such as Homer would represent that of Ulysses to have been, discovers itself likewise in the speech which he made to the ghost of Ajax on that occasion. "O Ajax!" says he, "will you keep your resentments even after death? What destructions hath this fatal armour brought upon the Greeks, by robbing them of you, who were their bulwark and defence? Achilles is not more bitterly lamented among us than you. Impute not then your death to any one but Jupiter, who out of his anger to the Greeks, took you away from among them : let me entreat you to approach me ; restrain the fierceness of your wrath, and the greatness of your soul, and hear what I have to say to you." Ajax, without making a reply, turned his back upon him, and retired into a crowd of ghosts.

Ulysses, after all these visions, took a view of those impious wretches who lay in tortures for the crimes they had committed upon the earth, whom he describes under the varieties of pain, as so many marks of divine vengeance, to deter others from following their example. He then tells us that notwithstanding he had a great curiosity to see the heroes that lived in the ages before him, the ghosts began to gather about him in such prodigious multitudes, and with such a confusion of voices, that his heart trembled as he saw himself amidst so great a scene of horrors. He adds, that he was afraid lest some hideous spectre should appear to him, that might terrify him to distraction ; and therefore withdrew in time.

I question not but my reader will be pleased with this description of a future state, represented by such a noble and fruitful imagination, that had nothing to direct it besides the light of nature, and the opinions of a dark and ignorant age.

No. 153. [ADDISON.

From *Thursday*, *March* 30, to *Saturday*, *April* 1, 1710.

Bambalio, clangor, stridor, taratantara, murmur.—FARN., Rhet.

From my own Apartment, March 31.

I have heard of a very valuable picture, wherein all the painters of the age in which it was drawn are represented sitting together in a circle, and joining in a concert of music. Each of them plays upon such a particular instrument as is the most suitable to his character, and expresses that style and manner of painting which is peculiar to him. The famous cupola-painter of those times, to show the grandeur and boldness of his figures, has a horn in his mouth, which he seems to wind with great strength and force. On the contrary, an eminent artist, who wrought up his pictures with the greatest accuracy, and gave them all those delicate touches which are apt to please the nicest eye, is represented as tuning a theorbo. The same kind of humour runs through the whole piece.

I have often from this hint imagined to myself, that different talents in discourse might be shadowed out after the same manner by different kinds of music ; and that the several conversable parts of mankind in this great city might be cast into proper characters and divisions, as they resemble several instruments that are in use among the masters of harmony. Of these therefore in their order, and first of the drum.

Your drums are the blusterers in conversation, that with a loud laugh, unnatural mirth, and a torrent of noise, domineer in public assemblies, overbear men of sense, stun their companions, and fill the place they are in with a rattling sound, that has seldom any wit, humour, or good breeding in it. The drum notwithstanding, by this boisterous vivacity, is very proper to impose upon the ignorant ; and in conversation with ladies who are not of the finest taste, often passes for a man of mirth and wit, and for wonderful pleasant company. I need not observe, that the emptiness of the drum very much contributes to its noise.

The lute is a character directly opposite to the drum, that sounds very finely by itself, or in a very small concert.

Its notes are exquisitely sweet, and very low, easily drowned
in a multitude of instruments, and even lost among a few,
unless you give a particular attention to it. A lute is seldom
heard in a company of more than five, whereas a drum will
show itself to advantage in an assembly of five hundred.
The lutenists therefore are men of a fine genius, uncommon reflection, great affability, and esteemed chiefly by
persons of a good taste, who are the only proper judges of
so delightful and soft a melody.

The trumpet is an instrument that has in it no compass
of music or variety of sound, but is notwithstanding very
agreeable, so long as it keeps within its pitch. It has not
above four or five notes, which are however very pleasing,
and capable of exquisite turns and modulations. The
gentlemen who fall under this denomination, are your men
of the most fashionable education and refined breeding,
who have learned a certain smoothness of discourse, and
sprightliness of air, from the polite company they have
kept ; but at the same time they have shallow parts, weak
judgments, and a short reach of understanding : a playhouse, a drawing-room, a ball, a visiting-day, or a Ring at
Hyde Park, are the few notes they are masters of, which
they touch upon in all conversations. The trumpet however is a necessary instrument about a Court, and a proper
enlivener of a concert, though of no great harmony by
itself.

Violins are the lively, forward, importunate wits that
distinguish themselves by the flourishes of imagination,
sharpness of repartee, glances of satire, and bear away the
upper part in every concert. I cannot however but observe
that, when a man is not disposed to hear music, there is
not a more disagreeable sound in harmony than that of a
violin.

There is another musical instrument, which is more

frequent in this nation than any other ; I mean your bass-viol, which grumbles in the bottom of the concert, and with a surly masculine sound strengthens the harmony, and tempers the sweetness of the several instruments that play along with it. The bass-viol is an instrument of a quite different nature to the trumpet, and may signify men of rough sense, and unpolished parts, who do not love to hear themselves talk, but sometimes break out with an agreeable bluntness, unexpected wit, and surly pleasantries, to the no small diversion of their friends and companions. In short, I look upon every sensible true-born Briton to be naturally a bass-viol.

As for your rural wits, who talk with great eloquence and alacrity of foxes, hounds, horses, quickset hedges, and six-bar gates, double ditches, and broken necks, I am in doubt, whether I should give them a place in the conversable world. However, if they will content themselves with being raised to the dignity of hunting-horns, I snall desire for the future that they may be known by that name.

I must not here omit the bagpipe species, that will entertain you from morning to night with the repetition of the few notes, which are played over and over, with the perpetual humming of a drone running underneath them. These are your dull, heavy, tedious storytellers, the load and burden of conversations, that set up for men of importance, by knowing secret history, and giving an account of transactions, that whether they ever passed in the world or not, does not signify a halfpenny to its instruction, or its welfare. Some have observed, that the northern parts of this island are more particularly fruitful in bagpipes.

There are so very few persons who are masters in every kind of conversation, and can talk on all subjects, that I don't know whether we should make a distinct species of them : nevertheless, that my scheme may not be defective, for the sake of those few who are endowed with such extra-ordinary talents, I shall allow them to be harpsichords, a kind of music which every one knows is a concert by itself.

As for your passing-bells, who look upon mirth as criminal, and talk of nothing but what is melancholy in itself, and mortifying to human nature, I shall not mention them.

I shall likewise pass over in silence all the rabble of man-kind that crowd our streets, coffee-houses, feasts, and public tables. I cannot call their discourse conversation, but rather something that is practised in imitation of it. For which reason, if I would describe them by any musical instru-ment, it should be by those modern inventions of the bladder and string, tongs and key, marrow-bone and cleaver.

My reader will doubtless observe, that I have only touched here upon male instruments, having reserved my female concert to another occasion. If he has a mind to know where these several characters are to be met with, I could direct him to a whole club of drums ; not to mention another of bagpipes, which I have before given some account of in my description of our nightly meetings in Sheer Lane. The lutes may often be met with in couples upon the banks of a crystal stream, or in the retreats of shady woods and flowery meadows ; which for different reasons are likewise the great resort of your hunting-horns. Bass-viols are frequently to be found over a glass of stale beer and a pipe of tobacco ; whereas those who set up for violins, seldom fail to make their appearance at Will's once every evening. You may meet with a trumpet anywhere on the other side of Charing Cross.

was likewise a very proper residence for everything that resembles death, the poet tells us, that Sleep, whom he represents as a near relation to Death, has likewise his habitation in these quarters, and describes in them a huge gloomy elm-tree, which seems a very proper ornament for the place, and is possessed by an innumerable swarm of Dreams, that hang in clusters under every leaf of it. He then gives us a list of imaginary persons, who very naturally lie within the shadow of the dream-tree, as being of the same kind of make in themselves, and the materials or (to use Shakespeare's phrase) the stuff of which dreams are made. Such are the shades of the giant with a hundred hands, and of his brother with three bodies ; of the double-shaped Centaur and Scylla ; the Gorgon with snaky hair ; the Harpy with a woman's face and lion's talons ; the seven-headed Hydra ; and the Chimæra, which breathes forth a flame, and is a compound of three animals. These several mixed natures, the creatures of imagination, are not only introduced with great art after the dreams ; but as they are planted at the very entrance, and within the very gates of those regions, do probably denote the wild deliriums and extravagances of fancy, which the Soul usually falls into when she is just upon the verge of death.

Thus far Æneas travels in an allegory. The rest of the description is drawn with great exactness, according to the religion of the heathens, and the opinions of the platonic philosophy. I shall not trouble my reader with a common dull story, that gives an account why the heathens first of all supposed a ferryman in hell, and his name to be Charon ; but must not pass over in silence the point of doctrine which Virgil has very much insisted upon in this book, that the souls of those who are un-buried, are not permitted to go over into their respective places of rest till they have wandered a hundred years

upon the banks of Styx. This was probably an invention
of the heathen priesthood, to make the people extremely
careful of performing proper rites and ceremonies to the
memory of the dead. I shall not, however, with the
infamous scribblers of the age, take an occasion from such
a circumstance, to run into declamations against priestcraft, but rather look upon it even in this light as a
religious artifice, to raise in the minds of men an esteem
for the memory of their forefathers, and a desire to
recommend themselves to that of posterity; as also to
excite in them an ambition of imitating the virtues of the
deceased, and to keep alive in their thoughts the sense
of the soul's immortality. In a word, we may say in
defence of the severe opinions relating to the shades of
unburied persons, what has been said by some of our
divines in regard to the rigid doctrines concerning the
souls of such who die without being initiated into our
religion, that supposing they should be erroneous, they
can do no hurt to the dead, and will have a good effect
upon the living, in making them cautious of neglecting
such necessary solemnities.

Charon is no sooner appeased, and the triple-headed dog
laid asleep, but Æneas makes his entrance into the dominions of Pluto. There are three kinds of persons
described as being situated on the borders ; and I can give
no reason for their being stationed there in so particular a
manner, but because none of them seem to have had a
proper right to a place among the dead, as not having
run out the whole thread of their days, and finished
the term of life that had been allotted them upon earth.
The first of these are the souls of infants, who are snatched
away by untimely ends : the second, are of those who are
put to death wrongfully, and by an unjust sentence ; and
the third, of those who grew weary of their lives, and laid

violent hands upon themselves. As for the second of
these, Virgil adds with great beauty, that Minos, the judge
of the dead, is employed in giving them a rehearing, and
assigning them their several quarters suitable to the parts
they acted in life. The poet, after having mentioned the
souls of those unhappy men who destroyed themselves,
breaks out into a fine exclamation: "Oh, how gladly,"
says he, "would they now endure life with all its miseries !
But the Destinies forbid their return to earth, and the
waters of Styx surround them with nine streams that
are unpassable." It is very remarkable, that Virgil,
notwithstanding self-murder was so frequent among
the heathens, and had been practised by some of the
greatest men in the very age before him, has here represented it as so heinous a crime. But in this particular
he was guided by the doctrines of his great master Plato,
who says on this subject, that a man is placed in his
station of life like a soldier in his proper post, which he
is not to quit whatever may happen, until he is called
off by his commander who planted him in it.

There is another point in the platonic philosophy,
which Virgil has made the groundwork of the greatest
part in the piece we are now examining, having with
wonderful art and beauty materialised, if I may so call
it, a scheme of abstracted notions, and clothed the most
nice refined conceptions of philosophy in sensible images
and poetical representations. The Platonists tell us, that
the Soul, during her residence in the body, contracts many
virtuous and vicious habits, so as to become a beneficent,
mild, charitable, or an angry, malicious, revengeful being :
a substance inflamed with lust, avarice, and pride ; or, on
the contrary, brightened with pure, generous, and humble
dispositions : that these and the like habits of virtue
and vice growing into the very essence of the Soul,

survive and gather strength in her after her dissolution :
that the torments of a vicious soul in a future state arise
principally from those importunate passions which are
not capable of being gratified without a body ; and that
on the contrary, the happiness of virtuous minds very
much consists in their being employed in sublime specu-
ations, innocent diversions, sociable affections, and all
he ecstasies of passion and rapture which are agreeable
to reasonable natures, and of which they gained a relish
in this life.

Upon this foundation, the poet raises that beautiful
description of the secret haunts and walks which he tells
is are inhabited by deceased lovers.

" Not far from hence," says he, " lies a great waste of
plains, that are called, the ' fields of melancholy.'   In these
grows a forest of myrtle, divided into many shady retirements and covered walks, and inhabited by the souls of
those who pined away with love.   The passion," says he,
' continues with them after death."   He then gives a list
of this languishing tribe, in which his own Dido makes
the principal figure, and is described as living in this soft
romantic scene with the shade of her first husband
Sichæus.[1]

The poet in the next place mentions another plain that
was peopled with the ghosts of warriors, as still delighting
in each other's company, and pleased with the exercise
of arms.   He there represents the Grecian generals and
common soldiers who perished in the siege of Troy as
drawn up in squadrons, and terrified at the approach of
Æneas, which renewed in them those impressions of fear
they had before received in battle with the Trojans.   He
afterwards likewise, upon the same notion, gives a view
of the Trojan heroes who lived in former ages, amidst a

[1] See No. 133.

visionary scene of chariots and arms, flowery meadows, shining spears, and generous steeds, which he tells us were their pleasures upon earth, and now make up their happiness in Elysium. For the same reason also, he mentions others as singing pæans, and songs of triumph, amidst a beautiful grove of laurel. The chief of the concert was the poet Musæus, who stood enclosed with a circle of admirers, and rose by the head and shoulders above the throng of shades that surrounded him. The habitations of unhappy spirits, to show the duration of their torments, and the desperate condition they are in, are represented as guarded by a fury, moated round with a lake of fire, strengthened with towers of iron, encompassed with a triple wall, and fortified with pillars of adamant, which all the gods together are not able to heave from their foundations. The noise of stripes, the clank of chains, and the groans of the tortured, strike the pious Æneas with a kind of horror. The poet afterwards divides the criminals into two classes : the first and blackest catalogue consists of such as were guilty of outrages against the gods ; and the next, of such who were convicted of injustice between man and man : the greatest number of whom, says the poet, are those who followed the dictates of avarice.

It was an opinion of the Platonists, that the souls of men having contracted in the body great stains and pollutions of vice and ignorance, there were several purgations and cleansings necessary to be passed through both here and hereafter, in order to refine and purify them.[1]

Virgil, to give this thought likewise a clothing of poetry, describes some spirits as bleaching in the winds, others as cleansing under great falls of waters, and others as purging in fire to recover the primitive beauty and purity of their natures.

[1] " Purify the soul from ignorance and vice " (folio).

It was likewise an opinion of the same sect of philosophers, that the souls of all men exist in a separate state,
long before their union with their bodies ; and that upon
their immersion into flesh, they forget everything which
passed in the state of pre-existence ; so that what we here
call knowledge, is nothing else but memory, or the recovery
of those things which we knew before.

In pursuance of this scheme, Virgil gives us a view of
several souls, who, to prepare themselves for living upon
earth, flock about the banks of the river Lethe, and swill
themselves with the waters of oblivion.

The same scheme gives him an opportunity of making
a noble compliment to his countrymen, where Anchises is
represented taking a survey of the long train of heroes
that are to descend from him, and giving his son Æneas an
account of all the glories of his race.

I need not mention the revolution of the platonic year,[1]
which is but just touched upon in this book ; and as I
have consulted no author's thoughts in this explication,
shall be very well pleased, if it can make the noblest piece
of the most accomplished poet more agreeable to my
female readers, when they think fit to look into Dryden's
translation of it.

[1] The Great or Platonic Year is the time in which the fixed stars
make their revolution.   See Cicero, " De Natura Deorum," ii. 20.

No. 155.   ° [ADDISON.

From *Tuesday, April 4,* to *Thursday, April 6,* 1710.

—— Aliena negotia curat,
Excussus propriis.—HOR., 2 Sat. iii. 19.

From my own Apartment, April 5.

There lived some years since within my neighbourhood a very grave person, an upholsterer,[1] who seemed a man of more than ordinary application to business. He was a very early riser, and was often abroad two or three hours before any of his neighbours. He had a particular carefulness in the knitting of his brows, and a kind of impatience in all his motions, that plainly discovered he was always intent on matters of importance. Upon my inquiry into his life and conversation, I found him to be the greatest newsmonger in our quarter ; that he rose before day to read the *Postman ;* and that he would take two or three turns to the other end of the town before his neighbours were up, to see if there were any Dutch mails come in. He had a wife and several children ; but was much more inquisitive to know what passed in Poland than in his own family, and was in greater pain and anxiety of mind for King Augustus' welfare than that of his nearest relations. He looked extremely thin in a dearth of news, and never enjoyed himself in a westerly wind. This indefatigable kind of life was the ruin of his shop ; for

[1] The original of the Political Upholsterer of Nos. 155; 160 and 178 is said to have been an Edward Arne, of Covent Garden. It is clear that he cannot—as some have said—be the same person as the Arne at whose house the Indian kings lodged (see No. 171). Steele was attacked in the *Examiner* (vol. i. No. 11, vol. iv. No. 40) for the liberties here taken by Addison.

218

about the time that his favourite prince left the crown of
Poland, he broke and disappeared.

·This man and his affairs had been long out of my mind,
till about three days ago, as I was walking in St. James's
Park, I heard somebody at a distance hemming after me :
and who should it be but my old neighbour the upholsterer ! I saw he was reduced to extreme poverty, by
certain shabby superfluities in his dress : for notwithstanding that it was a very sultry day for the time of the
year, he wore a loose great-coat and a muff, with a long
campaign-wig out of curl ; to which he had added the
ornament of a pair of black garters buckled under the
knee. Upon his coming up to me, I was going to
inquire into his present circumstances ; but was prevented
by his asking me, with a whisper, whether the last letters
brought any accounts that one might rely upon from
Bender ? I told him, none that I heard of ; and asked
him, whether he had yet married his eldest daughter ?
He told me, No. "But pray," says he, "tell me sincerely,
what are your thoughts of the King of Sweden ?" For
though his wife and children were starving, I found his
chief concern at present was for this great monarch. I
told him, that I looked upon him as one of the first heroes
of the age. "But pray," says he, "do you think there is
anything in the story of his wound ?" And finding me
surprised at the question, "Nay," says he, "I only propose
it to you." I answered, that I thought there was no
reason to doubt of it. "But why in the heel," says he,
"more than in any other part of the body ?" "Because,"
says I, "the bullet chanced to light there."

This extraordinary dialogue was no sooner ended, but
he began to launch out into a long dissertation upon the
affairs of the North ; and after having spent some time on
them, he told me, he was in a great perplexity how to

reconcile the *Supplement* with the *English Post*, and had been just now examining what the other papers say upon the same subject. "The *Daily Courant*," says he, "has' these words, 'We have advices from very good hands, that a certain prince has some matters of great importance under consideration.' This is very mysterious; but the *Postboy* leaves us more in the dark, for he tells us, that there are private intimations of measures taken by a certain prince, which time will bring to light. Now the *Postman*," says he, "who used to be very clear, refers to the same news in these words : 'The late conduct of a certain prince affords great matter of speculation.' This certain prince," says the upholsterer, "whom they are all so cautious of naming, I take to be" ———. Upon which, though there was nobody near us, he whispered something in my ear, which I did not hear, or think worth my while to make him repeat.

We were now got to the upper end of the Mall, where were three or four very odd fellows sitting together upon the bench. These I found were all of them politicians, who used to sun themselves in that place every day about dinner-time. Observing them to be curiosities in their kind, and my friend's acquaintance, I sat down among them.

The chief politician of the bench was a great asserter of paradoxes. He told us, with a seeming concern, that by some news he had lately read from Muscovy, it appeared to him that there was a storm gathering in the Black Sea, which might in time do hurt to the naval forces of this nation. To this he added, that for his part, he could not wish to see the Turk driven out of Europe, which he believed could not but be prejudicial to our woollen manufacture. He then told us, that he looked upon those extraordinary revolutions which had lately happened in these parts of the world, to have risen chiefly from two persons who were not much talked of; "and those," says he, "are Prince Menzikoff and the Duchess of Mirandola." He backed his assertions with so many broken hints, and such a show of depth and wisdom, that we gave ourselves up to his opinions.

The discourse at length fell upon a point which seldom escapes a knot of true-born Englishmen, whether in case of a religious war, the Protestants would not be too strong for the Papists? This we unanimously determined on the Protestant side. One who sat on my right hand, and, as I found by his discourse, had been in the West Indies, assured us, that it would be a very easy matter for the Protestants to beat the Pope at sea ; and added, that whenever such a war does break out, it must turn to the good of the Leeward Islands. Upon this, one who sat at the end of the bench, and, as I afterwards found, was the geographer of the company, said, that in case the Papists should drive the Protestants from these parts of Europe, when the worst came to the worst, it would be impossible to beat them out of Norway and Greenland, provided the Northern crowns hold together, and the Czar of Muscovy stand neuter.

He further told us for our comfort, that there were vast tracts of land about the Pole, inhabited neither by Protestants nor Papists, and of greater extent than all the Roman Catholic dominions in Europe.

When we had fully discussed this point, my friend the upholsterer began to exert himself upon the present negotiations of peace, in which he deposed princes, settled the bounds of kingdoms, and balanced the power of Europe, with great justice and impartiality.

I at length took my leave of the company, and was going away ; but had not been gone thirty yards, before the upholsterer hemmed again after me. Upon his advancing towards me, with a whisper, I expected to hear some secret piece of news which he had not thought fit to communicate to the bench; but instead of that, he desired me in my ear to lend him half a crown. In compassion to so needy a statesman, and to dissipate the confusion I found he was in, I told him, if he pleased, I would give him five shillings, to receive five pounds of him when the Great Turk was driven out of Constantinople; which he very readily accepted, but not before he had laid down to me the impossibility of such an event, as the affairs of Europe now stand.

This paper I design for the particular benefit of those worthy citizens who live more in a coffee-house than in their shops, and whose thoughts are so taken up with the affairs of the Allies, that they forget their customers.

No. 156.   [ADDISON.

From *Thursday, April 6*, to *Saturday, April 8*, 1710.

—— Sequiturque patrem non passibus æquis.
VIRG., Æn. ii. 724.

From my own Apartment, April 7.

We have already described out of Homer the voyage of Ulysses to the Infernal Shades, with the several adventures that attended it.[1] If we look into the beautiful romance published not many years since by the Archbishop of Cambray,[2] we may see the son of Ulysses bound on the same expedition, and after the same manner making his discoveries among the regions of the dead. The story of Telemachus is formed altogether in the spirit of Homer,

[1] See No. 152.   [2] Fénelon's "Télémaque."

and will give an unlearned reader a notion of that great poet's manner of writing, more than any translation of him can possibly do. As it was written for the instruction of a young prince, who may one day sit upon the throne of France, the author took care to suit the several parts of his story, and particularly the description we are now entering upon, to the character and quality of his pupil. For which reason, he insists very much on the misery of bad, and the happiness of good kings, in the account he has given of punishments and rewards in the other world.

We may however observe, notwithstanding the endeavours of this great and learned author to copy after the style and sentiments of Homer, that there is a certain tincture of Christianity running through the whole relation. The prelate in several places mixes himself with the poet ; so that his future state puts me in mind of Michael Angelo's " Last Judgment," where Charon and his boat are represented as bearing a part in the dreadful solemnities of that great day.

Telemachus, after having passed through the dark avenues of death in the retinue of Mercury, who every day delivers up a certain tale of ghosts to the ferryman of Styx, is admitted into the infernal bark. Among the companions of his voyage, is the shade of Nabopharzon, a king of Babylon, and tyrant of all the East. Among the ceremonies and pomps of his funeral, there were four slaves sacrificed, according to the custom of the country, in order to attend him among the shades. The author having described this tyrant in the most odious colours of pride, insolence, and cruelty, tells us, that his four slaves, instead of serving him after death, were perpetually insulting him with reproaches and affronts for his past usage ; that they spurned him as he lay upon the ground, and forced him to show his face, which he would fain have covered, as lying under all the confusions of guilt and infamy ; and in short, that they kept him bound in a chain, in order to drag him before the tribunal of the dead.

Telemachus, upon looking out of the bark, sees all the strand covered with an innumerable multitude of shades, who, upon his jumping ashore, immediately vanished. He then pursues his course to the palace of Pluto, who is described as seated on his throne in terrible majesty, with Proserpine by his side. At the foot of his throne was the pale hideous spectre, who, by the ghastliness of his visage, and the nature of the apparitions that surrounded him, discovers himself to be Death. His attendants are, Melancholy, Distrust, Revenge, Hatred, Avarice, Despair, Ambition, Envy, Impiety, with frightful Dreams, and waking Cares, which are all drawn very naturally in proper actions and postures. The author, with great beauty, places near his Frightful Dreams an assembly of phantoms, which are often employed to terrify the living, by appearing in the shape and likeness of the dead.

The young hero in the next place takes a survey of the different kinds of criminals that lay in torture among clouds of sulphur and torrents of fire. The first of these were such as had been guilty of impieties, which every one has a horror for : to which is added, a catalogue of such offenders that scarce appear to be faulty in the eyes of the vulgar. Among these, says the author, are malicious critics, that have endeavoured to cast a blemish upon the perfections of others ; with whom he likewise places such as have often hurt the reputation of the innocent, by passing a rash judgment on their actions, without knowing the occasion of them.

These crimes, says he, are more severely punished after death, because they generally meet with impunity upon earth.

Telemachus, after having taken a survey of several other wretches in the same circumstances, arrives at that region of torments in which wicked kings are punished. There are very fine strokes of imagination in the description which he gives of this unhappy multitude. He tells us, that on one side of them there stood a revengeful fury, thundering in their ears incessant repetitions of all the crimes they had committed upon earth, with the aggravations of ambition, vanity, hardness of heart, and all those secret affections of mind that enter into the composition of a tyrant. At the same time, she holds up to them a large mirror, in which every one sees himself represented in the natural horror and deformity of his character. On the other side of them stands another fury, that with an insulting derision repeats to them all the praises that their flatterers had bestowed upon them while they sat upon their respective thrones. She too, says the author, presents a mirror before their eyes, in which every one sees himself adorned with all those beauties and perfections in which they had been drawn by the vanity of their own hearts, and the flattery of others. To punish them for the wantonness of the cruelty which they formerly exercised, they are now delivered up to be treated according to the fancy and caprice of several slaves, who have here an opportunity of tyrannising in their turns.

The author having given us a description of these ghastly spectres, who, says he, are always calling upon Death, and are placed under the distillation of that burning vengeance which falls upon them drop by drop, and is never to be exhausted, leads us into a pleasing scene of groves, filled with the melody of birds, and the odours of a thousand different plants. These groves are represented as rising among a great many flowery meadows, and watered with streams that diffuse a perpetual freshness, in the midst of an eternal day, and a never-fading spring. This, says the author, was the habitation of those good princes who were friends of the gods, and parents of the people. Among these, Telemachus converses with the shade of one of his ancestors, who makes a most agreeable relation of the joys of Elysium, and the nature of its inhabitants. The residence of Sesostris among these happy shades, with his character and present employment, is drawn in a very lively manner, and with a great elevation of thought.

The description of that pure and gentle light which overflows these happy regions, and clothes the spirits of these virtuous persons, has something in it of that enthusiasm which this author was accused of by his enemies in the Church of Rome ; but however it may look in religion, it makes a very beautiful figure in poetry.

The rays of the sun, says he, are darkness in comparison with this light, which rather deserves the name of glory, than that of light. It pierces the thickest bodies, in the same manner as the sunbeams pass through crystal : it strengthens the sight instead of dazzling it ; and nourishes in the most inward recesses of the mind, a perpetual serenity that is not to be expressed. It enters and incorporates itself with the very substance of the soul : the spirits of the blessed feel it in all their senses, and in all their perceptions. It produces a certain source of peace and joy that arises in them for ever, running through all the faculties, and refreshing all the desires of the soul. External pleasures and delights, with all their charms and allurements, are regarded with the utmost indifference and neglect by these happy spirits who have this great principle of pleasure within them, drawing the whole mind to itself, calling off their attention from the most delightful objects, and giving them all the transports of inebriation, without the confusion and the folly of it.

I have here only mentioned some master-touches of this admirable piece, because the original itself is understood by the greater part of my readers. I must confess, I take a particular delight in these prospects of futurity, whether grounded upon the probable suggestions of a fine imagination, or the more severe conclusions of philosophy ; as a man loves to hear all the discoveries or conjectures relating to a foreign country which he is, at some time, to inhabit. Prospects of this nature lighten the burden of any present evil, and refresh us under the worst and lowest circumstances of mortality. They extinguish in us both the fear and envy of human grandeur. Insolence shrinks its head, Power disappears ; Pain, Poverty and Death fly before them. In short, the mind that is habituated to the lively sense of a hereafter, can hope for what is the most terrifying to the generality of mankind, and rejoice in what is the most afflicting.

No. 157.

[ADDISON.[1]

From *Saturday, April* 8, to *Tuesday, April* 11, 1710.

—— Facile est inventis addere.

From my own Apartment, April 10.

I was last night in an assembly of very fine women. How I came among them is of no great importance to the reader. I shall only let him know, that I was betrayed

[1] This paper is not included in Tickell's edition of Addison's Works ; but Steele ascribes it to Addison in his Dedication of " The Drummer" to Congreve.

into so good company by the device of an old friend, who had promised to give some of his female acquaintance a sight of Mr. Bickerstaff. Upon hearing my name mentioned, a lady who sat by me told me, they had brought together a female concert for my entertainment. "You must know," says she, "that we all of us look upon ourselves to be musical instruments,[1] though we do not yet know of what kind, which we hope to learn from you, if you will give us leave to play before you." This was followed by a general laugh, which I always look upon as a necessary flourish in the opening of a female concert. They then struck up together, and played a whole hour upon two grounds, viz., the Trial,[2] and the Opera. I could not but observe, that several of their notes were more soft, and several more sharp, than any that ever I heard in a male concert; though I must confess, there was not any regard to time, nor any of those rests and pauses which are frequent in the harmony of the other sex : besides, that the music was generally full, and no particular instrument permitted to play long by itself.

I seemed so very well pleased with what every one said, and smiled with so much compliance at all their pretty fancies, that though I did not put one word into their discourse, I have the vanity to think they looked upon me as very agreeable company. I then told them, that if I were to draw the picture of so many charming musicians, it should be like one I had seen of the Muses, with their several instruments in their hands. Upon which the lady kettledrum tossed back her head, and cried, "A very pretty simile !" The concert again revived ; in which, with nods, smiles, and approbations, I bore the part rather of one who beats the time, than of a performer.

I was no sooner retired to my lodgings, but I ran over

---

[1] See No. 153.   [2] The trial of Dr. Sacheverell.

in my thoughts the several characters of this fair assembly, which I shall give some account of, because they are various in their kind, and may each of them stand as a sample of a whole species.

The person who pleased me most was a flute, an instrument that, without any great compass, has something exquisitely sweet and soft in its sound : it lulls and soothes the ear, and fills it with such a gentle kind of melody, as keeps the mind awake without startling it, and raises a most agreeable passion between transport and indolence. In short, the music of the flute is the conversation of a mild and amiable woman, that has nothing in it very elevated, or at the same time anything mean or trivial.

I must here observe, that the hautboy is the most perfect of the flute species, which, with all the sweetness of the sound, has a great strength and variety of notes ; though at the same time I must observe, that the hautboy in one sex is as scarce as the harpsichord in the other.

By the side of the flute there sat a flageolet, for so I must call a certain young lady, who fancied herself a wit, despised the music of the flute as low and insipid, and would be entertaining the company with tart ill-natured observations, pert fancies, and little turns, which she imagined to be full of life and spirit. The flageolet therefore does not differ from the flute so much in the compass of its notes, as in the shrillness and sharpness of the sound. We must however take notice, that the flageolets among their own sex are more valued and esteemed than the flutes.

There chanced to be a coquette in the concert, that with a great many skittish notes, affected squeaks, and studied inconsistencies, distinguished herself from the rest of the company. She did not speak a word during the whole trial; but I thought she would never have done upon the opera. One while she would break out upon, "That hideous king!" then upon the "charming black-moor!" Then, "Oh that dear lion!" Then would hum over two or three notes; then run to the window to see what coach was coming. The coquette therefore I must distinguish by that musical instrument which is commonly known by the name of a kit, that is more jiggish than the fiddle itself, and never sounds but to a dance.

The fourth person who bore a part in the conversation was a prude, who stuck to the trial, and was silent upon the whole opera. The gravity of her censures, and composure of her voice, which were often attended with supercilious casts of the eye, and a seeming contempt for the lightness of the conversation, put me in mind of that ancient serious matronlike instrument the virginal.

I must not pass over in silence a Lancashire hornpipe, by which I would signify a young country lady, who with a great deal of mirth and innocence diverted the company very agreeably; and, if I am not mistaken, by that time the wildness of her notes is a little softened, and the redundancy of her music restrained by conversation and good company, will be improved into one of the most amiable flutes about the town. Your romps and boarding-school girls fall likewise under this denomination.

On the right hand of the hornpipe sat a Welsh harp, an instrument which very much delights in the tunes of old historical ballads, and in celebrating the renowned actions and exploits of ancient British heroes. By this instrument I therefore would describe a certain lady, who is one of those female historians that upon all occasions enters into pedigrees and descents, and finds herself related, by some offshoot or other, to almost every great family in England:

for which reason she jars and is out of tune very often in conversation, for the company's want of due attention and respect to her.

But the most sonorous part of our concert was a she-drum, or (as the vulgar call it) a kettledrum, who accompanied her discourse with motions of the body, tosses of the head, and brandishes of the fan. Her music was loud, bold, and masculine. Every thump she gave, alarmed the company, and very often set somebody or other in it a-blushing.

The last I shall mention was a certain romantic instrument called a dulcimer, who talked of nothing but shady woods, flowery meadows, purling streams, larks and nightingales, with all the beauties of the spring, and the pleasures of a country life. This instrument has a fine melancholy sweetness in it, and goes very well with the flute.

I think most of the conversable part of womankind may be found under one of the foregoing divisions; but it must be confessed, that the generality of that sex, notwithstanding they have naturally a great genius for being talkative, are not mistresses of more than one note; with which however, by frequent repetition, they make a greater sound than those who are possessed of the whole gamut, as may be observed in your larums or household scolds, and in your castanets or impertinent tittle-tattles, who have no other variety in their discourse but that of talking slower or faster.

Upon communicating this scheme of music to an old friend of mine, who was formerly a man of gallantry and a rover, he told me, that he believed he had been in love with every instrument in my concert. The first that smit him was a hornpipe, who lived near his father's house in the country; but upon his failing to meet her at an assize, according to appointment, she cast him off.

His next passion was for a kettledrum, whom he fell in
love with at a play ; but when he became 'acquainted
with her, not finding the softness of her sex in her conversation, he grew cool to her ; though at the same time
he could not deny, but that she behaved herself very much
like a gentlewoman. His third mistress was a dulcimer,
who he found took great delight in sighing and languishing, but would go no farther than the preface of matrimony ; so that she would never let a lover have any more
of her than her heart, which, after having won, he was
forced to leave her, as despairing of any further success.
" I must confess," says my friend, " I have often considered
her with a great deal of admiration ; and I find her
pleasure is so much in this first step of an amour, that her
life will pass away in dream, solitude, and soliloquy, till
her decay of charms makes her snatch at the worst man
that ever pretended to her. In the next place," says my
friend, "I fell in love with a kit,[1] who led me such a dance
through all the varieties of a familiar, cold, fond, and
indifferent behaviour, that the world began to grow cen-
sorious, though without any cause : for which reason, to
recover our reputations, we parted by consent. To mend my
hand," says he, " I made my next application to a virginal,
who gave me great encouragement, after her cautious
manner, till some malicious companion told her of my
long passion for the kit, which made her turn me off as a
scandalous fellow. At length, in despair," says he, "I betook
myself to a Welsh harp, who rejected me with contempt,
after having found that my great-grandmother was a
brewer's daughter." I found by the sequel of my friend's
discourse, that he had never aspired to a hautboy; that he
had been exasperated by a flageolet ; and that to this very
day, he pines away for a flute.

[1] See Nos. 34 and 160.

The Tatler

Upon the whole, having thoroughly considered how absolutely necessary it is, that two instruments, which are to play together for life, should be exactly tuned, and go in perfect concert with each other, I would propose matches between the music of both sexes, according to the following table of marriage :

1. Drum and kettledrum.
2. Lute and flute.
3. Harpsichord and hautboy.
4. Violin and flageolet.
5. Bass-viol and kit.
6. Trumpet and Welsh harp.
7. Hunting-horn and hornpipe.
8. Bagpipe and castanets.
9. Passing-bell and virginal.

Mr. Bickerstaff, in consideration of his ancient friendship and acquaintance with Mr. Betterton,[1] and great esteem for his merit, summons all his disciples, whether dead or living, mad or tame, Toasts, Smarts, Dappers, Pretty Fellows, Musicians or Scrapers, to make their appearance at the playhouse in the Haymarket on Thursday next ; when there will be a play acted for the benefit of the said Mr. Betterton.

[1] See Nos. 1, 71, 167.

No. 158.   « [ADDISON.

From *Tuesday, April* 11, to *Thursday, April* 13, 1710.

Faciunt næ intelligendo, ut nihil intelligant.
TER., Andria, Prologue, 17.

From my own Apartment, April 12.

Tom Folio[1] is a broker in learning, employed to get together good editions, and stock the libraries of great men. There is not a sale of books begins till Tom Folio is seen at the door. There is not an auction where his name is not heard, and that too in the very nick of time, in the critical moment, before the last decisive stroke of the hammer. There is not a subscription goes forward, in which Tom is not privy to the first rough draught of the proposals ; nor a catalogue printed, that does not come to him wet from the press. He is an universal scholar, so far as the title-page of all authors, knows the manuscripts in which they were discovered, the editions through which they have passed, with the praises or censures which they have received from the several members of the learned world. He has a greater esteem for Aldus and Elzevir, than for Virgil and Horace. If you talk of Herodotus, he breaks out into a panegyric upon Harry Stephans. He thinks he gives you an account of an author, when he tells you the subject he treats of, the name of the editor, and the year in which it was printed. Or if you draw him into further particulars, he cries up the goodness of the paper, extols the diligence of the

---

[1] The original of Tom Folio is supposed to be Thomas Rawlinson, a great book-collector, who lived in Gray's Inn, and afterwards in London House, Aldersgate Street, where he died, August 6, 1725, aged 44. His library and MSS. were sold between 1722 and 1734.

corrector, and is transported with the beauty of the letter. This he looks upon to be sound learning and substantial criticism. As for those who talk of the fineness of style, and the justness of thought, or describe the brightness of any particular passages ; nay, though they write themselves in the genius and spirit of the author they admire, Tom looks upon them as men of superficial learning, and flashy parts.

I had yesterday morning a visit from this learned idiot (for that is the light in which I consider every pedant), when I discovered in him some little touches of the cox-comb which I had not before observed. Being very full of the figure which he makes in the republic of letters, and wonderfully satisfied with his great stock of know-ledge, he gave me broad intimations, that he did not " believe " in all points as his forefathers had done. He then communicated to me a thought of a certain author upon a passage of Virgil's account of the dead, which I made the subject of a late paper.[1] This thought has taken very much among men of Tom's pitch and under-standing, though universally exploded by all that know how to construe Virgil, or have any relish of antiquity. Not to trouble my reader with it, I found upon the whole, that Tom did not believe a future state of rewards and punish-ments, because Æneas, at his leaving the empire of the dead, passed through the gate of ivory, and not through that of horn. Knowing that Tom had not sense enough to give up an opinion which he had once received, that he might avoid wrangling, I told him, that Virgil possibly had his oversights as well as another author. " Ah ! Mr. Bickerstaff," says he, " you would have another opinion of him, if you would read him in Daniel Heinsius' edition. I have perused him myself several times in that edition,"

[1] No. 154.

continued he ; " and after the strictest and most malicious
examination, could find but two faults in him : one of
them is in the ' Æneids,' where there are two commas
instead of a parenthesis ; and another in the third ' Georgic,'
where you may find a semicolon turned upside down."
"Perhaps," said I, " these were not Virgil's thoughts, but
those of the transcriber." "I do not design it," says
Tom, " as a reflection on Virgil : on the contrary, I know
that all the manuscripts 'reclaim' against such a punctuation.
Oh ! Mr. Bickerstaff," says he, " what would a man give
to see one simile of Virgil writ in his own hand ?" I
asked him which was the simile he meant ; but was
answered, " Any simile in Virgil." He then told me all
the secret history in the commonwealth of learning ; of
modern pieces that had the names of ancient authors
annexed to them ; of all the books that were now writing
or printing in the several parts of Europe ; of many
amendments which are made, and not yet published ; and
a thousand other particulars, which I would not have my
memory burdened with for a Vatican.

At length, being fully persuaded that I thoroughly
admired him, and looked upon him as a prodigy of learning,
he took his leave. I know several of Tom's class who are
professed admirers of Tasso without understanding a word
of Italian ; and one in particular, that carries a "Pastor Fido"
in his pocket, in which I am sure he is acquainted with no
other beauty but the clearness of the character.

There is another kind of pedant, who, with all Tom
Folio's impertinences, has greater superstructures and
embellishments of Greek and Latin, and is still more
unsupportable than the other, in the same degree as he is
more learned. Of this kind very often are editors,
commentators, interpreters, scholiasts, and critics ; and in
short, all men of deep learning without common sense.

These persons set a greater value on themselves for having
found out the meaning of a passage in Greek, than upon
the author for having written it ; nay, will allow the
passage itself not to have any beauty in it, at the same
time that they would be considered as the greatest men of
the age for having interpreted it. They will look with
contempt upon the most beautiful poems that have been
composed by any of their contemporaries ; but will lock
themselves up in their studies for a twelvemonth together,
to correct, publish, and expound, such trifles of antiquity
as a modern author would be contemned for. Men of the
strictest morals, severest lives, and the gravest professions,
will write volumes upon an idle sonnet that is originally in
Greek or Latin ; give editions of the most immoral authors,
and spin out whole pages upon the various readings of a
lewd expression. All that can be said in excuse for them,
is, that their works sufficiently show they have no taste of
their authors ; and that what they do in this kind, is out
of their great learning, and not out of any levity or
lasciviousness of temper.

A pedant of this nature is wonderfully well described in
six lines of Boileau,[1] with which I shall conclude his
character :

> " *Un Pédant enivré de sa vaine science,*
> *Tout hérissé de grec, tout bouffi d'arrogance,*
> *Et qui, de mille auteurs retenus mot pour mot,*
> *Dans sa tête entassés, n'a souvent fait qu'un sot,*
> *Croit qu'un livre fait tout, et que, sans Aristote,*
> *La raison ne voit goutte, et le bon sens radote.*"

[1] Satire iv.: "Les folies humaines."

No. 159.   • [Steele.

From *Thursday, April* 13, to *Saturday, April* 15, 1710.

Nitor in adversum, nec me qui cætera, vincit
Impetus.—Ovid., Met. ii. 72.

From my own Apartment, April 14.

The wits of this island, for above fifty years past, instead of correcting the vices of the age, have done all they could to inflame them. Marriage has been one of the common topics of ridicule that every stage-scribbler has found his account in ; for whenever there is an occasion for a clap, an impertinent jest upon matrimony is sure to raise it. This has been attended with very pernicious consequences. Many a country squire, upon his setting up for a man of the town, has gone home in the gaiety of his heart and beat his wife. A kind husband has been looked upon as a clown, and a good wife as a domestic animal, unfit for the company or conversation of the *beau monde.* In short, separate beds, silent tables, and solitary homes have been introduced by your men of wit and pleasure of the age.

As I shall always make it my business to stem the torrents of prejudice and vice, I shall take particular care to put an honest father of a family in countenance, and endeavour to remove all the evils out of that state of life, which is either the most happy, or most miserable, that a man can be placed in. In order to this, let us, if you please, consider the wits and well-bred persons of former times. I have shown in another paper,[1] that Pliny, who was a man of the greatest genius, as well as of the first quality of his

[1] No. 149.

age, did not think it below him to be a kind husband, and to treat his wife as a friend, companion and counsellor. I shall give the like instance of another, who in all respects was a much greater man than Pliny, and has written a whole book of letters to his wife. They are not so full of turns as those translated out of the former author, who writes very much like a modern, but are full of that beautiful simplicity which is altogether natural, and is the distinguishing character of the best ancient writers. The author I am speaking of, is Cicero; who, in the following passages which I have taken out of his letters,[1] shows, that he did not think it inconsistent with the politeness of his manners, or the greatness of his wisdom, to stand upon record in his domestic character.

These letters were written at a time when he was banished from his country, by a faction that then prevailed at Rome.

Cicero to Terentia.

I.

"I learn from the letters of my friends, as well as from common report, that you give incredible proofs of virtue and fortitude, and that you are indefatigable in all kinds of good offices. How unhappy a man am I, that a woman of your virtue, constancy, honour, and good nature, should fall into so great distresses upon my account; and that my dear Tulliola should be so much afflicted for the sake of a father, with whom she had once so much reason to be pleased! How can I mention little Cicero, whose first knowledge of things began with the sense of his own misery? If all this had happened by the decrees of fate, as you would kindly persuade me, I could have borne it. But, alas! it is all befallen me by my own

[1] "Epist." xiv. 1-4.

indiscretion, who thought I was beloved by those who envied me, and did not join with them who sought my friendship.——At present, since my friends bid me hope, I shall take care of my health, that I may enjoy the benefit of your affectionate services.——Plancius hopes we may some time or other come together into Italy. If I ever live to see that day ; if I ever return to your dear embraces ; in short, if I ever again recover you and myself, I shall think our conjugal piety very well rewarded.——As for what you write to me about selling your estate, consider (my dear Terentia), consider, alas ! what would be the event of it. If our present fortune continues to oppress us, what will become of our poor boy ? My tears flow so fast, that I am not able to write any further ; and I would not willingly make you weep with me.——Let us take care not to undo the child that is already undone : if we can leave him any-thing, a little virtue will keep him from want, and a little fortune raise him in the world. Mind your health, and let me know frequently what you are doing.——Remember me to Tulliola and Cicero.

II.

" Don't fancy that I write longer letters to any one than to yourself, unless when I chance to receive a longer letter from another, which I am indispensably obliged to answer in every particular. The truth of it is, I have no subject for a letter at present : and as my affairs now stand, there is nothing more painful to me than writing. As for you and our dear Tulliola, I cannot write to you without abundance of tears, for I see both of you miserable, whom I always wished to be happy, and whom I ought to have made so.——I must acknowledge, you have done everything for me with the utmost fortitude, and the utmost affection ; nor indeed is it more than I expected

from you ; though at the same time it is a great aggravation of my ill fortune, that the afflictions I suffer can be
relieved only by those which you undergo for my sake. For
honest Valerius has written me a letter, which I could not
read without weeping very bitterly ; wherein he gives me
an account of the public procession which you have made
for me at Rome.   Alas ! my dearest life, must then
Terentia, the darling of my soul, whose favour and recom-
mendations have been so often sought by others ; must my
Terentia droop under the weight of sorrow, appear in the
habit of a mourner, pour out floods of tears, and all this
for my sake ; for my sake, who have undone my family,
by consulting the safety of others !——As for what you
write about selling your house, I am very much afflicted,
that what is laid out upon my account may any way reduce
you to misery and want.   If we can bring about our design,
we may indeed recover everything ; but if Fortune persists in
persecuting us, how can I think of your sacrificing for me
the poor remainder of your possessions ?   No, my dearest
life, let me beg you to let those bear my expenses who are
able, and perhaps willing to do it ; and if you would show
your love to me, do not injure your health, which is already
too much impaired.   You present yourself before my eyes
day and night ; I see you labouring amidst innumerable
difficulties ; I am afraid lest you should sink under them ;
but I find in you all the qualifications that are necessary
to support you : be sure therefore to cherish your health,
that you may compass the end of your hopes and your
endeavours.——Farewell, my Terentia, my heart's desire,
farewell."

III.

" A ristocritus has delivered to me three of your letters,
which I have almost defaced with my tears.   Oh !
my Terentia, I am consumed with grief, and feel the weight

of your sufferings more than of my own.   I am more
miserable than you are, notwithstanding you are very much
so ; and that for this reason, because though our calamity
is common, it is my fault that brought it upon us.   I ought
to have died rather than have been driven out of the city :
I am therefore overwhelmed not only with grief, but with
shame.   I am ashamed that I did not do my utmost for
the best of wives, and the dearest of children.   You are
ever present before my eyes in your mourning, your affliction, and your sickness.   Amidst all which, there scarce
appears to me the least glimmering of hope.——However,
so long as you hope, I will not despair.——I will do what
you advise me.   I have returned my thanks to those friends
whom you mentioned, and have let them know, that you
have acquainted me with their good offices.   I am sensible
of Piso's extraordinary zeal and endeavours to serve me.
Oh ! would the gods grant that you and I might live
together in the enjoyment of such a son-in-law, and of our
dear children.——As for what you write of your coming
to me if I desire it, I would rather you should be where
you are, because I know you are my principal agent at
Rome.   If you succeed, I shall come to you : if not——.
But I need say no more.   Be careful of your health, and
be assured, that nothing is, or ever was, so dear to me as
yourself.   Farewell, my Terentia ; I fancy that I see you,
and therefore cannot command my weakness so far as to
refrain from tears."

IV.

" I don't write to you as often as I might, because not-
       withstanding I am afflicted at all times, I am quite
overcome with sorrow whilst I am writing to you, or
reading any letters that I receive from you.——If these
evils are not to be removed, I must desire to see you,

my dearest life, as soon as possible, and to die in your embraces; since neither the gods, whom you always religiously worshipped; nor the men, whose good I always promoted, have rewarded us according to our deserts.——What a distressed wretch am I! should I ask a weak woman, oppressed with cares and sickness, to come and live with me, or shall I not ask her? Can I live without you? But I find I must. If there be any hopes of my return, help it forward, and promote it as much as you are able. But if all that is over, as I fear it is, find out some way or other of coming to me. This you may be sure of, that I shall not look upon myself as quite undone whilst you are with me. But what will become of Tulliola? You must look to that; I must confess, I am entirely at a loss about her. Whatever happens, we must take care of the reputation and marriage of that dear unfortunate girl. As for Cicero, he shall live in my bosom and in my arms. I cannot write any further, my sorrows will not let me.——Support yourself, my dear Terentia, as well as you are able. We have lived and flourished together amidst the greatest honours: it is not our crimes, but our virtues that have distressed us.——Take more than ordinary care of your health; I am more afflicted with your sorrows than my own. Farewell, my Terentia, thou dearest, faithfullest, and best of wives."

Methinks it is a pleasure to see this great man in his family, who makes so different a figure in the Forum or Senate of Rome. Every one admires the orator and the consul; but for my part, I esteem the husband and the father. His private character, with all the little weaknesses of humanity, is as amiable as the figure he makes in public is awful and majestic. But at the same time that I love to surprise so great an author in his private walks, and to survey him in his most familiar lights, I think it would be barbarous to form to ourselves any idea of mean-spiritedness from these natural openings of his heart, and disburdening of his thoughts to a wife. He has written several other letters to the same person, but none with so great passion as these of which I have given the foregoing extracts.

It would be ill-nature not to acquaint the English reader, that his wife was successful in her solicitations for this great man, and saw her husband return to the honours of which he had been deprived, with all the pomp and acclamation that usually attended the greatest triumph.

No. 160. [Addison and Steele.

From *Saturday, April* 15, to *Tuesday, April* 18, 1710.

From my own Apartment, April 17.

A common civility to an impertinent fellow often draws upon one a great many unforeseen troubles ; and if one does not take particular care, will be interpreted by him as an overture of friendship and intimacy. This I was very sensible of this morning. About two hours before day, I heard a great rapping at my door, which continued some time, till my maid could get herself ready to go down and see what was the occasion of it. She then brought me up word, that there was a gentleman who seemed very much in haste, and said he must needs speak with me. By the description she gave me of him, and by his voice, which I could hear as I lay in my bed, I fancied him to be my old acquaintance the upholsterer,[1] whom I met the other day in St. James's Park. For

[1] See No. 155.

which reason, I bid her tell the gentleman, whoever he was, that I was indisposed, that I could see nobody, and that, if he had anything to say to me, I desired he would leave it in writing. My maid, after having delivered her message, told me that the gentleman said he would stay at the next coffee-house till I was stirring, and bid her be sure to tell me, that the French were driven from the Scarp, and that Douay was invested. He gave her the name of another town, which I found she had dropped by the way.

As much as I love to be informed of the success of my brave countrymen, I do not care for hearing of a victory before day, and was therefore very much out of humour at this unseasonable visit. I had no sooner recovered my temper, and was falling asleep, but I was immediately startled by a second rap ; and upon my maid's opening the door, heard the same voice ask her if her master was yet up ; and at the same time bid her tell me, that he was come on purpose to talk with me about a piece of home news that everybody in town will be full of two hours hence. I ordered my maid as soon as she came into the room, without hearing her message, to tell the gentleman, that whatever his news was, I would rather hear it two hours hence than now ; and that I persisted in my resolution not to speak with anybody that morning. The wench delivered my answer presently, and shut the door. It was impossible for me to compose myself to sleep after two such unexpected alarms ; for which reason I put on my clothes in a very peevish humour. I took several turns about my chamber, reflecting with a great deal of anger and contempt on these volunteers in politics, that undergo all the pain, watchfulness, and disquiet of a First Minister, without turning it to the advantage either of themselves or their country ; and yet it is surprising to

consider how numerous this species of men is. There is
nothing more frequent than to find a tailor breaking his
rest on the affairs of Europe, and to see a cluster of
porters sitting upon the Ministry. Our streets swarm
with politicians, and there is scarce a shop which is not
held by a statesman. As I was musing after this manner,
I heard the upholsterer at the door delivering a letter to
my maid, and begging her, in a very great hurry, to give
it to her master as soon as ever he was awake, which I
opened, and found as follows :

"MR. BICKERSTAFF,

" I was to wait upon you about a week ago, to let you
know, that the honest gentlemen whom you con-
versed with upon the bench at the end of the Mall, having
heard that I had received five shillings of you, to give you
a hundred pounds upon the Great Turk's being driven out
of Europe, desired me to acquaint you, that every one of
that company would be willing to receive five shillings, to
pay a hundred pounds on the same conditions. Our last
advices from Muscovy making this a fairer bet than it was
a week ago, I do not question but you will accept the
wager.

"But this is not my present business. If you remember, I whispered a word in your ear as we were
walking up the Mall, and you see what has happened
since. If I had seen you this morning, I would have told
you in your ear another secret. I hope you will be
recovered of your indisposition by to-morrow morning,
when I will wait on you at the same hour as I did this ;
my private circumstances being such, that I cannot well
appear in this quarter of the town after it is day.

" I have been so taken up with the late good news from
Holland, and expectation of further particulars, as well as

with other transactions, of which I will tell you more to-morrow morning, that I have not slept a wink these three nights.

" I have reason to believe that Picardy will soon follow the example of Artois, in case the enemy continue in their present resolution of flying away from us. I think I told you last time we were together my opinion about the Deulle.

" The honest gentlemen upon the bench bid me tell you, they would be glad to see you often among them. We shall be there all the warm hours of the day, during the present posture of affairs.

" This happy opening of the campaign will, I hope, give us a very joyful summer ; and I propose to take many a pleasant walk with you, if you will sometimes come into the Park ; for that is the only place in which I can be free from the malice of my enemies. Farewell till three o'clock to-morrow morning. I am,

" Your most humble Servant, &c.

" P.S. The King of Sweden is still at Bender."

I should have fretted myself to death at this promise of a second visit, if I had not found in his letter an intimation of the good news which I have since heard at large. I have however ordered my maid to tie up the knocker of my door in such a manner as she would do if I was really indisposed. By which means I hope to escape breaking my morning's rest.[1]

Since I have given this letter to the public, I shall communicate one or two more, which I have lately received

[1] The preceding portion of this paper is printed in Tickell's edition of Addison's Works.

from others of my correspondents. The following is from a Coquette, who is very angry at my having disposed of her in marriage to a Bass-viol :[1]

"Mr. Bickerstaff,

"I thought you would never have descended from the Censor of Great Britain, to become a match-maker. But pray, why so severe upon the Kit? Had I been a Jews-harp, that is nothing but tongue, you could not have used me worse. Of all things, a Bass-viol is my aversion. Had you married me to a Bagpipe, or a Passing-bell, I should have been better pleased. Dear Father Isaac, either choose me a better husband, or I will live and die a Dulcimer. In hopes of receiving satisfaction from you, I am yours, whilst

"Isabella Kit."

The pertness which this fair lady has shown in this letter, was one occasion of my joining her to the Bass-viol, which is an instrument that wants to be quickened by these little vivacities ; as the sprightliness of the Kit ought to be checked and curbed by the gravity of the Bass-viol.

My next letter is from Tom Folio,[2] who it seems takes it amiss that I have published a character of him so much to his disadvantage :

"Sir,

"I suppose you meant Tom Fool, when you called me Tom Folio in a late trifling paper of yours ; for I find, it is your design to run down all useful and solid learning. The tobacco-paper on which your own writings are usually printed,[3] as well as the incorrectness of the

---

[1] See No. 157.   [2] See No. 158.   [3] See No. 101.

press, and the scurvy letter, sufficiently show the extent of your knowledge. I question not but you look upon John Morphew to be as great a man as Elzevir ; and Aldus, to have been such another as Bernard Lintot.[1] If you would give me my revenge, I would only desire of you to let me publish an account of your library, which I daresay would furnish out an extraordinary catalogue.

"Tom Folio."

It has always been my way to baffle reproach with silence, though I cannot but observe the disingenuous proceedings of this gentleman, who is not content to asperse my writings, but has wounded, through my sides, those eminent and worthy citizens, Mr. John Morphew, and Mr. Bernard Lintot.[2]

---

[1] Bernard Lintot (1675–1736) was Jacob Tonson's principal rival in the publishing trade in the time of Queen Anne and George I.

[2] The author of a curious pamphlet, "The Critical Specimen," 1711, said he was much divided in his opinion, whether to prefer the every way excellent Mr. Jacob Tonson, junior, or Mr. Bernard Lintot to be his bookseller, for the latter of whom he had had a particular consideration since he received this eulogium from his honoured friend Isaac Bickerstaff, Esq.—This pamphlet purports to be a specimen of a proposed Life of Rinaldo Furioso, Critic of the Woful Countenance,—*i.e.*, John Dennis. It contains remarks upon the two good lines he wrote (*Spectator*, No. 47) upon the difficulty of distinguishing his comedies from his tragedies, &c. &c. There is, too, an allusion to the *Tatlers* and *Spectators* in the notice that the virtues of the critic are to be printed in a very small neat Elzevir character, and his extravagances in a noble large letter on royal paper.

No. 161.   *[ADDISON,

From *Tuesday, April* 18, to *Thursday, April* 20, 1710.

—— Nunquam Libertas gratior exstat
Quam sub rege pio ——
          CLAUDIAN, De Laudibus Stilichonis, iii. 113.

From my own Apartment, April 19.

I was walking two or three days ago in a very pleasing
retirement, and amusing myself with the reading of
that ancient and beautiful allegory, called "The Table of
Cebes."[1]   I was at last so tired with my walk, that I sat
down to rest myself upon a bench that stood in the midst
of an agreeable shade.   The music of the birds, that filled
all the trees about me, lulled me asleep before I was aware
of it ; which was followed by a dream, that I impute in
some measure to the foregoing author, who had made an
impression upon my imagination, and put me into his own
way of thinking.

I fancied myself among the Alps, and, as it is natural
in a dream, seemed every moment to bound from one
summit to another, till at last, after having made this
airy progress over the tops of several mountains, I arrived
at the very centre of those broken rocks and precipices.
I here, methought, saw a prodigious circuit of hills, that
reached above the clouds, and encompassed a large space
of ground, which I had a great curiosity to look into.   I
thereupon continued my former way of travelling through
a great variety of winter scenes, till I had gained the top
of these white mountains, which seemed another Alps of

[1] Cebes, of Thebes, was a disciple of Philolaus and Socrates.   His
Πίναξ is an account of a table on which human life, with all its
temptations and dangers, is represented symbolically.

snow. I looked down from hence into a spacious plain, which was surrounded on all sides by this mound of hills, and which presented me with the most agreeable prospect I had ever seen. There was a greater variety of colours in the embroidery of the meadows, a more lively green in the leaves and grass, a brighter crystal in the streams, than what I ever met with in any other region. The light itself had something more shining and glorious in it than that of which the day is made in other places. I was wonderfully astonished at the discovery of such a paradise amidst the wildness of those cold, hoary landscapes which lay about it ; but found at length, that this happy region was inhabited by the Goddess of Liberty ; whose presence softened the rigours of the climate, enriched the barrenness of the soil, and more than supplied the absence of the sun. The place was covered with a wonderful profusion of flowers, that without being disposed into regular borders and parterres, grew promiscuously, and had a greater beauty in their natural luxuriancy and disorder, than they could have received from the checks and restraints of art. There was a river that arose out of the south side of the mountain, that by an infinite number of turns and windings, seemed to visit every plant, and cherish the several beauties of the spring, with which the fields abounded. After having run to and fro in a wonderful variety of meanders, as unwilling to leave so charming a place, it at last throws itself into the hollow of a mountain, from whence it passes under a long range of rocks, and at length rises in that part of the Alps where the inhabitants think it the first source of the Rhone. This river, after having made its progress through those free nations, stagnates in a huge lake,[1] at the leaving of them, and no sooner enters into the regions of slavery, but

---

[1] The Lake of Geneva.

runs through them with an incredible rapidity, and takes its shortest way to the sea.

I descended into the happy fields that lay beneath me, and in the midst of them, beheld the goddess sitting upon a throne. She had nothing to enclose her but the bounds of her own dominions, and nothing over her head but the heavens. Every glance of her eye cast a track of light where it fell, that revived the spring, and made all things smile about her. My heart grew cheerful at the sight of her, and as she looked upon me, I found a certain confidence growing in me, and such an inward resolution as I never felt before that time.

On the left hand of the goddess sat the Genius of a Commonwealth, with the cap of liberty on her head, and in her hand a wand, like that with which a Roman citizen used to give his slaves their freedom. There was something mean and vulgar, but at the same time exceeding bold and daring, in her air; her eyes were full of fire, but had in them such casts of fierceness and cruelty, as made her appear to me rather dreadful than amiable. On her shoulder she wore a mantle, on which there was wrought a great confusion of figures. As it flew in the wind, I could not discern the particular design of them, but saw wounds in the bodies of some, and agonies in the faces of others; and over one part of it could read in letters of blood, " The Ides of March."

On the right hand of the goddess was the Genius of Monarchy. She was clothed in the whitest ermine, and wore a crown of the purest gold upon her head. In her hand she held a sceptre like that which is borne by the British monarchs. A couple of tame lions lay crouching at her feet : her countenance had in it a very great majesty without any mixture of terror : her voice was like the voice of an angel, filled with so much sweetness, and accompanied with such an air of condescension, as tempered the awfulness of her appearance, and equally inspired love and veneration into the hearts of all that beheld her.

In the train of the Goddess of Liberty were the several Arts and Sciences, who all of them flourished underneath her eye. One of them in particular made a greater figure than any of the rest, who held a thunderbolt in her hand, which had the power of melting, piercing, or breaking everything that stood in its way. The name of this goddess was Eloquence.

There were two other dependent goddesses, who made a very conspicuous figure in this blissful region. The first of them was seated upon a hill, that had every plant growing out of it, which the soil was in its own nature capable of producing. The other was seated in a little island, that was covered with groves of spices, olives, and orange-trees; and in a word, with the products of every foreign clime. The name of the first was Plenty, of the second, Commerce. The first leaned her right arm upon a plough, and under her left held a huge horn, out of which she poured a whole autumn of fruits. The other wore a rostral crown upon her head, and kept her eyes fixed upon a compass.

I was wonderfully pleased in ranging through this delightful place, and the more so, because it was not encumbered with fences and enclosures; till at length, methought, I sprung from the ground, and pitched upon the top of a hill, that presented several objects to my sight which I had not before taken notice of. The winds that passed over this flowery plain, and through the tops of the trees which were full of blossoms, blew upon me in such a continued breeze of sweets, that I was wonderfully charmed with my situation. I here saw all the inner declivities of that great circuit of mountains, whose outside was covered with snow, overgrown with huge forests of fir-trees, which indeed are very frequently found in other parts of the Alps. These trees were inhabited by storks, that came thither in great flights from very distant quarters of the world. Methought, I was pleased in my dream to see what became of these birds, when, upon leaving the places to which they make an annual visit, they rise in great flocks so high till they are out of sight ; and for that reason have been thought by some modern philosophers to take a flight to the moon. But my eyes were soon diverted from this prospect, when I observed two great gaps that led through this circuit of mountains, where guards and watches were posted day and night. Upon examination I found, that there were two formidable enemies encamped before each of these avenues, who kept the place in a perpetual alarm, and watched all opportunities of invading it.

Tyranny was at the head of one of these armies, dressed in an Eastern habit, and grasping in her hand an iron sceptre. Behind her was Barbarity, with the garb and complexion of an Ethiopian ; Ignorance with a turban upon her head ; and Persecution holding up a bloody flag, embroidered with fleurs-de-luce. These were followed by Oppression, Poverty, Famine, Torture, and a dreadful train of appearances, that made me tremble to behold them. Among the baggage of this army, I could discover racks, wheels, chains, and gibbets, with all the instruments art could invent to make human nature miserable.

Before the other avenue I saw Licentiousness, dressed in a garment not unlike the Polish cassock, and leading up a whole army of monsters, such as Clamour, with a hoarse voice and a hundred tongues ; Confusion, with a mis-shapen body and a thousand heads ; Impudence, with a forehead of brass ; and Rapine, with hands of iron. The tumult, noise, and uproar in this quarter were so very great, that they disturbed my imagination more than is consistent with sleep, and by that means awaked me.

No. 162.   [ADDISON.

From *Thursday*, *April* 20, to *Saturday*, *April* 22, 1710.

Tertius e cœlo cecidit Cato.—Juv., Sat. ii. 40.

From my own Apartment, April 21.

In my younger years I used many endeavours to get a place at Court, and indeed continued my pursuits till I arrived at my grand climacteric : but at length altogether despairing of success, whether it were for want of capacity, friends, or due application, I at last resolved to erect a new office, and for my encouragement, to place myself in it. For this reason, I took upon me the title and dignity of Censor of Great Britain, reserving to myself all such perquisites, profits, and emoluments as should arise out of the discharge of the said office.   These in truth have not been inconsiderable ; for, besides those weekly contributions which I receive from John Morphew, and those annual subscriptions which I propose to myself from the most elegant part of this great island, I daily live in a very comfortable affluence of wine, stale beer, Hungary water, beef, books, and marrow-bones, which I receive from many well-disposed citizens ; not to mention the forfeitures which accrue to me from the several offenders that appear before me on court-days.

Having now enjoyed this office for the space of a twelve-month, I shall do what all good officers ought to do, take a survey of my behaviour, and consider carefully whether I have discharged my duty, and acted up to the character with which I am invested.   For my direction in this par-

ticular, I have made a narrow search into the nature of the
old Roman censors, whom I must always regard, not only
as my predecessors, but as my patterns in this great employment ; and have several times asked my own heart
with great impartiality, whether Cato will not bear a more
venerable figure among posterity than Bickerstaff.

I find the duty of the Roman censor was twofold.
The first part of it consisted in making frequent reviews
of the people, in casting up their numbers, ranging them
under their several tribes, disposing them into proper
classes, and subdividing them into their respective
centuries.

In compliance with this part of the office, I have taken
many curious surveys of this great city. I have collected
into particular bodies the Dappers[1] and the Smarts,[2] the
Natural and Affected Rakes,[3] the Pretty Fellows and the
Very Pretty Fellows.[4] I have likewise drawn out in
several distinct parties your Pedants[5] and Men of Fire,[6]
your Gamesters[7] and Politicians.[8] I have separated Cits
from Citizens,[9] Freethinkers from Philosophers,[10] Wits
from Snuff-takers,[11] and Duellists from Men of Honour.[12]
I have likewise made a calculation of Esquires,[13] not only
considering the several distinct swarms of them that are
settled in the different parts of this town, but also that
more rugged species that inhabit the fields and woods,
and are often found in pothouses, and upon haycocks.

I shall pass the soft sex over in silence, having not yet
reduced them into any tolerable order ; as likewise the

---

[1] See No. 85.   [2] See Nos. 26, 28.   [3] See Nos. 27, 143.
[4] See Nos. 21, 22, 24.   [6] See No. 158.   [9] See No. 61.
[7] See Nos. 13, 14, 15, 56, &c.   [8] See Nos. 40, 155.
[9] See No. 25.   [10] See Nos. 108, 111, 135.
[11] See Nos. 35, 141.   [12] See Nos. 25, 26, 28, 29, 30, 39.
[13] See Nos. 19, 115.

softer tribe of lovers, which will cost me a great deal of time, before I shall be able to cast them into their several centuries and subdivisions.

The second part of the Roman censor's office was to look into the manners of the people, and to check any growing luxury, whether in diet, dress, or building. This duty likewise I have endeavoured to discharge, by those wholesome precepts which I have given my countrymen in regard to beef and mutton, and the severe censures which I have passed upon ragouts and fricassees.[1] There is not, as I am informed, a pair of red heels[2] to be seen within ten miles of London, which I may likewise ascribe, without vanity, to the becoming zeal which I expressed in that particular. I must own, my success with the petticoat[3] is not so great : but as I have not yet done with it, I hope I shall in a little time put an effectual stop to that growing evil. As for the article of building, I intend hereafter to enlarge upon it, having lately observed several warehouses, nay private shops, that stand upon Corinthian pillars, and whole rows of tin pots showing themselves, in order to their sale, through a sash-window.

I have likewise followed the example of the Roman censors, in punishing offences according to the quality of the offender. It was usual for them to expel a senator who had been guilty of great immoralities out of the senate-house, by omitting his name when they called over the list of his brethren. In the same manner, to remove effectually several worthless men who stand possessed of great honours, I have made frequent draughts of dead men[4] out of the vicious part of the nobility, and given them up to the new society of upholders, with the necessary orders for their interment.

---

[1] See No. 148.   [2] See No. 26.   [3] See No. 116.   [4] See Nos. 96, 110.

As the Roman censors used to punish the knights or gentlemen of Rome, by taking away their horses from them, I have seized the canes[1] of many criminals of figure, whom I had just reason to animadvert upon. As for the offenders among the common people of Rome, they were generally chastised, by being thrown out of a higher tribe, and placed in one which was not so honourable. My reader cannot but think I have had an eye to this punishment, when I have degraded one species of men into bombs, squibs, and crackers,[2] and another into drums, bass-viols, and bagpipes ;[3] not to mention whole packs of delinquents whom I have shut up in kennels, and the new hospital which I am at present erecting, for the reception of those my countrymen who give me but little hopes of their amendment, on the borders of Moorfields.[4] I shall only observe upon this last particular, that since some late surveys I have taken of this island, I shall think it necessary to enlarge the plan of the buildings which I design in this quarter.

When my great predecessor Cato the elder stood for the Censorship of Rome, there were several other competitors who offered themselves ; and to get an interest among the people, gave them great promises of the mild and gentle treatment which they would use towards them in that office. Cato on the contrary told them, he presented himself as a candidate, because he knew the age was sunk in immorality and corruption ; and that if they would give him their votes, he would promise them to make use of such a strictness and severity of discipline as should recover them out of it. The Roman historians, upon this occasion, very much celebrate the public-spiritedness of that people, who chose Cato for their censor, notwithstanding his method of recommending

[1] See No. 26. [2] See No. 88. [3] See No. 153. [4] See Nos. 62, 127.

himself. I may in some measure extol my own countrymen upon• the same account, who, without any respect
to party, or any application from myself, have made
such generous subscriptions for the Censor of Great
Britain, as will give a magnificence to my old age, and
which I esteem more than I would any post in Europe
of a hundred times the value. I shall only add, that
upon looking into my catalogue of subscribers, which I
intend to print alphabetically in the front of my Lucubrations, I find the names of the greatest beauties and wits in
the whole island of Great Britain, which I only mention
for the benefit of any of them who have not subscribed, it
being my design to close the subscription in a very short
time.

No. 163.   [ADDISON.

From *Saturday, April* 22, to *Tuesday, April* 25, 1710.

> Idem inficeto est inficetior rure,
> Simul poemata attigit ; neque idem unquam
> Æque est beatus, ac poema cum scribit :
> Tam gaudet in se, tamque se ipse miratur.
> Nimirum idem omnes fallimur ; neque est quisquam,
> Quem non in aliqua re videre Suffenum
> Possis.—CATULLUS, xxii. 14.

Will's Coffee-house, April 24.

I yesterday came hither about two hours before the
company generally make their appearance, with a
design to read over all the newspapers; but upon my sitting
down, I was accosted by Ned Softly, who saw me from a
corner in the other end of the room, where I found he
had been writing something. "Mr. Bickerstaff," says he,
"I observe by a late paper of yours, that you and I are

just of a humour ; for you must know, of all impertinences, there is nothing which I so much hate as news. I
never read a Gazette in my life ; and never trouble my
head about our armies, whether they win or lose, or in what
part of the world they lie encamped." Without giving me
time to reply, he drew a paper of verses out of his pocket,
telling me, that he had something which would entertain
me more agreeably, and that he would desire my judgment
upon every line, for that we had time enough before us
till the company came in.

Ned Softly is a very pretty poet, and a great admirer of
easy lines. Waller is his favourite : and as that admirable
writer has the best and worst verses of any among our
great English poets, Ned Softly has got all the bad ones
without book, which he repeats upon occasion, to show
his reading, and garnish his conversation. Ned is indeed a
true English reader, incapable of relishing the great and
masterly strokes of this art ; but wonderfully pleased with
the little Gothic ornaments of epigrammatical conceits,
turns, points, and quibbles, which are so frequent in the
most admired of our English poets, and practised by those
who want genius and strength to represent, after the
manner of the ancients, simplicity in its natural beauty
and perfection.

Finding myself unavoidably engaged in such a conversation, I was resolved to turn my pain into a pleasure, and
to divert myself as well as I could with so very odd a
fellow. "You must understand," says Ned, "that the
sonnet I am going to read to you was written upon a lady,
who showed me some verses of her own making, and is
perhaps the best poet of our age. But you shall hear it."
Upon which he began to read as follows :

" To Mira on her Incomparable Poems.

I.

" When dressed in laurel wreaths you shine,
  And tune your soft melodious notes,
You seem a sister of the Nine,
  Or Phœbus' self in petticoats.

II.

" I fancy, when your song you sing
  (Your song you sing with so much art),
Your pen was plucked from Cupid's wing ;
  For ah! it wounds me like his dart."

" Why," says I, " this is a little nosegay of conceits, a
very lump of salt : every verse has something in it that
piques ; and then the dart in the last line is certainly as
pretty a sting in the tail of an epigram (for so I think your
critics call it) as ever entered into the thought of a poet."
" Dear Mr. Bickerstaff," says he, shaking me by the hand,
" everybody knows you to be a judge of these things ; and
to tell you truly, I read over Roscommon's translation of
Horace's 'Art of Poetry' three several times, before I sat
down to write the sonnet which I have shown you. But
you shall hear it again, and pray observe every line of it,
for not one of them shall pass without your approbation.

" When dressed in laurel wreaths you shine.

"That is," says he, " when you have your garland on ;
when you are writing verses." To which I replied, " I
know your meaning : a metaphor ! " " The same," said
he, and went on :

" And tune your soft melodious notes.

" Pray observe the gliding of that verse ; there is scarce
a consonant in it : I took care to make it run upon liquids.

261

Give me your opinion of it." "Truly," said I, "I think it as good as the former." "I am very glad to hear you say so," says he ; "but mind the next :

> "*You seem a sister of the Nine.*

"That is," says he, "you seem a sister of the Muses ; for if you look into ancient authors, you will find it was their opinion, that there were nine of them." "I remember it very well," said I ; "but pray proceed."

> "*Or Phœbus' self in petticoats.*

"Phœbus," says he, "was the God of Poetry. These little instances, Mr. Bickerstaff, show a gentleman's reading. Then to take off from the air of learning, which Phœbus and the Muses have given to this first stanza, you may observe how it falls all of a sudden into the familiar ; 'in petticoats ! '

> "*Or Phœbus' self in petticoats.*"

"Let us now," says I, "enter upon the second stanza. I find the first line is still a continuation of the metaphor :

> "*I fancy, when your song you sing.*"

"It is very right," says he ; "but pray observe the turn of words in those two lines. I was a whole hour in adjusting of them, and have still a doubt upon me, whether in the second line it should be, 'Your song you sing' ; or, 'You sing your song'? You shall hear them both :

> "*I fancy, when your song you sing*
>   (*Your song you sing with so much art*).

Or,

> "*I fancy, when your song you sing*
>   (*You sing your song with so much art*)."

"Truly," said I, "the turn is so natural either way, that you have made me almost giddy with it." "Dear sir," said he, grasping me by the hand, "you have a great deal of patience ; but pray what do you think of the next verse :

> "*Your pen was plucked from Cupid's wing ?*"

"Think !" says I ; "I think you have made Cupid look like a little goose." "That was my meaning," says he ; "I think the ridicule is well enough hit off. But we now come to the last, which sums up the whole matter :

> "*For ah ! it wounds me like his dart.*

"Pray, how do you like that 'Ah !' Does it not make a pretty figure in that place ? 'Ah !' It looks as if I felt the dart, and cried out at being pricked with it :

> "*For ah ! it wounds me like his dart.*

"My friend Dick Easy,"[1] continued he, "assured me he would rather have written that 'Ah !' than to have been the author of the 'Æneid.' He indeed objected that I made Mira's pen like a quill in one of the lines, and like a dart in the other. But as to that——" "Oh! as to that," says I, "it is but supposing Cupid to be like a porcupine, and his quills and darts will be the same thing." He was going to embrace me for the hint ; but half a dozen critics coming into the room, whose faces he did not like, he conveyed the sonnet into his pocket, and whispered me in the ear, he would show it me again as soon as his man had written it over fair.

[1] Perhaps Henry Cromwell. See Nos. 47, 49, 165, and Mrs. Elizabeth Thomas' "Pylades and Corinna," i. 194.

No. 164.   ʳ [ȘTEELE.

From *Tuesday, April* 25, to *Thursday, April* 27, 1710.

Qui sibi promittit cives, urbem sibi curæ,
Imperium fore et Italiam, delubra Deorum,
Quo patre sit natus, num ignotâ matre inhonestus,
Omnes mortales curare et quærere cogit.
HOR., 1 Sat. vi. 34.

From my own Apartment, April 26.

I have lately been looking over the many packets of
letters which I have received from all quarters of Great
Britain, as well as from foreign countries, since my
entering upon the office of Censor, and indeed am very
much surprised to see so great a number of them, and
pleased to think that I have so far increased the revenue
of the Post Office.   As this collection will grow daily, I
have digested it into several bundles, and made proper
endorsements on each particular letter, it being my design,
when I lay down the work that I am now engaged in, to
erect a Paper Office, and give it to the public.[1]

I could not but make several observations upon reading
over the letters of my correspondents : as first of all, on
the different tastes that reign in the different parts of this
city.   I find, by the approbations which are given me, that
I am seldom famous on the same days on both sides of
Temple Bar ; and that when I am in the greatest repute
within the Liberties, I dwindle at the court end of the
town.   Sometimes I sink in both these places at the same

---

[1] This idea was carried out in 1725, when Charles Lillie published,
by Steele's permission, two volumes of " Original and genuine Letters
sent to the *Tatler* and *Spectator*, during the time those works were
publishing.   None of which have been before printed."   See No. 110.

time ; but for my comfort, my name has then been up in the districts of Wapping and Rotherhithe. Some of my correspondents desire me to be always serious, and others to be always merry. Some of them entreat me to go to bed and fall into a dream, and like me better when I am asleep than when I am awake : others advise me to sit all night upon the stars, and be more frequent in my astrological observations ; for that a vision is not properly a lucubration. Some of my readers thank me for filling my paper with the flowers of antiquity, others desire news from Flanders. Some approve my criticisms on the dead, and others my censures on the living. For this reason, I once resolved in the new edition of my works, to range my several papers under distinct heads, according as their principal design was to benefit and instruct the different capacities of my readers, and to follow the example of some very great authors, by writing at the head of each discourse, "Ad Aulam," "Ad Academiam," "Ad Populum," "Ad Clerum."

There is no particular in which my correspondents of all ages, conditions, sexes, and complexions, universally agree, except only in their thirst after scandal. It is impossible to conceive how many have recommended their neighbours to me upon this account, or how unmercifully I have been abused by several unknown hands, for not publishing the secret histories of cuckoldom that I have received from almost every street in town.

It would indeed be very dangerous for me to read over the many praises and eulogiums which come post to me from all the corners of the nation, were they not mixed with many checks, reprimands, scurrilities, and reproaches, which several of my good-natured countrymen cannot forbear sending me, though it often costs them twopence

or a groat before they can convey them to my hands :¹ so
that sometimes when I am put into the best humour in the
world, after having read a panegyric upon my performance,
and looked upon myself as a benefactor to the British
nation, the next letter perhaps I open, begins with, " You
old doting scoundrel;" "Are not you a sad dog?"
"Sirrah, you deserve to have your nose slit;" and the
like ingenious conceits. These little mortifications are
necessary to surpass that pride and vanity which naturally
arise in the mind of a received author, and enable me to
bear the reputation which my courteous readers bestow
upon me, without becoming a coxcomb by it. It was for
the same reason, that when a Roman general entered the
city in the pomp of a triumph, the commonwealth allowed
of several little drawbacks to his reputation, by conniving
at such of the rabble as repeated libels and lampoons upon
him within his hearing, and by that means engaged his
thoughts upon his weakness and imperfections, as well as on
the merits that advanced him to so great honours. The conqueror however was not the less esteemed for being a man
in some particulars, because he appeared as a god in others.

There is another circumstance in which my countrymen
have dealt very perversely with me; and that is, in
searching not only into my own life, but also into the
lives of my ancestors. If there has been a blot in my
family for these ten generations, it has been discovered by
some or other of my correspondents. In short, I find the
ancient family of the Bickerstaffs has suffered very much
through the malice and prejudice of my enemies. Some
of them twit me in the teeth with the conduct of my Aunt
Margery :¹ nay, there are some who have been so disingenuous, as to throw Maud the Milkmaid² into my dish,
notwithstanding I myself was the first who discovered that

¹ See Nos. 117, 186, Advertisements.   ² See No. 151.   ³ See No. 75.

266

alliance. I reap however many benefits from the malice of these my enemies, as they let me see my own faults, and give me a view of myself in the worst light ; as they hinder me from being blown up by flattery and self-conceit ; as they make me keep a watchful eye over my own actions, and at the same time make me cautious how I talk of others, and particularly of my friends and relations, or value myself upon the antiquity of my family.

But the most formidable part of my correspondents are those whose letters are filled with threats and menaces. I have been treated so often after this manner, that not thinking it sufficient to fence well, in which I am now arrived at the utmost perfection,[1] and carry pistols about me, which I have always tucked within my girdle ; I several months since made my will, settled my estate, and took leave of my friends, looking upon myself as no better than a dead man. Nay, I went so far as to write a long letter to the most intimate acquaintance I have in the world, under the character of a departed person, giving him an account of what brought me to that untimely end, and of the fortitude with which I met it. This letter being too long for the present paper, I intend to print it by itself very suddenly ; and at the same time I must confess, I took my hint of it from the behaviour of an old soldier in the Civil Wars, who was corporal of a company in a regiment of foot, about the same time that I myself was a cadet in the King's army.

This gentleman was taken by the enemy ; and the two parties were upon such terms at that time, that we did not treat each other as prisoners of war, but as traitors and rebels. The poor corporal being condemned to die, wrote

---

[1] It would hardly be possible for a man of Bickerstaff's age to acquire perfection in fencing after only a few months' practice. See No. 173 : "I first began to learn to push this last winter."

a letter to his wife when under sentence of execution. He writ on the Thursday, and was to be executed on the Friday : but considering that the letter would not come to his wife's hands till Saturday, the day after execution, and being at that time more scrupulous than ordinary in speaking exact truth, he formed his letter rather according to the posture of his affairs when she should read it, than as they stood when he sent it ; though it must be confessed, there is a certain perplexity in the style of it, which the reader will easily pardon, considering his circumstances :

"DEAR WIFE,

"Hoping you are in good health, as I am at this present writing, this is to let you know, that yesterday, between the hours of eleven and twelve, I was hanged, drawn and quartered. I died very penitently, and everybody thought my case very hard. Remember me kindly to my poor fatherless children.

"Yours till death,

"W. B."

It so happened, that this honest fellow was relieved by a party of his friends, and had the satisfaction to see all the rebels hanged who had been his enemies. I must not omit a circumstance which exposed him to raillery his whole life after. Before the arrival of the next post, that would have set all things clear, his wife was married to a second husband, who lived in the peaceful possession of her ; and the corporal, who was a man of plain understanding, did not care to stir in the matter, as knowing that she had the news of his death under his own hand, which she might have produced upon occasion.

.No. 165.   [ADDISON.

From *Thursday*, *April* 27, to *Saturday*, *April* 29, 1710.

From my own Apartment, April 28.

It has always been my endeavour to distinguish between
realities and appearances, and to separate true merit
from the pretence to it. As it shall ever be my study to
make discoveries of this nature in human life, and to
settle the proper distinctions between the virtues and
perfections of mankind, and those false colours and
resemblances of them that shine alike in the eyes of the
vulgar ; so I shall be more particularly careful to search into
the various merits and pretences of the learned world. This
is the more necessary, because there seems to be a general
combination among the pedants to extol one another's
labours, and cry up one another's parts ; while men of
sense, either through that modesty which is natural to
them, or the scorn they have for such trifling commendations, enjoy their stock of knowledge like a hidden treasure,
with satisfaction and silence. Pedantry indeed in learning
is like hypocrisy in religion, a form of knowledge without
the power of it, that attracts the eyes of the common
people, breaks out in noise and show, and finds its reward
not from any inward pleasure that attends it, but from the
praises and approbations which it receives from men.

Of this shallow species there is not a more importunate, empty, and conceited animal, than that which is
generally known by the name of a critic. This, in the
common acceptation of the word, is one that, without
entering into the sense and soul of an author, has a few
general rules, which, like mechanical instruments, he applies

269

Timothy, "is by no means just." "Pray," says she, "let my similes pass without a criticism. I must confess," continued she (for I found she was resolved to exasperate him), "I laughed very heartily at the last new comedy which you found so much fault with." "But, madam," says he, "you ought not to have laughed; and I defy any one to show me a single rule that you could laugh by." "Ought not to laugh!" says she: "pray, who should hinder me?" "Madam," says he, "there are such people in the world as Rapin, Dacier, and several others, that ought to have spoiled your mirth." "I have heard," says the young lady, "that your great critics are always very bad poets: I fancy there is as much difference between the works of one and the other, as there is between the carriage of a dancing-master and a gentleman. I must confess," continued she, "I would not be troubled with so fine a judgment as yours is; for I find you feel more vexation in a bad comedy than I do in a deep tragedy." "Madam," says Sir Timothy, "that is not my fault; they should learn the art of writing." "For my part," says the young lady, "I should think the greatest art in your writers of comedies is to please." "To please!" says Sir Timothy; and immediately fell a-laughing. "Truly," says she, "that is my opinion." Upon this, he composed his countenance, looked upon his watch, and took his leave.

I hear that Sir Timothy has not been at my friend's house since this notable conference, to the great satisfaction of the young lady, who by this means has got rid of a very impertinent fop.

I must confess, I could not but observe, with a great deal of surprise, how this gentleman, by his ill-nature, folly, and affectation, has made himself capable of suffering so many imaginary pains, and looking with such a senseless severity upon the common diversions of life.

No. 166. [STEELE.

From *Saturday, April* 29, to *Tuesday, May* 2, 1710.

—— Dicenda tacenda loquutus.—HOR., 1 Ep. vii. 72.

White's Chocolate-house, May 1.

The world is so overgrown with singularities in behaviour, and method of living, that I have no sooner laid before mankind the absurdity of one species of men, but there starts up to my view some new sect of impertinents that had before escaped notice. This afternoon, as I was talking with fine Mrs. Sprightly's porter, and desiring admittance upon an extraordinary occasion, it was my fate to be spied by Tom Modely riding by in his chariot. He did me the honour to stop, and asked what I did there of a Monday? I answered that I had business of importance, which I wanted to communicate to the lady of the house. Tom is one of those fools who look upon knowledge of the fashion to be the only liberal science ; and was so rough as to tell me, that a well-bred man would as soon call upon a lady (who keeps a day) at midnight, as on any day but that on which she professes being at home. There are rules and decorums which are never to be transgressed by those who understand the world ; and he who offends in this kind, ought not to take it ill if he is turned away, even when he sees the person look out at her window whom he inquires for. " Nay," said he, " my Lady Dimple is so positive in this rule, that she takes it for a piece of good breeding and distinction to deny herself with her own mouth. Mrs. Comma,[1] the great scholar, insists upon it ;

[1] " I have been informed by a relation of hers, that when Mrs. Mary Astell has accidentally seen needless visitors coming, whom she knew

and I myself have heard her assert, that a lord's porter, or a lady's woman, cannot be said to lie in that case, because they act by instruction ; and their words are no more their own, than those of a puppet."

He was going on with this ribaldry, when on a sudden he looked on his watch, and said, he had twenty visits to make, and drove away without further ceremony. I was then at leisure to reflect upon the tasteless manner of life, which a set of idle fellows lead in this town, and spend youth itself with less spirit, than other men do their old age. These expletives in human society, though they are in themselves wholly insignificant, become of some consideration when they are mixed with others. I am very much at a loss how to define, or under what character, distinction, or denomination, to place them, except you give me leave to call them the Order of the Insipids. This order is in its extent like that of the Jesuits, and you see of them in every way of life, and in every profession. Tom Modely has long appeared to me at the head of this species. By being habitually in the best company, he knows perfectly well when a coat is well cut, or a periwig well mounted.[1] As soon as you enter the place where he is, he tells the next man to him who is your tailor, and judges of you more from the choice of your periwig-maker than of your friend. His business in this world is to be well dressed ; and the greatest circumstance that is to be recorded in his annals is, that he wears twenty shirts a week. Thus, without ever speaking

to be incapable of discoursing upon any useful subject, she would look out of the window, and jestingly tell them (as Cato did Nasica), ' Mrs. Astell is not at home ' ; and in good earnest keep them out, not suffering such triflers to make inroads upon her more serious hours " (Ballard's " Memoirs of British Learned Ladies," 1775, p. 309). For Swift's attacks on Mary Astell, see Nos. 32, 63.

[1] " Monter une perruque " is a French barber's phrase.

reason among the men, or passion among the women, he is everywhere well received ; and without any one man's esteem, he has every man's indulgence.

This order has produced great numbers of tolerable copiers in painting, good rhymers in poetry, and harmless projectors in politics. You may see them at first sight grow acquainted by sympathy, insomuch that one who had not studied nature, and did not know the true cause of their sudden familiarities, would think that they had some secret intimation of each other, like the freemasons. The other day at Will's I heard Modely, and a critic of the same order, show their equal talents with great delight. The learned insipid was commending Racine's turns ; the genteel insipid, Devillier's curls.[1]

These creatures, when they are not forced into any particular employment, for want of ideas in their own imaginations, are the constant plague of all they meet with by inquiries for news and scandal, which makes them the heroes of visiting-days, where they help the design of the meeting, which is to pass away that odious thing called Time, in discourses too trivial to raise any reflections which may put well-bred persons to the trouble of thinking.

From my own Apartment, May 1.

I was looking out of my parlour window this morning,[2] and receiving the honours which Margery, the milkmaid to our lane, was doing me, by dancing before my door

---

[1] See Nos. 26, 29. Duvillier or Devillier was a hairdresser.

[2] May Day. In the *Spectator* (No. 365) Budgell says : "It is likewise on the first day of this month that we see the ruddy milkmaid exerting herself in a most sprightly manner under a pyramid of silver tankards, and like the virgin Tarpeia, oppressed by the costly ornaments which her benefactors lay upon her." Similarly, Misson ("Travels in England," p. 307) says : "On the first of May, and the five or six days following, all the pretty young country girls that serve the town with milk, dress themselves up very neatly, and borrow abundance of silver plate,

with the plate of half her customers on her head, when
Mr. Clayton,[1] the author of " Arsinoe," made me a visit,
and desired me to insert the following advertisement in
my ensuing paper :

The Pastoral Masque composed by Mr. Clayton,
author of " Arsinoe," will be performed on Wednesday
the 3rd instant, in the great room at York Buildings.[2]
Tickets are to be had at White's Chocolate-house,
St. James's Coffee-house in St. James's Street, and Young
Man's Coffee-house.[3]

Note. The tickets delivered out for the 27th of April
will be taken then.

When I granted his request, I made one to him, which
was, that the performers should put their instruments in
tune before the audience came in ; for that I thought the

whereof they make a pyramid, which they adorn with ribands and
flowers, and carry upon their heads, instead of their common milk-
pails. In this equipage, accompanied by some of their fellow milk-
maids, and a bagpipe and fiddle, they go from door to door, dancing
before the houses of their customers."

[1] " There is a Pastoral Masque to be performed on the 27th inst., in
York Buildings, for the benefit of Mr. Clayton, and composed by him.
This gentleman is the person who introduced the Italian opera into
Great Britain, and hopes he has pretensions to the favour of all lovers
of music, who can get over the prejudice of his being their country-
man " (*Tatler*, original folio, No. 163).

Thomas Clayton, in association with Haym and Dieuport, began a
series of operatic performances at Drury Lane Theatre in 1705, com-
mencing with " Arsinoe," which was a success. In 1707 he produced
a setting of Addison's " Rosamond," but it was played only three times.
The opera performances were continued until 1711, after which
Clayton gave concerts in York Buildings (see *Spectator*, No. 258). He
died about 1730.

[2] In the Strand. In 1713 Steele started a scheme for " a noble
entertainment for persons of refined taste," in York Buildings.

[3] At Charing Cross, with a back door into Spring Gardens.

resentment of the Eastern Prince, who, according to the old story, took " tuning " for " playing," to be very just and natural. He was so civil, as not only to promise that favour, but also to assure me, that he would order the heels of the performers to be muffled in cotton, that the artists in so polite an age as ours, may not intermix with their harmony a custom which so nearly resembles the stamping dances of the West Indians or Hottentots.

ADVERTISEMENTS.

A Bass-viol of Mr. Bickerstaff's acquaintance, whose mind and fortune do not very exactly agree, proposes to set himself to sale by way of lottery.[1] Ten thousand pounds is the sum to be raised, at threepence a ticket, in consideration that there are more women who are willing to be married than that can spare a greater sum. He has already made over his person to trustees for the said money to be forthcoming, and ready to take to wife the fortunate woman that wins him.

N.B. Tickets are given out by Mr. Charles Lillie, and Mr. John Morphew. Each adventurer must be a virgin, and subscribe her name to her ticket.[2]

Whereas the several churchwardens of most of the parishes within the bills of mortality, have in an earnest

[1] See Nos. 153, 157, 168.
[2] In the *Daily Courant* for Aug. 18, 1710, there was advertised as just published a pamphlet called "A Good Husband for Five Shillings ; or, Esquire Bickerstaff's Lottery for the London Ladies. Wherein those that want bedfellows, in an honest way, will have a fair chance to be well fitted." It was complained that husbands were scarce through the war. The title exhausts all that is of interest in the pamphlet, with the exception of the frontispiece, which represents a room in which a lottery is being drawn, with two wheels of fortune, &c.

manner applied themselves by way of petition, and have
also made a presentment of the vain and loose deportment
during divine service, of persons of too great figure in all
their said parishes for their reproof : And whereas it is
therein set forth, that by salutations given each other,
hints, shrugs, ogles, playing of fans, and fooling with
canes at their mouths, and other wanton gesticulations,
their whole congregation appears rather a theatrical
audience, than a house of devotion : It is hereby ordered,
that all canes, cravats, bosom-laces, muffs, fans, snuff-boxes,
and all other instruments made use of to give persons
unbecoming airs, shall be immediately forfeited and sold ;
and of the sum arising from the sale thereof, a ninth part
shall be paid to the poor, and the rest to the overseers.[1]

[1] Nichols notes that a correction in this number, intimated in the
following paper, was actually made in a copy before him, and concluded that there was sometimes more than one impression of the
original folio issue. This was certainly the case. There is a set of
the *Tatlers* in folio in the British Museum (press-mark 628 m 13) in
which many of the numbers are set up somewhat differently from
the ordinary issue (Nos. 4, 28, 29, 30, &c.). Sometimes there is a line
more or less in a column ; sometimes slightly different type is used
in one or two advertisements.

No. 167.

From *Tuesday*, *May* 2, to *Thursday*, *May* 4, 1710.

Segnius irritant animos demissa per aurem,
Quam quæ sunt oculis subjecta fidelibus——
Hor., Ars Poet. 180.

From my own Apartment, May 2.

Having received notice, that the famous actor Mr. Betterton[1] was to be interred this evening in the cloisters near Westminster Abbey, I was resolved to walk thither, and see the last office done to a man whom I had always very much admired, and from whose action I had received more strong impressions of what is great and noble in human nature, than from the arguments of the most solid philosophers, or the descriptions of the most charming poets I had ever read. As the rude and

[1] See Nos. 1, 71, 157. On the 25th of April 1710, there was given for Betterton's benefit, "The Maid's Tragedy" of Beaumont and Fletcher, in which he himself performed his celebrated part of Melantius. This, however, was the last time he was to appear on the stage, for, having been suddenly seized with the gout, and being impatient at the thought of disappointing his friends, he made use of outward applications to reduce the swellings of his feet, which enabled him to walk on the stage, though obliged to have his foot in a slipper. But the fomentations he had used occasioning a revulsion of the gouty humour to the nobler parts, threw the distemper up into his head, and terminated his life on the 28th of April. On the 2nd of May his body was interred with much ceremony in the cloister of Westminster.—"This day is published, 'The Life of Mr. Thomas Betterton'" (*Postboy*, Sept. 16 to 19, 1710). This book, attributed to Gildon, is dedicated to Richard Steele, Esq. "I have chosen," says the author, "to address this discourse to you, because the Art of which it treats is of your familiar acquaintance, and the graces of action and utterance come naturally under the consideration of a dramatic writer."

untaught multitude are no way wrought upon more effectually than by seeing public punishments and, executions,
so men of letters and education feel their humanity most
forcibly exercised, when they attend the obsequies of men
who had arrived at any perfection in liberal accomplishments.   Theatrical action is to be esteemed as such,
except it be objected, that we cannot call that an art
which cannot be attained by art.   Voice, stature, motion,
and other gifts, must be very bountifully bestowed by
Nature, or labour and industry will but push the unhappy
endeavourer, in that way, the further off his wishes.

Such an actor as Mr. Betterton ought to be recorded
with the same respect as Roscius among the Romans.
The greatest orator[1] has thought fit to quote his judgment, and celebrate his life.   Roscius was the example to
all that would form themselves into proper and winning
behaviour.   His action was so well adapted to the sentiments he expressed, that the youth of Rome thought they
wanted only to be virtuous to be as graceful in their
appearance as Roscius.   The imagination took a lively
impression of what was great and good ; and they who
never thought of setting up for the arts of imitation,
became themselves imitable characters.

There is no human invention so aptly calculated for the
forming a free-born people as that of a theatre.   Tully
reports that the celebrated player of whom I am speaking
used frequently to say, " The perfection of an actor is
only to become what he is doing."   Young men, who are
too unattentive to receive lectures, are irresistibly taken with
performances.   Hence it is, that I extremely lament the
little relish the gentry of this nation have at present for
the just and noble representations in some of our tragedies.
The operas which are of late introduced can leave no

[1] Cicero.

trace behind them that can be of service beyond the present moment. To sing and to dance are accomplishments very few have any thoughts of practising ; but to speak justly, and move gracefully, is what every man thinks he does perform, or wishes he did.

I have hardly a notion, that any performer of antiquity could surpass the action of Mr. Betterton in any of the occasions in which he has appeared on our stage. The wonderful agony which he appeared in, when he examined the circumstance of the handkerchief in "Othello" ; the mixture of love that intruded upon his mind upon the innocent answers Desdemona makes, betrayed in his gesture such a variety and vicissitude of passions, as would admonish a man to be afraid of his own heart, and perfectly convince him, that it is to stab it to admit that worst of daggers, jealousy. Whoever reads in his closet this admirable scene, will find that he cannot, except he has as warm an imagination as Shakespeare himself, find any but dry, incoherent, and broken sentences : but a reader that has seen Betterton act it, observes there could not be a word added ; that longer speeches had been unnatural, nay impossible, in Othello's circumstances. The charming passage in the same tragedy, 'where he tells the manner of winning the affection of his mistress, was urged with so moving and graceful an energy, that while I walked in the cloisters, I thought of him with the same concern as if I waited for the remains of a person who had in real life done all that I had seen him represent. The gloom of the place, and faint lights before the ceremony appeared, contributed to the melancholy disposition I was in ; and I began to be extremely afflicted, that Brutus and Cassius had any difference ; that Hotspur's gallantry was so unfortunate ; and that the mirth and good humour of Falstaff could not exempt him from the grave. Nay, this occasion in me, who look upon the distinctions amongst men to be merely scenical, raised reflections upon the emptiness of all human perfection and greatness in general·; and I· could not but regret, that the sacred heads which lie buried in the neighbourhood of this little portion of earth in which my poor old friend is deposited, are returned to dust as well as he, and that there is no difference in the grave between the imaginary and the real monarch. This made me say of human life itself with Macbeth :

> " To-morrow, to-morrow, and to-morrow,
> Creeps in a stealing pace from day to day,
> To the last moment of recorded time !
> And all our yesterdays have lighted fools
> To their eternal night !   Out, out short candle !
> Life's but a walking shadow, a poor player
> That struts and frets his hour upon the stage,
> And then is heard no more." [1]

The mention I have here made of Mr. Betterton, for whom I had, as long as I have known anything, a very great esteem and gratitude for the pleasure he gave me, can do him no good ; but it may possibly be of service to the unhappy woman he has left behind him,[2] to have it known, that this great tragedian was never in a scene half so moving as the circumstances of his affairs created at his departure. His wife, after the cohabitation of forty years in the strictest amity, has long pined away with a sense of his decay, as

---

[1] " Macbeth," act v. sc. 5, quoted inaccurately by Steele.
[2] Betterton married, in 1662, Maria Saunderson, an actress who seems to have been as good as she was clever. She lost her reason after the death of her husband, but recovered it before her death at the end of 1711. By her will she bequeathed to Mrs. Bracegirdle, Mrs. Barry, Mr. Doggett, Mr. Wilks, and Mr. Dent, twenty shillings a piece for rings ; and her husband's picture to Mrs. Anne Stevenson, whom she appointed her residuary legatee.

well in his person as his little fortune ; and in proportion to that, she has herself decayed both in her health and her reason. •Her husband's death, added to her age and infirmities, would certainly have determined her life, but that the greatness of her distress has been her relief, by a present deprivation of her senses. This absence of reason is her best defence against age, sorrow, poverty, and sickness. I dwell upon this account so distinctly, in obedience to a certain great spirit[1] who hides her name, and has by letter applied to me to recommend to her some object of compassion, from whom she may be concealed.

This, I think, is a proper occasion for exerting such heroic generosity ; and as there is an ingenuous shame in those who have known better fortune to be reduced to receive obligations, as well as a becoming pain in the truly generous to receive thanks in this case, both those delicacies are preserved ; for the person obliged is as incapable of knowing her benefactress, as her benefactress is unwilling to be known by her.

ADVERTISEMENT.

Whereas it has been signified to the Censor, that under the pretence that he has encouraged the Moving Picture,[2] and particularly admired the Walking Statue, some persons within the Liberties of Westminster have vended Walking Pictures, insomuch that the said pictures have within few days after sales by auction returned to the habitation of their first proprietors ; that matter has been narrowly looked into, and orders are given to Pacolet to take notice

[1] Possibly Lady Elizabeth Hastings (see Nos. 42, 49), or perhaps Queen Anne, though it is not likely that she consulted Steele by letter on the subject. The Queen gave Mrs. Betterton a pension on the death of her husband, "but," says Cibber, "she lived not to receive more than the first half year of it."

[2] See No. 129.

of all who are concerned in such frauds, with directions to
draw their pictures, that they may be hanged .in effigy, *in
terrorem* of all auctions for the future.   •

No. 168.   [STEELE.

From *Thursday, May 4*, to *Saturday, May 6*, 1710.

From my own Apartment, May 5.

Never was man so much teased, or suffered half the
uneasiness, as I have done this evening, between a
couple of fellows with whom I was unfortunately engaged
to sup, where there were also several others in company.
One of them is the most invincibly impudent, and the
other as incorrigibly absurd. Upon hearing my name,
the man of audacity, as he calls himself, began to assume
an awkward way of reserve, by way of ridicule upon me
as a Censor, and said, he must have a care of his
behaviour, for there would notes be writ upon all that
should pass. The man of freedom and ease (for such
the other thinks himself) asked me, whether my sister
Jenny was breeding or not? After they had done with
me, they were impertinent to a very smart, but well-bred
man, who stood his ground very well, and let the company
see they ought, but could not be out of countenance. I
look upon such a defence as a real good action ; for while
he received their fire, there was a modest and worthy
young gentleman sat secure by him, and a lady of the
family at the same time, guarded against the nauseous
familiarity of the one, and the more painful mirth of the
other. This conversation, where there were a thousand
things said not worth repeating, made me consider with
myself, how it is that men of these disagreeable characters

often go great lengths in the world, and seldom fail of outstripping men of merit ; nay, succeed so well, that with a · load of imperfections on their heads, they go on in opposition to general disesteem, while they who are every way their superiors, languish away their days, though possessed of the approbation and goodwill of all who know them.

If we would examine into the secret spring of action in the impudent and the absurd, we shall find, though they bear a great resemblance in their behaviour, that they move upon very different principles. The impudent are pressing, though they know they are disagreeable ; the absurd are importunate, because they think they are acceptable. Impudence is a vice, and absurdity a folly. Sir Francis Bacon talks very agreeably upon the subject of impudence.[1] He takes notice, that the orator being asked, what was the first, second, and third requisite, to make a fine speaker, still answered, "Action." This, said he, is the very outward form of speaking, and yet it is what with the generality has more force than the most consummate abilities. Impudence is to the rest of mankind of the same use which action is to orators.

The truth is, the gross of men are governed more by appearances than realities, and the impudent man in his air and behaviour undertakes for himself that he has ability and merit, while the modest or diffident gives himself up as one who is possessed of neither. For this reason, men of front carry things before them with little opposition, and make so skilful a use of their talent, that they can grow out of humour like men of consequence, and be sour, and make their satisfaction do them the same service as desert. This way of thinking has often furnished me with an apology for great men who confer

---

[1] Essay xii., "Of Boldness."

favours on the impudent.   In carrying on the government
of mankind, they are not to consider what men they
themselves approve in their closets and private conversations, but what men will extend themselves furthest, and
more generally pass upon the world for such as their
patrons want in such and such stations, and consequently
take so much work off the hands of those who employ
them.

Far be it that I should attempt to lessen the acceptance
which men of this character meet with in the world ; but
I humbly proposo only, that they who have merit of a
different kind, would accomplish themselves in some degree
with this quality of which I am now treating.   Nay, I allow
these gentlemen to press as forward as they please in the
advancement of their interests and fortunes, but not to
intrude upon others in conversation also : let them do
what they can with the rich and the great, as far as they
are suffered, but let them not interrupt the easy and
agreeable.   They may be useful as servants in ambition, but
never as associates in pleasure.   However, as I would still
drive at something instructive in every Lucubration, I must
recommend it to all men who feel in themselves an impulse
towards attempting laudable actions, to acquire such a
degree of assurance, as never to lose the possession of
themselves in public or private, so far as to be incapable
of acting with a due decorum on any occasion they are
called to.   It is a mean want of fortitude in a good
man, not to be able to do a virtuous action with as
much confidence as an impudent fellow does an ill one.
There is no way of mending such false modesty, but by
laying it down for a rule, that there is nothing shameful
but what is criminal.

The Jesuits, an order whose institution is perfectly
calculated for making a progress in the world, take care

to accomplish their disciples for it, by breaking them of all impertinent bashfulness, and accustoming then to a ready performance of all indifferent things. I remember in my travels, when I was once at a public exercise in one of their schools, a young man made a most admirable speech, with all the beauty of action, cadence of voice, and force of argument imaginable, in defence of the love of glory. We were all enamoured with the grace of the youth, as he came down from the desk where he spoke to present a copy of his speech to the head of the society. The principal received it in a very obliging manner, and bid him go to the market-place and fetch a joint of meat, for he should dine with him. He bowed, and in a trice the orator returned, full of the sense of glory in this obedience, and with the best shoulder of mutton in the market.

This treatment capacitates them for every scene of life. I therefore recommend it to the consideration of all who have the instruction of youth, which of the two is the most inexcusable, he who does everything by the mere force of his impudence, or who performs nothing through the oppression of his modesty? In a word, it is a weakness not to be able to attempt what a man thinks he ought, and there is no modesty but in self-denial.

P.S. Upon my coming home I received the following petition and letter:

"The humble petition of Sarah Lately:

"SHEWETH,

"That your petitioner has been one of those ladies who has had fine things constantly spoken to her in general terms, and lived, during her most blooming years, in daily expectation of declarations of marriage, but never had one made to her.

" That she is now in her grand climacteric ; which being above the space of four virginities, accounting at 15 years each,   •   .

" Your petitioner most humbly prays, that in the lottery for the Bass-viol [1] she may have four tickets, in consideration that her single life has been occasioned by the inconstancy of her lovers, and not through the cruelty or forwardness of your petitioner.

" And your Petitioner shall," &c.

"MR. BICKERSTAFF,   " *May* 3, 1710.

" According to my fancy, you took a much better way to dispose of a Bass-viol in yesterday's paper than you did in your table of marriage.[2]   I desire the benefit of a lottery for myself too——   The manner of it I leave to your own discretion : only if you can——allow the tickets at above five farthings a piece.   Pray accept of one ticket for your trouble, and I wish you may be the fortunate man that wins.

" Your very humble Servant till then,

"ISABELLA KIT."

I must own the request of the aged petitioner to be founded upon a very undeserved distress ; and since she might, had she had justice done her, been mother of many pretenders to this prize, instead of being one herself, I do readily grant her demand ; but as for the proposal of Mrs. Isabella Kit, I cannot project a lottery for her, until I have security she will surrender herself to the winner.

[1] See No. 166.   [2] See Nos. 157, 160.

No. 169.   [STEELE.

From *Saturday*, *May* 6, to *Tuesday*, *May* 9, 1710.

O rus ! Quando ego te aspiciam ? quandoque licebit ·
Nunc veterum libris, nunc somno, et inertibus horis,
Ducere sollicitæ jucunda oblivia vitæ ?
HOR., 2 Sat. vi. 60.

From my own Apartment, May 8.

The summer season now approaching, several of our family have invited me to pass away a month or two in the country, and indeed nothing could be more agreeable to me than such a recess, did I not consider that I am by two quarts a worse companion than when I was last among my relations : and I am admonished by some of our club, who have lately visited Staffordshire, that they drink at a greater rate than they did at that time. As every soil does not produce every fruit or tree, so every vice is not the growth of every kind of life ; and I have, ever since I could think, been astonished that drinking should be the vice of the country. If it were possible to add to all our senses, as we do to that of sight, by perspectives, we should methinks more particularly labour to improve them in the midst of the variety of beauteous objects which Nature has produced to entertain us in the country ; and do we in that place destroy the use of what organs we have ? As for my part, I cannot but lament the destruction that has been made of the wild beasts of the field, when I see large tracts of earth possessed by men who take no advantage of their being rational, but lead mere animal lives, making it their whole endeavour to kill in themselves all they have above beasts ; to wit, the use of reason, and taste of society. It is frequently boasted

The Tatler No. 169. May 9, 1710

in the writings of orators and poets, that it is to eloquence
and poesy we owe that we are drawn out of woods and
solitudes into towns and cities, and from a wild and savage
being become acquainted with the laws of humanity and
civility. If we are obliged to these arts for so great
service, I could wish they were employed to give us a
second turn ; that as they have brought us to dwell in
society (a blessing which no other creatures know), so
they would persuade us, now they have settled us, to lay
out all our thoughts in surpassing each other in those
faculties in which only we excel other creatures. But it is
at present so far otherwise, that the contention seems to
be, who shall be most eminent in performances wherein
beasts enjoy greater abilities than we have. I'll undertake,
were the butler and swineherd, at any true esquire's in
Great Britain, to keep and compare accounts of what wash
is drunk up in so many hours in the parlour and the pig-
sty, it would appear, the gentleman of the house gives
much more to his friends than his hogs.

This, with many other evils, arises from the error in
men's judgments, and not making true distinctions between
persons and things. It is usually thought, that a few
sheets of parchment, made before a male and female of
wealthy houses come together, give the heirs and descend-
ants of that marriage possession of lands and tenements ;
but the truth is, there is no man who can be said to
be proprietor of an estate, but he who knows how to
enjoy it. Nay, it shall never be allowed, that the land is
not a waste, when the master is uncultivated. Therefore,
to avoid confusion, it is to be noted, that a peasant with a
great estate is but an incumbent, and that he must be a
gentleman to be a landlord. A landlord enjoys what he
has with his heart, an incumbent with his stomach.
Gluttony, drunkenness, and riot, are the entertainments of

an incumbent ; benevolence, civility, social and human
virtues, the accomplishments of a landlord. Who, that
has any passion for his native country, does not think it
worse than conquered, when so large diversions of it are in
the hands of savages, that know no use of property but
to be tyrants ; or liberty, but to be unmannerly ? A
gentleman in a country life enjoys Paradise with a temper
fit for it ; a clown is cursed in it with all the cutting and
unruly passions man could be tormented with when he
was expelled from it.

There is no character more deservedly esteemed than
that of a country gentleman, who understands the station
in which heaven and nature have placed him. He is
father to his tenants, and patron to his neighbours, and is
more superior to those of lower fortune by his benevolence
than his possessions. He justly divides his time between
solitude and company, so as to use the one for the other.
His life is spent in the good offices of an advocate, a
referee, a companion, a mediator, and a friend. His
counsel and knowledge are a guard to the simplicity and
innocence of those of lower talents, and the entertainment
and happiness of those of equal. When a man in a
country life has this turn, as it is to be hoped thousands
have, he lives in a more happy condition than any is
described in the pastoral descriptions of poets, or the vainglorious solitudes recorded by philosophers.

To a thinking man it would seem prodigious, that the
very situation in a country life does not incline men to a
scorn of the mean gratifications some take in it. To
stand by a stream, naturally lulls the mind into composure
and reverence ; to walk in shades, diversifies that pleasure ;
and a bright sunshine makes a man consider all nature in
gladness, and himself the happiest being in it, as he is the
most conscious of her gifts and enjoyments. It would be

the most impertinent piece of pedantry imaginable to form our pleasures by imitation of others. I will not therefore mention Scipio and Lælius, who are generally produced on this subject as authorities for the charms of a rural life. He that does not feel the force of agreeable views and situations in his own mind, will hardly arrive at the satisfactions they bring from the reflections of others. However, they who have a taste that way, are more particularly inflamed with desire when they see others in the enjoyment of it, especially when men carry into the country a knowledge of the world as well as of nature. The leisure of such persons is endeared and refined by reflection upon cares and inquietudes. The absence of past labours doubles present pleasures, which is still augmented, if the person in solitude has the happiness of being addicted to letters. My cousin Frank Bickerstaff gives me a very good notion of this sort of felicity in the following letter :

"Sir,

" I write this to communicate to you the happiness I have in the neighbourhood and conversation of the noble lord whose health you inquired after in your last. I have bought that little hovel which borders upon his royalty ; but am so far from being oppressed by his greatness, that I who know no envy, and he who is above pride, mutually recommend ourselves to each other by the difference of our fortunes. He esteems me for being so well pleased with a little, and I admire him for enjoying so handsomely a great deal. He has not the little taste of observing the colour of a tulip, or the edging of a leaf of box, but rejoices in open views, the regularity of this plantation, and the wildness of another, as well as the fall of a river, the rising of a promontory, and all other objects fit to entertain a mind like his, that has been long versed in great and public amusements. The make of the soul is as much seen in leisure as in business. He has long lived in Courts, and been admired in assemblies, so that he has added to experience a most charming eloquence ; by which he communicates to me the ideas of my own mind upon the objects we meet with, so agreeably, that with his company in the fields, I at once enjoy the country, and a landscape of it. He is now altering the course of canals and rivulets, in which he has an eye to his neighbour's satisfaction, as well as his own. He often makes me presents by turning the water into my grounds, and sends me fish by their own streams. To avoid my thanks, he makes Nature the instrument of his bounty, and does all good offices so much with the air of a companion, that his frankness hides his own condescension, as well as my gratitude. Leave the world to itself, and come see us.

"Your affectionate Cousin,

"FRANCIS BICKERSTAFF."

No. 170.   [STEELE.

From *Tuesday, May* 9, to *Thursday, May* 11, 1710.

> Fortuna sævo læta negotio et
> Ludum insolentem ludere pertinax
> Transmutat incertos honores,
> Nunc mihi, nunc alii, benigna.
> HOR., 3 Od. xxix. 49.

From my own Apartment, May 10.

Having this morning spent some time in reading on the subject of the vicissitude of human life, I laid aside my book, and began to ruminate on the discourse

The Tatler   No. 170. May 11, 1710

which raised in me those reflections.   I believed it a very
good office to the world, to sit down and show others the
road in which I am experienced by my wanderings and
errors.   This is Seneca's way of thinking, and he had half
convinced me, how dangerous it is to our true happiness
and tranquillity to fix our minds upon anything which is in
the power of Fortune.   It is excusable only in animals
who have not the use of reason, to be catched by hooks
and baits.   Wealth, glory, and power, which the ordinary
people look up at with admiration, the learned and wise
know to be only so many snares laid to enslave them.
There is nothing further to be sought for with earnestness,
than what will clothe and feed us.   If we pamper ourselves
in our diet, or give our imaginations a loose in our desires,
the body will no longer obey the mind.   Let us think no
further than to defend ourselves against hunger, thirst,
and cold.   We are to remember, that everything else is
despicable, and not worth our care.   To want little is true
grandeur, and very few things are great to a great mind.
Those who form their thoughts in this manner, and
abstract themselves from the world, are out of the way of
Fortune, and can look with contempt both on her favours
and her frowns.   At the same time, they who separate
themselves from the immediate commerce with the busy
part of mankind, are still beneficial to them, while by their
studies and writings they recommend to them the small
value which ought to be put upon what they pursue with
so much labour and disquiet.   Whilst such men are
thought the most idle, they are the most usefully employed.
They have all things, both human and divine, under consideration.   To be perfectly free from the insults of
fortune, we should arm ourselves with their reflections.
We should learn, that none but intellectual possessions are
what we can properly call our own.   All things from

without are but borrowed. What Fortune gives us, is not ours ; and whatever she gives, she can take away.

· It is a common imputation to Seneca, that though he declaimed with so much strength of reason, and a stoical contempt of riches and power, he was at the same time one of the richest and most powerful men in Rome. I know no instance of his being insolent in that fortune, and can therefore read his thoughts on those subjects with the more deference. I will not give philosophy so poor a look, as to say it cannot live in courts ; but I am of opinion, that it is there in the greatest eminence, when amidst the affluence of all the world can bestow, and the addresses of a crowd who follow him for that reason, a man can think both of himself and those about him abstracted from these circumstances. Such a philosopher is as much above an anchorite, as a wise matron, who passes through the world with innocence, is preferable to the nun who locks herself up from it.

Full of these thoughts I left my lodgings, and took a walk to the Court end of the town ; and the hurry, and busy faces I met with about Whitehall, made me form to myself ideas of the different prospects of all I saw, from the turn and cast of their countenances. All, methought, had the same thing in view, but prosecuted their hopes with a different air : some showed an unbecoming eager- ness, some a surly impatience, some a winning deference, but the generality a servile complaisance.

I could not but observe, as I roved about the offices, that all who were still but in expectation, murmured at Fortune ; and all who had obtained their wishes, imme- diately began to say, there was no such being. Each believed it an act of blind chance that any other man was preferred, but owed only to service and merit what he had obtained himself. It is the fault of studious men to appear

in public with too contemplative a carriage ; and I began
to observe, that my figure, age, and dress, made me particular : for which reason I thought it better to refnove a
studious countenance from among busy ones, and take a
turn with a friend in the Privy Garden.[1]

When my friend was alone with me there, " Isaac," said
he, " I know you came abroad only to moralise and make
observations, and I will carry you hard by, where you shall
see all that you have yourself considered or read in authors,
or collected from experience, concerning blind Fortune and
irresistible Destiny, illustrated in real persons and proper
mechanisms. The Graces, the Muses, the Fates, all the
beings which have a good or evil influence upon human
life, are, you'll say, very justly figured in the persons
of women ; and where I am carrying you, you'll see
enough of that sex together, in an employment which will
have so important an effect upon those who are to receive
their manufacture, as will make them be respectively called
Deities or Furies, as their labour shall prove disadvantageous
or successful to their votaries." Without waiting for my
answer, he carried me to an apartment contiguous to the
Banqueting House, where there were placed at two long
tables a large company of young women, in decent and
agreeable habits, making up tickets for the lottery appointed
by the Government. There walked between the tables a
person who presided over the work. This gentlewoman
seemed an emblem of Fortune, she commanded as if unconcerned in their business ; and though everything was performed by her direction, she did not visibly interpose in

---

[1] Now Whitehall Gardens, between Parliament Street and the
Thames. There Pepys had the pleasure of seeing Lady Castlemaine
in 1662 : "In the Privy Garden saw the finest smocks and linen petticoats of my Lady Castlemaine's, laced with rich lace at the bottom ;
and did me good to look at them."

particulars. She seemed in pain at our near approach to her, and most to approve us, when we made her no advances. Her height, her mien, her gesture, her shape, and her countenance, had something that spoke both familiarity and dignity. She therefore appeared to me not only a picture of Fortune, but of Fortune as I liked her ; which made me break out in the following words :

"MADAM,

"I am very glad to see the fate of the many who now languish in expectation of what will be the event of your labours in the hands of one who can act with so impartial an indifference. Pardon me, that have often seen you before, and have lost you for want of the respect due to you. Let me beg of you, who have both the furnishing and turning of that wheel of lots, to be unlike the rest of your sex, repulse the forward and the bold, and favour the modest and the humble. I know you fly the importunate, but smile no more on the careless. Add not to the coffers of the usurer, but give the power of bestowing to the generous. Continue his wants who cannot enjoy or communicate plenty; but turn away his poverty, who can bear it with more ease than he can see it in another."

ADVERTISEMENT.

Whereas Philander signified to Clarinda by letter bearing date Thursday 12 o'clock, that he had lost his heart by a shot from her eyes, and desired she would condescend to meet him the same day at eight in the evening at Rosamond's Pond,[1] faithfully protesting, that in case she would not do him that honour, she might see the body of the said Philander the next day floating on the said lake of Love, and that he desired only three sighs upon view

[1] See No. 60.

of his said body : it is desired, if he has not made away with himself accordingly, that he would forthwith show himself to the coroner of the city of Westminster ; or Clarinda, being an old offender, will be found guilty of wilful murder.

No. 171.   [STEELE.

From *Thursday, May* 11, to *Saturday, May* 13, 1710.

> Alter rixatur de lana sæpe caprina,
> Propugnat nugis armatus.—
>   HOR., 1 Ep. xviii. 15.

Grecian Coffee-house, May 12.

It has happened to be for some days the deliberation at the learnedest board in this house, whence honour and title had its first original. Timoleon, who is very particular in his opinions, but is thought particular for no other cause but that he acts against depraved custom, by the rules of nature and reason, in a very handsome discourse gave the company to understand, that in those ages which first degenerated from simplicity of life, and natural justice, the wise among them thought it necessary to inspire men with the love of virtue, by giving them who adhered to the interests of innocence and truth, some distinguishing name to raise them above the common level of mankind. This way of fixing appellations of credit upon eminent merit, was what gave being to titles and terms of honour. " Such a name," continued he, " without the qualities which should give a man pretence to be exalted above others, does but turn him to jest and ridicule. Should one see another cudgelled, or scurvily treated, do you think a man so used would take it kindly to be called Hector, or Alexander? Everything must bear a proportion with the outward value that is set upon it; or instead of being long had in veneration, that very term of esteem will become a word of reproach." When Timoleon had done speaking, Urbanus pursued the same purpose, by giving an account of the manner in which the Indian kings,[1] who were lately in Great Britain, did honour to the person where they lodged. "They were placed," said he, "in a handsome apartment, at an upholsterer's in King Street, Covent Garden. The man of the house, it seems, had been very observant of them, and

[1] The four kings were Iroquois chiefs who had been persuaded by adjacent British colonists to come and pay their respects to Queen Anne, and satisfy themselves of the untruth of the assertion made by the Jesuits, that the English and all other nations were vassals to the French king. They were said also to have been told that the Saviour was born in France and crucified in England. The names of the kings, according to Boyer's "Annals," were: Tee Yee Neen Ho Ga Prow, and Sa Ga Yean Qua Prah Ton, of the Maquas; Elow Oh Kaom, and Oh Nee Yeath Ton No Prow, of the River Sachem, and the Ganajohhore Sachem. They had an audience of the Queen on April 19, 1710, and were afterwards entertained by the Lords Commissioners of the Admiralty, the Duke of Ormonde, &c., until their departure for Boston on the 8th of May. See Addison's paper in the *Spectator*, No. 50, and Swift's remark upon it in the "Journal to Stella," April 28, 1711. A concert at York Buildings on May 1, 1710, "for the entertainment of the Emperor of the Mobocks and the three Indian kings," was advertised in No. 165 of the *Tatler*. The kings were lodged at the Two Crowns and Cushion, the house of an upholsterer in Covent Garden, probably Thomas Arne, the father of Dr. Thomas Arne the musician, and Mrs. Cibber, the actress. The following advertisement appeared at the end of No. 250, dated Nov. 14, 1710, and with some variation was reprinted in Nos. 253, 256, and 267 of the original edition: "This is to give notice, that the metzotinto-prints, by John Simmonds, in whole lengths, of the four Indian kings, that are done from the original pictures drawn by John Verelst, which her Majesty has at her palace at Kensington, are now to be delivered to subscribers, and sold at the Rainbow and Dove, the corner of Ivy Bridge in the Strand."

ready in their service. These just and generous princes, who act according to the dictates of natural justice, thought it proper to confer some dignity upon their landlord before they left his house. One of them had been sick during his residence there, and having never before been in a bed, had a very great veneration for him who made that engine of repose, so useful and so necessary in his distress. It was consulted among the four princes, by what name to dignify his great merit and services. The Emperor of the Mohocks, and the other three kings, stood up, and in that posture recounted the civilities they had received, and particularly repeated the care which was taken of their sick brother. This, in their imagination, who are used to know the injuries of weather, and the vicissitudes of cold and heat, gave them very great impressions of a skilful upholsterer, whose furniture was so well contrived for their protection on such occasions. It is with these less instructed (I will not say less knowing) people, the manner of doing honour, to impose some name significant of the qualities of the person they distinguish, and the good offices received from him. It was therefore resolved, to call their landlord Cadaroque, which is the name of the strongest fort in their part of the world. When they had agreed upon the name, they sent for their landlord, and as he entered into their presence, the Emperor of the Mohocks taking him by the hand, called him Cadaroque. After which the other three princes repeated the same word and ceremony."

Timoleon appeared much satisfied with this account, and having a philosophic turn, began to argue against the modes and manners of those nations which we esteem polite, and express himself with disdain at our usual method of calling such as are strangers to our innovations, barbarous. " I have," says he, "so great a deference for the

distinction given by these princes, that Cadaroque shall be
my upholsterer——" He was going on, but the intended discourse was interrupted by Minucio, who sat
near him, a small philosopher, who is also somewhat of
a politician ; one of those who sets up for knowledge by
doubting, and has no other way of making himself considerable, but by contradicting all he hears said. He has,
besides much doubt and spirit of contradiction, a constant
suspicion as to State affairs. This accomplished gentleman, with a very awful brow, and a countenance full ot
weight, told Timoleon, that it was a great misfortune
men of letters seldom looked into the bottom of things.
" Will any man," continued he, " persuade me, that this
was not from the beginning to the end a concerted
affair ? Who can convince the world, that four kings
shall come over here, and lie at the Two Crowns and
Cushion,¹ and one of them fall sick, and the place be called
King Street, and all this by mere accident ? No, no :
to a man of very small penetration, it appears, that Tee
Yee Neen Ho Ga Row, Emperor of the Mohocks, was
prepared for this adventure beforehand. I do not care
to contradict any gentleman in his discourse ; but I must
say, however, Sa Ga Yeath Rua Geth Ton, and E Tow
Oh Koam, might be surprised in this matter ; nevertheless,
Ho Nec Yeth Taw No Row knew it before he set foot on
the English shore."

Timoleon looked steadfastly at him for some time,
then shaked his head, paid for his tea, and marched off.
Several others who sat around him, were in their turns
attacked by this ready disputant. A gentleman who was
at some distance, happened in discourse to say it was four
miles to Hammersmith. " I must beg your pardon," says
Minucio, " when we say a place is so far off, we do not

---

¹ Arne's shop.

mean exactly from the very spot of earth we are in, but from the town where we are ; so that you must begin your account from the end of Piccadilly ; and if you do so, I'll lay any man ten to one, it is not above three good miles off." Another, about Minucio's level of understanding, began to take him up in this important argument, and maintained, that considering the way from Pimlico at the end of St. James's Park, and the crossing from Chelsea by Earl's Court, he would stand to it, that it was full four miles. But Minucio replied with great vehemence, and seemed so much to have the better of the dispute, that this adversary quitted the field, as well as the other. I sat till I saw the table almost all vanished, where, for want of discourse, Minucio asked me, how I did ? To which I answered, "Very well." "That's very much," said he ; "I assure you, you look paler than ordinary." "Nay," thought I, "if he won't allow me to know whether I am well or not, there is no staying for me neither." Upon which I took my leave, pondering as I went home at this strange poverty of imagination, which makes men run into the fault of giving contradiction. They want in their minds entertainment for themselves or their company, and therefore build all they speak upon what is started by others ; and since they cannot improve that foundation, they strive to destroy it. The only way of dealing with these people is to answer in monosyllables, or by way of question. When one of them tells you a thing that he thinks extraordinary, I go no further than, " Say you so, sir ? Indeed! Heyday !" or "Is it come to that !" These little rules, which appear but silly in the repetition, have brought me with great tranquillity to this age. And I have made it an observation, that as assent is more agreeable than flattery, so contradiction is more odious than culumny.

ADVERTISEMENT.

Mr. Bickerstaff's aërial messenger has brought him a report of what passed at the auction of pictures which was in Somerset House Yard on Monday last, and finds there were no "screens" present, but all transacted with great justice.

N.B. All false buyers at auctions being employed only to hide others, are from this day forward to be known in Mr. Bickerstaff's writings by the word "screens."

No. 172. [STEELE.

From *Saturday, May* 13, to *Tuesday, May* 16, 1710.

Quid quisque vitet, nunquam homini satis
Cautum est in horas.—HOR., 2 Od. xiii. 13.

From my own Apartment, May 15.

When a man is in a serious mood, and ponders upon his own make, with a retrospect to the actions of his life, and the many fatal miscarriages in it, which he owes to ungoverned passions, he is then apt to say to himself, that experience has guarded him against such errors for the future : but nature often recurs in spite of his best resolutions, and it is to the very end of our days a struggle between our reason and our temper, which shall have the empire over us. However, this is very much to be helped by circumspection, and a constant alarm against the first onsets of passion. As this is in general a necessary care to make a man's life easy and agreeable to himself, so it is more particularly the duty of such as are engaged in friend-ship and more near commerce with others. Those who have their joys, have also their griefs in proportion, and none can extremely exalt or depress friends, but friends. The harsh things which come from the rest of the world, are received and repulsed with that spirit which every honest man bears for his own vindication ; but unkindness in words or actions among friends, affects us at the first instant in the inmost recesses of our souls. Indifferent people, if I may so say, can wound us only in heterogeneous parts, maim us in our legs or arms ; but the friend can make no pass but at the heart itself. On the other side, the most impotent assistance, the mere well-wishes of a friend, gives a man constancy and courage against the most prevailing force of his enemies. It is here only a man enjoys and suffers to the quick. For this reason, the most gentle behaviour is absolutely necessary to maintain friend-ship in any degree above the common level of acquaintance. But there is a relation of life much more near than the most strict and sacred friendship, that is to say, marriage. This union is of too close and delicate a nature to be easily conceived by those who do not know that condition by experience. Here a man should, if possible, soften his passions ; if not for his own ease, in compliance to a creature formed with a mind of a quite different make from his own. I am sure, I do not mean it an injury to women, when I say there is a sort of sex in souls. I am tender of offending them, and know it is hard not to do it on this subject ; but I must go on to say, that the soul of a man and that of a woman are made very unlike, according to the employments for which they are designed. The ladies will please to observe, I say, our minds have different, not superior qualities to theirs. The virtues have respectively a masculine and a feminine cast. What we call in men wisdom, is in women prudence. It is a partiality to call one greater than the other. A prudent woman is in the same class of honour as a wise man, and the scandals in the way of both are equally dangerous. But to make this state anything but a burden, and not hang a weight upon our very beings, it is very proper each of the couple should frequently remember, that there are many things which grow out of their very natures that are pardonable, nay becoming, when considered as such, but without that reflection must give the quickest pain and vexation. To manage well a great family is as worthy an instance of capacity, as to execute a great employment ; and for the generality, as women perform the considerable part of their duties as well as men do theirs, so in their common behaviour, those of ordinary genius are not more trivial than the common rate of men ; and in my opinion, the playing of a fan is every whit as good an entertainment as the beating a snuff-box.

But however I have rambled in this libertine manner of writing by way of essay, I now sat down with an intention to represent to my readers, how pernicious, how sudden, and how fatal surprises of passion are to the mind of man ; and that in the more intimate commerces of life they are most liable to arise, even in our most sedate and indolent hours. Occurrences of this kind have had very terrible effects ; and when one reflects upon them, we cannot but tremble to consider what we are capable of being wrought up to against all the ties of nature, love, honour, reason, and religion, though the man who breaks through them all, had, an hour before he did so, a lively and virtuous sense of their dictates. When unhappy catastrophes make up part of the history of princes, and persons who act in high spheres, or are represented in the moving language and well-wrought scenes of tragedians, they do not fail of striking us with terror ; but then they affect us only in a transient manner, and pass through our imaginations, as incidents in which our fortunes are too

humble to be concerned, or which writers form for the
ostentation of their own force ; or, at most, as things fit
rather to exercise the powers of our minds, than to create
new habits in them. Instead of such high passages, I was
thinking it would be of great use (if anybody could hit it)
to lay before the world such adventures as befall persons
not exalted above the common level. This, methought,
would better prevail upon the ordinary race of men, who
are so prepossessed with outward appearances, that they
mistake fortune for nature, and believe nothing can relate
to them that does not happen to such as live and look like
themselves.

The unhappy end of a gentleman whose story an
acquaintance of mine was just now telling me, would be
very proper for this end if it could be related with all the
circumstances as I heard it this evening ; for it touched
me so much, that I cannot forbear entering upon it.

Mr. Eustace,[1] a young gentleman of a good estate near
Dublin in Ireland, married a lady of youth, beauty, and
modesty, and lived with her in general with much ease and
tranquillity ; but was in his secret temper impatient of
rebuke : she is apt to fall into little sallies of passion, yet
as suddenly recalled by her own reflection on her fault,
and the consideration of her husband's temper. It happened, as he, his wife, and her sister, were at supper
together about two months ago, that in the midst of a
careless and familiar conversation, the sisters fell into a
little warmth and contradiction. He, who was one of that

---

[1] " Last Sunday Mr. Francis Eustace committed a most barbarous
murder on the body of his wife, by giving her seven or eight stabs
with his sword, of which she died instantly. He jumped out of the
window, and falling on a palisado pale, tore his legs and thighs in such
a manner that he was forced to have them dressed by the surgeon, who
is since sent to Newgate for letting him escape, and a proclamation is
issued out for apprehending him " (*British Mercury*, 1710).

sort of men who are never unconcerned at what passes before them, fell into an outrageous passion on the side of the sister. The person about whom they disputed was so near, that they were under no restraint from running into vain repetitions of past heats : on which occasion all the aggravations of anger and distaste boiled up, and were repeated with the bitterness of exasperated lovers. The wife observing her husband extremely moved, began to turn it off, and rally him for interposing between two people who from their infancy had been angry and pleased with each other every half-hour. But it descended deeper into his thoughts, and they broke up with a sullen silence. The wife immediately retired to her chamber, whither her husband soon after followed. When they were in bed, he soon dissembled a sleep, and she, pleased that his thoughts were composed, fell into a real one. Their apartment was very distant from the rest of their family, in a lonely country house. He now saw his opportunity, and with a dagger he had brought to bed with him, stabbed his wife in the side. She awaked in the highest terror ; but immediately imagined it was a blow designed for her husband by ruffians, began to grasp him, and strive to awake and rouse him to defend himself. He still pretended himself sleeping, and gave her a second wound.

She now drew open the curtains, and by the help of moonlight saw his hand lifted up to stab her. The horror disarmed her from further struggling ; and he, enraged anew at being discovered, fixed his poniard in her bosom. As soon as he believed he had despatched her, he attempted to escape out of the window : but she, still alive, called to him not to hurt himself ; for she might live. He was so stung with the insupportable reflection upon her goodness and his own villainy, that he jumped to the bed, and wounded her all over with as much rage as if every blow was provoked by new aggravations. In this fury of mind he fled away. His wife had still strength to go to her sister's apartment, and give her an account of this wonderful tragedy; but died the next day. Some weeks after, an officer of justice, in attempting to seize the criminal, fired upon him, as did the criminal upon the officer. Both their balls took place, and both immediately expired.

No. 173.　　　　　　　　　　[STEELE.

From *Tuesday*, *May* 16, to *Thursday*, *May* 18, 1710.

———— Sapientia prima est
Stultitia caruisse.—HOR., 1 Ep. i. 41.

Sheer Lane, May 17.

When I first began to learn to push[1] this last winter, my master had a great deal of work upon his hands to make me unlearn the postures and motions which I had got by having in my younger years practised backsword, with a little eye to the single falchion. "Knock-down"[2] was the word in the Civil Wars, and we generally added to this skill the knowledge of the Cornish hug, as well as the grapple, to play with hand and foot. By this means I was for defending my head when the French gentleman was making a full pass at my bosom, insomuch that he told me I was fairly killed seven times in one morning, without having done my master any other mischief than one knock on the pate. This was a great misfortune to me; and I believe I may say, without vanity, I am the first who ever pushed so erroneously, and yet conquered the prejudice of education so well, as to make my passes so clear, and

[1] Fence.　　　[2] Hence the phrase, "a knock-down argument."

recover hand and foot with that agility, as I do at this day. The truth of it is, the first rudiments of education are given very indiscreetly by most parents, as much with relation to the more important concerns of the mind, as in the gestures of the body. Whatever children are designed for, and whatever prospects the fortune or interest of their parents may give them in their future lives, they are all promiscuously instructed the same way ; and Horace and Virgil must be thrummed by a boy as well before he goes to an apprenticeship as to the University. This ridiculous way of treating the under-aged of this island has very often raised both my spleen and mirth, but I think never both at once so much as to-day. A good mother of our neighbourhood made me a visit with her son and heir, a lad somewhat above five foot, and wants but little of the height and strength of a good musketeer in any regiment in the service. Her business was to desire I would examine him, for he was far gone in a book, the first letters of which she often saw in my papers. The youth produced it, and I found it was my friend Horace. It was very easy to turn to the place the boy was learning in, which was the fifth Ode of the first Book, to Pyrrha. I read it over aloud, as well because I am always delighted when I turn to the beautiful parts of that author, as also to gain time for considering a little how to keep up the mother's pleasure in her child, which I thought barbarity to interrupt. In the first place I asked him, who this same Pyrrha was ? He answered very readily, she was the wife of Pyrrhus, one of Alexander's captains. I lifted up my hands. The mother curtsies. " Nay," says she, " I knew you would stand in admiration."——" I assure you," continued she, " for all he looks so tall, he is but very young. Pray ask him some more, never spare him." With that I took the liberty to ask him, what was the

character of this gentlewoman? He read the three first
verses :

> *Quis multa gracilis te puer in rosa*
> *Perfusus liquidis urget odoribus,*
>   *Grato, Pyrrha, sub antro?* [1]

and very gravely told me, she lived at the sign of the
Rose in a cellar. I took care to be very much astonished
at the lad's improvements ; but withal advised her, as soon
as possible, to take him from school, for he could learn no
more there. This very silly dialogue was a lively image
of the impertinent method used in breeding boys without
genius or spirit, to the reading things for which their heads
were never framed. But this is the natural effect of a
certain vanity in the minds of parents, who are wonderfully delighted with the thought of breeding their children
to accomplishments, which they believe nothing but want
of the same care in their own fathers prevented them from
being masters of. Thus it is, that the part of life most
fit for improvement is generally employed in a method
against the bent of Nature ; and a lad of such parts as are
fit for an occupation, where there can be no calls out of
the beaten path, is two or three years of his time wholly
taken up in knowing how well Ovid's mistress became
such a dress ; how such a nymph for her cruelty was
changed into such an animal ; and how it is made generous
in Æneas to put Turnus to death, gallantries that can no
more come within the occurrences of the lives of ordinary
men, than they can be relished by their imaginations.
However, still the humour goes on from one generation
to another ; and the pastrycook here in the lane the
other night told me, he would not yet take away his son
from his learning, but has resolved, as soon as he had a
little smattering in the Greek, to put him apprentice to a

[1] Horace, 1 Od. v. 1.

soap-boiler. These wrong beginnings determine our success in the world ; and when our thoughts are originally falsely biasèd, their agility and force do but carry us the further out of our way in proportion to our speed. But we are half-way our journey when we have got into the right road. If all our days were usefully employed, and we did not set out impertinently, we should not have so many grotesque professors in all the arts of life, but every man would be in a proper and becoming method of distinguishing or entertaining himself suitably to what Nature designed him. As they go on now, our parents do not only force us upon what is against our talents, but our teachers are also as injudicious in what they put us to learn. I have hardly ever since suffered so much by the charms of any beauty, as I did before I had a sense of passion, for not apprehending that the smile of Lalage was what pleased Horace ;[1] and I verily believe, the stripes I suffered about *digito male pertinaci*[2] has given that irreconcilable aversion, which I shall carry to my grave, against coquettes.

As for the elegant writer of whom I am talking, his excellences are to be observed as they relate to the different concerns of his life ; and he is always to be looked upon as a lover, a courtier, or a man of wit. His admirable odes have numberless instances of his merit in each of these characters. His epistles and satires are full of proper notices for the conduct of life in a Court ; and what we call good breeding, most agreeably intermixed with his morality. His addresses to the persons who favour him are so inimitably engaging, that Augustus

[1] See 1 Od. xxii. 23 :
> "Dulce ridentem Lalagen amabo,
> Dulce loquentem."

[2] Horace, 1 Od. ix. 24.

complained of him for so seldom writing to him, and
asked him, whether he was afraid posterity should read
their names together?   Now for the generality of men to
spend much time in such writings, is as pleasant a folly as
any he ridicules.   Whatever the crowd of scholars may
pretend, if their way of life, or their own imaginations, do
not lead them to a taste of him, they may read, nay write,
fifty volumes upon him, and be just as they were when
they began.   I remember to have heard a great painter
say, there are certain faces for certain painters, as well as
certain subjects for certain poets.   This is as true in the
choice of studies, and no one will ever relish an author
thoroughly well, who would not have been fit company for
that author had they lived at the same time.   All others
are mechanics in learning, and take the sentiments of
writers like waiting-servants, who report what passed at
their master's table ; but debase every thought and expression, for want of the air with which they were uttered.

No. 174.   [STEELE.

From *Thursday, May* 18, to *Saturday, May* 20, 1710.

Quem mala stultitia, et quæcunque inscitia veri,
Cæcum agit, insanum Chrysippi porticus et grex
Autumat.—HOR., 2 Sat. iii. 43.

From my own Apartment, May 19.

The learned Scotus, to distinguish the race of mankind,
gives every individual of that species what he calls
a " seity," something peculiar to himself, which makes him
different from all other persons in the world.   This par-
ticularity renders him either venerable or ridiculous,
according as he uses his talents, which always grow out

into faults, or improve into virtues. In the office I have undertaken, you are to observe, that I have hitherto presented only the more insignificant and lazy part of mankind under the denomination of "dead men," together with the degrees towards non-existence, in which others can neither be said to live nor be defunct, but are only animals merely dressed up like men, and differ from each other but as flies do by a little colouring or fluttering of their wings. Now as our discourses heretofore have chiefly regarded the indolent part of the species, it remains that we do justice also upon the impertinently active and enterprising. Such as these I shall take particular care to place in safe custody, and have used all possible diligence to run up my edifice in Moorfields for that service.[1]

We who are adept in astrology, can impute it to several causes in the planets, that this quarter of our great city is the region of such persons as either never had, or have lost, the use of reason. It has indeed been time out of mind the receptacle of fools as well as madmen. The care and information of the former I assign to other learned men, who have for that end taken up their habitation in those parts ; as, among others, to the famous Dr. Trotter, and my ingenious friend Dr. Langham.[2] These oraculous proficients are day and night employed in deep searches, for the direction of such as run astray after their lost goods: but at present they are more particularly serviceable to their country, in foretelling the fate of such as have chances in the public lottery. Dr. Langham shows a peculiar generosity on this occasion, taking only one half-crown for a prediction, eighteenpence of which to be paid out of the prizes ; which method the doctor is willing to comply with in favour of every adventurer in the whole

---

[1] See Nos. 125, 127, 175.
[2] Two of the numerous astrologers who lived in Moorfields.

lottery. Leaving therefore the whole generation of such inquirers to such *literati* as I have now mentioned, we are to proceed towards peopling our house, which we have erected with the greatest cost and care imaginable.

It is necessary in this place to premise, that the superiority and force of mind which is born with men of great genius, and which, when it falls in with a noble imagination, is called " poetical fury," does not come under my consideration ; but the pretence to such an impulse without natural warmth, shall be allowed a fit object of this charity ; and all the volumes written by such hands shall be from time to time placed in proper order upon the rails of the unhoused booksellers within the district of the college[1] (who have long inhabited this quarter), in the same manner as they are already disposed soon after their publication. I promise myself from these writings my best opiates for those patients whose high imaginations, and hot spirits, have waked them into distraction. Their boiling tempers are not to be wrought upon by my gruels and juleps, but must ever be employed, or appear to be so, or their recovery will be impracticable. I shall therefore make use of such poets as preserve so constant a mediocrity as never to elevate the mind into joy, or depress it into sadness, yet at the same time keep the faculties of the readers in suspense, though they introduce no ideas of their own. By this means, a disordered mind, like a broken limb, will recover its strength by the sole benefit of being out of use, and lying without motion. But as reading is not an entertainment that can take up the full time of my patients, I have now in pension a proportionable number of storytellers, who are by turns to walk about the galleries of the house, and by their narra-

---

[1] During the first half of the eighteenth century the walls of Bedlam were made use of by dealers in second-hand books.

tions second the labours of my pretty good poets.
There are ₊among these storytellers some that have so
earnest• countenances, and weighty brows, that they will
draw a madman, even when his fit is just coming on, into
a whisper, and by the force of shrugs, nods, and busy
gestures, make him stand amazed so long as that we may
have time to give him his broth without danger.

But as Fortune has the possession of men's minds, a
physician may cure all the sick people of ordinary degree
in the whole town, and never come into reputation.   I
shall therefore begin with persons of condition ; and the
first I shall undertake, shall be the Lady Fidget, the
general visitant, and Will Voluble, the fine talker.
These persons shall be first locked up, for the peace of
all whom the one visits, and all whom the other talks to.

The passion which first touched the brain of both these
persons was envy ; and has had such wondrous effects,
that to this, Lady Fidget owes that she is so courteous ;
to this, Will Voluble that he is eloquent.   Fidget has
a restless torment in hearing of any one's prosperity, and
cannot know any quiet till she visits her, and is eyewitness
of something that lessens it.   Thus her life is a continual
search after what does not concern her, and her companions speak kindly even of the absent and the unfortunate, to tease her.   She was the first that visited
Flavia after the small-pox, and has never seen her since
because she is not altered.   Call a young woman handsome in her company, and she tells you, it is a pity she
has no fortune : say she is rich, and she is as sorry that
she is silly.   With all this ill nature, Fidget is herself
young, rich, and handsome ; but loses the pleasure of all
those qualities, because she has them in common with
others.

To make up her misery, she is well-bred, she hears

commendations till she is ready to faint for want of venting herself in contradictions. This madness is not expressed by the voice ; but is uttered in the eyes and features : its first symptom is upon beholding an agreeable object, a sudden approbation immediately checked with dislike.

This lady I shall take the liberty to conduct into a bed of straw and darkness, and have some hopes, that after long absence from the light, the pleasure of seeing at all may reconcile her to what she shall see, though it proves to be never so agreeable.

My physical remarks on the distraction of envy in other persons, and particularly in Will Voluble, is interrupted by a visit from Mr. Kidney,[1] with advices which will bring matter of new disturbance to many possessed with this sort of disorder, which I shall publish to bring out the symptoms more kindly, and lay the distemper more open to my view.

St. James's Coffee-house, May 19.

This evening a mail from Holland brought the following advices :

From the Camp before Douay,[2] May 26, N.S.   On the 23rd the French assembled their army, and encamped with their right near Bouchain, and their left near Crevecœur. Upon this motion of the enemy, the Duke of Marlborough and Prince Eugene made a movement with their army on the 24th, and encamped from Arlieux

---

[1] The waiter ; see No. 1.
[2] Douay capitulated on the 25th of June, after a fifty-four days siege, which cost the Allies eight thousand men. Two English regiments were cut to pieces at a sortie made by the besieged French troops. Two years later Douay was recaptured by Villars.

to Vitry and Isez-Esquerchien, where they are so advantageously posted, that they not only cover the siege, secure
our convoys of provisions, forage, and ammunition, from
Lille and Tournay, and the canals and dykes we have made
to turn the water of the Scarp and La Cense to Bouchain ;
but are in a readiness, by marching from the right, to
possess themselves of the field of battle marked out betwixt
Vitry and Montigny, or from the left to gain the lines of
circumvallation betwixt Fierin and Dechy : so that whatever way the enemy shall approach to attack us, whether
by the plains of Lens, or by Bouchain and Valenciennes,
we have but a very small movement to make, to possess
ourselves of the ground on which it will be most advantageous to receive them. The enemy marched this morning
from their left, and are encamped with their right at Oisy,
and their left towards Arras, and, according to our advices,
will pass the Scarp to-morrow, and enter on the plains of
Lens, though several regiments of horse, the German and
Liège troops, which are destined to compose part of their
army, have not yet joined them. If they pass the Scarp,
we shall do the like at the same time, to possess ourselves
with all possible advantage of the field of battle : but if
they continue where they are, we shall not remove, because
in our present station we sufficiently cover from all insults
both our siege and convoys.

Monsieur Villars cannot yet go without crutches, and
it is believed will have much difficulty to ride. He and
the Duke of Berwick are to command the French army,
the rest of the marshals being only to assist in council.

Last night we entirely perfected four bridges over the
avant fossé at both attacks ; and our saps are so far
advanced, that in three or four days batteries will be raised
on the *glacis*, to batter in breach both the outworks and
ramparts of the town.

The Tatler

No. 175. May 23, 1710

Letters from the Hague of the 27th, N.S., say, that the Deputies of the States of Holland, who set out for Gertruy-denburg on the 23rd, to renew the conferences with the French Ministers, returned on the 26th, and had communicated to the States-General the new overtures that were made on the part of France, which it is believed, if they are in earnest, may produce a general treaty.

No. 175. [STEELE.

From *Saturday*, May 20, to *Tuesday*, May 23, 1710.

From my own Apartment, May 22.

In the distribution of the apartments in the new Bedlam, proper regard is had to the different sexes, and the lodgings accommodated accordingly. Among other necessaries, as I have thought fit to appoint storytellers to soothe the men, so I have allowed tale-bearers to indulge the intervals of my female patients. But before I enter upon disposing of the main of the great body that wants my assistance, it is necessary to consider the human race abstracted from all other distinctions and considerations except that of sex. This will lead us to a nearer view of their excellences and imperfections, which are to be accounted the one or the other, as they are suitable to the design for which the persons so defective or accomplished came into the world.

To make this inquiry aright, we must speak of the life of people of condition, and the proportionable applications to those below them will be easily made, so as to value the whole species by the same rule. We will begin with the woman, and behold her as a virgin in her father's house. This state of her life is infinitely more delightful

than that of her brother at the same age. While she is
entertained with learning melodious airs at her spinet, is
led round a room in the most complaisant manner to a
fiddle, who is entertained with applauses of her beauty and
perfection in the ordinary conversation she meets with :
the young man is under the dictates of a rigid school-
master or instructor, contradicted in every word he speaks,
and curbed in all the inclinations he discovers. Mrs.
Elizabeth is the object of desire and admiration, looked
upon with delight, courted with all the powers of
eloquence and address, approached with a certain worship,
and defended with a certain loyalty. This is her case as
to the world : in her domestic character, she is the companion, the friend, and confidante of her mother, and the
object of a pleasure something like the love between angels,
to her father. Her youth, her beauty, her air, are by him
looked upon with an ineffable transport beyond any other
joy in this life, with as much purity as can be met with in
the next.

Her brother William, at the same years, is but in the
rudiments of those acquisitions which must gain him
esteem in the world. His heart beats for applause among
men, yet is he fearful of every step towards it. If he
proposes to himself to make a figure in the world, his
youth is damped with a prospect of difficulties, dangers,
and dishonours ; and an opposition in all generous attempts,
whether they regard his love or his ambition.

In the next stage of life she has little else to do, but
(what she is accomplished for by the mere gifts of nature)
to appear lovely and agreeable to her husband, tender to
her children, and affable to her servants : but a man, when
he enters into this way, is but in the first scene, far from
the accomplishment of his designs. He is now in all
things to act for others as well as himself. He is to have

The Tatler   No. 175. May 23, 1710

industry and frugality in his private affairs, and integrity and addresses in public. To these qualities, he must add a courage and resolution to support his other abilities, lest he be interrupted in the prosecution of his just endeavours, in which the honour and interest of posterity are as much concerned as his own personal welfare.

This little sketch may in some measure give an idea of the different parts which the sexes have to act, and the advantageous as well as inconvenient terms on which they are to enter upon their several parts of life. This may also be some rule to us in the examination of their conduct. In short, I shall take it for a maxim, that a woman who resigns the purpose of being pleasing, and the man who gives up the thoughts of being wise, do equally quit their claim to the true causes of living ; and are to be allowed the diet and discipline of my charitable structure to reduce them to reason.

On the other side, the woman who hopes to please by methods which should make her odious, and the man who would be thought wise by a behaviour that renders him ridiculous, are to be taken into custody for their false industry, as justly as they ought for their negligence.

N.B. Mr. Bickerstaff is taken extremely ill with the toothache, and cannot proceed in this discourse.

St. James's Coffee-house, May 22.

Advices from Flanders of the 30th instant, N.S., say, that the Duke of Marlborough having intelligence of the enemy's passing the Scarp on the 29th in the evening, and their march towards the plains of Lens, had put the Confederate army in motion, which was advancing towards the camp on the north side of that river between Vitry and Henin-Lietard. The Confederates, since the

320

approach of the enemy, have added several new redoubts to their camp, and drawn the cannon out of the lines of circumvallation in a readiness for the batteries.

It is not believed, notwithstanding these appearances, that the enemy will hazard a battle for the relief of Douay ; the siege of which place is carried on with all the success that can be expected, considering the difficulties they meet with occasioned by the inundations. On the 28th at night we made a lodgment on the salient angle of the glacis of the second counterscarp, and our approaches are so far advanced, that it is believed the town will be obliged to surrender before the 8th of the next month.

No. 176. [STEELE.

From *Tuesday*, *May* 23, to *Thursday*, *May* 25, 1710.

Nullum numen abest, si sit Prudentia.
Juv., Sat. x. 365.

From my own Apartment, May 23.

This evening, after a little ease from the raging pain caused by so small an organ as an aching tooth, under which I had behaved myself so ill as to have broke two pipes and my spectacles, I began to reflect with admiration on those heroic spirits, which in the conduct of their lives seem to live so much above the condition of our make, as not only under the agonies of pain to forbear any intemperate word or gesture, but also in their general and ordinary behaviour to resist the impulses of their very blood and constitution. This watch over a man's self, and the command of his temper, I take to be the greatest of human perfections, and is the effect of a strong and resolute mind. It is not only the most expedient practice for carrying on our own designs, but is also very deservedly the most amiable quality in the sight of others. It is a winning deference to mankind, which creates an immediate imitation of itself whenever it appears, and prevails upon all (who have to do with a person endued with it) either through shame or emulation. I do not know how to express this habit of mind, except you will let me call it equanimity. It is a virtue, which is necessary at every hour, in every place, and in all conversations, and is the effect of a regular and exact prudence. He that will look back upon all the acquaintances he has had in his whole life, will find he has seen more men capable of the greatest employments and performances, than such as could in the general bent of their carriage act otherwise than according to their own complexion and humour. But the indulgence of ourselves in wholly giving way to our natural propensity, is so unjust and improper a licence, that when people take it up, there is very little difference, with relation to their friends and families, whether they are good- or ill-natured men : for he that errs by being wrought upon by what we call the sweetness of his temper, is as guilty as he that offends through the perverseness of it.

It is not therefore to be regarded what men are in themselves, but what they are in their actions. Eucrates[1] is the best-natured of all men ; but that natural softness has effects quite contrary to itself, and for want of due bounds to his benevolence, while he has a will to be a friend to all, he has the power of being such to none. His constant inclination to please makes him never fail of doing so ; though (without being capable of falsehood) he is a friend only to those who are present ; for the same humour which makes him the best companion, renders

[1] Eucrates reminds us in some respects of Steele himself.

him the worst correspondent. It is a melancholy thing to consider, that the most engaging sort of men in conversation are frequently the most tyrannical in power, and least to be depended upon in friendship. It is certain this is not to be imputed to their own disposition ; but he that is to be led by others, has only good luck if he is not the worst, though in himself the best man living. For this reason, we are no more wholly to indulge our good than our ill dispositions. I remember a crafty old cit, one day speaking of a well-natured young fellow who set up with a good stock in Lombard Street, " I will," says he, " lay no more money in his hands, for he never denied me anything." This was a very base, but with him a prudential reason for breaking off commerce : and this acquaintance of mine carried this way of judging so far, that he has often told me, he never cared to deal with a man he liked, for that our affections must never enter into our business.

When we look round us in this populous city, and consider how credit and esteem are lodged, you find men have a great share of the former, without the least portion of the latter. He who knows himself for a beast of prey, looks upon others in the same light, and we are so apt to judge of others by ourselves, that the man who has no mercy, is as careful as possible never to want it. Hence it is, that in many instances men gain credit by the very contrary methods by which they do esteem ; for wary traders think every affection of the mind a key to their cash.

But what led me into this discourse was my impatience of pain ; and I have, to my great disgrace, seen an instance of the contrary carriage in so high a degree, that I am out of countenance that I ever read Seneca. When I look upon the conduct of others in such occur-

rences, as well as behold their equanimity in the general
tenor of their life, it very much abates the self-love, which
is seldom well-governed by any sort of men, 'and least of
all by us authors.

The fortitude of a man who brings his will to the
obedience of his reason is conspicuous, and carries
with it a dignity in the lowest state imaginable. Poor
Martius,[1] who now lies languishing in the most violent
fever, discovers in the faintest moments of his distemper
such a greatness of mind, that a perfect stranger who
should now behold him, would indeed see an object
of pity, but at the same time that it was lately an object of
veneration. His gallant spirit resigns, but resigns with an
air that speaks a resolution which could yield to nothing
but fate itself. This is conquest in the philosophic sense ;
but the empire over ourselves is, methinks, no less laudable in common life, where the whole tenor of a man's
carriage is in subservience to his own reason, and conformity
both to the good sense and inclination of other men.

Aristæus'[2] is, in my opinion, a perfect master of himself
in all circumstances. He has all the spirit that man can
have, and yet is as regular in his behaviour as a mere
machine. He is sensible of every passion, but ruffled by
none. In conversation, he frequently seems to be less
knowing to be more obliging, and chooses to be on a
level with others rather than oppress with the superiority
of his genius. In friendship he is kind without profession ;
in business, expeditious without ostentation. With the
greatest softness and benevolence imaginable, he is impartial in spite of all importunity, even that of his own
good nature. He is ever clear in his judgment ; but in

[1] Perhaps Cornelius Wood. See No. 144.
[2] In writing of Aristæus, Steele seems to have had Addison in his
mind. His friend had recently left London for Ireland.

complaisance to his company, speaks with doubt, and never shows confidence in argument, but to support the sense of another.* Were such an equality of mind the general endeavour of all men, how sweet would be the pleasures of conversation? He that is loud would then understand, that we ought to call a constable, and know, that spoiling good company is the most heinous way of breaking the peace. We should then be relieved from these zealots in society, who take upon them to be angry for all the company, and quarrel with the waiters to show they have no respect for anybody else in the room. To be in a rage before you, is in a kind being angry with you. You may as well stand naked before company, as to use such familiarities; and to be careless of what you say, is the most clownish way of being undressed.

Sheer Lane, May 24.

When I came home this evening, I found the following letters; and because I think one a very good answer to the other, as well as that it is the affair of a young lady, it must be immediately dismissed :

"SIR,

" I have a good fortune, partly paternal and partly acquired. My younger years I spent in business; but age coming on, and having no more children than one daughter, I resolved to be a slave no longer : and accordingly I have disposed of my effects, placed my money in the funds, bought a pretty seat in a pleasant country ; am making a garden, and have set up a pack of little beagles. I live in the midst of a good many well-bred neighbours, and several well-tempered clergymen. Against a rainy day I have a little library ; and against the gout in my stomach a little good claret. With all this I am the miserablest man in the world; not that I've lost the relish of any of these pleasures, but am distracted with such a multiplicity of entertaining objects, that I am lost in the variety. I am in such a hurry of idleness, that I do not know with what diversion to begin. Therefore, sir, I must beg the favour of you, when your more weighty affairs will permit, to put me in some method of doing nothing; for I find Pliny makes a great difference betwixt *Nihil agere* and *Agere nihil*; and I fancy, if you would explain him, you would do a very great kindness to many in Great Britain, as well as to

" Your humble Servant,

" J. B."

"SIR,

"The enclosed is written by my father in one of his pleasant humours. He bids me seal it up, and send you a word or two from myself, which he won't desire to see till he hears of it from you. Desire him before he begins his method of doing nothing, to have nothing to do; that is to say, let him marry off his daughter. I am,

" Your gentle Reader,

"S. B."

No. 177.

[Steele.

From *Thursday, May 25*, to *Saturday, May 27*, 1710.

—— Male si palpere, recalcitrat undique tutus.
                                        Hor., 2 Sat. i. 20.

Sheer Lane, May 26.

The ingenious Mr. Penkethman,[1] the comedian, has lately left here a paper or ticket, to which is affixed a small silver medal, which is to entitle the bearer to see one-and-twenty plays at his theatre for a guinea. Greenwich is the place where, it seems, he has erected his house ; and his time of action is to be so contrived, that it is to fall in with going and returning with the tide : besides, that the bearer of this ticket may carry down with him a particular set of company to the play, striking off for each person so introduced one of his twenty-one times of admittance. In this warrant of his, he has made me a high compliment in a facetious distich, by way of dedication of his endeavours, and desires I would recommend them to the world. I must needs say, I have not for some time seen a properer choice than he has made of a patron : who more fit to publish his work than a novelist[2] ? who to recommend it than a censor ? This honour done me, has made me turn my thoughts upon the nature of dedications in general, and the abuse of that custom, as well by a long practice of my predecessors, as the continued folly of my contemporary authors.

In ancient times, it was the custom to address their works to some eminent for their merit to mankind, or particular patronage of the writers themselves, or knowledge in the matter of which they treated. Under these

---

[1] See No. 4.   [2] Writer of news.

327

regards, it was a memorable honour to both parties, and a
very agreeable record of their commerce with each other.
These applications were never stuffed with impertinent
praises, but were the native product of their esteem, which
was implicitly received, or generally known to be due to
the patron of the work : but vain flourishes came into the
world, with other barbarous embellishments ; and the
enumeration of titles, and great actions, in the patrons
themselves, or their sires, are as foreign to the matter in
hand as the ornaments are in a Gothic building.   This
is clapping together persons which have no manner of
alliance, and can for that reason have no other effect than
making both parties justly ridiculous.   What pretence is
there in Nature for me to write to a great man, and tell
him, " My lord, because your Grace is a duke, your Grace's
father before you was an earl, his lordship's father was a
baron, and his lordship's father both a wise and a rich
man, I, Isaac Bickerstaff, am obliged, and could not possibly
forbear addressing to you the following treatise."   Though
this is the plain exposition of all I could possibly say to
him with a good conscience, yet the silly custom has so
universally prevailed, that my lord duke and I must
necessarily be particular friends from this time forward, or
else I have just room for being disobliged, and may turn
my panegyric into a libel.   But to carry this affair still
more home, were it granted that praises in dedications
were proper topics, what is it that gives a man authority
to commend, or what makes it a favour to me that he
does commend me ?   It is certain, that there is no praise
valuable but from the praiseworthy.   Were it otherwise,
blame might be as much in the same hands.   Were the
good and evil of fame laid upon a level among mankind,
the judge on the bench, and the criminal at the bar, would
differ only in their stations ; and if one's word is to pass

as much as the other's, their reputation would be much alike to the jury. Pliny,[1] speaking of the death of Martial, expresses himself with great gratitude to him for the honours done him in the writings of that author ; but he begins it with an account of his character, which only made the applause valuable. He indeed in the same Epistle says, it is a sign we have left off doing things which deserve praise, when we think commendation impertinent. This is asserted with a just regard to the persons whose good opinion we wish for ; otherwise reputation would be valued according to the number of voices a man has for it, which are not always to be insured on the more virtuous side. But however we pretend to model these nice affairs, true glory will never attend anything but truth ; and there is something so peculiar in it, that the very self-same action done by different men cannot merit the same degree of applause. The Roman, who was surprised in the enemy's camp before he had accomplished his design, and thrust his bare arm into a flaming pile, telling the general, there were many as determined as himself who (against sense of danger) had conspired his death, wrought in the very enemy an admiration of his fortitude, and a dismission with applause.[2] But the condemned slave who represented him in the theatre, and consumed his arm in the same manner, with the same resolution, did not raise in the spectators a great idea of his virtue, but of him whom he imitated in an action no way differing from that of the real Scævola, but in the motive to it.

Thus true glory is inseparable from true merit, and whatever you call men, they are no more than what they are in themselves ; but a romantic sense has crept into the minds of the generality, who will ever mistake words and appearances for persons and things.

[1] "Epist." iii. 21.   [2] Livy, ii. 12.

The Tatler

The simplicity of the ancients was as conspicuous in the address of their writings, as in any other monuments they have left behind them. Cæsar and Augustus were much more high words of respect, when added to occasions fit for their characters to appear in, than any appellations which have ever been since thought of. The latter of these great men had a very pleasant way of dealing with applications of this kind. When he received pieces of poetry which he thought had worth in them, he rewarded the writer ; but where he thought them empty, he generally returned the compliment made him with some verses of his own.

This latter method I have at present occasion to imitate. A female author has dedicated a piece to me,[1] wherein she would make my name (as she has others) the introduction of whatever is to follow in her book ; and has spoke some panegyrical things which I know not how to return, for want of better acquaintance with the lady, and consequently being out of a capacity of giving her praise or blame. All therefore that is left for me, according to the foregoing rules, is to lay the picture of a good and evil woman before her eyes, which are but mere words if they do not concern her. Now you are to observe, the way in a dedication is to make all the rest of the world as little like the person we address to as possible, according to the following epistle :

"MADAM,

"But, M——

"—— *Memorabile nullum*
Fœminea in pœna est.——"[2]

---

[1] Mrs. Manley's "Memoirs of Europe . . . by the translator of the New Atalantis.'" See Nos. 35, 63.

[2] "—— Nullum memorabile nomen
Fœminea in pœna est."—"Æneid," ii. 583-4.

No. 178.

Sheer Lane, May 29.

When we look into the delightful history of the most ingenious Don Quixote of the Mancha, and consider the exercises and manner of life of that renowned gentleman, we cannot but admire the exquisite genius and discerning spirit of Michael Cervantes, who has not only painted his adventurer with great mastery in the conspicuous parts of his story, which relate to love and honour, but also intimated in his ordinary life, economy, and furniture, the infallible symptoms he gave of his growing frenzy, before he declared himself a knight-errant. His hall was furnished with old lances, halberds, and morions ; his food, lentils ; his dress, amorous. He slept moderately, rose early, and spent his time in hunting. When by watchfulness and exercise he was thus qualified for the hardships of his intended peregrinations, he had nothing more to do but to fall hard to study ; and before he should apply himself to the practical part, get into the methods of making love and war by reading books of knighthood. As for raising tender passion in him, Cervantes reports [1] that he was wonderfully delighted with a smooth intricate sentence ; and when they listened at his study-door, they could frequently hear him read aloud, "The reason of the unreasonableness, which against my reason is wrought, doth so weaken my reason, as with all reason I do justly complain on your beauty." Again, he would pause till he came to another charming sentence, and with the most pleasing accent imaginable be

[1] "Don Quixote," Part I. chap. i.

331

loud at a new paragraph : " The high heavens, which, with
your divinity, do fortify you divinely with the stars, make
you deserveress of the deserts that your greatness deserves."
With these, and other such passages (says my author) the
poor gentleman grew distracted, and was breaking his brains
day and night to understand and unravel their sense.

As much as the case of this distempered knight is
received by all the readers of his history as the most
incurable and ridiculous of all phrensies, it is very certain
we have crowds among us far gone in as visible a madness
as his, though they are not observed to be in that condition. As great and useful discoveries are sometimes
made by accidental and small beginnings, I came to the
knowledge of the most epidemic ill of this sort, by falling
into a coffee-house where I saw my friend the upholsterer,[1]
whose crack[2] towards politics I have heretofore mentioned.
This touch in the brain of the British subject is as certainly
owing to the reading newspapers, as that of the Spanish
worthy above mentioned to the reading works of chivalry.
My contemporaries the novelists[3] have, for the better
spinning out paragraphs, and working down to the end of
their columns, a most happy art in saying and unsaying,
giving hints of intelligence, and interpretations of indifferent actions, to the great disturbance of the brains of
ordinary readers. This way of going on in the words, and
making no progress in the sense, is more particularly the
excellence of my most ingenious and renowned fellow-
labourer, the *Postman*[4] ; and it is to this talent in him

---

[1] See Nos. 155, 160.
[2] In the *Spectator*, No. 251, Addison applies the word to a crazy
person : " A crack and a projector."
[3] Writers of newspapers.
[4] The *Postman* was edited by a French Protestant named Fontive,
whom Dunton describes as " the glory and mirror of news-writers ; a
very grave, learned, orthodox man."

that I impute the loss of my upholsterer's intellects. That unfortunate tradesman has for years past been the chief orator in ragged assemblies, and the reader in alley coffee-houses. He was yesterday surrounded by an audience of that sort, among whom I sat unobserved through the favour of a cloud of tobacco, and saw him with the *Postman* in his hand, and all the other papers safe under his left elbow. He was intermixing remarks, and reading the Paris article of May 30, which says that "it is given out that an express arrived this day, with advice, that the armies were so near in the plain of Lens, that they cannonaded each other." (" Ay, ay, here we shall have sport.") "And that it was highly probable the next express would bring us an account of an engagement." (" They are welcome as soon as they please.") " Though some others say, that the same will be put off till the 2nd or 3rd of June, because the Marshal Villars expects some further reinforcements from Germany, and other parts, before that time." (" What-a-pox does he put it off for ? Does he think our horse is not marching up at the same time? But let us see what he says further.") " They hope that Monsieur Albergotti,[1] being encouraged by the presence of so great an army, will make an extraordinary defence." (" Why then I find, Albergotti is one of those that love to have a great many on their side. Nay, I'll say that for this paper, he makes the most natural inferences of any of them all.") " The Elector of Bavaria being uneasy to be without any command, has desired leave to come to Court to communicate a certain project to his Majesty. Whatever it be, it is said that prince is suddenly expected, and then we shall have a more certain account of his project, if this report has any foundation." (" Nay, this paper never imposes upon us, he goes upon

---

[1] Albergotti was then holding Douay for Lewis XIV.

sure grounds ; for he won't be positive the Elector has a project, or that he will come, or if he does come at all ; for he doubts, you see, whether the report has any foundation.")

What makes this the more lamentable is, that this way of writing falls in with the imagination of the cooler and duller part of her Majesty's subjects. The being kept up with one line contradicting another, and the whole, after many sentences of conjecture, vanishing in a doubt whether there is anything at all in what the person has been reading, puts an ordinary head into a vertigo, which his natural dulness would have secured him from. Next to the labours of the *Postman*, the upholsterer took from under his elbow honest Ichabod Dawks' *Letter*,[1] and there, among other speculations, the historian takes upon him to say that " it is discoursed that there will be a battle in Flanders before the armies separate, and many will have it to be to-morrow, the great battle of Ramillies being fought on a Whit Sunday." A gentleman who was a wag in this company laughed at the expression, and said, " By Mr. Dawks' favour, I warrant ye, if we meet them on Whit Sunday, or Monday, we shall not stand upon the day[2] with them, whether it be before or after the holidays." An admirer of this gentleman stood up, and told a neighbour at a distant table the conceit, at which indeed we were all very merry. These reflections in the writers of the transactions of the times, seize the noddles of such as were not born to have thoughts of their own, and consequently lay a weight upon everything which they read in print. But

---

[1] See No. 18. The news-letter was printed to imitate hand-writing.

[2] Cf. " Macbeth," act iii. sc. 4 :
　　" Stand not upon the order of your going,
　　But go at once ! "

Mr. Dawks concluded his paper with a courteous sentence, which was very well taken and applauded by the whole company. "We wish," says he, "all our customers a merry Whitsuntide, and many of them." Honest Ichabod is as extraordinary a man as any of our fraternity, and as particular. His style is a dialect between the familiarity of talking and writing, and his letter such as you cannot distinguish whether print or manuscript, which gives us a refreshment[1] of the idea from what has been told us from the press by others. This wishing a good tide had its effect upon us, and he was commended for his salutation, as showing as well the capacity of a bellman as an historian. My distempered old acquaintance read in the next place the account of the affairs abroad in the *Courant* ;[2] but the matter was told so distinctly, that these wanderers thought there was no news in it ; this paper differing from the rest as a history from a romance. The tautology, the contradictions, the doubts, and wants of confirmations, are what keep up imaginary entertainments in empty heads, and produce neglect of their own affairs, poverty, and bankruptcy, in many of the shop-statesmen ; but turn the imaginations of those of a little higher orb into deliriums of dissatisfaction, which is seen in a continual fret upon all that touches their brains, but more particularly upon any advantage obtained by their country, where they are considered as lunatics, and therefore tolerated in their ravings.

What I am now warning the people of is, that the newspapers of this island are as pernicious to weak heads in England as ever books of chivalry to Spain ; and therefore shall do all that in me lies, with the utmost care and vigilance imaginable, to prevent these growing evils. A flaming instance of this malady appeared in my old

---

[1] A *réchauffé*.   [2] See No. 18.

acquaintance at this time, who, after he had done reading all his papers, ended with a thoughtful air, " If we should have a peace, we should then know for certain whether it was the King of Sweden that lately came to Dunkirk.'' I whispered him, and desired him to step aside a little with me. When I had opportunity, I decoyed him into a coach, in order for his more easy conveyance to Moor-fields. The man went very quietly with me ; and by that time he had brought the Swede from the defeat by the Czar to the Boristhenes, we were passing by Will's Coffee-house, where the man of the house beckoned to us. We made a full stop, and could hear from above a very loud voice swearing, with some expressions towards treason, that the subject in France was as free as in England. His distemper would not let him reflect, that his own dis course was an argument of the contrary. They told him, one would speak with him below. He came immediately to our coach-side. I whispered him, that I had an order to carry him to the Bastile. He immediately obeyed with great resignation : for to this sort of lunatic, whose brain is touched for the French, the name of a gaol in that kingdom has a more agreeable sound than that of a paternal seat in this their own country. It happened a little unluckily bringing these lunatics together, for they immediately fell into a debate concerning the greatness of their respective monarchs ; one for the King of Sweden, the other for the Grand Monarch of France. This gentleman from Will's is now next door to the upholsterer, safe in his apartment in my Bedlam, with proper medica-ments, and the *Mercure Galant*[1] to soothe his imagination that he is actually in France. If therefore he should escape to Covent Garden again, all persons are desired to lay hold of him, and deliver him to Mr. Morphew, my

[1] See No. 67.

overseer. At the same time, I desire all true subjects to forbear discourse with him, any otherwise than when he begins to fight a battle for France, to say, "Sir, I hope to see you in England."

No. 179. [STEELE.

From *Tuesday, May* 30, to *Thursday, June* 1, 1710.

—— O ! quis me gelidis sub montibus Hæmi
Sistat, et ingenti ramorum protegat umbra ?
VIRG., Georg. ii. 488.[1]

From my own Apartment, May 31.

In this parched season, next to the pleasure of going into the country, is that of hearing from it, and partaking the joys of it in description, as in the following letter :

"SIR,

"I believe you will forgive me, though I write to you a very long epistle, since it relates to the satisfaction of a country life, which I know you would lead, if you could. In the first place I must confess to you, that I am one of the most luxurious men living ; and as I am such, I take care to make my pleasures lasting, by following none but such as are innocent and refined, as well as, in some measure, improving. You have in your labours been so much concerned to represent the actions and passions of mankind, that the whole vegetable world has almost escaped your observation : but sure there are gratifications to be drawn from thence, which deserve to be recommended. For your better information, I wish you could visit your old friend in Cornwall : you would be

---

[1] The correct reading is, "O, qui me gellidis in vallibus," &c.

pleased to see the many alterations I have made about my house, and how much I have improved my estate without raising the rents of it.

"As the winter engrosses with us near a double portion of the year (the three delightful vicissitudes being crowded almost within the space of six months), there is nothing upon which I have bestowed so much study and expense, as in contriving means to soften the severity of it, and, if possible, to establish twelve cheerful months about my habitation. In order to this, the charges I have been at in building and furnishing a greenhouse will, perhaps, be thought somewhat extravagant by a great many gentlemen whose revenues exceed mine. But when I consider, that all men of any life and spirit have their inclinations to gratify, and when I compute the sums laid out by the generality of the men of pleasure (in the number of which I always rank myself) in riotous eating and drinking, in equipage and apparel, upon wenching, gaming, racing and hunting ; I find, upon the balance, that the indulging of my humour comes at a reasonable rate.

"Since I communicate to you all incidents serious and trifling, even to the death of a butterfly, that fall out within the compass of my little empire, you will not, I hope, be ill pleased with the draught I now send you of my little winter paradise, and with an account of my way of amusing myself and others in it.

"The younger Pliny, you know, writes a long letter to his friend Gallus,[1] in which he gives him a very particular plan of the situation, the conveniences, and the agreeableness of his villa. In my last, you may remember, I promised you something of this kind. Had Pliny lived in a northern climate, I doubt not but we should have found a very complete orangery amongst his Epistles ; and I, prob-

[1] "Epist." ii. 17.

338

ably, should have copied his model, instead of building after my own fancy, and you had been referred to him for the• history of my late exploits in architecture : by which means my performances would have made a better figure, at least in writing, than they are like to make at present. •

"The area of my greenhouse is a hundred paces long, fifty broad, and the roof thirty feet high. The wall toward the north is of solid stone. On the south side, and at both the ends, the stonework rises but three feet fròm the ground, excepting the pilasters, placed at convenient distances to strengthen and beautify the building. The intermediate spaces are filled up with large sashes of the strongest and most transparent glass. The middle sash (which is wider than any of the others) serves for the entrance, to which you mount by six easy steps, and descend on the inside by as many. This opens and shuts with greater ease, keeps the wind out better, and is at the same time more uniform than folding-doors.

"In the middle of the roof there runs a ceiling thirty feet broad from one end to the other. This is enlivened by a masterly pencil, with all the variety of rural scenes and prospects, which he has peopled with the whole tribe of sylvan deities. Their characters and their stories are so well expressed, that the whole seems a collection of all the most beautiful fables of the ancient poets translated into colours. The remaining spaces of the roof, ten feet on each side of the ceiling, are of the clearest glass, to let in the sky and clouds from above. The building points full east and west, so that I enjoy the sun while he is above the horizon. His rays are improved through the glass, and I receive through it what is desirable in a winter-sky, without the coarse alloy of the season, which is a kind of sifting or straining the weather. My greens and

339

flowers are as sensible as I am of this benefit : they flourish and look cheerful as in the spring, while their fellow creatures abroad are starved to death. I must add, that a moderate expense of fire, over and above the contributions I receive from the sun, serves to keep this large room in a due temperature ; it being sheltered from the cold winds by a hill on the north, and a wood on the east.

" The shell, you see, is both agreeable and convenient ; and now you shall judge, whether I have laid out the floor to advantage. There goes through the whole length of it a spacious walk of the finest gravel, made to bind and unite so firmly, that it seems one continued stone ; with this advantage, that it is easier to the foot, and better for walking, than if it were what it seems to be. At each end of the walk, on the one and on the other side of it, lies a square plot of grass of the finest turf and brightest verdure. What ground remains on both sides, between these little smooth fields of green, is flagged with large quarries of white marble, where the blue veins trace out such a variety of irregular windings through the clear surface, that these bright plains seem full of rivulets and streaming meanders. This to my eye, that delights in simplicity, is inexpressibly more beautiful than the chequered floors which are so generally admired by others. Upon the right and upon the left, along the gravel walk, I have ranged interchangeably the bay, the myrtle, the orange and the lemon trees, intermixed with painted hollies, silver firs, and pyramids of yew ; all so disposed, that every tree receives an additional beauty from its situation ; besides the harmony that rises from the disposition of the whole, no shade cuts too strongly, or breaks in harshly upon the other ; but the eye is cheered with a mild rather than gorgeous diversity of greens.

"The borders of the four grass plots are garnished with pots of flowers : those delicacies of Nature create two senses at once, and leave such delightful and gentle impressions upon the brain, that I cannot help thinking them of equal force with the softest airs of music, toward the smoothing of our tempers. In the centre of every plot is a statue. The figures I have made choice of are a Venus, an Adonis, a Diana, and an Apollo ; such excellent copies, as to raise the same delight as we should draw from the sight of the ancient originals.

"The north wall would have been but a tiresome waste to the eye, if I had not diversified it with the most lively ornaments, suitable to the place. To this intent, I have been at the expense to lead over arches from a neighbouring hill a plentiful store of spring water, which a beautiful Naiad, placed as high as is possible in the centre of the wall, pours out from an urn. This, by a fall of above twenty foot, makes a most delightful cascade into a basin, that opens wide within the marble floor on that side. At a reasonable distance, on either hand of the cascade, the wall is hollowed into two spreading scallops, each of which receives a couch of green velvet, and forms at the same time a canopy over them. Next to them come two large aviaries, which are likewise let into the stone. These are succeeded by two grottoes, set off with all the pleasing rudeness of shells and moss, and cragged stones, imitating in miniature rocks and precipices, the most dreadful and gigantic works of Nature. After the grottoes, you have two niches, the one inhabited by Ceres, with her sickle and sheaf of wheat ; and the other by Pomona, who, with a countenance full of good cheer, pours a bounteous autumn of fruits out of her horn. Last of all come two colonies of bees, whose stations lying east and west, the one is saluted by the rising, the other by the setting sun. These, all of them being placed at proportioned intervals, furnish out the whole length of the wall ; and the spaces that lie between are painted in fresco, by the same hand that has enriched my ceiling.

"Now, sir, you see my whole contrivance to elude the rigour of the year, to bring a northern climate nearer the sun, and to exempt myself from the common fate of my countrymen. I must detain you a little longer, to tell you, that I never enter this delicious retirement, but my spirits are revived, and a sweet complacency diffuses itself over my whole mind. And how can it be otherwise, with a conscience void of offence, where the music of falling waters, the symphony of birds, the gentle humming of bees, the breath of flowers, the fine imagery of painting and sculpture : in a word, the beauties and the charms of nature and of art court all my faculties, refresh the fibres of the brain and smooth every avenue of thought. What pleasing meditations, what agreeable wanderings of the mind, and what delicious slumbers, have I enjoyed here ! And when I turn up some masterly writer to my imagination, methinks here his beauties appear in the most advantageous light, and the rays of his genius shoot upon me with greater force and brightness than ordinary. This place likewise keeps the whole family in good humour, in a season wherein gloominess of temper prevails universally in this island. My wife does often touch her lute in one of the grottoes, and my daughter sings to it, while the ladies with you, amidst all the diversions of the town, and in the most affluent fortunes, are fretting and repining beneath a lowering sky for they know not what. In this greenhouse we often dine, we drink tea, we dance country dances ; and what is the chief pleasure of all, we entertain our neighbours in it, and by this

means contribute very much to mend the climate five or
six miles about us.   I am,

> " Your most humble Servant,
>
> " T. S." [1]

No. 180.   [STEELE.

From *Thursday, June* 1, to *Saturday, June* 3, 1710.

Stultitiam patiuntur opes.—Hor., 1 Ep. xviii. 29.

From my own Apartment, June 2.

I have received a letter which accuses me of partiality
in the administration of the Censorship, and says,
that I have been very free with the lower part of mankind,
but extremely cautious in representations of matters which
concern men of condition.   This correspondent takes upon
him also to say, the upholsterer was not undone by turning politician, but became bankrupt by trusting his goods
to persons of quality ; and demands of me, that I should
do justice upon such as brought poverty and distress upon
the world below them, while they themselves were sunk
in pleasures and luxury, supported at the expense of those
very persons whom they treated with a negligence, as if

[1] Thomas Smith, who voted against Steele's expulsion, was member
for the borough of Eye, and may have been the person who wrote
this letter, to which the initials of his name are subscribed.   In the
preface to the *Examiner,* the first number of which was published
Aug. 3, 1710, there is the following passage : " All descriptions of
stage-players and statesmen, the erecting of greenhouses, the forming
of constellations, the beaus' red heels, and the furbelows of the ladies,
shall remain entire to the use and benefit of their first proprietor."
    The description of stage-players and statesmen, here mentioned, is
an allusion to Downes' letter.   See No. 193.

they did not know whether they dealt with them or not. This is a very heavy accusation, both of me and such as the man aggrieved accuses me of tolerating. For this reason, I resolved to take this matter into consideration, and upon very little meditation could call to my memory many instances which made this complaint far from being groundless. The root of this evil does not always proceed from injustice in the men of figure, but often from a false grandeur which they take upon them in being unacquainted with their own business, not considering how mean a part they act when their names and characters are subjected to the little arts of their servants and dependants. The overseers of the poor are a people who have no great reputation for the discharge of their trust, but are much less scandalous than the overseers of the rich. Ask a young fellow of a great estate, who was that odd fellow spoke to him in a public place? He answers, "One that does my business." It is, with many, a natural consequence of being a man of fortune, that they are not to understand the disposal of it; and they long to come to their estates, only to put themselves under new guardianship. Nay, I have known a young fellow who was regularly bred an attorney, and was a very expert one till he had an estate fallen to him. The moment that happened, he who could before prove the next land he cast his eye upon his own, and was so sharp, that a man at first sight would give him a small sum for a general receipt, whether he owed him anything or not : such a one, I say, have I seen, upon coming to an estate, forget all his diffidence of mankind, and become the most manageable thing breathing. He immediately wanted a stirring man to take upon him his affairs, to receive and pay, and do everything which he himself was now too fine a gentleman to understand. It is pleasant to consider, that he who would have got an estate had he not come to one, will certainly starve because one fell to him : but such contradictions are we to ourselves, and any change of life is·insupportable to some natures.

It is a mistaken sense of superiority, to believe a figure or equipage gives men precedence to their neighbours. Nothing can create respect from mankind, but laying obligations upon them ; and it may very reasonably be concluded, that if it were put into a due balance, according to the true state of the account, many who believe themselves in possession of a large share of dignity in the world, must give place to their inferiors. The greatest of all distinctions in civil life is that of debtor and creditor, and there needs no great progress in logic to know which, in that case, is the advantageous side. He who can say to another, " Pray, master," or " Pray, my lord, give me my own," can as justly tell him, " It is a fantastical distinction you take upon you, to pretend to pass upon the world for my master or lord, when at the same time that I wear your livery, you owe me wages ; or, while I wait at your door, you are ashamed to see me till you have paid my bill."

The good old way among the gentry of England to maintain their pre-eminence over the lower rank, was by their bounty, munificence, and hospitality ; and it is a very unhappy change, if at present, by themselves or their agents, the luxury of the gentry is supported by the credit of the trader. This is what my correspondent pretends to prove out of his own books, and those of his whole neighbourhood. He has the confidence to say, that there is a mug-house near Long Acre, where you may every evening hear an exact account of distresses of this kind. One complains, that such a lady's finery is the occasion that his own wife and daughter appear so long in the same gown : another, that all the furniture of her visiting apartment are no more hers, than the scenery of a play are the proper goods of the actress. Nay, at the lower end of the same table, you may hear a butcher and poulterer say, that at their proper charge all that family has been maintained since they last came to town.

The free manner in which people of fashion are discoursed on at such meetings, is but a just reproach for their failures in this kind ; but the melancholy relations of the great necessities tradesmen are driven to, who support their credit in spite of the faithless promises which are made them, and the abatement which they suffer when paid, by the extortion of upper servants, is what would stop the most thoughtless man in the career of his pleasures, if rightly represented to him.

If this matter be not very speedily amended, I shall think fit to print exact lists of all persons who are not at their own disposal, though above the age of twenty-one ; and as the trader is made bankrupt for absence from his abode, so shall the gentleman for being at home, if, when Mr. Morphew calls, he cannot give him an exact account of what passes in his own family. After this fair warning, no one ought to think himself hardly dealt with, if I take upon me to pronounce him no longer master of his estate, wife, or family, than he continues to improve, cherish, and maintain them upon the basis of his own property, without incursions upon his neighbour in any of these particulars.

According to that excellent philosopher Epictetus, we are all but acting parts in a play ; and it is not a distinction in itself to be high or low, but to become the parts we are to perform. I am by my office prompter on this occasion, and shall give those who are a little out in their parts such soft hints as may help them to proceed, without letting it be known to the audience they were out : but if they run quite out of character, they must be called off the stage, and receive parts more suitable to their genius.

Servile complaisance shall degrade a man from his honour and quality, and haughtiness be yet more debased. Fortune shall no longer appropriate distinctions, but Nature direct us in the disposition both of respect and discountenance. As there are tempers made for command, and others for obedience; so there are men born for acquiring possessions, and others incapable of being other than mere lodgers in the houses of their ancestors, and have it not in their very composition to be proprietors of anything. These men are moved only by the mere effects of impulse : their goodwill and disesteem are to be regarded equally, for neither is the effect of their judgment. This loose temper is that which makes a man, what Sallust so well remarks to happen frequently in the same person, to be covetous of what is another's, and profuse of what is his own.[1] This sort of men is usually amiable to ordinary eyes ; but in the sight of reason, nothing is laudable but what is guided by reason. The covetous prodigal is of all others the worst man in society : if he would but take time to look into himself, he would find his soul all over gashed with broken vows and promises, and his retrospect on his actions would not consist of reflections upon those good resolutions after mature thought, which are the true life of a reasonable creature, but the nauseous memory of imperfect pleasures, idle dreams, and occasional amusements. To follow such dissatisfying pursuits, is it possible to suffer the ignominy of being unjust ? I remember in Tully's Epistle, in the recommendation of a man to an affair which had no manner of relation to money, it is said, " You may trust him, for he is a frugal man." It is certain, he who has not a regard to strict justice in the commerce of life, can be capable of no good action in any other kind ; but he who lives below his income, lays up every moment of life armour against a

---

[1] " Alieni appetens, sui profusus " (" Bell. Cat." cap. i.).

347

base world, that will cover all his frailties while he is so
fortified, and exaggerate them when he is naked and
defenceless.

ADVERTISEMENT.

A stage-coach sets out exactly at six from Nando's
Coffee-house [1] to Mr. Tiptoe's dancing school, and returns
at eleven every evening, for 16*d*.

N.B. Dancing-shoes not exceeding four inches height in
the heel, and periwigs not exceeding three feet in length,
are carried in the coach-box gratis.

No. 181. [STEELE.

From *Saturday,* *June* 3, to *Tuesday,* *June* 6, 1710.

—— Dies, ni fallor, adest, quem semper acerbum,
Semper honoratum (sic di voluistis), habebo.
VIRG., Æn. v. 49.

From my own Apartment, June 5.

There are those among mankind, who can enjoy no
relish of their being, except the world is made
acquainted with all that relates to them, and think everything lost that passes unobserved ; but others find a solid
delight in stealing by the crowd, and modelling their life
after such a manner, as is as much above the approbation
as the practice of the vulgar. Life being too short to
give instances great enough of true friendship or goodwill, some sages have thought it pious to preserve a certain
reverence for the manes of their deceased friends, and have
withdrawn themselves from the rest of the world at certain
seasons, to commemorate in their own thoughts such of
their acquaintance who have gone before them out of this

[1] See No. 142.

life : and indeed, when we are advanced in years, there is not a more pleasing entertainment, than to recollect in a gloomy moment the many we have parted with that have been dear and agreeable to us, and to cast a melancholy thought or two after those with whom, perhaps, we have indulged ourselves in whole nights of mirth and jollity. With such inclinations in my heart I went to my closet yesterday in the evening, and resolved to be sorrowful ; upon which occasion, I could not but look with disdain upon myself, that though all the reasons which I had to lament the loss of many of my friends are now as forcible as at the moment of their departure, yet did not my heart swell with the same sorrow which I felt at that time ; but I could, without tears, reflect upon many pleasing adventures I have had with some who have long been blended with common earth. Though it is by the benefit of nature that length of time thus blots out the violence of afflictions ; yet with tempers too much given to pleasure, it is almost necessary to revive the old places of grief in our memory, and ponder step by step on past life, to lead the mind into that sobriety of thought which poises the heart, and makes it beat with due time, without being quickened with desire, or retarded with despair, from its proper and equal motion. When we wind up a clock that is out of order, to make it go well for the future, we do not immediately set the hand to the present instant, but we make it strike the round of all its hours, before it can recover the regularity of its time. "Such," thought I, " shall be my method this evening ; and since it is that day of the year which I dedicate to the memory of such in another life as I much delighted in when living, an hour or two shall be sacred to sorrow and their memory, while I run over all the melancholy circumstances of this kind which have occurred to me in my whole life."

The Tatler No. 181. June 6, 1710

The first sense of sorrow I ever knew was upon the death of my father,[1] at which time I was not quite five years of age ; but was rather amazed at what all the house meant, than possessed with a real understanding why nobody was willing to play with me. I remember I went into the room where his body lay, and my mother sat weeping alone by it. I had my battledore in my hand, and fell a beating the coffin, and calling " Papa " ; for I know not how I had some slight idea that he was locked up there. My mother catched me in her arms, and transported beyond all patience of the silent grief she was before in, she almost smothered me in her embrace, and told me in a flood of tears, papa could not hear me, and would play with me no more, for they were going to put him under ground, whence he could never come to us again. She was a very beautiful woman, of a noble spirit, and there was a dignity in her grief amidst all the wildness of her transport, which, methought, struck me with an instinct of sorrow, which, before I was sensible of what it was to grieve, seized my very soul, and has made pity the weakness of my heart ever since. The mind in infancy is, methinks, like the body in embryo, and receives impressions so forcible, that they are as hard to be removed by reason, as any mark with which a child is born is to be taken away by any future application. Hence it is, that good nature in me is no merit ; but having been so frequently overwhelmed with her tears before I knew the cause of any affliction, or could draw defences from my own judgment, I imbibed commiseration, remorse, and an unmanly gentleness of mind, which has since ensnared me into ten thousand calamities, and

---

[1] Steele's father, Richard Steele, was a Dublin solicitor. His mother, whose maiden name was Elinor Sheyles, had married Thomas Symes, of Dublin, as her first husband.

from whence I can reap no advantage, except it be, that in such a humour as I am now in, I can the better indulge myself in the softnesses of humanity, and enjoy that sweet anxiety which arises from the memory of past afflictions.[1]

We that are very old, are better able to remember things which befell us in our distant youth, than the passages of later days. For this reason it is, that the companions of my strong and vigorous years present themselves more immediately to me in this office of sorrow. Untimely or unhappy deaths are what we are most apt to lament, so little are we able to make it indifferent when a thing happens, though we know it must happen. Thus we groan under life, and bewail those who are relieved from it. Every object that returns to our imagination raises different passions according to the circumstance of their departure. Who can have lived in an army, and in a serious hour reflect upon the many gay and agreeable men that might long have flourished in the arts of peace, and not join with the imprecations of the fatherless and widow on the tyrant to whose ambition they fell sacrifices? But gallant men, who are cut off by the sword, move rather our veneration than our pity, and we gather relief enough from their own

[1] Thackeray has compared the treatment of Death by Swift, Addison, and Steele. After speaking of Addison's "lovely serenity" and Swift's "savage indignation," he turns to Steele : "The third, whose theme is Death, too, and who will speak his word of mortal as Heaven teaches him, leads you up to his father's coffin, and shows you his beautiful mother weeping, and himself an unconscious little boy wondering at her side. His own natural tears flow as he takes your hand, and confidingly asks for your sympathy ; 'See how good and innocent and beautiful women are,' he says, 'how tender little children ! Let us love these and one another, brother—God knows we have need of love and pardon ! ' " ("English Humourists," 1864, 158-9).

contempt of death, to make it no evil, which was approached with so much cheerfulness, and attended with so much honour. But when we turn our thoughts from the great parts of life on such occasions, and instead of lamenting those who stood ready to give death to those from whom they had the fortune to receive it ; I say, when we let our thoughts wander from such noble objects, and consider the havoc which is made among the tender and the innocent, pity enters with an unmixed softness, and possesses all our souls at once.

Here (were there words to express such sentiments with proper tenderness) I should record the beauty, innocence, and untimely death, of the first object my eyes ever beheld with love. The beauteous virgin ! How ignorantly did she charm, how carelessly excel ! O Death ! thou hast right to the bold, to the ambitious, to the high, and to the haughty, but why this cruelty to the humble, to the meek, to the undiscerning, to the thoughtless ?[1] Nor age, nor business, nor distress, can erase the dear image from my imagination. In the same week, I saw her dressed for a ball, and in a shroud. How ill did the habit of Death become the pretty trifler ? I still behold the smiling earth —A large train of disasters were coming on to my memory, when my servant knocked at my closet door, and interrupted me with a letter, attended with a hamper of wine, of the same sort with that which is to be put to sale on Thursday next at Garraway's Coffee-house.[2] Upon the receipt of it, I sent for three of my friends. We are so

---

[1] The unsuspecting.

[2] "Notice is hereby given, that 46 hogsheads and one half of extraordinary French claret will be put up to sale, at £20 per hogshead, at Garraway's Coffee-house in Exchange Alley, on Thursday the 8th instant, at three in the afternoon, and to be tasted in a vault under Messrs. Lane and Harrison's, in Sweething's Lane, Lombard Street, from this day till the time of sale," &c. (No. 181, Advertisement).

intimate, that we can be company in whatever state of mind we meet, and can entertain each other without expecting always to rejoice. The wine we found to be generous and warming, but with such a heat as moved us rather to be cheerful than frolicsome. It revived the spirits without firing the blood. We commended it till two of the clock this morning, and having to-day met a little before dinner, we found, that though we drank two bottles a man, we had much more reason to recollect than forget what had passed the night before.

No. 182. [Steele.

From *Tuesday, June 6*, to *Thursday, June 8*, 1710.

Spectaret populum ludis attentius ipsis.—Hor., 2 Ep. i. 197.

Sheer Lane, June 7.

The town grows so very empty, that the greater number of my gay characters are fled out of my sight into the country. My beaus are now shepherds, and my belles wood-nymphs. They are lolling over rivulets, and covered with shades, while we who remain in town hurry through the dust about impertinences, without knowing the happiness of leisure and retirement. To add to this calamity, even the actors are going to desert us for a season, and we shall not shortly have so much as a landscape or frost-scene to refresh ourselves within the midst of our fatigues. This may not perhaps be so sensible a loss to any other as to me ; for I confess it is one of my greatest delights to sit unobserved and unknown in the gallery, and entertain myself either with what is personated on the stage, or observe what appearances present themselves in the audience. If there were no other good con-

sequences in a playhouse, than that so many persons of
different ranks and conditions are placed there in their
most pleasing aspects, that prospect only would be very
far from being below the pleasures of a wise man.   There
is not one person you can see, in whom, if you look with
an inclination to be pleased, you may not behold something worthy or agreeable.   Our thoughts are in our
features ; and the visage of those in whom love, rage,
anger, jealousy or envy, have their frequent mansions,
carries the traces of those passions wherever the amorous,
the choleric, the jealous, or the envious, are pleased to
make their appearance.   However, the assembly at a play
is usually made up of such as have a sense of some elegance
in pleasure, by which means the audience is generally composed of those who have gentle affections, or at least of
such as at that time are in the best humour you can ever
find them.   This has insensibly a good effect upon our
spirits ; and the musical airs which are played to us, put
the whole company into a participation of the same
pleasure, and by consequence for that time equal in
humour, in fortune, and in quality.   Thus far we gain
only by coming into an audience ; but if we find added to
this, the beauties of proper action, the force of eloquence,
and the gaiety of well-placed lights and scenes, it is being
happy, and seeing others happy for two hours ; a duration
of bliss not at all to be slighted by so short-lived a
creature as man.   Why then should not the duty of the
player be had in much more esteem than it is at present ?
If the merit of a performance be to be valued according to
the talents which are necessary to it, the qualifications of a
player should raise him much above the arts and ways of
life which we call mercenary or mechanic.   When we look
round a full house, and behold so few that can (though
they set themselves out to show as much as the persons on

the stage do) come up to what they would appear even in dumb show, how much does the actor deserve our approbation, who adds to the advantage of looks and motions the tone of voice, the dignity, the humility, the sorrow, the triumph suitable to the character he personates?

It may possibly be imagined by severe men, that I am too frequent in the mention of the theatrical representations; but who is not excessive in the discourse of what he extremely likes? Eugenio can lead you to a gallery of fine pictures, which collection he is always increasing : Crassus through woods and forests, to which he designs to add the neighbouring counties. These are great and noble instances of their magnificence. The players are my pictures, and their scenes my territories. By communicating the pleasure I take in them, it may in some measure add to men's gratifications this way, as viewing the choice and wealth of Eugenio and Crassus augments the enjoyments of those whom they entertain, with a prospect of such possessions as would not otherwise fall within the reach of their fortunes.

It is a very good office one man does another, when he tells him the manner of his being pleased ; and I have often thought, that a comment upon the capacities of the players would very much improve the delight that way, and impart it to those who otherwise have no sense of it.

The first of the present stage are Wilks,[1] and Cibber,[2] perfect actors in their different kinds. Wilks has a

---

[1] See No. 14.

[2] Colley Cibber, actor and dramatist, was born in 1671. He was admirable alike as an actor of comic parts and a critic of acting, and some of his comedies are excellent. In 1714 Cibber became associated with Steele in the management of Drury Lane Theatre. After his retirement from the stage in 1733 he published his famous "Apology" (1740). He died in 1757. Steele wrote several times in his praise in the *Spectator* (Nos. 370, 546).

singular talent in representing the graces of Nature, Cibber the deformity in the affectation of them.   Were I a writer of plays, I should never employ either of them in parts which had not their bent this way.   This is seen in the inimitable strain and run of good humour which is kept up in the character of Wildair,[1] and in the nice and delicate abuse of understanding in that of Sir Novelty.[2] Cibber, in another light, hits exquisitely the flat civility of an affected gentleman-usher, and Wilks the easy frankness of a gentleman.

If you would observe the force of the same capacities in higher life, can anything be more ingenuous than the behaviour of Prince Harry when his father checks him ? Anything more exasperating, than that of Richard, when he insults his superiors ? To beseech gracefully, to approach respectfully, to pity, to mourn, to love, are the places wherein Wilks may be made to shine with the utmost beauty : to rally pleasantly, to scorn artfully, to flatter, to ridicule, and to neglect, are what Cibber would perform with no less excellence.

When actors are considered with a view to their talents, it is not only the pleasure of that hour of action which the spectators gain from their performance, but the opposition of right and wrong on the stage would have its force in the assistance of our judgments on other occasions.   I have at present under my tutelage a young poet, who, I design, shall entertain the town the ensuing winter.   And as he does me the honour to let me see his comedy as he writes it, I shall endeavour to make the parts fit the genius of the several actors, as exactly as their habits can their bodies : and because the two I have mentioned are to perform the principal parts, I have prevailed with the house to let " The

---

[1] Sir Harry Wildair, in Farquhar's " Constant Couple."
[2] Sir Novelty Fashion, in Cibber's " Love's Last Shift."

Careless Husband "¹ be acted on Tuesday next, that my young author may have a view of a play which is acted to perfection, both by them and all concerned in it, as being born within the walls of the theatre, and written with an exact knowledge of the abilities of the performers. Mr. Wilks will do his best in this play, because it is for his own benefit ; and Mr. Cibber, because he writ it. Besides which, all the great beauties we have left in town, or within call of it, will be present, because it is the last play this season. This opportunity will, I hope, inflame my pupil with such generous notions from seeing this fair assembly as will be then present, that his play may be composed of sentiments and characters proper to be presented to such an audience. His drama at present has only the outlines drawn. There are, I find, to be in it all the reverent offices of life, such as regard to parents, husbands, and honourable lovers, preserved with the utmost care ; and at the same time that agreeableness of behaviour, with the intermixture of pleasing passions as arise from innocence and virtue, interspersed in such a manner, as that to be charming and agreeable shall appear the natural conse-quence of being virtuous. This great end is one of those I propose to do in my Censorship ; but if I find a thin house, on an occasion when such a work is to be promoted, my pupil shall return to his commons at Oxford, and Sheer Lane and the theatres be no longer correspondents.

¹ In this play, produced in 1705, Wilks was Sir Charles Easy ; Cibber, Lord Foppington ; and Mrs. Oldfield, Lady Betty Modish. In his " Apology " Cibber said that it was only just to place to the account of Mrs. Oldfield a large share of the favourable reception accorded to " The Careless Husband."

No. 183.   ₍[STEELE.

From *Thursday, June 8,* to *Saturday, June* 10, 1710.

—— Fuit hæc sapientia quondam,
Publica privatis secernere.
                              HOR., Ars Poët. 396.

From my own Apartment, June 9.

When men look into their own bosoms, and consider the generous seeds which are there planted, that might, if rightly cultivated, ennoble their lives, and make their virtue venerable to futurity ; how can they, without tears, reflect on the universal degeneracy from that public spirit, which ought to be the first and principal motive of all their actions ? In the Grecian and Roman nations, they were wise enough to keep up this great incentive; and it was impossible to be in the fashion without being a patriot. All gallantry had its first source from hence ; and to want a warmth for the public welfare was a defect so scandalous, that he who was guilty of it had no pretence to honour or manhood. What makes the depravity among us in this behalf the more vexatious and irksome to reflect upon, is, that the contempt of life is carried as far amongst us as it could be in those memorable people ; and we want only a proper application of the qualities which are frequent among us to be as worthy as they. There is hardly a man to be found who will not fight upon any occasion which he thinks may taint his own honour. Were this motive as strong in everything that regards the public, as it is in this our private case, no man would pass his life away without having distinguished himself by some gallant instance of his zeal towards it in the respective incidents of his life and profession. But it is so far otherwise, that there cannot at present be a more ridiculous animal than one who seems to regard the good of others. He in civil life whose thoughts turn upon schemes which may be of general benefit, without further reflection, is called a " projector " ; and the man whose mind seems intent upon glorious achievements, a " knight-errant." The ridicule among us runs strong against laudable actions. Nay, in the ordinary course of things, and the common regards of life, negligence of the public is an epidemic vice. The brewer in his excise, the merchant in his customs, and for aught we know the soldier in his muster-rolls, think never the worse of themselves for being guilty of their respective frauds towards the public. This evil is come to such a fantastical height, that he is a man of a public spirit, and heroically affected to his country, who can go so far as even to turn usurer with all he has in her funds. There is not a citizen in whose imagination such a one does not appear in the same light of glory as Codrus, Scævola, or any other great name in old Rome. Were it not for the heroes of so much per cent. as have regard enough for themselves and their nation to trade with her with their wealth, the very notion of public love would long ere now have vanished from among us. But however general custom may hurry us away in the stream of a common error, there is no evil, no crime, so great as that of being cold in matters which relate to the common good. This is in nothing more conspicuous than in a certain willingness to receive anything that tends to the diminution of such as have been conspicuous instruments in our service. Such inclinations proceed from the most low and vile corruption of which the soul of man is capable. This effaces not only the practice, but the very approbation of honour and virtue ; and has had such an effect that, to speak freely, the very sense of public good has no longer a part even in our conversations. Can then the most generous motive of life, the good of others, be so easily banished from the breast of man ? Is it possible to draw all our passions inward ? Shall the boiling heat of youth be sunk in pleasures, the ambition of manhood in selfish intrigues ? Shall all that is glorious, all that is worth the pursuit of great minds, be so easily rooted out ? When the universal bent of a people seems diverted from the sense of their common good and common glory, it looks like a fatality, and crisis of impending misfortune.

The generous nations we just now mentioned understood this so very well, that there was hardly an oration ever made which did not turn upon this general sense, that the love of their country was the first and most essential quality in an honest mind. Demosthenes, in a cause wherein his fame, reputation, and fortune were embarked, puts his all upon this issue : " Let the Athenians," says he, " be benevolent to me, as they think I have been zealous for them." This great and discerning orator knew there was nothing else in nature could bear him up against his adversaries, but this one quality of having shown himself willing or able to serve his country. This certainly is the test of merit ; and the first foundation for deserving goodwill, is having it yourself. The adversary of this orator at that time was Æschines, a man of wily arts and skill in the world, who could, as occasion served, fall in with a national start of passion, or sullenness of humour (which a whole nation is sometimes taken with as well as a private man), and by that means divert them from their common sense, into an aversion for receiving anything in its true light. But when Demosthenes had awaked his audience with that one hint of judging by the general tenor of his life towards them, his services bore down his opponent before him, who fled to the covert of his mean arts till some more favourable occasion should offer, against the superior merit of Demosthenes.

It were to be wished, that love of their country were the first principle of action in men of business, even for their own sakes ; for when the world begins to examine into their conduct, the generality, who have no share in, or hopes of any part in power or riches, but what is the effect of their own labour or property, will judge of them by no other method, than that of how profitable their administration has been to the whole.   They who are out of the influence of men's fortune or favour, will let them stand or fall by this one only rule ; and men who can bear being tried by it, are always popular in their fall : those who cannot suffer such a scrutiny, are contemptible in their advancement.

But I am here running into shreds of maxims from reading Tacitus this morning, which has driven me from my recommendation of public spirit, which was the intended purpose of this Lucubration.   There is not a more glorious instance of it, than in the character of Regulus. This same Regulus was taken prisoner by the Carthagenians, and was sent by them to Rome, in order to demand some Punic noblemen who were prisoners in exchange for himself, and was bound by an oath that he would return to Carthage if he failed in his commission.   He proposes this to the Senate, who were in suspense upon it ; which Regulus observing (without having the least notion of putting the care of his own life in competition with the public good), desired them to consider that he was old, and almost useless ; that those demanded in exchange were men of daring tempers, and great merit in military affairs, and wondered they would make any doubt of permitting him to go back to the short tortures prepared for him at Carthage, where he should have the advantage of ending a long life both gloriously and usefully. This generous advice was consented to, and he took his leave of his country and his weeping friends to go to certain death, with that cheerful composure, as a man, after the fatigue of business in a Court or a city, retires to the next village for the air.

No. 184.   [Steele.

From *Saturday, June* 10, to *Tuesday, June* 13, 1710.

Una de multis face nuptiali
Digna.—Hor., 3 Od. xi. 33.

From my own Apartment, June 12.

There are certain occasions of life which give propitious omens of the future good conduct of it, as well as others which explain our present inward state, according to our behaviour in them. Of the latter sort are funerals ; of the former, weddings. The manner of our carriage when we lose a friend, shows very much our temper, in the humility of our words and actions, and a general sense of our destitute condition, which runs through all our deport-ment. This gives a solemn testimony of the generous affection we bore our friends, when we seem to disrelish everything now we can no more enjoy them, or see them partake in our enjoyments. It is very proper and human to put ourselves as it were in their livery after their decease, and wear a habit unsuitable to prosperity, while those we loved and honoured are mouldering in the grave. As this is laudable on the sorrowful side ; so on the other, incidents of success may no less justly be represented and acknowledged in our outward figure and carriage. Of all such occasions, that great change of a single life into marriage is the most important, as it is the source of all relations, and from whence all other friendship and commerce do principally arise. The general intent of both sexes is to dispose of themselves happily and honourably in this state ; and as all the good qualities we have are exerted to make our way into it, so the best appearance, with regard to their minds, their persons, and their fortunes, at the first entrance into it, is a due to each other in the married pair, as well as a compliment to the rest of the world. It was an instruction of a wise lawgiver, that unmarried women should wear such loose habits which, in the flowing of their garb, should incite their beholders to a desire of their persons ; and that the ordinary motion of their bodies might display the figure and shape of their limbs in such a manner, as at once to preserve the strictest decency, and raise the warmest inclinations.

This was the economy of the legislator for the increase of people, and at the same time for the preservation of the genial bed. She who was the admiration of all who beheld her while unmarried, was to bid adieu to the pleasure of shining in the eyes of many, as soon as she took upon her the wedded condition. However, there was a festival of life allowed the new-married, a sort of intermediate state between celibacy and matrimony, which continued certain days. During that time, entertainments, equipages, and other circumstances of rejoicing, were encouraged, and they were permitted to exceed the common mode of living, that the bride and bridegroom might learn from such freedoms of conversation to run into a general conduct to each other, made out of their past and future state, so to temper the cares of the man and the wife with the gaieties of the lover and the mistress.

In those wise ages the dignity of life was kept up, and

on the celebration of such solemnities there were no impertinent whispers and senseless interpretations put upon the unaffected cheerfulness or accidental seriousness of the bride ; but men turned their thoughts upon the general reflections, upon what issue might probably be expected from such a couple in the succeeding course of their life, and felicitated them accordingly upon such prospects.

I must confess, I cannot from any ancient manuscripts, sculptures, or medals, deduce the rise of our celebrated custom of throwing the stocking ; but have a faint memory of an account a friend gave me of an original picture in the palace of Aldobrandini in Rome. This seems to show a sense of this affair very different from what is usual among us. It is a Grecian wedding, and the figures represented are, a person offering sacrifice, a beautiful damsel dancing, and another playing on the harp. The bride is placed in her bed, the bridegroom sits at the foot of it, with an aspect which intimates his thoughts were not only entertained with the joys with which he was surrounded, but also with a noble gratitude, and divine pleasure in the offering, which was then made to the gods to invoke their influence on his new condition. There appears in the face of the woman a mixture of fear, hope, and modesty ; in the bridegroom, a well-governed rapture. As you see in great spirits grief which discovers itself the more by forbearing tears and complaints, you may observe also the highest joy is too big for utterance, the tongue being of all the organs the least capable of expressing such a circumstance. The nuptial torch, the bower, the marriage song, are all particulars which we meet with in the allusions of the ancient writers ; and in every one of them something is to be observed which denotes their industry to aggrandise and adorn this occasion above all others.

With us all order and decency in this point is per-
verted by the insipid mirth of certain animals we usually
call "wags." These are a species of all men the most
insupportable. One cannot without some reflection say,
whether their flat mirth provokes us more to pity or to
scorn; but if one considers with how great affectation
they utter their frigid conceits, commiseration immediately
changes itself into contempt.

A wag is the last order even of pretenders to wit and
good humour. He has generally his mind prepared to
receive some occasion of merriment, but is of himself
too empty to draw any out of his own set of thoughts,
and therefore laughs at the next thing he meets, not
because it is ridiculous, but because he is under a necessity of laughing. A wag is one that never in its life saw a
beautiful object, but sees what it does see in the most low
and most inconsiderable light it can be placed. There
is a certain ability necessary to behold what is amiable
and worthy of our approbation, which little minds want,
and attempt to hide by a general disregard to everything
they behold above what they are able to relish. Hence it
is, that a wag in an assembly is ever guessing how well
such a lady slept last night, and how much such a young
fellow is pleased with himself. The wag's gaiety consists
in a certain professed ill-breeding, as if it were an excuse
for committing a fault, that a man knows he does so.
Though all public places are full of persons of this order,
yet, because I will not allow impertinence and affectation
to get the better of native innocence and simplicity of
manners, I have, in spite of such little disturbers of public
entertainments, persuaded my brother Tranquillus and his
wife my sister Jenny, in favour of Mr. Wilks, to be at the
play to-morrow evening.

They, as they have so much good sense as to act

naturally, without regard to the observation of others,
will not, I hope, be discomposed if any of the fry of wags
should take upon them to make themselves merry upon
the occasion of their coming, as they intend, in their
wedding clothes.   My brother is a plain, worthy, and
honest man, and as it is natural for men of that turn
to be mightily taken with sprightly and airy women, my
sister has a vivacity which may perhaps give hopes to
impertinents, but will be esteemed the effect of innocence
among wise men.   They design to sit with me in the
box, which the house have been so complaisant to offer
me whenever I think fit to come thither in my public
character.[1]

I do not in the least doubt, but the true figure of conjugal affection will appear in their looks and gestures.
My sister does not affect to be gorgeous in her dress, and
thinks the happiness of a wife is more visible in a cheerful
look than a gay apparel.   It is a hard task to speak of
persons so nearly related to one with decency, but I may
say, all who shall be at the play will allow him to have the
mien of a worthy English gentleman ; her, that of a
notable and deserving wife.

[1] See Nos. 120, 122. "I remember Mr. Bickerstaff at the playhouse, and with what a modest, decent gravity he behaved himself"
(*Examiner*, vol. iii. No. 46). This passage occurs in a notice of
Addison's "Cato," where it is said that on the first night a crowd of
silly people "were drawn up under the leading of the renowned
Ironside, and appointed to clap at his signals. . . . The *Spectator*
never appeared in public with a worse grace."

No. 185.   [STEELE.

From *Tuesday, June* 13, to *Thursday, June* 15, 1710.

Notitiam primosque gradus vicinia fecit ;
Tempore crevit amor, tædæ quoque jure coissent ;
Sed vetuere patres, quod non potuere vetare,
Ex æquo captis ardebant mentibus ambo.
                                        OVID, Met. iv. 59.

From my own Apartment, June 14.

As soon as I was up this morning, my man gave me the following letter, which, since it leads to a subject that may prove of common use to the world, I shall take notice of with as much expedition as my fair petitioner could desire :

" MR. BICKERSTAFF,

" Since you have so often declared yourself a patron of the distressed, I must acquaint you, that I am daughter to a country gentleman of good sense, and may expect £3000 or £4000 for my fortune. I love and am beloved by Philander, a young gentleman who has an estate of £500 per annum, and is our near neighbour in the country every summer. My father, though he has been a long time acquainted with it, constantly refuses to comply with our mutual inclinations : but what most of all torments me, is, that if ever I speak in commendation of my lover, he is much louder in his praises than myself ; and professes that it is out of pure love and esteem for Philander, as well as his daughter, that he can never consent we should marry each other ; when (as he terms it) we may both do so much better. It must indeed be confessed, that two gentlemen of considerable fortunes, made

367

their addresses to me last winter, and Philander (as I have since learned) was offered a young heiress with £15,000, but it seems we could neither of us think, that accepting those matches would be doing better than remaining constant to our first passion. Your thoughts upon the whole may perhaps have some weight with my father, who is one of your admirers, as is

"Your humble Servant,

"SYLVIA.

" P.S. You are desired to be speedy, since my father daily presses me to accept of what he calls an 'advantageous offer.' "

There is no calamity in life that falls heavier upon human nature than a disappointment in love, especially when it happens between two persons whose hearts are mutually engaged to each other. It is this distress which has given occasion to some of the finest tragedies that were ever written, and daily fills the world with melancholy, discontent, frenzy, sickness, despair, and death. I have often admired at the barbarity of parents, who so frequently interpose their authority in this grand article of life. I would fain ask Sylvia's father, whether he thinks he can bestow a greater favour on his daughter, than to put her in a way to live happily? Whether a man of Philander's character, with £500 per annum, is not more likely to contribute to that end, than many a young fellow whom he may have in his thoughts with so many thousands? Whether he can make amends to his daughter by any increase of riches, for the loss of that happiness she proposes to herself in her Philander? Or whether a father should compound with his daughter to be miserable, though she were to get £20,000 by the bargain? I suppose he would have her reflect with esteem on his memory after his death ; and does he think this a proper method to make her do so, when, as often as she thinks on the loss of her Philander, she must at the same time remember him as the cruel cause of it ? Any transient ill-humour is soon forgotten ; but the reflection of such a cruelty must continue to raise resentments as long as life itself ; and by this one piece of barbarity, an indulgent father loses the merit of all his past kindnesses. It is not impossible but she may deceive herself in the happiness which she pro-poses from Philander ; but as in such a case she can have no one to blame but herself, she will bear the disappoint-ment with greater patience ; but if she never makes the experiment, however happy she may be with another, she will still think she might have been happier with Phil-ander. There is a kind of sympathy in souls that fits them for each other ; and we may be assured, when we see two persons engaged in the warmths of a mutual affection, that there are certain qualities in both their minds which bear a resemblance to one another. A generous and constant passion in an agreeable lover, where there is not too great a disparity in other circumstances, is the greatest blessing that can befall the person beloved ; and if overlooked in one, may perhaps never be found in another. I shall conclude this with a celebrated instance of a father's indulgence in this particular, which, though carried to an extravagance, has something in it so tender and amiable, as may justly reproach the hardness of temper that is to be met with in many a British father.

Antiochus, a prince of great hopes, fell passionately in love with the young Queen Stratonice, who was his mother-in-law, and had bore a son to the old King Seleucus his father. The prince finding it impossible to extinguish his passion, fell sick, and refused all manner of nourishment, being determined to put an end to that life which was become insupportable.

Erasistratus the physician soon found that love was his distemper ; and observing the alteration in his pulse and countenance whenever Stratonice made him a visit, was soon satisfied that he was dying for his young mother-in-law.   Knowing the old king's tenderness for his son, when he one morning inquired of his health, he told him, that the prince's distemper was love ; but that it was incurable, because it was impossible for him to possess the person whom he loved. The king, surprised at this account, desired to know how his son's passion could be incurable ? "Why, sir," replied Erasistratus, " because he is in love with the person I am married to."

The old king immediately conjured him by all his past favours to save the life of his son and successor.   "Sir," said Erasistratus, "would your majesty but fancy yourself in my place, you would see the unreasonableness of what you desire ! "   " Heaven is my witness," said Seleucus, " I could resign even my Stratonice to save my Antiochus." At this the tears ran down his cheeks, which when the physician saw, taking him by the hand, "Sir," says he, "if these are your real sentiments, the prince's life is out of danger ; it is Stratonice for whom he dies." Seleucus immediately gave orders for solemnising the marriage ; and the young queen, to show her obedience, very generously exchanged the father for the son.

No. 186. [Steele.

From *Thursday, June* 15, to *Saturday, June* 17, 1710.

Emitur sola virtute potestas.
  • Claudian, De Tertio Consulatu Honorii, 188.

Sheer Lane, June 16.

As it has been the endeavour of these our labours to extirpate from among the polite or busy part of mankind, all such as are either prejudicial or insignificant to society ; so it ought to be no less our study to supply the havoc we have made by an exact care of the growing generation. But when we begin to inculcate proper precepts to the children of this island, except we could take them out of their nurses' arms, we see an amendment is almost impracticable ; for we find the whole species of our youth and grown men is incorrigibly prepossessed with vanity, pride, or ambition, according to the respective pursuits to which they turn themselves : by which means the world is infatuated with the love of appearances instead of things. Thus the vain man takes praise for honour, the proud man ceremony for respect, the ambitious man power for glory. These three characters are, indeed, of very near resemblance, but differently received by mankind. Vanity makes men ridiculous ; pride, odious ; and ambition, terrible. The foundation of all which is, that they are grounded upon falsehood : for if men, instead of studying to appear considerable, were in their own hearts possessors of the requisites for esteem, the acceptance they otherwise unfortunately aim at would be as inseparable from them, as approbation is from truth itself. By this means they would have some rule to walk by ; and they

371

may ever be assured, that a good cause of action will certainly receive a suitable effect. It may be a useful hint in such cases for a man to ask of himself, whether he really is what he has a mind to be thought?[1] If he is, he need not give himself much further anxiety. "What will the world say?" is the common question in matters of difficulty; as if the terror lay wholly in the sense which others, and not we ourselves, shall have of our actions. From this one source arise all the impostors in every art and profession, in all places, among all persons in conversation, as well as in business. Hence it is, that a vain fellow takes twice as much pains to be ridiculous, as would make him sincerely agreeable.

Can any one be better fashioned, better bred, or has any one more good nature, than Damasippus? But the whole scope of his looks and actions tends so immediately to gain the good opinion of all he converses with, that he loses it for that only reason. As it is the nature of vanity to impose false shows for truths, so does it also turn real possessions into imaginary ones. Damasippus, by assuming to himself what he has not, robs himself of what he has.

There is nothing more necessary to establish reputation, than to suspend the enjoyment of it. He that cannot bear the sense of merit with silence, must of necessity destroy it : for fame being the general mistress of mankind, whoever gives it to himself, insults all to whom he relates any circumstances to his own advantage. He is considered as an open ravisher of that beauty, for whom all others pine in silence. But some minds are so incapable of any temperance in this particular, that on every second in their discourse you may observe an earnestness in their eyes, which shows they wait for your approbation, and perhaps the next instant cast an eye on a glass to see how they

[1] See Nos. 30, 39, 138.

like themselves. Walking the other day in a neighbouring Inn of Court, I saw a more happy and more graceful orator than I ever before had heard or read of. A youth, of about nineteen years of age, was in an Indian night-gown and laced cap pleading a cause before a glass : the young fellow had a very good air, and seemed to hold his brief in his hand rather to help his action, than that he wanted notes for his further information. When I first began to observe him, I feared he would soon be alarmed; but he was so zealous for his client, and so favourably received by the court, that he went on with great fluency to inform the bench, that he humbly hoped they would not let the merit of the cause suffer by the youth and in-experience of the pleader ; that in all things he submitted to their candour ; and modestly desired they would not conclude, but that strength of argument and force of reason may be consistent with grace of action and comeli-ness of person.

To me, who see people every day in the midst of crowds (whomsoever they seem to address to) talk only to themselves and of themselves, this orator was not so extravagant a man as perhaps another would have thought him ; but I took part in his success, and was very glad to find he had in his favour judgment and costs without any manner of opposition.

The effects of pride and vanity are of consequence only to the proud and the vain, and tend to no further ill than what is personal to themselves, in preventing their pro-gress in anything that is worthy and laudable, and creating envy instead of emulation of superior virtue. These ill qualities are to be found only in such as have so little minds, as to circumscribe their thoughts and designs within what properly relates to the value which they think due to their dear and amiable selves : but ambition, which is the

third great impediment to honour and virtue, is a fault of
such as think themselves born for moving in a higher
orb, and prefer being powerful and mischievous te being
virtuous and obscure.   The parent of this mischief in life,
so far as to regulate it into schemes, and make it possess a
man's whole heart, without his believing himself a demon,
was Machiavelli.   He first taught, that a man must necessarily appear weak to be honest.   Hence it gains upon
the imagination, that a great is not so despicable as a
little villain ; and men are insensibly led to a belief, that
the aggravation of crimes is the diminution of them.
Hence the impiety of thinking one thing and speaking
another.   In pursuance of this empty and unsatisfying
dream, to betray, to undermine, to kill in themselves all
natural sentiments of love to friends or country, is the
willing practice of such as are thirsty of power, for any
other reason than that of being useful and acceptable to
mankind.

ADVERTISEMENT.

Whereas Mr. Bickerstaff has lately received a letter out
of Ireland, dated June 9, importing that he is grown very
dull, for the postage of which Mr. Morphew charges one
shilling ; and another without date of place or time, for
which he the said Morphew charges twopence : it is
desired, that for the future his courteous and uncourteous
readers will go a little further in expressing their good and
ill-will, and pay for the carriage of their letters, otherwise
the intended pleasure or pain which is designed for
Mr. Bickerstaff will be wholly disappointed.

No. 187.   [STEELE.

From *Saturday, June* 17, to *Tuesday, June* 20, 1710.

—— Pudet hæc opprobria nobis
.Et dici potuisse et non potuisse refelli.
                                        OVID, Met. i. 758.

From my own Apartment, June 19.

Pasquin of Rome to Isaac Bickerstaff of London.[1]

" Hᴵs Holiness is gone to Castel Gandolpho, much discomposed at some late accounts from the mis-
sionaries in your island : for a committee of cardinals,
which lately sat for the reviving the force of some obsolete
doctrines, and drawing up amendments to certain points of
faith, have represented the Church of Rome to be in great
danger, from a treatise written by a learned Englishman,
which carries spiritual power much higher than we could
have dared to have attempted even here. His book is
called, ' An Epistolary Discourse, proving from the Scrip-
tures and the First Fathers, that the Soul is a Principle
naturally Mortal : wherein is proved, that none have the
Power of giving this Divine immortalising Spirit since the
Apostles, but the Bishops.' By Henry Dodwell, A.M.[2]
The assertion appeared to our *literati* so short and effectual

---

[1] See No. 129. In Lillie's "Letters sent to the *Tatler* and
Spectator" (i. 56) there is a letter from "Orontes" to Mr. Bickerstaff,
dated July 6, 1710, referring to this and to No. 190, in which the
writer says : "You would do yourself a grand favour, if you would
break off acquaintance with the Italian Pasquin, and not disturb yourself with principles which are as far above your thoughts as the
probability of your discovering the philosopher's stone." A censor
should not be among the factions.
[2] See No. 118.

a method of subjecting the laity, that it is feared auricular confession and absolution will not be capable of keeping the clergy of Rome in any degree of greatness, in competition with such teachers whose flocks shall receive this opinion. What gives the greater jealousy here is, that in the catalogue of treatises which have been lately burnt within the British territories, there is no mention made of this learned work ; which circumstance is a sort of implication, that the tenet is not held erroneous, but that the doctrine is received amongst you as orthodox. The youth of this place are very much divided in opinion, whether a very memorable quotation which the author repeats out of Tertullian, be not rather of the style and manner of Meursius ? *In illo ipso voluptatis æstu quo genitale virus expellitur, nonne aliquid de anima quoque, sentimus exire, atque, adeo marcessimus et devigescimus cum lucis detrimento ?* This piece of Latin goes no further than to tell us how our fathers got us, so that we are still at a loss how we afterwards commence eternal ; for *creando infunditur, et infundendo creatur*, which is mentioned soon after, may allude only to flesh and blood as well as the former. Your readers in this city, some of whom have very much approved the warmth with which you have attacked free-thinkers, atheists, and other enemies to religion and virtue, are very much disturbed that you have given them no account of this remarkable dissertation : and I am employed by them to desire you would with all possible expedition send me over the ceremony of the creation of souls, as well as a list of all the mortal and immortal men within the dominions of Great Britain. When you have done me this favour, I must trouble you for other tokens of your kindness, and particularly I desire you would let me have the religious handkerchief,[1] which is of late so

---

[1] Handkerchiefs printed with pictures of Dr. Sacheverell.

much worn in England, for I have promised to make a present of it to a courtesan of a French Minister.

' " Letters from the frontiers of France inform us, that a young gentleman[1] who was to have been created a cardinal on the next promotion, has put off his design of coming to Rome so soon as was intended, having, as it is said, received letters from Great Britain, wherein several virtuosi of that island have desired him to suspend his resolutions towards a monastic life, till the British grammarians shall publish their explication of the words ' indefeasible ' and ' revolution.' According as these two hard terms are made to fit the mouths of the people, this gentleman takes his measures for his journey hither.

" Your ' New Bedlam ' has been read and considered by some of your countrymen among us ; and one gentleman, who is now here as a traveller, says your design is impracticable, for that there can be no place large enough to contain the number of your lunatics. He advises you therefore to name the ambient sea for the boundary of your hospital. If what he says be true, I do not see how you can think of any other enclosure ; for according to his discourse, the whole people are taken with a vertigo ; great and popular actions are received with coldness and discontent ; ill news hoped for with impatience ; heroes in your service are treated with calumny, while criminals pass through your towns with acclamations.[2]

[1] The Pretender.

[2] Dr. Sacheverell received many popular ovations while he was suspended from preaching : " Lest these brethren in iniquity [the *Observator* and the *Review*] should not prove sufficient to poison the nation, sow sedition plentifully, and ripen rebellion to a fruitful harvest of blood and rapine, a third person [the *Tatler*] who for a considerable time hath diverted the Town with the most useful and pleasing amusements our age ever produced, hath joined in the cry with them, in hopes, no doubt, that by his additional strength they shall become

"This Englishman went on to say, you seemed at
present to flag under a satiety of success, as if you wanted
misfortune as a necessary vicissitude.   Yet, alas !, though
men have but a cold relish of prosperity, quick is the
anguish of the contrary fortune.   He proceeded to make
comparisons of times, seasons, and great incidents.   After
which he grew too learned for my understanding, and
talked of Hanno the Carthaginian, and his irreconcilable
hatred to the glorious commander Hannibal.   Hannibal,
said he, was able to march to Rome itself, and brought
that ambitious people, which designed no less than the

such a formidable Triumvirate that all opposition must fall before
them, and the Church irresistibly submit to that fate which the other
two have so long endeavoured to procure by their seditious popular
harangues. . . . Our third gentleman is pleased to tell us, ' *That great
and popular actions,*' &c.   This is a subtle way to create jealousies and
divisions amongst us, noways becoming the character of a gentleman,
or an ingenuous education.   Pray, sir, speak plain, and don't instil
your poison secretly, and stab in the dark.   What heroes in our service
are treated with calumny ?   Who do you mean by your Hanno and
Hannibal ?   All the nation owns and glories in the noble actions of
our great Duke of Marlborough " (*Moderator*, No. 13, June 30 to
July 3, 1710).   The next number of the *Moderator*, No. 14, is upon
the same subject, and is largely occupied with a discussion of the legal
question mentioned in the *Tatler*, No. 190.   The writer speaks of the
brains of the common people, who are too apt to censure the actions
of their superiors, as " set on work by a person who has gained their
esteem by his learned Lucubrations."   " They are assured that a gentleman of his bright parts and learning must be intimately acquainted
with persons of the first rank and quality, from whom he learns these
high and important secrets which he thus generously communicates to
the world."   If any one, therefore, pretends that the author's meaning
is that the " Duke of Marlborough is likely to be ruined by the Lord
Treasurer's converting to other uses that money which our Senate
voted for our General's service, who is to be blamed for the vile asper-
sion ?"   Ministers should take care that the spreaders of such false
reports shall know to their cost that the Act respecting false and
slanderous news is still in force.

empire of the world, to sue for peace in the most abject
and servile manner ; when faction at home detracted from
the glory of his actions, and after many artifices, at last
prevailed with the Senate to recall him from the midst of
his victories, and in the very instant when he was to reap
the benefit of all his toils, by reducing the then common
enemy of all nations which had liberty to reason. When
Hannibal heard the message of the Carthaginian senators
who were sent to recall him, he was moved with a generous
and disdainful sorrow, and is reported to have said,
' Hannibal then must be conquered not by the arms of the
Romans, whom he has often put to flight, but by the
envy and detraction of his countrymen. Nor shall Scipio
triumph so much in his fall as Hanno, who will smile to
have purchased the ruin of Hannibal, though attended
with the fall of Carthage.'[1]

" I am, Sir, &c.

" PASQUIN."

Will's Coffee-house, June 19.

There is a sensible satisfaction in observing the countenance and action of the people on some occasions. To
gratify myself in this pleasure, I came hither with all speed
this evening with an account of the surrender of Douay.
As soon as the battle-critics[2] heard it, they immediately
drew some comfort, in that it must have cost us a great
deal of men. Others were so negligent of the glory of
their country, that they went on in their discourse on the

---

[1] The conclusion of Pasquin's letter alludes to the following allegorical piece, the publication of which was just then recent : " The
History of Hannibal and Hanno, &c., collected from the best authors,
by A. M., Esq." It is reprinted in " The Life and Posthumous
Writings " of Arthur Maynwaring, 1715. See No. 190.

[2] See No. 65.

full house which is to be at " Othello " on Thursday, and the curiosity they should go with to see Wilks play a part so very different from what he had ever before appeared in, together with the expectation that was raised in the gay part of the town on that occasion.

This universal indolence and inattention among us to things that concern the public, made me look back with the highest reverence on the glorious instances in antiquity, of a contrary behaviour in the like circumstances. Harry English, upon observing the room so little roused on the news, fell into the same way of thinking. "How unlike," said he, " Mr. Bickerstaff, are we to the old Romans ! There was not a subject of their State but thought himself as much concerned in the honour of his country, as the first officer of the commonwealth. How do I admire the messenger, who ran with a thorn in his foot to tell the news of a victory to the Senate ! He had not leisure for his private pain, till he had expressed his public joy ; nor could he suffer as a man, till he had triumphed as a Roman."

No. 188.   [STEELE.

From *Tuesday, June* 20, to *Thursday, June* 22, 1710.

Quæ regio in terris nostri non plena laboris ?
VIRG., Æn. i. 460.

From my own Apartment, June 21.

I was this morning looking over my letters that I have lately received from my several correspondents ; some of which referring to my late papers, I have laid aside, with an intent to give my reader a sight of them. The first criticises upon my greenhouse, and is as follows :

"Mr. Bickerstaff,　　　"South Wales, *June* 7.

"This letter comes to you from my orangery, which I intend to reform as much as I can, according to your ingenious model, and shall only beg of you to communicate to me your secret of preserving grass-plots in a covered room ;[1] for in the climate where my country-seat lies, they require rain and dews as well as sun and fresh air, and cannot live upon such fine food as your 'sifted weather.' I must likewise desire you to write over your greenhouse the following motto :

> "*Hic ver perpetuum, atque alienis mensibus æstas.*

instead of your

> "*O ! qui me gelidis sub montibus Hæmi*
> *Sistat, et ingenti ramorum protegat umbrâ !*[2]

which, under favour, is the panting of one in summer after cool shades, and not of one in winter after a summer-house. The rest of your plan is very beautiful ; and that your friend who has so well described it may enjoy it many winters, is the hearty wish of

　　　　　　"His and your Unknown," &c.

This oversight of a grass-plot in my friend's green-house, puts me in mind of a like inconsistency in a celebrated picture, where Moses is represented as striking a rock, and the Children of Israel quenching their thirst at the waters that flow from it, and run through a beautiful landscape of groves and meadows, which could not flourish in a place where water was to have been found only by a miracle.

[1] See No. 179.　[2] Virgil, "Georg." ii. 488 ("In vallibus Hæmi ").

The next letter comes to me from a Kentish yeoman, who is very angry with me for my advice to parents, occasioned by the amours of Sylvia and Philander, as related in my paper, No. 185 :

"SQUIRE BICKERSTAFF,

"I don't know by what chance one of your *Tatlers* is got into my family, and has almost turned the brains of my eldest daughter Winifred, who has been so undutiful as to fall in love of her own head, and tells me a foolish heathen story that she has read in your paper to persuade me to give my consent. I am too wise to let children have their own wills in a business like marriage. It is a matter in which neither I myself, nor any of my kindred, were ever humoured. My wife and I never pretended to love one another like your Sylvias and Philanders ; and yet if you saw our fireside, you would be satisfied we are not always a-squabbling. For my part, I think that where man and woman come together by their own good liking, there is so much fondling and fooling, that it hinders young people from minding their business. I must therefore desire you to change your note, and instead of advising us old folks, who perhaps have more wit than yourself, to let Sylvia know, that she ought to act like a dutiful daughter, and marry the man that she does not care for. Our great-grandmothers were all bid to marry first, and love would come afterwards ; and I don't see why their daughters should follow their own inventions. I am resolved Winifred shan't.

"Yours," &c.

This letter is a natural picture of ordinary contracts, and of the sentiments of those minds that lie under a kind of intellectual rusticity. This trifling occasion made me

run over in my imagination the many scenes I have
observed of the married condition, wherein the quintessence
of pleasure and pain are represented as they accompany
that state, and no other. It is certain, there are a thousand
thousand like the above-mentioned yeoman and his wife,
who are never highly pleased or distasted in their whole
lives : but when we consider the more informed part of
mankind, and look upon their behaviour, it then appears
that very little of their time is indifferent, but generally
spent in the most anxious vexation, or the highest satisfaction. Shakespeare has admirably represented both the
aspects of this state in the most excellent tragedy of
"Othello." In the character of Desdemona, he runs
through all the sentiments of a virtuous maid and a
tender wife. She is captivated by his virtue, and faithful
to him, as well from that motive, as regard to her own
honour. Othello is a great and noble spirit, misled by
the villany of a false friend to suspect her innocence, and
resents it accordingly. When after the many instances of
passion the wife is told her husband is jealous, her simplicity makes her incapable of believing it, and say, after
such circumstances as would drive another woman into
distraction,

> *I think the sun where he was born*
> *Drew all such humours from him.*[1]

This opinion of him is so just, that his noble and tender
heart beats itself to pieces before he can affront her with
the mention of his jealousy ; and owns, this suspicion has
blotted out all the sense of glory and happiness which
before it was possessed with, when he laments himself in
the warm allusions of a mind accustomed to entertainments
so very different from the pangs of jealousy and revenge.
How moving is his sorrow, when he cries out as follows :

[1] "Othello," act iii. sc. 4.

" *I had been happy, if the general camp,*
Pioneers and all, had tasted her sweet body,
So I had nothing known. Oh now ! for ever
Farewell the tranquil mind ! Farewell content,
Farewell the plumèd troops, and the big wars,
That make ambition virtue ! Oh farewell !
Farewell the neighing steed and the shrill trump,
The spirit-stirring drum, th' ear-piercing fife,
The royal banner, and all quality,
Pride, pomp, and circumstance of glorious war !
And oh ye mortal engines ! whose rude throats
The immortal Jove's dread clamours counterfeit,
Farewell ! Othello's occupation's gone." [1]

I believe I may venture to say, there is not in any other part of Shakespeare's works more strong and lively pictures of nature than in this. I shall therefore steal incog. to see it, out of curiosity to observe how Wilks and Cibber touch those places where Betterton[2] and Sandford[3] so very highly excelled. But now I am got into a discourse of acting, with which I am so professedly pleased, I shall conclude this paper with a note I have just received from the two ingenious friends, Mr. Penkethman[4] and Mr. Bullock: [5]

"SIR,

" Finding by your paper, No. 182, that you are drawing parallels between the greatest actors of the age ; as you have already begun with Mr. Wilks and Mr. Cibber, we desire you would do the same justice to your humble Servants,

"WILLIAM BULLOCK, and

"WILLIAM PENKETHMAN."

For the information of posterity, I shall comply with this letter, and set these two great men in such a light as Sallust has placed his Cato and Cæsar.

Mr. William Bullock and Mr. William Penkethman are of the same age, profession, and sex. They both distinguish themselves in a very particular manner under the discipline of the crabtree, with this only difference, that Mr. Bullock has the most agreeable squawl, and Mr. Penkethman the more graceful shrug. Penkethman devours a cold chicken with great applause ; Bullock's talent lies chiefly in asparagus. Penkethman is very dexterous at conveying himself under a table ; Bullock is no less active at jumping over a stick. Mr. Penkethman has a great deal of money, but Mr. Bullock is the taller man.

No. 189.   [STEELE.

From *Thursday, June 22,* to *Saturday, June 24,* 1710.

> Est in juvencis, est in equis patrum
> Virtus ; neque imbellem feroces
> Progenerant aquilæ columbam.
> HOR., 4 Od. iv. 30.

From my own Apartment, June 23.

Having lately turned my thoughts upon the consideration of the behaviour of parents to children in the great affair of marriage,[1] I took much delight in turning over a bundle of letters which a gentleman's steward in the country had sent me some time ago. This parcel is a collection of letters written by the children of the family to which he belongs to their father, and contain all the little passages of their lives, and the new ideas they received

[1] See No. 185.

as their years advanced. There is in them an account of their diversions as well as their exercises ; and what I thought very remarkable, is, that two sons of the family, who now make considerable figures in the world, gave omens of that sort of character which they now bear, in the first rudiments of thought which they show in their letters. Were one to point out a method of education, one could not, methinks, frame one more pleasing or improving than this ; where the children get a habit of communicating their thoughts and inclinations to their best friend with so much freedom, that he can form schemes for their future life and conduct from an observation of their tempers, and by that means be early enough in choosing their way of life, to make them forward in some art or science at an age when others have not determined what profession to follow. As to the persons concerned in this packet I am speaking of, they have given great proofs of the force of this conduct of their father in the effect it has had upon their lives and manners. The elder, who is a scholar, showed from his infancy a propensity to polite studies, and has made a suitable progress in literature ; but his learning is so well woven into his mind, that from the impressions of it, he seems rather to have contracted a habit of life, than manner of discourse. To his books he seems to owe a good economy in his affairs, and a complacency in his manners, though in others that way of education has commonly a quite different effect. The epistles of the other son are full of accounts of what he thought most remarkable in his reading. He sends his father for news the last noble story he had read. I observe, he is particularly touched with the conduct of Codrus, who plotted his own death, because the oracle had said, if he were not killed, the enemy should prevail over his country. Many other incidents in his little letters

give omens of a soul capable of generous undertakings ;
and what makes it the more particular is, that this gentleman had, in the present war, the honour and happiness of
doing an action for which only it was worth coming into
the world.   Their father is the most intimate friend they
have, and they always consult him rather than any other,
when any error has happened in their conduct through
youth and inadvertency.   The behaviour of this gentleman
to his sons has made his life pass away with the pleasures
of a second youth ; for as the vexations which men receive
from their children hasten the approach of age and double
the force of years ; so the comforts which they reap from
them are balm to all other sorrows, and disappoint the
injuries of time.   Parents of children repeat their lives in
their offspring, and their concern for them is so near, that
they feel all their sufferings and enjoyments as much as if
they regarded their own proper persons.   But it is generally so far otherwise, that the common race of squires in
this kingdom use their sons as persons that are waiting
only for their funerals, and spies upon their health and
happiness ; as indeed they are by their own making them
such.   In cases where a man takes the liberty after this
manner to reprehend others, it is commonly said, "Let him
look at home."   I am sorry to own it ; but there is one
branch of the house of the Bickerstaffs, who have been as
erroneous in their conduct this way as any other family
whatsoever.   The head of this branch is now in town, and
has brought up with him his son and daughter (who are
all the children he has) in order to be put some way into
the world, and see fashions.   They are both very ill-bred
cubs, and having lived together from their infancy without
knowledge of the distinctions and decencies that are proper
to be paid to each other's sex, they squabble like two
brothers.   The father is one of those who knows no better

than that all pleasure is debauchery, and imagines, when
he sees a man become his estate, that he will certainly
spend it.   This branch are a people who never had among
them one man eminent either for good or ill ; however,
have all along kept their heads just above water, not by a
prudent and regular economy, but by expedients in the
matches they have made into their house.   When one of
the family has, in the pursuit of foxes, and in the entertainment of clowns, run out the third part of the value of
his estate, such a spendthrift has dressed up his eldest son,
and married what they call a good fortune, who has supported the father as a tyrant over them, during his life, in
the same house or neighbourhood.   The son in succession
has just taken the same method to keep up his dignity,
till the mortgages he has ate and drank himself into,
have reduced him to the necessity of sacrificing his son
also, in imitation of his progenitor.   This had been for
many generations the whole that had happened in the
family of Sam. Bickerstaff, till the time of my present
cousin Samuel, the father of the young people we have just
now spoken of.

Samuel Bickerstaff, Esq., is so happy, as that by several
legacies from distant relations, deaths of maiden sisters,
and other instances of good fortune, he has, besides his
real estate, a great sum of ready money.   His son at the
same time knows he has a good fortune, which the father
cannot alienate, though he strives to make him believe
he depends only on his will for maintenance.   Tom is
now in his nineteenth year, Mrs. Mary in her fifteenth.
Cousin Samuel, who understands no one point of good
behaviour as it regards all the rest of the world, is an
exact critic in the dress, the motion, the looks and gestures
of his children.   What adds to their misery is, that he is
excessively fond of them, and the greatest part of their

time is spent in the presence of this nice observer.   Their
life is one continued constraint.   The girl never turns her
head, but she is warned not to follow the proud minxes
of the town.   The boy is not to turn fop, or be quarrel-
some ; at the same time not to take an affront.   I had
the good fortune to dine with him to-day, and heard his
fatherly table-talk as we sat at dinner, which, if my
memory does not fail me, for the benefit of the world, I
shall set down as he spoke it, which was much as follows,
and may be of great use to those parents who seem to
make it a rule, that their children's turn to enjoy the
world is not to commence till they themselves have
left it.

" Now, Tom, I have bought you chambers in the Inns
of Court.   I allow you to take a walk once or twice a day
round the garden.   If you mind your business, you need
not study to be as great a lawyer as Coke upon Littleton.
I have that that will keep you ; but be sure you keep an
exact account of your linen.   Write down what you give
out to your laundress, and what she brings home again.
Go as little as possible to the other end of the town ; but
if you do, come home early.   I believe I was as sharp as
you for your years, and I had my hat snatched off my head
coming home late at a shop by St. Clement's Church, and
I don't know from that day to this who took it.   I do not
care if you learn to fence a little, for I would not have you
be made a fool of.   Let me have an account of everything
every post ; I am willing to be at that charge, and I think
you need not spare your pains.   As for you, daughter
Molly, don't mind one word that is said to you in London,
for it is only for your money."[1]

---

[1] It has been suggested that the latter part of this paper may refer
to Dr. Gilbert Budgell and his son Eustace, Addison's cousin. (See

No. 190.　　　　　{STEELE.

From *Saturday, June 24,* to *Tuesday, June 27,* 1710.

—— Timeo Danaos et dona ferentes.- VIRG., Æn. ii. 49.

Sheer Lane, June 26.

There are some occasions in life, wherein regards to a man's self is the most pitiful and contemptible of all passions ; and such a time certainly is when the true public spirit of a nation is run into a faction against their friends and benefactors. I have hinted heretofore some things which discover the real sorrow I am in at the observation, that it is now very much so in Great Britain, and have had the honour to be pelted with several epistles to expostulate with me on that subject ; [1] among others, one from a person of the number of those they call Quakers, who seems to admonish me out of pure zeal and goodwill. But as there is no character so unjust as that of talking in party upon all occasions, without respect to merit or worth on the contrary side, so there is no part we can act so justifiable as to speak our mind when we see things urged to extremity, against all that is praiseworthy or valuable in life, upon general and groundless suggestions. But if I have talked too frankly upon such reflections, my correspondent has laid before me, after his way, the error of it in a

"Grand Magazine," i. 391, *seq.* ; and Cibber's "Lives of the Poets," vol. v.)　On the death of his father in 1711, Eustace Budgell came into possession of an estate of £950 a year.

[1] Swift may have been among those who protested at the introduction of politics into the *Tatler* (see No. 187), and Nichols thought that he was the writer of the letter signed "Aminadab" in this number. In June 1710, the fall of the Whigs was rapidly approaching.

manner that makes me indeed thankful for his kindness, but the more inclinable to repeat the imprudence from the necessity of the circumstance :

"The 23rd of the 6th month,
" FRIEND ISAAC,   which is the month *June.*

" Forasmuch as I love thee, I cannot any longer refrain declaring my mind unto thee concerning some things. Thou didst thyself indite the epistle inserted in one of thy late Lucubrations, as thou wouldst have us call them : for verily thy friend of stone,[1] and I speak according to knowledge, hath no fingers ; and though he hath a mouth, yet speaketh he not therewith ; nor yet did that epistle at all come unto thee from the mansion-house of the Scarlet Whore. It is plain therefore, that the truth is not in thee : but since thou wouldst lie, couldst thou not lie with more discretion ? Wherefore shouldst thou insult over the afflicted, or add sorrow unto the heavy of heart ? Truly this gall proceedeth not from the spirit of meekness. I tell thee moreover, the people of this land be marvellously given to change ; insomuch that it may likely come to pass, that before thou art many years nearer to thy dissolution, thou mayest behold him sitting on a high place whom thou now laughest to scorn : and then how wilt thou be glad to humble thyself to the ground, and lick the dust of his feet, that thou mayest find favour in his sight ? If thou didst meditate as much upon the Word as thou dost upon the profane scribblings of the wise ones of this generation, thou wouldst have remembered what happened unto Shimei, the son of Gera the Benjamite, who cursed the good man David in his distress.[2] David pardoned his transgression, yet was he afterwards taken as in a snare by the words of his own mouth, and fell by the sword of

[1] Pasquin. See Nos. 129, 130, 187.   [2] 2 Sam. xvi. 13.

Solomon the chief ruler.[1]   Furthermore, I do not remember to have heard in the days of my youth and vanity,
when, like thine, my conversation was with the Gentiles,
that the men of Rome, which is Babylon, ever sued unto
the men of Carthage for tranquillity, as thou dost aver :
neither was Hannibal, the son of Hamilcar, called home by
his countrymen, till these saw the sword of their enemies
at their gates ; and then was it not time for him, thinkest
thou, to return ?   It appeareth therefore that thou dost
prophecy backwards ; thou dost row one way, and look
another ; and indeed in all things art thou too much a
time-server ; yet seemest thou not to consider what a day
may bring forth.   Think of this, and take tobacco.

" Thy Friend,

" Aminadab."

   If the zealous writer of the above letter has any meaning, it is of too high a nature to be the subject of my
Lucubrations.   I shall therefore waive such high points,
and be as useful as I can to persons of less moment than
any he hints at.   When a man runs into a little fame in
the world, as he meets with a great deal of reproach which
he does not deserve, so does he also a great deal of esteem
to which he has in himself no pretensions.   Were it
otherwise, I am sure no one would offer to put a law case
to me : but because I am an adept in physic and astrology,
they will needs persuade me that I am no less a proficient in
all other sciences.   However, the point mentioned in the
following letter is so plain a one, that I think I need not
trouble myself to cast a figure to be able to discuss it.

[1] 1 Kings ii. 36.

"MR. BICKERSTAFF,

"It is some years ago since the entail of the estate of our family was altered, by passing a fine in favour of me (who now am in possession of it) after some others deceased. The heirs-general, who live beyond sea, were excluded by this settlement, and the whole estate is to pass in a new channel after me and my heirs. But several tenants of the lordship persuade me to let them hereafter hold their lands of me according to the old customs of the barony, and not oblige them to act by the limitations of the last settlement. This, they say, will make me more popular among my dependants, and the ancient vassals of the estate, to whom any deviation from the line of succession is always invidious.

"Yours," &c.

"SIR,   "Sheer Lane, *June* 24.

"You have by the fine a plain right, in which none else of your family can be your competitor ; for which reason, by all means demand vassalage upon that title. The contrary advice can be given for no other purpose in nature but to betray you, and favour other pretenders, by making you place a right which is in you only, upon a level with a right which you have in common with others. I am,

"Sir,

"Your most faithful

"Servant till death,

"I. B."

There is nothing so dangerous or so pleasing, as compliments made to us by our enemies : and my correspondent tells me, that though he knows several of those who give him this counsel were at first against passing the fine in favour of him ; yet is he so touched with their homage to him, that he can hardly believe they have a mind to set it aside, in order to introduce the heirs-general into his estate.

These are great evils ; but since there is no proceeding with success in this world, without complying with the arts of it, I shall use the same method as my correspondent's tenants did with him, in relation to one whom I never had a kindness for ; but shall, notwithstanding, presume to give him my advice.

> "*Isaac Bickerstaff, Esq., of Great Britain, to Lewis XIV. of France.*

"Sir,

"Your Majesty will pardon me while I take the liberty to acquaint you, that some passages written from your side of the water do very much obstruct your interests. We take it very unkindly that the prints of Paris are so very partial in favour of one set of men among us, and treat the others as irreconcilable to your interests. Your writers are very large in recounting anything which relates to the figure and power of one party, but are dumb when they should represent the actions of the other. This is a trifling circumstance many here are apt to lay some stress upon ; therefore I thought fit to offer it to your consideration before you despatch the next courier.

"I. B."[1]

---

[1] " The Tories happen now to have other work upon their hands, and are not at leisure to return the civilities that are paid them ; however, having had the honour of a letter from the King of France . . . they have sent in their answer to me, and desire me to forward it ; but I am at a loss how to do this, unless my brother the *Tatler* will convey

No. 191.   [Steele.

From *Tuesday*, *June* 27, to *Thursday*, *June* 29, 1710.

------ Propter vitam vivendi perdere causas.—Juv., Sat. viii. 84.

From my own Apartment, June 28.

Of all the evils under the sun, that of making vice commendable is the greatest : for it seems to be the basis of society, that applause and contempt should be always given to proper objects. But in this age we behold things for which we ought to have an abhorrence, not only received without disdain, but even valued as motives of emulation. This is naturally the destruction of simplicity of manners, openness of heart, and generosity of temper. When one gives oneself the liberty to range, and run over in one's thoughts the different geniuses of men which one meets in the world, one cannot but observe, that most of the indirection and artifice which is used among men, does not proceed so much from a degeneracy in Nature, as an affectation of appearing men of consequence by such practices. By this means it is, that a cunning man is so far from being ashamed of being esteemed such, that he secretly rejoices in it. It has been a sort of maxim, that the greatest art is to conceal art ; but I know not how, among some people we meet with, their greatest cunning is to appear cunning. There is Polypragmon[1] makes it the whole business of his life to be thought a

it under his cover, for I protest I know no man in England but him that holds a correspondence with his Christian Majesty " (*Examiner,* No. 2, August 10, 1710).

   [1] In reply to this suggestion that the character of Polypragmon was meant for Harley, Steele said, in the *Guardian*, No. 53 : " I drew it as the most odious image I could paint of ambition. . . . Whoever seeks

cunning fellow, and thinks it a much greater character to
be terrible than agreeable. When it has once entered into
a man's head to have an ambition to be thought crafty, all
other evils are necessary consequences. To deceive is the
immediate endeavour of him who is proud of the capacity
of doing it. It is certain, Polypragmon does all the ill he
possibly can, but pretends to much more than he performs. He is contented in his own thoughts, and hugs
himself in his closet, that though he is locked up there
and doing nothing, the world does not know but that he
is doing mischief. To favour this suspicion, he gives half-
looks and shrugs in his general behaviour, to give you to
understand that you don't know what he means. He is
also wonderfully adverbial in his expressions, and breaks
off with a "perhaps" and a nod of the head, upon matters of
the most indifferent nature. It is a mighty practice with

employment for his own private interest, vanity, or pride, and not for
the good of his prince and country, has his share in the picture of
Polypragmon ; and let this be the rule in examining that description,
and I believe the Examiner will find others to whom he would rather
give a part of it, than to the person on whom I believe he bestows it,
because he thinks he is the most capable of having his vengeance on
me. . . . . I have not, like him, fixed odious images on persons, but
on vices." To this the *Examiner* (vol. iv. No. 2) replied : "He
would insinuate, that Timon and Polypragmon are general characters,
and stand for a whole species, or, as he quaintly words it, for Knights
of the Shire. If this be true, why did he not before now silence the
industrious clamours of his party, who both in print and public conversation applied those characters to persons of the first rank, though
without any regard to the rules of resemblance ?" The writer of
"Annotations on the *Tatler*," 1710, in the preface to the second part,
regretted that Steele had become a politician, and said, in allusion to
Steele's experiments in alchemy : "Turning statesman and drudging
for the Philosopher's Stone, are toils not altogether unlike each other ;
buffeting with fire, labouring in smoke, wearing out of lungs, and
tiring oneself with expectation, are misfortunes common to both these
projects ; 'tis converting real gold to dross, out of a prospect of converting dross into real gold."

men of this genius to avoid frequent appearance in public,
and to be as mysterious as possible when they do come
into company.   There is nothing to be done, according to
them, the common way ; and let the matter in hand be
what it will, it must be carried with an air of importance,
and transacted, if we may so speak, with an ostentatious
secrecy.   These are your persons of long heads, who would
fain make the world believe their thoughts and ideas are
very much superior to their neighbours', and do not value
what these their neighbours think of them, provided they
do not reckon them fools.   These have such a romantic
touch in business, that they hate to perform anything like
other men.   Were it in their choice, they had rather bring
their purposes to bear by overreaching the persons they
deal with, than by a plain and simple manner.   They
make difficulties for the honour of surmounting them.
Polypragmon is eternally busied after this manner, with no
other prospect, than that he is in hopes to be thought the
most cunning of all men, and fears the imputation of want
of understanding much more than that of the abuse of it.
But alas ! how contemptible is such an ambition, which is
the very reverse of all that is truly laudable, and the very
contradiction to the only means to a just reputation, simplicity of manners ?   Cunning can in no circumstance
imaginable be a quality worthy a man except in his own
defence, and merely to conceal himself from such as are
so ; and in such cases it is no longer craft, but wisdom.
The monstrous affectation of being thought artful immediately kills all thoughts of humanity and goodness,
and gives men a sense of the soft affections and impulses
of the mind (which are imprinted in us for our mutual
advantage and succour) as of mere weaknesses and follies.
According to the men of cunning, you are to put off the
nature of a man as fast as you can, and acquire that of a

demon, as if it were a more eligible character to be a powerful enemy than an able friend. But it ought to be a mortification to men affected this way, that there wants but little more than instinct to be considerable in it ; for when a man has arrived at being very bad in his inclination, he has not much more to do, but to conceal himself, and he may revenge, cheat, and deceive, without much employment for understanding, and go on with great cheerfulness with the high applause of being a prodigious cunning fellow. But indeed, when we arrive at that pitch of false taste, as not to think cunning a contemptible quality, it is, methinks, a very great injustice that pick-pockets are had in so little veneration, who must be admirably well turned, not only for the theoretic, but also the practical behaviour of cunning fellows. After all the endeavour of this family of men whom we call cunning, their whole work falls to pieces, if others will lay down all esteem for such artifices, and treat it as an unmanly quality, which they forbear to practise only because they abhor it. When the spider is ranging in the different apartments of his web, it is true that he only can weave so fine a thread ; but it is in the power of the merest drone that has wings to fly through and destroy it.

Will's Coffee-house, June 28.

Though the taste of wit and pleasure is at present but very low in this town, yet there are some that preserve their relish undebauched with common impressions, and can distinguish between reality and imposture. A gentleman was saying here this evening, that he would go to the play to-morrow night to see heroism, as it has been represented by some of our tragedians, represented in burlesque. It seems, the play of " Alexander " is to be then turned into ridicule for its bombast, and other false

ornaments in the thought as well as the language.[1] The
bluster Alexander makes, is as much inconsistent with the
character of a hero, as the roughness of Clytus is an instance
of the sincerity of a bold artless soldier.   To be plain is
not to be rude, but rather inclines a man to civility and
deference ; not indeed to show it in the gestures of the
body, but in the sentiments of the mind.   It is, among
other things, from the impertinent figures unskilful dra-
matists draw of the characters of men, that youth are
bewildered and prejudiced in their sense of the world, of
which they have no notions but what they draw from
books and such representations.   Thus talk to a very
young man, let him be of never so good sense, and he
shall smile when you speak of sincerity in a courtier, good
sense in a soldier, or honesty in a politician. The reason
of this is, that you hardly see one play wherein each of
these ways of life is not drawn by hands that know nothing
of any one of them : and the truth is so far of the opposite
side to what they paint, that it is more impracticable to
live in esteem in Courts than anywhere else without sincerity.   Good sense is the great requisite in a soldier, and
honesty the only thing that can support a politician.
This way of thinking made the gentleman of whom I was
just now speaking say, he was glad any one had taken
upon him to depreciate such unnatural fustian as the
tragedy of " Alexander."   The character of that prince
indeed was, that he was unequal, and given to intemper-
ance ; but in his sober moments, when he had warm in
his imagination the precepts of his great instructor, he was
a pattern of generous thoughts and dispositions, in opposi-

---

[1] A burlesque of Lee's " Rival Queens ; or, the Death of Alexander
the Great," by Cibber, called "The Rival Queans ; or, the Humours
of Alexander the Great," was acted at Drury Lane in 1710, but not
printed until 1729.

tion to the strongest desires which are incident to a youth and conqueror. But instead of representing that hero in the glorious character of generosity and chastity, in his treatment of the beauteous family of Darius, he is drawn all along as a monster of lust, or of cruelty ; as if the way to raise him to the degree of a hero were to make his character as little like that of a worthy man as possible. Such rude and indigested draughts of things are the proper objects of ridicule and contempt, and depreciating Alexander, as we have him drawn, is the only way of restoring him to what he was in himself. It is well contrived of the players to let this part be followed by a true picture of life, in the comedy called, " The Chances,"[1] wherein Don John and Constantia are acted to the utmost perfection. There need not be a greater instance of the force of action than in many incidents of this play, where indifferent passages, and such that conduce only to the tacking of the scenes together, are enlivened with such an agreeable gesture and behaviour, as apparently shows what a play might be, though it is not wholly what a play should be.

No. 192. [ADDISON.

From *Thursday, June* 29, to *Saturday, July* 1, 1710.

Tecum vivere amem, tecum obeam libens.—HOR., 3 Od. ix. 24.

From my own Apartment, June 30.

Some years since I was engaged with a coachful of friends to take a journey as far as the Land's End. We were very well pleased with one another the first day, every one endeavouring to recommend himself by his good

[1] An adaptation of Beaumont and Fletcher's comedy, by the Duke of Buckingham, 1682.

humour and complaisance to the rest of the company. This good correspondence did not last long; one of our party was soured the very first evening by a plate of butter which had not been melted to his mind, and which spoiled his temper to such a degree, that he continued upon the fret to the end of our journey. A second fell off from his good humour the next morning, for no other reason that I could imagine, but because I chanced to step into the coach before him, and place myself on the shady side. This however was but my own private guess, for he did not mention a word of it, nor indeed of anything else, for three days following. The rest of our company held out very near half the way, when of a sudden Mr. Sprightly fell asleep; and instead of endeavouring to divert and oblige us, as he had hitherto done, carried himself with an unconcerned, careless, drowsy behaviour, till we came to our last stage. There were three of us who still held up our heads, and did all we could to make our journey agreeable; but, to my shame be it spoken, about three miles on this side Exeter, I was taken with an unaccountable fit of sullenness, that hung upon me for above threescore miles; whether it were for want of respect, or from an accidental tread upon my foot, or from a foolish maid's calling me " The old gentleman," I cannot tell. In short, there was but one who kept his good humour to the Land's End.

There was another coach that went along with us, in which I likewise observed, that there were many secret jealousies, heartburnings, and animosities: for when we joined companies at night, I could not but take notice, that the passengers neglected their own company, and studied how to make themselves esteemed by us, who were altogether strangers to them; till at length they grew so well acquainted with us, that they liked us as little as they did one another. When I reflect upon this journey, I often fancy it to be a picture of human life, in respect to the several friendships, contracts, and alliances that are made and dissolved in the several periods of it. ᶜThe most delightful and most lasting engagements are generally those which pass between man and woman ; and yet upon what trifles are they weakened, or entirely broken ? Sometimes the parties fly asunder, even in the midst of courtship, and sometimes grow cool in the very honey month. Some separate before the first child, and some after the fifth ; others continue good till thirty, others till forty ; while some few, whose souls are of a happier make, and better fitted to one another, travel on together to the end of their journey in a continual intercourse of kind offices and mutual endearments.

When we therefore choose our companions for life, if we hope to keep both them and ourselves in good humour to the last stage of it, we must be extremely careful in the choice we make, as well as in the conduct on our own part. When the persons to whom we join ourselves can stand an examination, and bear the scrutiny, when they mend upon our acquaintance with them, and discover new beauties the more we search into their characters, our love will naturally rise in proportion to their perfections.

But because there are very few possessed of such accomplishments of body and mind, we ought to look after those qualifications both in ourselves and others, which are indispensably necessary towards this happy union, and which are in the power of every one to acquire, or at least to cultivate and improve. These, in my opinion, are cheerfulness and constancy. A cheerful temper joined with innocence will make beauty attractive, knowledge delightful, and wit good-natured. It will lighten sickness, poverty, and affliction ; convert ignorance into an amiable simplicity, and render deformity itself agreeable.

Constancy is natural to persons of even tempers and uniform dispositions, and may be acquired by those of the greatest fickleness, violence, and passion, who consider seriously the terms of union upon which they come together, the mutual interest in which they are engaged, with all the motives that ought to incite their tenderness and compassion towards those who have their dependence upon them, and are embarked with them for life in the same state of happiness or misery. Constancy, when it grows in the mind upon considerations of this nature, becomes a moral virtue, and a kind of good nature, that is not subject to any change of health, age, fortune, or any of those accidents which are apt to unsettle the best dispositions that are founded rather in constitution than in reason. Where such a constancy as this is wanting, the most inflamed passion may fall away into coldness and indifference, and the most melting tenderness degenerate into hatred and aversion. I shall conclude this paper with a story that is very well known in the North of England.

About thirty years ago, a packet-boat that had several passengers on board was cast away upon a rock, and in so great danger of sinking, that all who were in it endeavoured to save themselves as well as they could, though only those who could swim well had a bare possibility of doing it. Among the passengers there were two women of fashion, who seeing themselves in such a disconsolate condition, begged of their husbands not to leave them. One of them chose rather to die with his wife than to forsake her; the other, though he was moved with the utmost compassion for his wife, told her, that for the good of their children it was better one of them should live, than both perish. By a great piece of good luck, next to a miracle, when one of our good men had taken the last and long farewell in order to save himself, and the other held in his arms the person that was dearer to him than life, the ship was preserved. It is with a secret sorrow and vexation of mind that I must tell the sequel of the story, and let my reader know, that this faithful pair who were ready to have died in each other's arms, about three years after their escape, upon some trifling disgust, grew to a coldness at first, and at length fell out to such a degree, that they left one another and parted for ever. The other couple lived together in an uninterrupted friendship and felicity; and what was remarkable, the husband whom the shipwreck had like to have separated from his wife, died a few months after her, not being able to survive the loss of her.

I must confess, there is something in the changeableness and inconstancy of human nature, that very often both dejects and terrifies me. Whatever I am at present, I tremble to think what I may be. While I find this principle in me, how can I assure myself that I shall be always true to my God, my friend, or myself? In short, without constancy there is neither love, friendship, nor virtue in the world.

No. 193.   [STEELE.[1]

From *Saturday, July* 1, to *Tuesday, July* 4, 1710.

Qui didicit, patriæ quid debeat et quid amicis,
Quo sit amore parens, quo frater amandus, et hospes . . .
Scribere[2] personæ scit convenientia cuique.

HOR., Ars Poet. 312.

Will's Coffee-house, July 3.

I have of late received many epistles, wherein the writers treat me as a mercenary person, for some late hints concerning matters which they think I should not have touched upon but for sordid considerations. It is apparent, that my motive could not be of that kind ; for when a man declares himself openly on one side, that party will take no more notice of him, because he is sure ; and the set of men whom he declares against, for the same reason are violent against him. Thus it is folly in a plain-dealer to expect, that either his friends will reward him, or his enemies forgive him. For which reason, I thought it was the shortest way to impartiality, to put myself beyond further hopes or fears, by declaring myself, at a time when the dispute is not about persons and parties, but things and causes. To relieve myself from the vexation which naturally attends such reflections, I came hither this evening to give my thoughts quite a new turn, and converse with men of pleasure and wit, rather than those of business and intrigue. I had hardly entered the room, when I was accosted by Mr. Thomas Doggett, who desired my favour in relation to the play which was to be acted for his benefit on Thursday. He pleased me in saying it

[1] The authorship of the greater part of this paper is uncertain ; see note on next page.   [2] " Reddere " (Horace).

was " The Old Bachelor,"[1] in which comedy there is a
necessary circumstance observed by the author, which
most other poets either overlook or do not understand,
that is to say, the distinction of characters. It is very
ordinary with writers to indulge a certain modesty of
believing all men as witty as themselves, and 'making all
the persons of the play speak the sentiments of the author,
without any manner of respect to the age, fortune, or
quality of him that is on the stage. Ladies talk like
rakes, and footmen make similes : but this writer knows
men, which makes his plays reasonable entertainments,
while the scenes of most others are like the tunes between
the acts. They are perhaps agreeable sounds, but they
have no ideas affixed to them. Doggett thanked me for
my visit to him in the winter,[2] and, after his comical
manner, spoke his request with so arch a leer, that I
promised the droll I would speak to all my acquaintance
to be at his play.

Whatever the world may think of the actors, whether
it be that their parts have an effect on their lives, or whatever it is, you see a wonderful benevolence among them
towards the interests and necessities of each other. Doggett
therefore would not let me go, without delivering me a
letter from poor old Downes the prompter,[3] wherein that

[1] See No. 9.
[2] See Nos. 120, 122. In the continuation of the *Tatler* which
Swift and Harrison conducted (No. 28, March 24, 1710–11) there is
this passage : " The person produced as mine in the playhouse, last
winter, did in no wise appertain to me. It was such a one, however,
as agreed well with the impression my writings had made, and served
the purpose I intended it for : which was to continue the awe and
reverence due to the character I was vested with, and at the same
time to let my enemies see how much I was the delight and favourite
of this town," &c.
[3] This letter, in ridicule of Harley's newly formed Ministry, has been
attributed to the joint authorship of Anthony Hepley (see No. 11) and

retainer to the theatre desires my advice and assistance in
a matter of concern to him.   I have sent him my private
opinion for his conduct ; but the stage and the State
affairs being so much canvassed by parties and factions, I
shall for some time hereafter take leave of subjects which
relate to either of them, and employ my care in consideration of matters which regard that part of mankind who
live without interesting themselves with the troubles or
pleasures of either.   However, for a mere notion of the
present posture of the stage, I shall give you the letter at
large as follows :

"HONOURED SIR,   "*July* 1, 1710.

"Finding by divers of your late papers, that you are a
friend to the profession of which I was many years
an unworthy member, I the rather make bold to crave
your advice, touching a proposal that has been lately made
me of coming into business, and the sub-administration of
stage affairs.   I have, from my youth, been bred up behind
the curtain, and been a prompter from the time of the

Temple Stanyan.   Harley is supposed to be the gentleman referred to
in the letter, and Downes, it has been suggested, is Thomas Osborne,
first Duke of Leeds.   Steele expressly disavowed responsibility for the
letter from Downes the prompter.   In No. 53 of the *Guardian* he
wrote : "Old Downes is a fine piece of raillery, of which I wish I had
been author.   All I had to do in it, was to strike out what related to
a gentlewoman about the Queen, whom I thought a woman free from
ambition, and I did it out of regard to innocence."   And in the Preface
to the *Tatler*, he said that this letter was by an unknown correspondent.   A writer in the *Examiner* (vol. iv. No. 2) mentions Old
Downes among the sufferers of figure under our author's satire.   The
same writer, or another in the same paper, expresses himself in the
following words : "Steele broke his own maxim for trifles in which
his country had no manner of concern ; and by entering into party
disputes, violated the most solemn repeated promises and that perfect
neutrality he had engaged to maintain.   As a proof that I did not
wrong him, he now openly takes upon himself Downes' letter, by

Restoration.[1] I have seen many changes, as well of scenes
as of actors, and have known men within my remembrance
arrive to the highest dignities of the theatre, who made
their entrance in the quality of mutes, joint-stools, flower-
pots, and tapestry hangings. It cannot be unknown to
the nobility and gentry, that a gentleman of the Inns of
Court, and a deep intriguer, had some time since worked
himself into the sole management and direction of the
theatre.[2] Nor is it less notorious, that his restless ambition, and subtle machinations, did manifestly tend to the
extirpation of the good old British actors, and the introduction of foreign pretenders; such as harlequins, French
dancers, and Roman singers; which, though they im-
poverished the proprietors, and imposed on the audience,
were for some time tolerated, by reason of his dexterous
insinuations, which prevailed upon a few deluded women,
especially the vizard masks, to believe that the stage was
in danger. But his schemes were soon exposed, and the
great ones that supported him withdrawing their favour,
he made his exit, and remained for a season in obscurity.
During this retreat the Machiavelian was not idle, but

wishing the raillery (as he calls it) were his own." In the "Essays
Divine, Moral, and Political" (1714), p. 42, Swift is made to say, "I
advised him [Steele] to the publishing that letter from Downes the
prompter, which was the beginning of his ruin, though I here declare
I did not write it." Forster ("Biographical Essays," 3rd ed.) con-
cludes that this fictitious letter was certainly by Mainwaring himself. In the "Journal to Stella" (Oct. 22, 1710), Swift wrote: "He
[Steele] has lost his place of Gazetteer, three hundred pounds a year,
for writing a *Tatler*, some months ago, against Mr. Harley, who gave it
him at first, and raised the salary from sixty to three hundred pounds."
See also Swift's "The Importance of the *Guardian* considered."

[1] John Downes was prompter to "The Duke's Servants" until
1706. In 1708 he published his valuable "Roscius Anglicanus, or an
Historical Review of the Stage."

[2] Christopher Rich, who began life as an attorney. See Nos. 12, 99.

secretly fomented divisions, and wrought over to his side
some of the inferior actors, reserving a trap-door to himself, to which only he had a key.   This entrance secured,
this cunning person, to complete his company, bethought
himself of calling in the most eminent of strollers from
all parts of the kingdom.   I have seen them all ranged
together behind the scenes ; but they are many of them
persons that never trod the stage before, and so very
awkward and ungainly, that it is impossible to believe the
audience will bear them.   He was looking over his catalogue of plays, and indeed picked up a good tolerable set
of grave faces for counsellors, to appear in the famous
scene of ' Venice Preserved,' when the danger is over ;
but they being but mere outsides, and the actors having a
great mind to play ' The Tempest,' there is not a man of
them, when he is to perform anything above dumb show,
is capable of acting with a good grace so much as the part
of Trinculo.   However, the master persists in his design,
and is fitting up the old ' storm ' ; but I am afraid he will
not be able to procure able sailors or experienced officers
for love or money.

   " Besides all this, when he comes to cast the parts, there
is so great a confusion amongst them for want of proper
actors, that for my part I am wholly discouraged.   The
play with which they design to open is, ' The Duke and
No Duke ' ;[1] and they are so put to it, that the master
himself is to act the conjurer, and they have no one for
the general but honest George Powell.[2]

   " Now, sir, they being so much at a loss for the *dramatis
personæ*, viz., the persons to enact, and the whole frame
of the house being designed to be altered, I desire your
opinion, whether you think it advisable for me to undertake to prompt them ?   For though I can clash swords

---

[1] A farce by Nahum Tate, 1685.   [2] See No. 3.

when they represent a battle, and have yet lungs enough
to huzza their victories, I question, if I should prompt
them right, whether they would act accordingly⸱ I am

"Your Honour's most humble Servant,

"J. DOWNES.

" P.S. Sir, since I writ this, I am credibly informed,
that they design a new house in Lincoln's Inn Fields, near
the Popish chapel,[1] to be ready by Michaelmas next ;
which indeed is but repairing an old one that has already
failed. You know the honest man who kept the office is
gone already."

[1] The theatre built by Betterton and his friends in 1695, in Portugal
Row, Lincoln's Inn Fields, was pulled down and rebuilt by Christopher Rich in 1714. The Roman Catholic Church here referred to
was in Duke (now Sardinia) Street, on the west side of the square.

www.ingramcontent.com/pod-product-compliance
Lightning Source LLC
Chambersburg PA
CBHW030822110726
47900CB00006B/1708